Augustine planted a hip against the end of the counter and tipped his head at Harlow, those stormy eyes of his taking her measure.

"You want to see the house now?"

"I can wait until it's light out." Traipsing through this big house with him in the dark seemed like a bad idea. Besides, there was no point falling in love with *anything* here. She was selling the house. Had to. A stain on his shirt caught her eye, giving her a chance to happily change the subject. She pointed at his chest. "Is that blood?"

He glanced at Lally, who met his gaze, then tucked her head down and busied herself with washing a bowl. "Must have cut myself. I should change."

Harlow watched him go. That blood was fresh, his shirt still damp with it, but the shirt wasn't cut, so any injury had been to his bare skin. She knew from personal experience that fae healed quickly. That wound should have scabbed over before he'd had a chance to put his shirt back on.

For once, she didn't need to touch someone to know they were lying.

Praise for HOUSE OF COMARRÉ:

"Kristen Painter's *Blood Rights* is dark and rich with layer after delicious layer. This spellbinding series will have you begging for more!"

—Gena Showalter, *New York Times* bestselling author

"Prophecy, curses, and devilish machination combine for a spellbinding debut of dark romance and pulse-pounding adventure."

—*Library Journal* (Starred Review)

"Painter scores with this one. Passion and murder, vampires and courtesans—original and un-put-downable. Do yourself a favor and read this one."

—Patricia Briggs, *New York Times* bestselling author

"Gripping, gritty, and imaginative. If you love dangerous males, kick-ass females, and unexpected twists, this is the series for you! Kristen Painter's engaging voice, smart writing, and bold, explosive plot blew me away. Prepare to lose some sleep!"

—Larissa Ione, *New York Times* bestselling author

"A world full of rich potential. Excellent!"

—P. C. Cast, *New York Times* bestselling author

"Kristen Painter brings a sultry new voice to the vampire genre, one that beckons with quiet passion and intrigue."

—L.A. Banks, *New York Times* bestselling author

"Exciting and interesting!"   —*RT Book Reviews* on *Bad Blood*

"The romance is tense and fresh...I highly recommend this if you enjoy fantasy and want an original take on vampires."

—*USA Today*'s Happy Ever After on *Blood Rights*

HOUSE
OF THE
RISING SUN

HOUSE OF THE RISING SUN

CRESCENT CITY: BOOK I

Kristen Painter

www.orbitbooks.net

Orbit
Hachette Book Group
237 Park Avenue, New York, NY 10017
HachetteBookGroup.com

First Edition: May 2014

Orbit is an imprint of Hachette Book Group, Inc. The Orbit name and logo are trademarks of Little, Brown Book Group Limited.

The Hachette Speakers Bureau provides a wide range of authors for speaking events. To find out more, go to www.hachettespeakersbureau.com or call (866) 376-6591.

The publisher is not responsible for websites (or their content) that are not owned by the publisher.

The characters and events in this book are fictitious. Any similarity to real persons, living or dead, is coincidental and not intended by the author.

Library of Congress Cataloging-in-Publication Data

Painter, Kristen L.
    [First Edition.]
    House of the rising sun / Kristen Painter.
        pages cm. — (Crescent city ; Book 1)
    Summary: "Augustine lives the perfect life in the Haven city of New Orleans. He rarely works a real job, spends most of his nights with a different human woman, and resides in a spectacular Garden District mansion paid for by retired movie star Olivia Goodwin, who has come to think of him as an adopted son, providing him room and board and whatever else he needs. But when Augustine returns home to find Olivia's been attacked by vampires, he knows his idyllic life has comes to an end. It's time for revenge—and to take up the mantle of the city's Guardian." —Provided by publisher.
        ISBN 978-0-316-27827-0 (pbk.) — ISBN 978-1-4789-8159-6 (audio download) — ISBN 978-0-316-27828-7 (ebook)   1. Vampires—Fiction.   2. Paranormal fiction.   3. Murder—Fiction.   I. Title.
    PS3616.A337845H68 2014
    813'.6—dc23
                                        2013047302

10 9 8 7 6 5 4 3 2 1

RRD-C

Printed in the United States of America

For Elaine—thank you for all your support

Prologue

New Orleans, Louisiana, 2040

Why can't we take the streetcar?" Walking home from church at night was always a little scary for Augustine, especially when they had to go past the cemetery.

"You know why," Mama answered. "Because we don't have money for things like that. Not that your shiftless father would help out. Why I expect anything from that lying, manipulative piece of…" She grunted softly and shook her head.

Augustine had never met his father, but from what Mama had told him, which wasn't much, his father didn't seem like a very nice man. Just once, though, Augustine would like to meet him to see what he looked like. Augustine figured he must look like his father, because he sure didn't look like Mama. Maybe if they met, he'd also ask his father why he never came around. Why he didn't want to be part of their family. Why Mama cried so much.

With a soft sigh, he held Mama's hand a little tighter, moving closer to her side. Unlike him, Mama only had five fingers on each hand, not six. She didn't have gray skin or horns like him, either. She didn't like his horns much. She kept them filed down so his hair hid the stumps. He jammed his free hand into his jacket pocket, the move jogging him to the side a little.

"Be careful, Augustine. You're going to make me trip."

"Sorry, Mama." The sidewalks were all torn up from the tree

roots poking through them. The moon shone through those big trees with their twisty branches and clumps of moss, and cast shadows that looked like creatures reaching toward them. He shivered, almost tripping over one of the roots.

She jerked his arm. "Pay attention."

"Yes, Mama." But paying attention was what had scared him in the first place. He tried shutting his eyes, picking his feet up higher to avoid the roots.

Next thing he knew, his foot caught one of those roots and he was on his hands and knees, the skin on his palms burning from where he'd scraped them raw on the rough sidewalk. His knee throbbed with the same pain, but he wouldn't cry, because he was almost nine and he was a big boy. Old enough to know that he must also control the powers inside him that wanted to come out whenever he felt angry or hurt or excited.

"Oh, Augustine! You ripped your good pants." Mama grabbed his hand and tugged him to his feet.

"I'm sorry about my pants." He stood very still, trying not to cause any more trouble. Mama got so angry, so fast. "My knee hurts."

With a sigh, Mama crouched down, pulled a tissue from her purse, spit on it and began to dab at the blood. "It will be okay. It's just a little scrape. And you heal...quickly."

The dabbing hurt worse, but he kept quiet, biting at his cheek. He looked at his hands, opening his twelve fingers wide. Already the scrapes there were fading. It was because of his fae blood, which he wasn't supposed to talk about. He dropped his hands and stared at the tall cemetery wall next to them. On the other side of that wall were a lot of dead people. In New Orleans, no one could be buried underground because of the water table. He'd learned that in school.

The wind shook the tree above their heads, making the

shadows crawl toward them. He inched closer to her and pointed at the cemetery. "Do you think there's ghosts in there, Mama?"

She stood, ignoring his pointing to brush dirt off his jacket. "Don't be silly. You know ghosts aren't real."

The cemetery gates creaked. She turned, then suddenly put him behind her. Around the side of her dress, Augustine could see a big shape almost on them, smell something sour and sweaty, and hear heavy breathing. Mama reached for Augustine, jerking them both back as the man grabbed for her.

The man missed, but Mama's heart was going *thump, thump, thump*. That was another fae thing Augustine wasn't supposed to talk about, being able to hear extra-quiet sounds like people's hearts beating.

"C'mere, now," the man growled. Even in the darkness, Augustine's sharp fae eyes could see the man's teeth were icky.

Mama swung her purse at him. "Leave us alone!"

"Us?" The man grunted, his gaze dropping to Augustine. Eyes widening for a second, he snorted. "Your runt's not going to ruin my fun."

"I'm not a runt," Augustine said. Fear made his voice wobble, but he darted out from behind his mother anyway, planting himself in front of her.

The man swatted Augustine away with a meaty hand.

Augustine hit the cemetery wall, cracking his head hard enough to see stars. But with the new pain came anger. And heat. The two mixed together like a storm in his belly, making him want to do…something. He tried to control it, but the man went after Mama next, grabbing her and pushing her to the ground. Then the man climbed on top of her.

She cried out and the swirling inside Augustine became a hurricane dragging him along in its winds. Without really knowing what he was doing, he leaped onto the man's back. The hard muscle and bone he expected seemed soft and squishy. He grabbed fistfuls of the man's jacket—but his hands met roots and dirt and shards of concrete instead.

Mama's eyes blinked up at him, wide and fearful. She seemed a little blurry. Was he crying? And how was he seeing her when he was on the man's back? And why had everything gone so quiet? Except for a real loud *tha-thump, tha-thump, tha-thump,* everything else sounded real far away. He pushed to his knees, expecting them to sting from his fall, but he felt nothing. And the man attacking his mother was somehow . . . gone.

"Don't, Augustine." She shook her head as she scrabbled backward. "Don't do this."

"Don't do what, Mama?" He reached for her but the hand that appeared before him was too big. And only had five fingers. He stuck his other hand out and saw the same thing. "What's happening to me, Mama?"

"Get out of him, Augustine." She got to her feet, one trembling hand clutching the crucifix on her necklace. "Let the man go."

He stood and suddenly he was looking down at his mother. Down. How was he doing that? He glanced at his body. But it wasn't his body, it was the man's.

"I don't understand." But he had an idea. Was this one of the powers he had? One of the things he was supposed to control? He didn't know how to get out. Was he trapped? He only wanted to protect his mother, he didn't want to be this man!

The storm inside him welled up in waves. The heat in his belly was too much. He didn't understand this new power. He wanted to be himself. He wanted to be out. Panic made bigger waves, hot swells that clogged his throat so he couldn't take deep breaths. The thumping noise got louder.

The man's hands reached up to claw at Augustine, at his own skin.

Mama backed away, her fingers in the sign of the cross. He cried out to her for help. He was too hot, too angry, too scared—

A loud, wet pop filled his ears and he fell to his hands and knees again, this time covered in sticky red ooze and smoking hunks of flesh. The thumping noise was gone. Around him was more sticky red, lumps of flesh and pieces of white bone. All he could think about was the time he and Nevil Tremain had stuffed a watermelon full of firecrackers. Except this was way worse. And blowing up the watermelon hadn't made him feel like throwing up. Or smelled like burnt metal. He sat back, wiped at his face and eyes and tried to find his mother. She was a few feet away, but coming closer.

"You killed that man." She stood over him looking more angry than afraid now. "You possessed that man like a demon." She pointed at him. "You're just like your father, just like that dirty fae-blooded liar."

Augustine shook his head. "That man was hurting you—"

"Yes, you saved me, but you took his *life*, Augustine." She looked around, eyes darting in all directions. "*Sturka*," she muttered, a fae curse word Augustine had once gotten slapped for saying.

"I didn't mean to, I was trying to help—"

"And who's next? Are you going to help me that way too someday?"

He was crying now, unable to help himself. "No, Mama, no. I would never hurt you."

She grabbed him by his shirt and yanked him to his feet. "Act human, not like a freak, do you understand? If people could see what you really looked like..." Fear clouded her eyes.

He nodded, sniffling, hating the smell of the blood he was

covered in. He didn't want to be a freak. He really didn't. "I can act human. I promise."

She let go of his shirt, her lip slightly curled as she looked him over. "This was your father's blood that caused this. Not mine."

"Not yours," Augustine repeated. Mama looked human but was part smokesinger, something he knew only because he'd overheard an argument she'd had with his father on the phone once. He'd learned other things that way, too. Like that his father was something called shadeux fae. But not just part. All of him. And he'd lied to Mama about that. Used magic to make Mama think he was human. To seduce her.

"I never want to hear or see anything fae ever again or I will put you out of my house. I live as human and while you're under my roof, so will you. Am I clear?"

The thought of being without her made his chest ache. She was all he had. His world. "Yes, Mama."

But keeping his fae side hidden was impossible and five years later, put him out is exactly what she did.

Chapter One

Procrastination assassinates opportunity.
—Elektos Codex, 4.1.1

New Orleans, 2068

Augustine trailed his fingers over the silky shoulder of one of his mocha-skinned bedmates. He dare not wake her, or her sister sleeping on the other side of him, or he feared he'd never get home in time for lunch with his dear Olivia. He felt a twinge of guilt that he'd spent his first night back in New Orleans in the company of "strange" women, as Olivia would call them, but only a twinge. A man had needs, after all.

The woman sighed contentedly at his touch, causing him to do the same. Last night had been just the right amount of fun to welcome him home. He eased onto his back and folded his arms behind his head, a satisfied smile firmly in place. The Santiago sisters from Mobile, Alabama, had earned their sleep.

Outside the Hotel Monteleone, the city was just waking up. Delivery trucks rumbled through the Quarter's narrow streets, shopkeepers washed their sidewalks clean of last night's revelries and the bitter scent of chicory coffee filled the air with a seductive, smoky darkness. Day or night, there was no mistaking the magic of New Orleans. And damn, he'd missed it.

His smile widened. He wasn't much for traveling and that's all he'd done these past few months. Things had gotten hot

after he'd given his estranged brother's *human* friend entrance
to the fae plane. Ditching town was the only way to keep the
Elektos off his back. The damn fae high council had never liked
him much. Violating such a sacred rule as allowing a mortal
access to the fae plane had shot him to the top of their blacklist.

Smile fading, he sighed. If two and a half months away
wasn't enough, then he'd have to figure something else out. He
didn't like being away from Livie for so long. He could imagine
the size of her smile when he strolled in this afternoon. She'd
been more of a mother to him than his own had, not a feat
that required much effort, but Olivia had saved him from the
streets. From himself.

There wasn't much he wouldn't do for her.

With that thought, he extricated himself from the bedcovers and his sleeping partners and began the hunt for his clothing. When he'd dressed, he stood before the vanity mirror and
finger-combed his hair around his recently grown-out horns.
They followed the curve of his skull, starting near his forehead,
then arching around to end with sharp points near his cheek-
bones. He preferred them ground down, but growing them out
had helped him blend with the rest of the fae population. Most
fae also added ornate silver bands and capped the tips in filigree,
but he wasn't into that.

His jeans, black T-shirt and motorcycle boots weren't much
to look at, but the horns were all it took for most mortal women
to go positively weak. Standard fae-wear typically included a lot
of magically enhanced leather, which was perfect for a city like
NOLA, where being a little theatrical was almost expected, but
you had to have plastic for spendy gear like that.

Satisfied, he walked back to the women who'd been his
unsuspecting welcome-home party and stood quietly at the side
of the bed.

Pressing his fingertips together, he worked the magic that

ran in his veins, power born of the melding of his smokesinger and shadeux fae bloodlines, power that had blossomed when he'd finally opened himself up to it. Power he'd learned to use through trial and error and the help of a good friend.

He smiled. It would be great to see Dulcinea again, too.

Slowly, he drew his fingers apart and threads of smoke spun out between them. The strands twisted and curled between his fingers until the nebulous creation took the shape of a rose.

Gentle heat built in the bones of his hands and arms, a pleasurable sensation that gave him great satisfaction.

The form solidified further, then Augustine flicked one wrist to break the connection. With that free hand, he grasped the stem. The moment he touched it, the stem went green and royal purple filled the flower's petals. He lifted it to his nose, inhaling its heady perfume. Fae magic never ceased to amaze him. He tucked the flower behind his ear and quickly spun another, then laid the blooms on the sisters' pillows.

Pleased with his work, he picked up his bag, pulled a black compact from the pocket of his jeans and flipped it open to reveal a mirror. The mirror was nothing special, just a piece of silver-backed glass, but that was all any fae needed to travel from one place to another.

"Thanks for a wonderful evening, ladies," he whispered. Focusing on his reflection, he imagined himself back at Livie's. The familiar swirl of vertigo tugged at him as the magic drew him through.

A second later, when he glanced away from his reflection, he was home.

Harlow Goodwin held paper documents so rarely that if the stark white, unrecycled stock in her hands were anything else than the death knell to her freedom, she'd be caressing it with her bare fingers, willing to risk any residual emotions left from the person who'd last touched it—it wasn't like she could read objects the way she could people or computers, but every once in a while, if the thing had been touched by someone else recently, something leaked through. In this case, she kept her gloves on. This wasn't any old paper, this was the judgment that was about to bring an abrupt and miserable end to life as she knew it.

They couldn't even have the decency to wait to deliver it until after she'd had her morning coffee. For once, she wished it had been another of her mother's missives pleading with her to come for a visit.

She read the sum again. Eight hundred fifty thousand dollars. Eight five zero zero zero zero. She'd heard it in court when the judge had pronounced her sentence, but seeing it in black-and-white, in letters that couldn't be backspaced over and deleted, made the hollowness inside her gape that much wider.

How in the hell was she going to pay off eight hundred and fifty freaking thousand dollars? Might as well have been a million. Or a hundred million. She couldn't pay it, even if she wanted to. That queasy feeling came over her again, like she might hurl the ramen noodles she'd choked down for dinner. Moments like this, not having a father cut through her more sharply than ever. She knew that if her mother had allowed him into her life, he'd be here, taking care of her. He'd know what to do, how to handle it. That's what fathers did, wasn't it?

At least that's what Harlow's father did in her fantasies. And fantasies were all she had, because Olivia Goodwin hadn't only kept that secret from the paparazzi; she'd also kept it from her daughter.

Oh, Harlow had tried to find him. She'd searched every possibility she could think of, traced her mother's path during the month of her conception, but her mother had been on tour for a movie premiere. Thirty-eight cities in twelve different countries. The number of men she could have come in contact with was staggering.

Harlow's father, whoever he was, remained a mystery.

Heart aching with the kind of loss she'd come to think of as normal, she tossed the papers onto her desk, collapsed onto her unmade bed and dropped her head into her hands. The five-monitor computer station on her desk hummed softly, a sound she generally considered soothing, but today it only served to remind her of how royally she'd been duped. Damn it.

The client who'd hired her to test his new security system and retrieve a set of files had actually given her false information. She'd ended up hacking into what she'd belatedly guessed was his rival's company and accessing their top-secret formula for a new drug protocol. Shady SOB.

She shuddered, thinking what her punishment might have been if she'd actually delivered that drug formula into her client's hands, but a sixth sense had told her to get out right after she'd accessed the file. Something in her head had tripped her internal alarms, something she'd be forever grateful for if only it had gone off sooner. She'd ditched the info and hurriedly erased her presence. Almost. Obviously not enough to prevent herself from being caught.

Times like this she cursed the "gift" she'd been born with. Well, the first one, the ability to feel people's emotions through touch, that one she always cursed. And really it was more than emotion. She saw images, heard sounds, even picked up scents from people. Which all added up to an intense overload—sometimes pleasurable but too often painful—that she preferred not to deal with. The second gift was the way she seemed to be able to read computers. She didn't know how else to describe it, but they responded to her like she could speak binary code without even trying. Finding her way into a motherboard took no more effort than opening a door. That gift had given her a career. A slightly questionable one at times. But a job was a job. Except when it brought her clients like this last one.

A client who was now in the wind, the twenty large she'd charged him not even a down payment on her fine. She should have known something was up when he'd paid in cash, his courier a shifty-eyed sort who was probably as much fae as he was something else. She shuddered. That cash, tucked away in a backpack under the bed, was the only thing the court hadn't been able to seize. Everything else was frozen solid until she paid the fine or did her time.

She flopped back on the bed and folded her arms over her eyes. She was about as screwed as a person could get.

Her eyes closed but it didn't stop her brain from filling her head with the one name she was doing her best not to think about.

The one person capable of helping her. The one person who'd been the greatest source of conflict in her life.

Olivia Goodwin.

Her mother.

Harlow hadn't *really* spoken to her mother in years. Not since their last big fight and Olivia's umpteenth refusal to share any information about her biological father. For Harlow, it was difficult to say what hurt worse—not knowing who her father was or her mother not understanding the gaping hole inside Harlow where her father was missing and yet her mother somehow thinking she could still make things okay between them.

The cycle usually started with Olivia barraging Harlow with pleas to move to New Orleans. Harlow ignored them until she finally believed things might be different this time and countered with a request of her own. Her father's name. Because that's all she needed. A name. With her computer skills, there was no question she'd be able to find him after that. But without a name...every clue she'd followed had led to a dead end. But that small request was all it took to shut Olivia down and destroy Harlow's hope. The next few months would pass without them talking at all.

Then Olivia would contact her again.

Harlow *had* made one attempt at reconciliation, but that had dissolved just like the rest of them. After that, their communication became very one-sided. Emails and calls and letters from her mother went unanswered except for an occasional response to let Olivia know she was still alive and still *not* interested in living in New Orleans.

She loved her mother. But the hurt Olivia had caused her was deep.

If her mother was going to help now, the money would come with strings attached. Namely Harlow agreeing to drop the topic of her father.

The thought widened the hole in her heart a little more. If she agreed to never ask about him again, she'd have to live with the same unbearable sense of not knowing she'd carried all her life. And if she didn't agree, her mother probably wouldn't give her the money, which meant Harlow was going to jail. A life lesson, her mother would call it.

A deep sigh fluttered the hair trapped between her cheeks and her forearms. Was she really going to do this? The drive from Boston to New Orleans would take a minimum of twenty-four hours, but flying meant being trapped in a closed space with strangers. It also meant putting herself on the CCU's radar, and until her fine was paid, she wasn't supposed to leave the state. At least she had a car. Her little hybrid might be a beater, but it would get her to Louisiana and there'd be no one in the car but her.

Another sigh and she pulled her arms away from her face to stare at the ceiling. If her mother refused her the money, which was a very real possibility, Harlow would be in jail in a month's time. Her security gone, her freedom gone, forced to live in a cell with another person.

She sat up abruptly. Would they let her keep her gloves in prison? What if her cell mate...touched her? That kind of looming threat made her want to do something rebellious. The kind of thing she'd only done once before at a Comic Con where her costume had given her a sense of anonymity and some protection from skin-to-skin contact.

She wanted one night of basic, bone-deep pleasure of her choosing. One night of the kind of fun that didn't include sitting in front of her monitors, leveling up one of her Realm of Zauron characters to major proportions. Not that that kind of fun wasn't epic. It was basically her life. But she needed something more, the kind of memory that would carry her through her incarceration.

One night of *careful* physical contact with another living, breathing *male* being.

The thought alone was enough to raise goose bumps on her skin. She'd do it the same way she had at Comic Con. A couple of good, stiff drinks and the alcohol would dull her senses and make being around so many people bearable. With a good buzz, she could stand being touched. Maybe even find it enjoyable, if things went well. Which was the point.

She was going to New Orleans. The city was practically built on senseless fun and cheap booze, right? If there was ever a place to have one last night of debauchery before heading to the big house, New Orleans seemed custom made for it.

On her Life Management Device, the one she could no longer afford and that would soon be turned off, she checked the weather. Unseasonably warm in New Orleans. Leaving behind the snowpocalypse of Boston wouldn't be such a hardship, but she wasn't about to ditch her long sleeves just for a little sunshine. On the rare occasions she had to leave her apartment, she liked as much skin covered as possible.

She jumped off the bed, grabbed her rolling bag and packed. Just the necessities—travel laptop with holoscreen and gaming headset, some clothes, toiletries and the cash. Not like she'd be gone long. She changed into her favorite Star Alliance T-shirt, set her security cameras, locked down her main computer and servers and grabbed her purse. She took a deep breath and one last look at her apartment. It was only for a few days. She could do this.

A few minutes later she was in the car, a jumbo energy drink in the cup holder and the nav on her LMD directing her toward Louisiana.

Augustine tucked away his traveling mirror and inhaled the comforting scent of home. The weeks of rarely staying in one spot for longer than a few nights had worn thin. He'd tried a stint in Austin, Texas, another fae Haven city, but a week there and he'd begun to feel eyes on him. Being back in New Orleans was pure happiness. This was the only ground he'd ever considered home, and this house, the estate of retired movie star Olivia Goodwin, was the only place that had ever *felt* like home.

Protecting Olivia and this place was why he'd run to begin with, but she knew he hadn't been the cause of the trouble. Not really. That landed squarely on the shoulders of his estranged half brother, Mortalis. They shared a father but that was about it. They'd never seen eye to eye on anything. Mortalis disapproved of Augustine's life in more ways than he could count and took every opportunity, rare as they were, to make that known.

Despite that, Augustine had helped one of Mortalis's very pretty, very persuasive female friends gain access to the fae plane, specifically the Claustrum, the max-security prison where the fae kept the worst of their kind. Livie had agreed it had been the right thing to do, but she hadn't really understood the consequences.

The sounds of female voices reached his ears. Olivia and Lally, her companion and housekeeper, were out on the back porch enjoying the unseasonably warm weather. He set his bag down and moved softly from the hall and into the kitchen. Their voices were louder now, filtering in through the screen door along with the afternoon breeze. Ice clinked in glasses and the scent of mint and bourbon followed.

He smiled. Livie loved herself a julep on the porch. He leaned in close to the screen, but left the door closed. "Miss me so much you have to drink away your sorrows, huh?"

Both women jumped in their rockers, clutching at their hearts and slopping bourbon and soda over the rims of their glasses.

Olivia shook her cane at him, her shock widening into an unstoppable grin. "Augustine Robelais, how dare you sneak up on two old women like that." She threw her head back and laughed. "Oh, Augie, you're home. Praise our lady Elizabeth Taylor. Get out here and let me hug your neck."

He pushed through the screen door and scooped Livie into his arms. She squeezed him hard, her form somehow frailer than he remembered. He whispered into her silver-white bob, "I missed you more than I have words for."

"And I, you, *cher.*" Her hand cupped the back of his head as she kissed his cheek. "I am so glad you're home." She released him, her amber eyes glittering with tears.

He turned to Lally and caught her in a hug as she stood. "I'm sure you didn't miss cleaning up after me, huh?"

Lally clung to him, her voice catching when she finally spoke. "Silly child." She patted his back as she let him go and sat down.

"I had so much free time, I read half Miss Olivia's library." She laughed. "I'm still not used to seeing you with your horns grown out, but I'm happy to have you back, no matter what you look like."

He leaned against the porch railing. The warmth of their love was almost palpable, soothing the ache in his heart from being away. "I appreciate that. I'll be grinding the horns off soon enough."

A wash of concern took away Livie's smile. "Everything all right then? Didn't have any trouble did you? No run-ins with any Elektos?"

"Not a bit." He couldn't stop smiling. Even the air smelled better. "How about you?"

She snorted softly. "Nothing I couldn't handle."

Which meant they'd been here. That knocked the smile off his face. Anger fueled a fire in his belly, but for her sake he just nodded. Obviously she didn't want to talk about it right now. Or maybe just not around Lally, but there wasn't much Olivia kept from her.

"You home to stay, Mr. Augustine?" Lally looked hopeful.

"Yes." He sighed and tipped his head back, inhaling the earthy, heady scent of the Garden District. Tiny green tips were beginning to show on the trees. In a few weeks, spring would overtake the place. "I hope I never have to run again." He would, though, if it meant keeping these two women safe.

"Good." Lally smiled. "We had enough of you bein' gone."

"That we did." Livie sipped her mint julep, then held it up to him. "You want a drink, darling?"

"No, I'm good. All I really want is to sleep in my own bed."

She took another sip before setting the drink down. "Well, I'll be. You mean you're not heading into the Quarter to see what young thing you might woo into your arms for the night?"

He laughed. Olivia didn't need to know he'd already been

there. "I thought I'd take one night off. Besides, tomorrow night is *Nokturnos*. I'll do plenty of wooing then."

"Is that tomorrow? With you gone, I guess it slipped my mind." She looked at Lally. "Did you realize it was the new moon?"

"I knew that much, but I can't be bothered with the rest." Lally waved her hand. "All that mask wearing and kissing strangers and carrying on like fools. Humans do enough of that during Mardi Gras."

Augustine raised a brow. "We don't carry on like—well, okay, a little bit like fools, but it's the fae New Year. There's got to be some celebration. Plus the fae need their own party before the tourists invade for carnival and the town isn't ours anymore. This is a big one, too. Since the covenant's been broken and humans know we exist, it's the first *Nokturnos* we can celebrate publicly." He shook his finger at Olivia. "You've got a good bit of haerbinger blood in your system, Ms. Goodwin. You should be celebrating, too."

She waved him off. "Please, *cher*. I've had enough celebrating in my days."

"My lands," Lally exclaimed with a smirk. "You sure came back from your sojourn with a lot of sass, didn't you, Mr. Augustine? Hmph."

He laughed.

"I missed this, I surely did." Lally tipped her head up toward Augustine. "So you'll be kissing a stranger tomorrow evening? Guess that's not much different than most of your evenings." She laughed, clearly tickled with herself.

"And I'm the one full of sass?" But he grinned. "Hey, you want me to have good luck for the New Year, don't you?" A yawn caught him off guard. Before he'd returned home, sleep had eluded him the last few nights, replaced by nightmares so real, they'd driven him to return home. Probably earlier than was prudent, but enough was enough.

Livie immediately looked concerned. "You really are tired, aren't you, *cher*?"

He hadn't slept much last night, either, but he wasn't about to tell them that. He scratched the base of one horn. "You know how it is when you're not in your own bed. It's just not the same."

Lally nodded. "I hear that. You going to make it till supper, Mr. Augustine, or should I put up a plate for you?"

"Depends on what you're fixing."

"Nothing special. Just a little RB-and-R and some hot sausage."

"Nothing special." He snorted. "You know I love red beans and rice. Especially yours. Yes to supper, but first I should probably run down to Jackson Square and see if Dulcinea is around. Let her know I'm back." He'd stayed clear of the Quarter's main areas last night, too, keeping as low a profile as he could without becoming completely invisible to the pretty tourist girls he so enjoyed.

Lally stood. "I'll just go take another sausage out of the freezer."

After she left, Livie gave him a sly smile. "I'm sure Dulcinea's missed you."

He rolled his eyes. "You know it's not like that between us."

"Mm-hmm. I know what you two get up to." She swirled the liquid in her glass. "I know you're both adults and consenting and all that."

He knew what Olivia was hinting at, but the past was the past. "We're just friends."

"Friends with benefits, that's what they used to call it in my day." She lifted her glass to her lips as Lally came back out.

"Y'all still talking about Miss Dulcinea?"

"Yes, why?" Augustine answered.

Lally settled into her chair and pointed toward the back corner of the yard. "She was out here one night. Just sitting in the gazebo past the pool there. I gave her a little wave, but she didn't wave back. Didn't see her again after that, but the next night, a stray cat showed up. Sleek gray thing with darker stripes and these two different-colored eyes that just looked right through a person's soul."

Augustine looked at Livie the same time she looked at him and in unison, they both said, "Dulcinea."

She was one of the oddest fae he knew, not just personality-wise, but because even she didn't know her bloodlines other than that they included fae and varcolai, or shifter. The strange stew of her lineage had given her some rare powers, including the ability to take on random animal forms. In othernatural terms, she was a remnant, a label applied to anyone with mixed othernatural heritage. But in the neighborhood, most called her a changeling.

Lally sat back, resting her arms across her plump stomach. "I figured that was her."

He nodded. "Thanks for letting me know."

She lifted one hand to shake a finger at him. "You definitely should go see that girl. She's pining for you."

Augustine laughed. "Dulce pines for no one. Except maybe this city." It was nice to know she'd kept an eye on Olivia and Lally while he'd been gone. He hadn't asked her to do that and was a little surprised she had, but then maybe he wasn't. Nothing Dulcinea did could really be considered shocking.

Chapter Two

Augustine strolled toward Jackson Square with a little extra swagger in his step despite his sleeplessness. That was the power of being home again, of being back where he belonged with Livie. But the closer to the square he got, the deeper the invasive itch of the iron fencing dug into him. Iron was a fae's worst nightmare, a death sentence in great enough quantities, which was why most of the ironwork in New Orleans had been replaced over the years with look-alike aluminum. He shook the itch off. He wouldn't let it bother him. Not even the tourists plowing past could ruin his mood. It was too beautiful a day, too good to be home and too hard to be grumpy in a city that had so much going for it.

Ahead of him, under her customary black umbrella, sat Dulcinea, her back to him. She kept to the square's far side to put as much distance between herself and the iron fencing as possible, but he still didn't know how she could take such prolonged exposure. For a fae, being so close to that much iron was like having your skin peeled off. Slowly. But that was Dulcinea. One of a kind.

A fat strand of bloodred yarn tied back her silvery gray dreads so that the beads, feathers and bones woven into the matted strands clinked against one another when she moved. That slip of red was the only color she wore. The rest of her outfit from her long, flowy dress to her casually torn leggings to her combat boots was black or a shade of gray. Combined with her dusty gray skin and her nearly six foot height, she made a striking figure. One that looked very much the mystical fortune-teller. And the tourists loved every inch of her, even her bicolored eyes, one blue, one green.

Since the breaking of the covenant that had enabled mortals to see all the othernatural creatures around them, New Orleans had enjoyed a boom in visitors interested in gawking at the fae that called the Haven city home.

Dulcinea was very happy to take advantage, literally, of those visitors. And was doing just that as he approached.

She had a victim—ah, tourist—at her table, her fae tarot cards laid out between them, no doubt spinning some grand tale that would result in the tourist forking over more money to hear what else their future might hold, or where their great-aunt Sally had buried a stash of gold coins or what numbers they should play in next week's lottery. It seemed likely to Augustine that Dulcinea's mulligan stew of a gene pool must hold a healthy dollop of haerbinger fae, the same as Livie's did, because both women had a good knack for knowing the truth about a person.

Dulcinea just embellished the truth with liberal abandon as befitted the needs of the poor sap in front of her. He sidled closer to listen.

"This card means death." She tapped one black-painted fingernail on the tarot card. The female tourist gasped, fear obvious in her eyes. Dulcinea raised her hand. "This death is not yours." She passed her hand dramatically through the air. "It's the death of all ill will against you. The death of your enemies' desire to bring harm against you."

"My enemies?" The woman wore jeans with a matching jean jacket and a bright white T-shirt that read "I got Bourbon on Drunk Street." Her fingers strayed to the St. Christopher medal around her neck. "I don't feel like I have any enemies."

Dulcinea leveled her gaze at the woman, cocking her head

slightly. "I see someone at your church. Another woman. She has dark hair and is a bit meddlesome." Dulcinea squinted and tapped the side of her head like she was on the verge of a psychic breakthrough. "She desires to..."

The woman's mouth went open. "Helen Kettell! I knew it. My coconut cream cake outsells her German chocolate every year at the bake sale." The woman covered her mouth with her hand for a moment. "What's she planning?"

Augustine snorted. Dulcinea glanced back, her eyes lighting when she saw him. She turned to the woman and sat forward in her chair. "You'll have to come back tomorrow. I'm closed."

"What? Closed? But you're talking to me right now."

"And now I'm not." Dulcinea jumped up and walked toward Augustine, ignoring the sputtering woman behind her. She flung her arms wide. "Gussie!"

He laughed, even though he'd kill anyone else who tried to call him that. "Hey, Dulce. I didn't mean to interrupt."

"You didn't. I was done." She kissed him on the mouth, then stepped back and grinned, crinkling the skin around her heavily lined eyes. "Really good to have you back in town. I guess you were too busy last night to say hello."

So she had seen him. Not surprising. "Yeah, well, I'm here now." He shook his head at the lip-to-lip contact. Also not surprising. "And it's good to be back. I owe you one for checking on Olivia and Lally while I was gone."

She hitched up one shoulder. "You would have done the same for me."

"You know it." Not that Dulcinea seemed to have any family for him to check on. She claimed not to know anything about her parents and that she was raised as an orphan by a distant aunt until she'd ended up in the same gang as him. Then the crew had become her family. He looked at her now-deserted table. "Business been good?"

"Crazy good, but I can only stand so much contact with *these* people." She hissed at a couple as they passed by, causing them to shrink back and almost run into another artist's stall. Then she gave the side eye to one of her competitors. "And then there's *that* one."

Augustine turned to look. Right in front of the fence, under a beautiful ivory pavilion, sat a woman who was as sleek and sophisticated as Dulcinea was not. "Ah." He nodded. "Giselle."

"Witch," Dulcinea spat.

Augustine smirked. "That's not much of an epithet considering she is one." Giselle Vincent wasn't *just* a witch. As the daughter of New Orleans's coven leader and High Wizard, she was witch royalty. Her father, Evander, was a fourth-level wizard and the final authority when it came to all things witchy in NOLA. Well, until the Elektos got involved. They were *really* the final authority due to the treaty established after the messy business of the curse.

He could see why Dulcinea would feel threatened by her, though. Giselle's reputation also made her one of the most sought-after fortune-tellers. Combine that with her rank and yeah, Dulcinea wouldn't be Giselle's bestie anytime soon.

"Yeah, well the High Priestess of Mean can get bent for all I care."

"What's she done to you?" Dulcinea and Giselle had never been friendly, but this blatant animosity was something new.

"I overheard her telling some tourists I have bedbugs living in my hair." Dulcinea flicked two fingers at Giselle in some sort of Dulcinea sign language for *suck it.*

Augustine popped a brow. "Do you really think she'd say that? Maybe I should have a talk with her." When they ran the streets as part of the same crew, he wouldn't have hesitated to come to Dulcinea's defense, but now that they were living more separate lives, he didn't want to overstep.

"No. Don't say anything. When it's time, I'll deal with her."

Giselle looked up, pushing her long black hair out of the way. From under the fringe of heavy bangs, her dark eyes pierced straight into Augustine. He held her gaze. She might be a witch, but she didn't scare him. Actually, she was kind of hot in an untouchable, pristine way. He couldn't imagine her hair messed up or her pristine white outfits dirty or wrinkled. Or maybe he could. He pulled his gaze back to Dulcinea. "If you're sure."

"I am. Leave the freak to me," Dulcinea added. "I mean, who wears white in this city? It's witchcraft, I tell you." She made crazy eyes. "Witchcraft."

"O-kay, how about we get you out of here for a bit?" He rolled his shoulders uncomfortably. "Forget Giselle, I think being next to all this iron is starting to affect you."

She stared at the fence for a second. "Yeah, that is kind of bothersome. Whatevs." Then she turned to him and smiled brightly. "Let's go drink. But not *Belle's*. I don't go there much anymore."

Dulcinea's standard hangout, *La Belle et la Bête*, was the same as the rest of the othernatural population in town because it was the oldest othernatural bar in town and specifically designed to keep mortal eyes from prying. He'd ask why not there later. "Fine with me. I need to be a little more inconspicuous at the moment anyway."

"Elektos doesn't know you're back, huh?"

"Nope." He looked at her a little harder. "Is that why you stopped going to *Belle's*? Were the Elektos hassling you about me?"

"Nobody hassles me. Except for you." She winked. "It was just...this and that. You know. C'mon. I know a good place." Without another word, she turned and started walking.

Damn, the Elektos going after her made him mad. He could understand the high council looking for him at Olivia's, but bothering his friends crossed a line. He jumped to catch up with her. "I'm sorry about that. Anything else going on?"

"Yes, but…" She shot him a look. "When we're settled." Then Dulcinea's gaze traveled higher. "I like the full-on horns. I bet those fae-loving female tourists do, too. You letting them grow now?"

He touched one self-consciously. In truth, he was kind of over them. "I'm not keeping them this way. Just did it to blend."

She shrugged. "Your head."

They crossed the street and swerved through a few blocks of tourists until she pushed through a nondescript wood door. A simple hand-painted sign above read "Stella's." He followed after her. The place was lit mostly by a bunch of holovisions showing various sporting events. The few solar tubes there looked like they hadn't held a full charge in years, which was fine with Augustine because he wasn't sure the place would hold up to bright light. The sticky floor grabbed at his boots with every step and dust coated the Mardi Gras beads that hung off the beer signs.

Dulcinea had already found a spot at the bar. He took the stool beside her, hoping nothing in the joint was communicable. "Nice place."

"Isn't it?" She perked up. "Stella's is my other joint. They leave you alone in here."

"They leave a lot alone in here by the looks of it."

The bartender stopped leaning and walked toward them, nodding at Dulcinea. "The usual?"

She held up two fingers. "Double it."

"Really," Augustine started, "you come here that often? What's your usual?" With Dulcinea, nothing was a given. Once upon a time, it had been white Russians, heavy on the white.

"I come here enough, I guess."

"Must have started since I left because you've never brought me here."

"You're too fancy for joints like this." She stuck her tongue out at him.

"Fancy?"

"Yeah, you like the kind of places where the beautiful people hang out." She batted her lashes at him, then gave him a wry smile. "I guess I should say the beautiful women. That you then seduce and take home."

"Hey, now." He pointed a finger at her. "I never take them home. It's their hotel or nothing."

She laughed. "You're such a man whore."

He waggled his eyebrows. "That didn't stop you from taking a dip in this pool." A dip that had happened ages ago and only that one time, as they'd quickly come to the mutual understanding that being friends was more valuable.

The bartender set two bottles of Abita, the local beer, down in front of them, answering the question about what her usual was. She took a long pull off hers before responding. "That's because I liked to swim and your pool was always open. Also, we were young and stupid."

"That we were." He sipped his beer. "Dulce, you know you could swim in any pool you wanted." She might be odd, but there were plenty of humans who'd developed a fae fetish since the covenant had fallen and to them there was no such thing as a normal fae anyway. Something he'd taken full advantage of.

She leaned in, clinking her bottle against his. "Maybe, but I don't want some mouth breather following me around, mooneyed and dopey with love. I want what I want until I don't want it anymore." She tipped her bottle in his direction. "With you, it was just like you said. We were young and dumb. No emotional strings. Just like all those tourist chicks you pick up. Except I never tried to hunt you down afterwards."

He nodded, slightly sobered by her frankness. "None of them have tried to hunt me down."

"That you know about." She set her beer on the bar, her expression growing earnest. "I really *am* glad you're back. Things are getting a little hinky in town."

"This about what you wouldn't tell me outside?"

She glanced around, but the few other patrons in the bar were some distance away and definitely not interested in what they were doing. "Vamps."

Not what he'd wanted to hear. He shook his head. He hadn't seen a single vampire on his walk here, despite the fact that they could daywalk within the limits of the Orleans parish thanks to a nearly two-century-old curse leveled against the city by a heartbroken witch. "Is that why you were over at Olivia's?"

She kind of half shrugged. "That and you were gone. Figured it couldn't hurt." The label on her bottle slowly disappeared under her fingernails. "Khell's got his hands full, but you ask me? It's his people to blame. I'm sure there's a soft spot in his ranks."

"So someone's getting greased, letting them in." Bribes were as much a part of New Orleans history as the vampires, but Augustine had thought the new Guardian, Khell, wouldn't have stood for that garbage. He didn't know Khell well, but the guy seemed a by-the-book type. Maybe his lieutenants were dirty. Augustine shook his head. Maybe? More like definitely. Few people in this city turned down a bribe.

Her odd eyes went a little darker. "Worse. I think one of them might be *bringing* the vampires in. Promising *La Ville Éternelle Nuit* to whoever can pay the price."

"Damn. That *is* hinky." *La Ville Éternelle Nuit* was what the vampires called New Orleans—except they didn't really know it was New Orleans they were referring to as the City of Eternal Night. After the witch had her heart broken by her fae lover and cursed the city into becoming a vampire playground, the ruling Elektos had been able to temper the curse with a secondary spell that erased the memory of New Orleans from a vampire's mind when they left.

Now *La Ville Éternelle Nuit* existed in vampire legends, more a myth than a real place. Like Atlantis or the Lost City of Gold.

Still, there was something in the witch's curse that caused the city to act like a beacon to the pasty bloodsuckers, drawing them to the place over and over to the point that New Orleans had at one time seemed synonymous with vampires.

Even in current times, the leeches managed to evade the fae checkpoints and bribe their way in on occasion. They might not understand why this place held such allure, but the draw remained. Eliminating the original witch's curse would probably be the only way to break it, but so far no one had found a way to do that.

"Told ya." She emptied her bottle.

He was only halfway through his, but he took a good swig in an effort to catch up. "Just one more reason I'm glad I never got sucked into that Guardian business. Bunch of hypocrites. You can't tell me Khell doesn't know what's going on right under his nose."

"Maybe he does. Maybe he doesn't. Just giving you a heads-up, I know you're out and about a lot. You might run into one."

"I appreciate the intel. I'll keep my eyes open." He squinted at her. "You haven't had any issues, have you?"

She smiled, eyes glinting. "You know I never go anywhere without a reasonable amount of steel strapped to me somewhere." She swung her leg out to rub against his. "Care to check the blade currently sheathed to my inner thigh?"

He snorted. "I believe you." He had a dagger in his boot but that was it, unlike the old days when he wore as much weaponry as he could, like the rest of his crew. Seemed it was a habit Dulcinea hadn't broken. Wasn't that unusual, really. Most fae went out pretty heavy, but he was trying to put that part of his life behind him for Livie's sake. Besides, when you had the amounts of smokesinger and shadeux blood that he did, weapons were extraneous. Some days he wondered what Mortalis or their father could have taught him, considering he'd learned to master his skills on his own and with some help from Dulcinea, but he was already lethal. What more could there be? "Maybe there's a bright side to these vamps in town."

"For real?"

"Well, if Khell and the Elektos are busy with that issue, maybe they won't care that I'm back."

She stared at him like he'd suddenly sprouted a third nostril. "Dude, you let a human into the Claustrum. They're never going to let that go."

He sighed. "That's what I was afraid of."

"But," she added, "they are plenty racked with this other business. Maybe if you catch a vamp or two, the Elektos would let things slide. You know, perform a couple of good-faith stakings."

He shook his head. "That's not my way anymore, you know that. I'm a lover, not a fighter."

"You used to be both. Hey, you going to do *Nokturnos* this year? Or you think the Elektos will be watching for you?"

"I'm sure they will be, but I'll have a mask on so how are they going to find me? I wouldn't miss it."

"Cool. Meet me at Mena's beforehand and we'll grab some dinner, then do a little pub run before the festivities get under way."

"It's a date."

She gave him a look, then inhaled, lifting herself up slightly. "Okay, I gotta run. This is on me." She slapped some plastic bills down on the bar top, hopped off her stool and without so much as another word, she left.

Typical Dulcinea. He sat awhile longer, thinking about what

she'd said. It wasn't a bad idea for him to bag and tag a few of the vampire intruders—if he could find any. Bringing the vamps in could help, but it would also put him squarely in the Elektos's crosshairs. Not only would they know he was in town, but they might get the wild idea that he was angling for the Guardianship next time it came open.

He crossed himself, a habit instilled by his mother and one he'd yet to shake. He hadn't meant to wish any ill will toward Khell. Although no doubt the Guardian was under orders to bring Augustine in, probably alive but with the Elektos, that wasn't a guarantee.

Someone behind him dropped a bottle. The pop of shattering glass set his nerves on edge. He shouldn't be out anyway. He slipped off the bar stool and headed for the john.

Once inside the cramped stall, he pulled his mirror from his pocket and left Stella's behind for a dinner of Lally's RB&R, followed by his bed and a long night of hopefully dreamless sleep.

"Please tell me you're kidding." Harlow stared at the fourth desk clerk she'd talked to in the last hour and a half. Driving twenty-four hours nonstop wasn't really as fun as it sounded, even while listening to the entire *Lord of the Rings* trilogy. Her last energy drink had worn off in Mississippi. Now every blink felt like sandpaper scraping her eyes. On top of that, she was being forced to talk to people. And they were *everywhere* in this crowded city. "I called from the last hotel. *You* said there were rooms."

He sighed like he didn't have the time for the conversation. "*You* didn't speak with me."

"Whoever I spoke with said there were rooms. They said they

would hold one. I gave them my credit number." A risk considering it might alert the CCU she was out of town, but as soon as she was in her room, she'd log on and take care of that.

He sighed. "Your name again?"

"Harlow Goodwin." She rubbed at her eyes, which only made them worse. All she wanted was a bed.

His brows rose. "Any relation to Olivia Goodwin? She lives here, you know."

"No relation, sorry." It wasn't fair to use the power of her mother's name when they weren't even on speaking terms.

"Ah, yes, Miss Goodwin. I see now. Your card was denied. Not that it matters. We are completely booked."

"Denied? That can't be—oh." She'd forgotten about the freeze on her assets. Damn, damn, damn. "I have cash."

His smile was syrupy. "Good for you. Perhaps the next hotel can help you."

"The next? This is the fourth one I've been to. I need to sleep now. Why are there no rooms?"

His expression screwed up into something akin to disbelief. "I expect the entire Quarter is booked. Tonight is *Nokturnos*."

Whatever that was. "You must have something."

With a sniff, he tapped the keyboard in front of him again. "Nothing." His fingers stopped and his gaze flicked across the screen. "Wait..." More tapping.

"Wait? For what? Did you find something? I'll take anything."

"It looks like I have one *suite* left." His emphasis made it plain he thought the room was well out of her price range. Which it was, but that didn't mean she deserved his attitude.

That alone made her want to take it. "And how much is this *suite*?"

"Twenty-two hundred."

"A night." Of course, it was a night. Lack of sleep was making her dumb. "For that kind of money, it should come with a butler."

"It does. And a chef, should you require one."

"For real?"

He looked up. "Yes."

"Wow. I don't need that much attention, but I'll take it." If she was going to jail, she might as well have a little luxury first. Anyway, she'd only be here two nights, tops. And if she was going to entertain some strange man for one last night of fun before she was locked up, why not do it in style?

He looked skeptical. "And how will you be paying for that, Miss Goodwin, since your credit was declined?"

She dug into her leather jacket and pulled out one of the rolls of plastic she'd brought for this very reason. "I said I had cash. If that's okay with you"—she read his name tag—"Milton."

He watched as she counted off bills, smacking them down on the counter so the plastic coating slapped the granite with a satisfactory *thwap*. His smile was half the size of his original one. "Very good, Miss Goodwin. I'll just take care of that for you."

"Thanks. Make sure you give me a receipt."

He nodded, then started pecking away at his keyboard. She turned to inspect the rest of the patrons milling about the lobby. There were so many. She cringed and tried to shake off the first twinges of a panic attack. None of these people cared what she was doing, none of them were bothered by her presence, so she shouldn't let them bother her. She concentrated on the details of the situation, a technique that often helped. A lot of them carried elaborate masks, some covered in feathers and sequins, some leather, some papier-mâché and spangles. "Is there some kind of party going on?" she asked without looking at him.

"Yes, ma'am. The *Nokturnos* I mentioned."

A sense of victory rose in her that he'd answered without

condescension. Amazing what a stack of plastic would do for a person's attitude. "It's a masked ball type thing?"

"It takes place in the streets, much like Mardi Gras, but there are no floats. Just general revelry and drinking. And beads, of course."

She turned to face him. "So a standard night in New Orleans?"

He smiled, genuinely this time. "Sort of. From what I understand, it's considered good luck if you kiss a stranger during *Nokturnos*. Wearing a mask when you go out means you're game."

She checked out the people carrying masks again. "How about that. And it starts tonight?"

"Yes. One night only, that of the first new moon before Mardi Gras."

She'd planned on going to see her mother first, but maybe it was better to save that unpleasant, inevitable business until after she'd had her fun, especially if the streets were going to be filled with willing strangers tonight. Hopefully not so filled she couldn't handle it. She'd deal with it later, though. All she wanted now was sleep. She checked her watch. Not quite 1 p.m. "What time does this thing start?"

He checked a piece of paper on the desk. "The new moon sets at eleven forty-three p.m., marking the beginning of the fae New Year, but *Nokturnos* really starts at sunset."

The word *fae* sent a jolt through her, reminding her she was in their territory now. Her mother's territory. "Good. Thanks." She had some time to sleep and recover from the drive. She could go out and have her night of fun before she faced her mother.

After that, she probably wouldn't need a reason to drink.

Chapter Three

Augustine rolled over and stretched, smiling as he did. Last night's sleep had been amazing. Deep, dreamless and restful. He stared out the big leaded-glass window that lit up his entire attic apartment, contentment washing over him. He'd have to deal with the Elektos at some point, but right now, he was just happy to be here. One day at a time. No reason to get worked up about what hadn't happened yet.

With that thought, he extricated himself from the bedcovers and blinked at the clock on his nightstand. Already well past lunch.

He stretched lazily and scratched his chest, standing for a moment before the vanity mirror. He frowned at his horns. Well, he was home now. After *Nokturnos*, he'd grind them down again.

Home. The word filled him with all kinds of satisfaction. He snapped the covers straight on the bed, sending dust motes swirling through the sunlight filtering in through the big window. Damn, it was good to be back.

Now all he really needed was a long, hot shower before lunch with Livie, something he'd missed while he'd been away.

Livie might be getting on in years, but she had enough fae blood in her to keep her sharp and spry, and her stories about her life as a famous actress never failed to entertain. Living with her was about the easiest thing he'd ever done and easy was sort of his life motto. He shucked his sleep pants and headed for the bath.

He rounded the corner into the white-tiled bath and nearly ran into Lally. If Olivia was like a mother to him, Lally was like his older, sweetly bossy, well-meaning sister. Fluffy white towels filled one arm.

"Lands, child, I'm so used to you not being here, you gave me a scare!" She clapped her hand to her chest, her fingers tangling in the gold chain that disappeared beneath the neck of her blue housedress. Then, as if she'd suddenly realized he was in his altogether, she canted her eyes toward the ceiling and handed him a towel. "Mr. Augustine, I do *not* need to see your business *again*. I've already seen it too many times."

He held the folded towel in front of himself. "You're the only woman who's ever said that, Lally." He kissed her cheek as he slid past. "It's good to be back."

She left the room, but lingered by the door, gaze aimed away from him. "You promise you're here to stay?"

"Yes." No matter what he had to do to make that true. "I said that yesterday and I meant it—did something happen while I was gone?"

She hesitated long enough for him to question her answer. "No, just that Miss Olivia missed you something awful. Now, hurry up. You already missed breakfast and I am just about to serve lunch." Eyes still averted, she started for the stairs, then hesitated. "I know you've got your *Nokturnos* tonight, but it's Valentine's Day today, in case you didn't realize. *And* you missed Christmas. And regular human folks' New Year."

He grinned. "If you think I came back without a present for you or Olivia, you don't know me very well, Lally Hughes."

With a little smile, she left, pulling the door shut behind her.

A hot shower later and he was in jeans and a long sleeve T-shirt headed down to the dining room and the delicious aromas of Lally's cooking. When he'd been traveling, the memories of her food had made his mouth water. Now his stomach grumbled along with it. His present for Lally was tucked under his arm, the one for Olivia clutched in his hand.

And there at the bottom of the stairs stood the woman herself in all her glory, which this morning meant a fringed peacock-printed caftan and turquoise turban.

Olivia Goodwin leaned on her cane, face beaming up at him. "How did you sleep, my darling? Or did you slip out of bed and end up in someone else's dreams?"

He laughed, winding his arm around her in a quick hug. He'd missed her scent of lemon verbena perfume. "Not last night. I stayed in my own bed and slept like a rock. It was just what I needed."

"Alas, think of all the poor girls who missed out."

He hitched his mouth to one side.

She lifted a brow as she disengaged herself from his embrace. "What?"

"Tonight's *Nokturnos*. I'll make up for it. At least twice."

She swatted him with her crystal-topped cane, amber eyes wide in pretend shock. "Oh, Augie, you're a scoundrel."

He held his free hand to his heart, splaying his six fingers over his chest. "You know I aim to please."

She shook her head, but her smile said she wasn't mad about anything. "C'mon, *cher*, let's eat. Lally's made shrimp and grits."

"Hot damn. I think besides you and her, that's the thing I missed the most." She laughed along with him. "But first, I have something for you." He handed over the square black box, keeping the larger package tucked under his arm. "Merry Christmas. I'm sorry I couldn't be here. And I guess happy Valentine's Day, too."

"Augie, you shouldn't have. But that doesn't mean I'm not glad you did." She smiled as she opened it, revealing the marcasite fleur-de-lis pendant he'd picked up in an antiques store. It wasn't much, simple costume jewelry, but it had reminded him of her the moment he'd seen it. Which was fortunate, because it was all he could afford. "It's lovely. I adore it!" She held the box out to him. "Put it on me, Augie."

He fastened the chain around her neck, then he stood back to admire it. "Bright and sparkly, just like you."

She glanced over at the rococo gold-framed hall mirror. "Perfect accessory for lunch, don't you think?" She tucked her arm through his. "Let's go."

Augustine walked her into the dining room. "I cannot tell you how poorly I've eaten since I've been away." A bit of a lie, but nothing could compare to Lally's cooking or the style of food he was used to. He helped Olivia into her chair, then took the seat across from her.

Lally came out from the kitchen with two covered plates, putting one down in front of each of them. "There's more where that came from, so eat up." She added a boat of her famous redeye gravy, then started pouring iced tea.

He set the remaining present on the table. "Merry Christmas, Lally."

"For me?" She smiled at him like she didn't know better. The woman had learned a lot from Olivia. Too much. "Should I open it now?"

"Go on, you know you want to." He laughed.

Livie touched her necklace. "Augie gave me this. Isn't it beautiful?"

"Gorgeous, Miss Olivia. The boy's got taste." Lally tore into the wrapping. "Oh," she exclaimed. "You know how I love these!" She held up the cookbook for Olivia to see, then shook her head at Augustine. "You shouldn't have. Real books are too dear."

He waved off her protests. "There was a great vintage

bookshop in…one of the places I was." Neither of them was supposed to know where he'd gone. "I got a really good deal on it." He'd traded a few shifts as night watchman.

Lally hugged the book to her chest. "I love it. It's going right on my shelf." She disappeared into the kitchen, humming to herself and smiling.

"That was sweet of you, Augie." Livie helped herself to the gravy, but her attention was clearly on Augustine. "How was your time away *really?*"

"Horrible. Awful." He stuffed a forkful of grits into his mouth. The creamy, salty goodness mixed with the bacon pieces Lally sprinkled over the shrimp just about did him in. "But this is fixing me right up."

"Austin's a nice town—"

He gave her a stern look. "Olivia."

She held her hands up. "*If* that's where you were. At least it's a Haven city like New Orleans."

He sighed, refusing to answer. She *knew* that was one of the places he'd been. She'd forced it out of him with that way of hers before he'd left.

She sipped her iced tea. "Sorry to hear your visit was so disagreeable. Were the people you met there unkind?"

"No, they were very nice. Now stop digging. You already know too much." He sat back. "Regardless of where I was, it wasn't here." He winked. "Nothing compares to New Orleans and the life I have here with you, Olivia."

She smiled, as he knew she would. "I love you, too, Augustine."

He drizzled more gravy over his grits. "Fill me in on everything I was too tired to hear last night. What have I missed?"

It was all the opening she needed. "Mr. Chalmers's beagle had a litter of five pups, but they've all been spoken for. Wendell, the boudin man down at the farmers' market? His daughter's getting married to a lawyer in New York. Can you imagine? Like there aren't plenty of nice boys right here in town. A New York lawyer. Pfft. Probably a vampire. What else…oh, of course, everyone's gearing up for Mardi Gras in a few weeks…"

Augustine just nodded and listened and ate, enjoying every minute of her banter. "What about the Elektos? Did they hassle you much? Tell the truth." He knew they must have based on his conversation with Lally and Olivia's reluctance to talk about it. "How many times did they come by?" He hoped not as much as he suspected.

She sighed and squeezed a wedge of lemon into her tea. "After the first few weeks, they stopped asking for you, but they kept a car outside for at least a month after that. I told them you'd left for good and I had no idea where you'd gone, but you know how the high council is."

"Yeah, I do. They're a stubborn lot."

"And thick as cold grits." She shook her head. "There's been a rash of vampires in the city lately, killing tourists and causing havoc, and that's been enough to distract them. Once that started, they left me alone."

He nodded. "Dulcinea mentioned the vamps, but I was in the Quarter last night and I didn't see any."

She shrugged. "If Dulcinea knows about them, they must be here, *cher*. I'm sure Khell has things under control, though. He's turned out to be a decent Guardian, despite some people's misgivings."

Augustine snorted and stabbed a shrimp. "How decent can he be if these vampires are running amok?"

"You said you didn't see any. Maybe he's cleared them out."

"Maybe." He didn't exactly doubt Khell's abilities as Guardian—sure, maybe he wasn't the typical gung ho idiot that usually took over, but if he was involved in bringing the vampires into the city, that was just crazy. Granted, anyone who took on that amount of responsibility had to have a good dollop of crazy in their blood, but being a traitor was a different kind of crazy. Still, who ever took on the Guardianship thinking they could actually protect the whole damn city?

She pushed her plate away. "What are your plans for the rest of the day?"

"Hang out with you until I head off to *Nokturnos*." That earned him another smile. "I need a mask, though. You got anything in the prop room?" Livie's stash of old film props was so endless, she kept a room in the house just to store them in, rotating the pieces on display every few months.

"Let me think." She tapped her chin. "I know I've got a plague doctor's mask in there somewhere, but you won't want that. Covers up your mouth." Her eyes widened and her hand came down to lightly smack the table. "Remember that fantasy movie I did? *Legend of the Mist*? I kept the Serpent King's mask. It's gorgeous. Glossy black leather scales tipped with metallic blues and purples. Look for a box labeled with the movie title."

"Sounds perfect, but I have to ask—how exactly did you end up with the leading man's mask?"

Her mouth bunched to one side in a coy smile. "Let's just say he left it in my trailer after the wrap party and leave it at that."

After Augustine dug out the mask, he spent the rest of the afternoon lounging on the front porch with Olivia, probably not the smartest place to be if the Elektos was still hunting him, but they'd figure out he was home sooner or later and he was so damn tired of looking over his shoulder. Better to confront them and have it out. He lay on the big upholstered swing while Livie sat in her rocker with her gardening catalogs. She found a thousand new flowers to plant and wanted his opinion on all of them. It was a nice way to pass the day and when Lally came out with a pitcher of Olivia's favorite spiked lemonade, he woke with a start, only realizing then that he'd drifted off. "Livie, you shouldn't have let me sleep."

"I might have drifted off a bit myself there. This warm weather will do that to a person." She pushed herself upright in the rocker and accepted a glass from Lally.

She held the tray out to him next. "No, thanks, Lally. I have a long night ahead of me."

She started back into the house, pausing at the door. "Leftovers for dinner all right with you, Miss Olivia?"

"Perfectly fine," Livie answered. "Hate to waste food. Especially when it's as good as yours." She pointed to the settee next to her rocker. "Don't go, Lally. Sit a spell with us. You should look at the varieties of tomatoes in this catalog."

Augustine sat up. "I should get ready. I'm supposed to meet Dulcinea for some pregame." He second-guessed the look on Livie's face. "You want me to stay for dinner? I will. Dulcinea will understand if I'm late."

"No, no. You go and have fun." She sipped her lemonade as Lally took a seat. "You need to spend time with your friends after being gone so long. Tell Dulcinea I said hello."

"Will do." He headed inside and jogged up the stairs to get ready, the anticipation of the night already dancing over his skin. *Nokturnos* was the start of the fae New Year, the chance to begin fresh. To wish for better things. He grinned.

Something told him tonight was going to be all kinds of interesting.

Olivia stared at the bowl before her, her mind on Augustine.

"What's wrong?" Lally asked. "Not in the mood for leftovers after all? You know they say gumbo really don't get good until

it's a few days old. I can make you something else, if you want,
though."

"The gumbo's fine." She forced a smile and nodded toward
the chair on her right. "Stop fussing over me and have your dinner." She glanced toward the front of the house. "I'm not sure
Augustine should have come back so soon."

"Tell him not to go out then. He'll stay home if you ask."
Lally took the seat, her face full of compassion.

"No, no, it's *Nokturnos*. I can't do that to him. Besides, he
deserves a night of fun after being away so long, not sitting
nursemaid with an old woman."

"Miss Olivia." Lally's scolding tone was a familiar one these
days. Maybe Augie's absence had affected Olivia more than
she'd realized. "Don't talk like that. He came back because
he was worried about you. Because he missed you and missed
being home."

Olivia looked away, not wanting to see pity on her friend's
face. "I know. But those are the wrong reasons. If the Elektos
wants to try him for his crime, he'll have to run again. Maybe
for good."

"Maybe you..." Lally hesitated, her hands coming up to
smooth the cloth napkin at the place setting.

"Maybe I could what?"

Lally cleared her throat. "If it was me and I had your means,
I'd offer the Elektos a little... *incentive* to leave that child alone."

Olivia laughed. "That is the New Orleans way, isn't it?"
Her laughter died off. "Truth is, I already tried that, but they
refused. And it was a very generous incentive. I fear they want
to make an example of him."

"Because he's refused them so many times?"

Olivia nodded. "Can you blame him for not wanting to be
Guardian? It's a tremendous amount of responsibility."

Judgment lifted Lally's brows and she pursed her lips. "Miss

Olivia, he'd shy from it even if there was no responsibility at all. You coddle that boy, turned him from a thug to a slug."

"Now, Lally…"

She sat back in her chair. "You know I'm right."

Olivia sighed. "I can't help it. He's been through so much. And changed so much—for me! You remember what he was like when I found him? Rougher 'an broken glass around the edges and full of bluster. He'd fight over a sideways glance." He'd been practically feral, but he'd responded so quickly to kind words and affection she knew there was more to him. That there was hope for him. "I don't want to make the same mistakes twice."

"Miss Harlow." Olivia's daughter's name spilled tentatively from Lally's lips like she knew she might be overstepping.

"Yes. Harlow." Olivia pushed her spoon through the gumbo, the recipe for which had been in Lally's family for generations and was a closely guarded secret. "She's my great failure. And Augustine has been my second chance. I love my daughter, but sadly, my refusal to part with certain information means she doesn't feel the same way about me."

Lally tipped her head a tiny bit. "Miss Olivia, why don't you just tell the child her daddy's name? She's a grown woman. She can make her own decisions about—"

"*No.*" The word shot out of Olivia's mouth like the crack of a gunshot. "You know how I feel about him. That man is poison. I won't have him infecting my daughter."

Lally sat back, her fingers fiddling with the chain around her neck. "Maybe you could explain that to her. Have you talked to her lately?"

"I called her last night. She didn't answer. I talk to her blessed voicemail more than I talk to her." At the sharp edge in her own voice, Olivia put on one of her best actress smiles and raised her gaze to meet Lally's. "What say we forget about dinner and have us a couple of mint juleps out on the porch? Take in the evening air?"

But Lally's soft smile didn't quite erase the sadness in her eyes. "You know, you can choose your friends, but you can't choose your family. Be thankful for Mr. Augustine. Don't feel guilty about him. Look at the life you took him from. The life you gave him. Take pride in that."

"I don't feel guilty. And you're right. Again." She'd be a mess without Lally. The woman was a gem. "He would have died on the streets running with that gang, acting like the world was out to get him."

Lally clucked her tongue. "In some ways, it mighta been. He was a hard case, that one. But you changed that boy for the better. So what if he's not big on responsibility. He's not hustling or robbing or jacking people up. That's something good you done."

"Thank you, Lally. You're a dear friend and I don't know what I'd do without you to talk me out of my head sometimes." She pushed to her feet with the help of her cane, something she didn't need so much as she enjoyed the use of a good prop. "Now, what say you we go get reacquainted with that other friend of ours, Mr. Jim Beam."

Chapter Four

D ude." Dulcinea whistled appreciatively when Augustine showed her the mask Olivia had given him to wear. "That is gorgeous. And with your horns? Super badass. You're going to have females all over you."

"You think?" He took another look at the mask. He'd had his doubts when he'd dug it out of the box. The Serpent King might be better saved for Halloween. "It doesn't strike you as a little intimidating?"

She waved her hand at it. "Chicks dig scary as long as the scary is also hot and willing to protect them. Don't you ever read any romance novels? Alpha male and all that. Especially in that outfit."

"That much I know." His getup of leather pants, black T-shirt, long leather coat and motorcycle boots would have been too much for the unseasonably warm days they'd been having, but the night held just enough chill to make him comfortable. And in a city like NOLA on a night like *Nokturnos*, leathers of some sort were almost expected if you were fae. "But don't tell me you aren't going to have men trailing you like toms in heat. Let me see your mask."

Over her outfit, which could only be described as a chain-mail catsuit, she wore a hip purse. She dug into that, pulled something out and unfurled it, holding in her hands a slip of filigreed silver leather so finely done it resembled liquid metal.

At second glance, he realized it was tooled in the shape of a cat's face. He grinned. "Beautiful. And very you. Prepare to beat them off with a stick."

"Why do you think I brought you?" She laughed and jerked her thumb toward Mena's. "Let's grab something to eat."

In no real rush, they took their time at dinner catching up and enjoying each other's uncomplicated company. It was good their one-time fling hadn't ruined anything, Augustine thought. Dulcinea was too good a friend to lose.

She pushed her plate away and glanced toward the window. "Sun's down. Streets are filling up. You ready to go celebrate the New Year?"

He finished his beer and sat back in his chair. "Born ready, baby."

They paid their bill and took to the streets, masks on. The crowds were thick as expected but not nearly what they'd be during Mardi Gras. Augustine took Dulcinea's hand and pulled her through the throng toward Bourbon Street. Without saying it, both understood they'd only be together until one of them found a partner for the evening, but until then they'd stick to each other's side, celebrating *Nokturnos* like they had since they'd run the streets with the rest of their crew.

Bourbon was just as it always was—loud and boisterous and full of people. The fae in attendance were mostly local but there were probably some who'd come to town for the event, plus a ton of human tourists, looking for a night of all-out fun. Some of the tourists were probably here to gawk, but any fae living in New Orleans either got used to that or stayed out of the Vieux Carré.

"Let's get another drink," Dulcinea shouted over the strains of "Sweet Home Alabama" pouring from one of the bars.

"I'll buy you a drink, kitty cat." A well-oiled tourist grinned at Dulcinea, his lids already heavy with alcohol. His friends hooted their approval of his idea, their LSU T-shirts giving them away for the college boys they were.

"And so it begins," Augustine muttered.

Dulcinea raised herself to her full height and notched her head to look down at him. In her platform boots, she was easily over six feet. "How generous. And how broad-minded you are."

"Broad-minded?" The guy looked baffled.

"Not to care that I'm a man." She leaned in and batted her lashes at him. "Do you want your good-luck kiss now or—"

"What?" His eyes widened. "No!" Laughing, his friends hauled him away and in seconds, they were swept away with the next wave of people.

Augustine shook his head. "You're awful."

Her smirk said she disagreed. "Awful funny, you mean. He was just a kid. I'd break him in two. Better he think the rejection was his idea."

He snorted softly. "Yeah, but sooner or later, one of them's going to get riled up about it."

One shoulder lifted in casual defiance. "Like I said, that's why I brought you."

"Dulce, I can't get into a fight tonight. If it weren't for this mask, I wouldn't even be here. I just want to have some fun, not give the Elektos another reason to come after me."

"Understood." She lifted a finger. "But I can't help it if men are drawn to me like cats to cream." She made flourishes with both hands up and down her body as if to illustrate her charms. "*This* is a lot to contain."

He crossed his arms and tried not to smile. "If you're trying to contain it, you might have worn something besides skintight chain mail."

"Pfft. Spoilsport. You didn't exactly wear a sack." She planted her hands on her hips, causing a small traffic jam as the crowd flowed around her. "Besides, it was laundry day."

"Well, if nothing else was clean you really had no choice."

Laughing, he grabbed her arm. "C'mon, crazy woman, let's get that drink."

The line for beer moved quickly and a few minutes later, they had to-go cups and were heading for an empty span of wall between a T-shirt shop and the walk-up window of a pizza joint. They propped themselves there and settled in to observe.

Dulcinea tipped her cup toward the crowd. "That one, with the purple feather mask and the low-cut shirt. Talk about her cup runneth over."

Augustine shook his head. "Also trying too hard. Look at all those beads. We're the only two who haven't seen her boobs." His turn. He pointed to a tall guy wearing a white half mask and a black cape. "That one there."

"The Phantom?" She snorted. "Spare me the dramatics. He's got potential stalker written all over him."

They went back and forth, eliminating the passersby until suddenly Dulce straightened, her gaze zeroing in on a man in the crowd. "Hell-o, beautiful." She made a soft noise deep in her throat that sounded half purr, half meow. "Mama likes." She motioned to Augustine without looking at him. "See you tomorrow."

"Later." And just like that, he was alone. He hung there a while longer, sipping his beer and assessing the crowd. Plenty of them assessed him right back, but he didn't bite. He wasn't sure who he was looking for, but he'd know her when he saw her. The right one to start his new year off perfectly. The right one to celebrate his return home. He grinned, thinking about the fun that awaited him.

A trio of masked human lovelies walked past, slanting their eyes at him and preening in their glitter masks and feather boas. They smiled back.

Now that was just too hard to ignore. He'd at least test the waters. "Ladies."

They stopped a few feet away and waved by wiggling their fingers at him. "Hi," they answered in unison.

And suddenly he realized his folly. He never should have limited himself to *one*.

"I don't know about this." Harlow adjusted the mask over her face. The T-shirt shops were filled with cheap masks, but her mind-set of doing it up big wouldn't let her settle for a five-dollar bit of felt and glitter. Of course, now that she was standing in the small boutique the concierge had recommended wearing a much more expensive handmade mask, the cheap ones weren't sounding quite as bad.

"Wait until you see it on," the saleslady said. "It suits you beautifully." She brought a mirror over and set it in front of Harlow.

She turned to look. And stopped still. "Wow. Shiny. That is much better than expected." The raven mask was more of a headdress, its sleek black feathers cascading down over her hair and shoulders, but the small beak sat just over her nose, leaving her mouth and chin exposed. Add in her black bat-wing sweater, leggings and side-buckle boots and she almost looked like some kind of bird superhero person.

Not at all like herself. This might actually work.

"You have the right-color eyes for that piece," the saleslady added.

"Thanks." Her amber eyes, another gift from her mother she could have done without, seemed genuinely birdlike behind the mask. Her normal smoky makeup only played that up.

"You might like these, too." The saleswoman set a pair of black feather-trimmed gloves on the counter.

Harlow picked them up. Even through the gloves she had

on she could tell these new ones were beautiful quality, not just some costume add-on. "Has anyone else tried these on?"

"No. They just came in a few days ago."

Harlow peeled her gloves off and tried them. They fit like they'd been made for her. "I'll take them and the mask." She peeled off a few bills and handed them over.

"Would you like me to box it all up?"

"No, I'm going to wear it. But I probably should get a box to take it home in." She glanced behind her. The streets were already full of people. She didn't relish the idea of having to go back to her hotel just to drop off a package. If she didn't get some liquid courage into her system, she just might chicken out, like she almost had at Comic Con.

As if reading her mind, the saleswoman said, "We can send the box to your hotel for you, if you like. I can put your old gloves in there as well."

"That would be great." Harlow typed her info into the tablet the woman placed on the counter, then tucked her change into the inside pocket of her leggings before adjusting the waistband of her sweater over them again. "Thank you."

"Thank you. And happy *Nokturnos*."

"Uh, yeah. Same to you." The second Harlow opened the door, the noise of the street hit her. Music from every direction, laughter, whooping and hollering, distant horns blowing and the occasional cheer. On the way over, the chaos of it all had almost turned her around, but now, wearing the mask gave her a sense of anonymity that raised her courage. *Just like Comic Con.* She repeated it like a mantra.

The shop door closed behind her but she stayed still, taking it all in for a moment, enjoying the strange new sense of boldness flowing through her. She laughed as a random thought occurred to her—this really was like Comic Con, except a lot of these people weren't pretending; they really were the creatures they appeared to be.

She stepped into the street and started walking with no real destination in mind. She dodged people as they came toward her and focused on the details. What would her superhero name be? Ravenwoman? The Claw? Hawktress? Nightwing? That was a good one. Of course, it already belonged to DC Comics, but so what, she liked it. Nightwing it was.

Now it was time for Nightwing to get a drink. Harlow made her way to the first walk-up window she came to and took a place in line with a comfortable distance away from the next person. She kept her eyes on the menu and the task of deciding what her poison would be. Something sweet, maybe, so it would go down fast and easy. That seemed to describe most of the drinks listed.

The people around her were all in groups, joking and having fun and clearly not on their first drink. They seemed to be lacking in the general understanding of personal space, too. Mask or not, she was questioning her decision to come out alone. Finally, her turn to order came. "Can I have a peach smash?"

The counter girl nodded. "You want a floater with that?"

"What's a floater?"

"We add a shot of tequila, dark rum or 151 on top."

"One Fifty-One." If she had any hope of making it through the night successfully, she was going to need all the alcoholic help she could get. She paid for the drink, then stuck near the side of the counter while she waited for it to be ready. The guys next to her catcalled to the women walking by.

None of them seemed to mind. Some of the women actually yelled back.

Harlow leaned against the wall and shook her head. All likeness to Comic Con aside, this was still so not her scene. She hated being touched because of the flood of emotions that meant enduring. Because of that, she'd developed a basic dis-like of crowds, but sex... sex only meant one other person. She could handle that, and had, but the opportunity to engage in that sort of activity rarely came along when you worked from home and did your best to leave that home as little as possible. Maybe she should call it a night, take her drink back to the hotel and meet up with her guild for a raid.

But then a guy walked by in a black and white striped out-fit, number stenciled over his chest and a black mask covering his eyes like a bandit and the reminder that jail loomed in her future stomped on her doubts. This might be her last chance for a long time to exercise her complete and utter personal freedom. Her last chance at some real fun.

"Peach smash!" the counter girl called out.

Harlow raised her hand. "That's me."

"Here you go." The girl behind the counter slid the peach smash toward Harlow.

"Thanks." She grabbed the tall plastic cup, used the straw to stir the 151 into the rest of the drink, then latched on to it and took a long sip. Fortified, she headed into the crowd with a slightly improved attitude. All she needed to do was make some friends, right? How hard could that be? The place was crawling with people looking to get friendly. What did you say to make friends? And you weren't online?

"Nice mask." Some guy coming toward her pointed at her headdress.

"Thanks." Be friendly, she reminded herself. "You, too." Not really. His looked like one of those cheap five-dollar ones. She downed some more of the peach smash, hoping it would help her missing social gene kick in.

He slowed, his friends all busy with women of their own. "Hey what kind of bird are you?" His mouth bent in a lecherous grin. "A swallow?"

"Really? Is that supposed to get me hot and bothered? Because, um, *no*." She sighed and walked away.

"Hey!" he yelled after her.

She ignored him and took another long sip of her drink as she kept going. Obviously, she'd had a very different idea about the kind of night this was going to be and the kind of guy she might meet out here. Someone... nice. And not just looking to get some action. Of course, that was kind of what *she* was doing. She just didn't want to do it with a Neanderthal. Heading back to the hotel was starting to look better and better. But she'd shelled out the cash for this mask. She caught a few of the feathers floating around her shoulders and rubbed her gloved fingers over them, imagining their silkiness.

Maybe she could turn it into something for the next Comic Con she went to. At least then she'd be among her own kind. What character could she use this for? Some kind of—she stopped abruptly, causing a small collision of people behind her. What was she thinking? There was no next Comic Con. Not for her. Unless they held one in prison.

Traffic flowed around her, human, fae or otherwise, and none of them had any idea the mess she was in. None of them would likely care, either. And yet, she was contemplating choosing one of them to spend one of her remaining nights of freedom with in exchange for what? Some consensual fun?

She was a grown woman acting like a horny college girl on spring break. Sad. Maybe she'd just forget the hooking up part, walk around a little more while she finished her drink and enjoy the fact that no matter how sad she was, she still wasn't as pathetic as some of these actual college kids. Most of whom appeared to be drunker than humanly possible. Hmm. The fact that she was contemplating walking around in this madness meant the alcohol was kicking in. She started to cut through the crowd to get to the sidewalk when two guys came tearing past her chasing each other.

The second clipped her shoulder hard as he went by, spinning her around and knocking her drink out of her hand. As she fell, a high-pitched shriek cut through the chaos. A hand clamped down on her forearm, catching her before she hit the ground and pulling her upright.

She glanced behind her, unable to believe she hadn't hit the cobblestones.

"You okay?"

"Yeah, I'm—" She turned to see who her benefactor was. Tall, dark and—judging by the horns—definitely fae. She ignored the trippy shiver of desire the sight of him inspired. Her body was betraying her over a guy who was fae? Wow. That was so not awesome.

"Are you kidding me?" A soggy brunette in a red glitter mask wiped peach smash out of her cleavage. She glared at Harlow from the side of her mysterious serpent-masked hero. "You spilled your drink all over me, you little—"

He interrupted her. "It wasn't her fault, Ginger."

Ginger? Harlow clamped her mouth shut, sensing this was not the time for snark. "Sorry about that. A guy ran into me and—"

"Whatever," the blonde on the other side of him said. She wore the same kind of red glitter mask as the brunette. She sighed and looked at him, her mouth pouty as she stroked her hand down his chest, her fingers dancing over what looked like hard, trim muscle. Fae, yes. Repulsive, no. "Can we go now?"

"Yeah, my buzz is wearing off," added a third girl, this one a redhead in yet another red glitter mask.

Did this guy buy in bulk? "I should go." She turned to leave, then realized he still had hold of her arm as the heat and pressure of his grip sank through her sleeve and into her skin. When she glanced at his hand, he released her.

His little half smile was sort of endearing. "Sorry. You still didn't answer. Are you okay?"

Was he really that concerned? She couldn't imagine he was trying to pick her up when his dance card was obviously full. "I'm fine, thanks."

"Let me buy you another drink."

Before Harlow could answer, the blonde spoke up again. "For real? C'mon, baby, we want to party."

He turned to her, but not before a look of impatience darkened his stormy gray-green eyes. "Why don't you three go ahead to the hotel? That way Ginger can clean up. I'll be right there."

"You sure?" The blonde's hands wrapped his bicep like she was afraid to let him go. She sure loved to touch him.

He looked back at Harlow, mischief in his gaze. "Sure."

She smiled, unable to help herself. Nothing about his answer sounded like he had any intention of meeting up with them.

As the trio melted into the crowd, he offered her his arm. "So how about that drink?"

She didn't take it. "You're ditching Charlie's Angels for me?"

He shrugged. "This is going to make me sound like the world's biggest creeper, but I could have those girls any night of the week, any week of the year. This is *Nokturnos*. They're not who I want to spend tonight with."

"And I am?" She was trying hard not to feel flattered and failing.

"You put time and thought into your mask. They didn't. That says a lot to me."

She put a few points on his side of the scoreboard. "I'll accept that."

"Have you been to New Orleans before?"

"No."

"How's your night going so far?"

"Not great." Although she'd gotten the start of a good buzz before she'd lost her drink. That was something.

He extended his arm again. "I can fix that. I love this city and I'd be happy to turn your night around."

She almost reached for his arm, then hesitated once more. "How do you know I even care how the rest of this night goes?"

He smiled full-on and her breath caught in her throat. *Oh my.* Why did fae men have to be so pretty? He tipped his head in toward her like he was about to share a secret. "I'm going with the mask again. You spent a lot of money on that so I'm assuming you planned on having fun tonight. Right or wrong?"

She took his arm, her hand sliding over an expanse of muscle that explained pretty thoroughly why the blonde had had a hard time letting go. "I'll give you another point for being perceptive."

He laughed. "I'll take it. So what were you drinking? One of those fruity frozen things, right?"

"Are you psychic, too?"

"Not hard to smell what my date was covered in."

She rolled her lips in to keep from laughing again. "That really wasn't my fault."

"I know. It was mine." He glanced at her. "I bet those guys a hundred bucks I could beat them to the end of Bourbon Street."

"But you weren't running."

"Nope. They were bothering the girls I was with. Seemed like an easy way to get rid of them." He shrugged. "It worked."

She just shook her head as he steered them through the crowd and toward another drink stand. He bought her a drink and got a beer for himself, then they started back down the street.

She took a long pull on the straw, trying to get as much of it in her system as she could. If she was going to kiss this guy, which seemed like the best idea of the night so far, she'd need the alcohol to tamp down her ability to read his emotions or he'd probably short-circuit something in her brain. "By the way, my name is—"

"Stop right there. No names on *Nokturnos*."

"Really? Why not?"

"The belief is that you ensure yourself good luck for the rest of the year if you kiss a stranger. If you tell me your name, you're no longer a stranger."

That was fine with her. "Okay, I bought a mask, I guess I'll play. What should I call you?"

He glanced back the way the girls had gone. "How about Charlie?"

She laughed. "I like it. And I'll be Angel."

He snorted. "That's the spirit. That is a really great mask, by the way."

"Yours, too. It's actually beautiful. Is that a weird thing to say to a guy?"

Before he could answer, loud whoops and shrieks caught their attention. A new group of revelers swept toward them, somehow noisier and more raucous than everyone else. They were all male, throwing beads and grabbing at every woman they passed. She froze, panicking. It was suddenly too much, the crowd, the noise, the— Charlie took her hand, pulled her through the crush and down a quieter side street where he brought them to a stop near a wall. The broad expanse of his back shielded her from the crowd behind them.

She felt like she should thank him, but didn't. Instead, she tried to explain. "I'm ... not always so great with crowds."

He nodded. "I sensed that."

"You did? How?"

He laughed softly. "The horns aren't part of the mask, sweetheart. I'm fae if you hadn't figured that out. Your pulse went into alarm mode when that group started toward us."

Damn it. She'd tried to gloss over his being fae so much she actually had. Hopefully her heart was still beating fast enough to cover the new twinge of panic his reminder brought on. She did her best to play it off. "Yeah, of course you would have heard that. I guess I just didn't realize you'd be able to pick up on it in all the rest of that noise."

He bent in closer, the scent of something warm and smoky filling her nose. "You okay?"

It was easy to believe the softness in his eyes was genuine concern. Too easy. She blew out a breath and shifted so that her back was flat against the wall. "I'm fine. Just needed a break from all that."

He sidled up against the wall next to her so that his bicep touched her shoulder. "It is nuts, huh? You should see it at Mardi Gras."

She could do without that. "I can't even imagine." The horror.

"It's the most fun you'll ever have."

Not repulsive but definitely crazy. Still, if her courage held out, the night might not be a total wash. Emboldened by the alcohol, she pressed him. "I thought being the most fun I'll ever have was your job?"

His head swiveled around and the look on his face was price-lessly stunned. Then he burst out laughing. "Just when I have you figured out."

She turned a little toward him. "Did you think I was going to cut and run?"

"Something like that."

She swallowed, holding on to her intoxication like a safety blanket. "And miss the kiss that's going to bring me good luck for the rest of the year?"

His lips slowly parted and his tongue came out to lick them. He cleared his throat. "It *is* almost moonset."

Do it, she wanted to shout. *Before my courage sobers up.* But he didn't need any further encouraging.

He pulled her against him, his legs straddling hers, his back against the wall and her weight leaning into him. One hand came up like he was going to cup her chin but she caught it with her gloved hand and pushed it to the wall. The kiss would be enough contact without his fingers on her skin.

Deep in his throat he made a sound of approval. Good. Let him think she wanted to be the aggressor. She lifted her face to his, hoping that would be enough.

It was.

Chapter Five

Augustine found Angel's upturned mouth a second after she offered it to him. Her sudden control of the situation spiked heat along his bones with a mix of pain and pleasure unlike anything he'd felt before. The female in charge wasn't new to him, but there was something so *untried* about her that her move shocked him. Even kissing her felt like tasting forbidden fruit. Sweet, ripe, juicy fruit.

His free hand slid up her rib cage until the curve of her breast stopped him. He stayed there, unwilling to go farther without some sign from her. Then her other hand came up to grip one of his horns and he inhaled at the caress of her silk-clad fingers on that sensitive area. The sensation only made him kiss her with greater hunger, eager to show her what she was doing to him. How odd that she could fire him up while at the same time kissing him with the tentativeness of someone unused to such intimacy. Even her fingers seemed to twine with his in a questing way that bordered on exploratory.

The awareness of her innocence flared into a thousand different things inside him, but the strongest of them was the sudden desire to protect her, to keep her innocent, to have her for himself. The want of those things pulsed within him, dark as dying stars.

She gasped and pushed away from him, her hand untangling from his instantly. Her mouth was open and her breath was coming as hard as the thumps of her heartbeat. Fear and regret tinged her amber eyes with a feral orange gleam. One gloved hand wiped at her mouth as she backed away. "I have to go."

"Wait." He reached for her, unsure of what had happened but thick with the need for her to stay. "Angel, come back to me."

"No," she whispered, her voice ragged. "Leave me alone, fae." And then she turned and ran down the dark street.

He wanted to chase her, to make her explain, but that wasn't his way. If a woman said no, she said no and he stopped right there. But no did little to ease his curiosity about what he'd done to upset her. And nothing to quench the fire she'd ignited in him.

He tore his mask off and stared after her, but she was long gone. Her words, *"Leave me alone, fae,"* echoed in his head. He frowned at the strangeness of her word choice. Not that he hadn't been called fae before in a derogatory way. Since the covenant had been broken, it happened more than he liked, but there were worse things to be called. It wasn't a big deal, except that it was an odd thing to hear from the mouth of another fae. At least he thought she was fae. With those eyes...

With a soft snort, he slipped his mask back on. Angel might not want him, but tonight was *Nokturnos*. There were plenty of other women looking for company. But even as the thought entered his mind, it lacked appeal. He wanted Angel. Ridiculous that he'd want a woman who didn't want him, but there it was. Her sense of innocence combined with her sharp wit and the knowledge that her trust would be hard-won only piqued his interest. After having that small taste of her, she was all he could think about.

It would be sunrise before he headed home, but the only company he'd be sharing the rest of his evening with came in a bottle.

Chapter Six

If there was anything last night had taught Harlow, it was that straying from her comfort zone rarely produced positive results. And yet here she was anyway. At her mother's house. With the early morning sun beating down on her like a punishment. If Olivia had only relented and given her the information about her father she'd begged for, they'd have a very different relationship. But no, Mother knew best. And now Harlow was finally going to have to capitulate and agree to let the issue of her paternity rest if she wanted Olivia's help. Somehow, she would have to find a way to ignore the empty place in her heart that she'd lived with her entire life. Resigned to the reality of what lay ahead, she pushed her sunglasses back on her nose, stopped leaning against her car and walked to the front door.

At least this part of New Orleans was blissfully quiet. A few blocks down, a woman walked her dog. Other than that, the streets were empty.

The house was impossibly beautiful, but Harlow hadn't expected anything less. Olivia Goodwin lived her life in a very certain way, with a very certain style. One Harlow had long ago forsaken. What would her life have been like if she'd let the issue of her father drop when she was a teenager? Would she be someone different now? Would she have embraced her fae side?

What would her life have been like if she'd known her father? Had a parent who understood her need to be *human*? Because she was sure her father was strictly human for no other reason than that she'd believed it for so long it had become part of his canon. Part of why she denied her fae side as much as she did. Part of why she clung to being human. His human blood in her veins was the only thing of him she had. Her only connection.

And she was about to give up any chance of solidifying that connection to save her own skin. That was if her mother wouldn't hold the years of estrangement against her, but that hope was as thin as the whole in her heart was large.

Feeling like a traitor to the father she'd never known, she stood in front of the big, leaded-glass doors and lifted her hand to knock. She was trembling a little. Not because she was afraid to see her mother, but because real-life confrontation on this scale scared the breath out of her. Online she was a warrior. In person... not so much. As she rapped her knuckles on the glass, she wished she could do this wearing her mask from last night. There was such comfort in anonymity.

An older African-American woman came to the door. The housekeeper and her mother's companion. Eulalie, if Harlow remembered correctly. She opened the door. "Can I help you, miss?" Then her mouth went slack and she blinked hard. Her hand went to her throat. "Miss Harlow?"

Harlow nodded. "Hello, Eulalie. Is my mother home?"

"Lands, child. I cannot believe—" Eulalie smoothed the skirt of her flowered dress and straightened. "She sure is. We're just fixin' to have breakfast. You come on in now." She opened the door wider.

"I'd rather wait here." Something about entering her mother's house without her mother knowing about it didn't feel right. She'd wait until Olivia invited her in. If that happened.

Eulalie didn't close the door. "All right then. I'll go fetch her."

"Thanks." She sat in one of the rockers to wait, the smoky scent of bacon and strong coffee wafting out from the house and making her stomach grumble with upset. It was probably a combination of last night's alcohol and this morning's nerves, coupled with the sense that she was about to lose her father.

But she'd be lying if she said there wasn't another man on her mind as well. The man who'd kissed her. Man, fae, whatever he was. She rolled her eyes. If she wanted a memory to take to prison, she'd certainly gotten herself one.

Why on earth had she decided to pick a guy who was fae? Silly female hormones. Sure, what she'd been able to see of him—and feel of him—had been undeniably amazing, but fae? His kiss had poured emotions into her she'd never expected to feel. The way his desire to possess her had just poured into her veins...she shivered at the memory, trying unsuccessfully to shut it out. To make matters worse, she'd dreamed of him, her bare hands gripping those horns of his while he—she blew out a hard breath in an attempt to alleviate the rising flush of warmth.

At least she'd never have to see him again. Whether her mother said yes or no about the money, she was going home today. If the CCU found out she'd left the state, she'd be in worse trouble than she already was.

A soft inhale brought her head up. Olivia stood on the porch, eyes liquid in a way Harlow hoped meant good things. "Harlow?"

She stood, her heart bumping against her rib cage in an attempt to break free. Her gut said run. Instead, she pushed her sunglasses up onto her head. "Hi. Mom." The word tasted so strange. "It's nice to see you." It was. She hadn't seen Olivia in a long time.

Olivia's hair was silver-white now, making her look older than Harlow remembered, but she still looked healthy and full of life. Something Harlow had always envied.

Olivia's knuckles tightened around the head of the cane she was using. "What brings you here after all these years?"

Harlow exhaled a soft, whooshing breath and began. There was no good place, really, so she just jumped in and prayed it made sense. "The work I do, with computers, I had a client who hired me to do some backdoor stuff, except I didn't know it was backdoor stuff until I got in there and then I got out too late and the CCU tracked me—or someone did—and—"

"CCU?" Olivia's brow wrinkled.

"Cyber Crimes Unit." That put a label on things, didn't it? "They...prosecuted me and so now I have this fine I can't pay and I didn't know where else to turn and..." Harlow took a breath, her mouth dry with anxiety. "I'm sorry that this is what's brought me here. I know how that makes me look."

"Do you?" Olivia planted her cane in front of her and put both hands on the crystal capping the end. "You don't answer the phone when I call. You barely answer the emails I send."

"I know and I'll try to be better, I really will—"

"It's been years since I last saw you and then you granted me a grand total of forty-five minutes for lunch with the excuse that you had *things* to do and now you show up on my door asking for money? This is why you've finally come to see me?"

Harlow swallowed down her embarrassment. "I know, Mom, I know. But you know why things are like this between us. Why I don't answer your calls or your emails. All I've ever asked is to know who my father—"

"How much is this fine?"

Harlow blinked into the sunlight, on the verge of tears she'd sworn she wouldn't shed. That's always how it was when the subject of her father came around. A screeching dead end. "Eight hundred and fifty thousand dollars."

Olivia's expression never faltered. "That is quite a sum of money. What happens if you don't pay it?"

"It's a huge sum of money." Harlow's sense of hope spiraled downward. "But without it, I go to prison."

"For how long?"

Harlow's answer was soft, her voice verging on a tremor that reflected what was going on inside her. "Two years." Speaking things had such a way of making them real.

Olivia was quiet a long moment. Then her brows rose, the look on her face far less horrified than Harlow imagined it would be. "Just think, I'd know exactly where you were, and exactly when I could come visit you. I'd probably see you more in those two years than I have in the last twenty."

"You'd let me...go to prison?" A chill dropped through Harlow, leaving her numb and desperate. "I'm willing to stop asking about my father." As the words left her mouth, part of Harlow's soul cried out.

"Are you willing to move here, too?"

Harlow swallowed. "Maybe. We could...talk about it. I guess."

"Somehow I doubt that." Olivia's mouth bent in disbelief. "I haven't decided anything yet. I need time to take this all in." Olivia turned toward the door. "I'll give you my answer at breakfast tomorrow. Eight a.m."

"I kind of need to go home today—"

Olivia paused, her eyes sharp with something dark. "Then I can give you my answer right now, but you're not going to like it."

"But, as I was going to say, I would be happy to change my plans so I can make breakfast." Happy wasn't exactly what she'd be, but she didn't see any other choice. Besides, it was the right thing to do. A little personal time in exchange for whatever Olivia was willing to give her...that was fair.

"Good." Olivia nodded, her look of disapproval fading.

Unable to stop herself, Harlow reached out and grabbed her mother's hand. Her voice came out a broken whisper. "Please,

Mom. Just give me a hint about my father? Anything, his initials, his place of birth—"

"He's dead." Olivia's gaze softened as if she suddenly realized the impact of her words. "I'm sorry. But it's time to let the past go, Harlow." She squeezed Harlow's hand, then released it.

Barely breathing from the shock of her mother's confession, Harlow stood there openmouthed and numb. "Dead?"

"Yes, and don't ask for details. Just let it go. Please." Olivia sighed. "I'll see you tomorrow." Then she walked back into the house and shut the door, leaving Harlow alone.

Harlow wanted desperately to get back to her car, but for two or three minutes she stood there, frozen to the spot. Her emotions warred over what was worse—the death of a father she'd never known or her mother about to let her go to prison. The news about her father was such a shock she couldn't process it. The possibility that her mother might actually let her go to jail was a reality she'd expected, but then again, maybe she hadn't. Not really.

How could her father be dead when she'd never had a chance to know him? Her heart hurt so much she thought she might vomit right there on the porch. How could her mother just drop that kind of news on her? What was so awful about her father that Olivia didn't want Harlow to even know his initials? The ache in her chest expanded throughout her body. She'd never had a father and she'd barely had a mother and now she was about to go to prison.

The hollowness inside her swelled to fill the space where her hope had once lived. Queasy with emotions she never wanted to feel again, she shuffled to her car and drove back to the hotel and her ghastly expensive room, where she sat, lights off, and stared out the window seeing very little but the bleakness of her future.

⚜

Olivia wept into her coffee, her appetite gone. Lally sat beside her, their plates untouched, the food cold. "After all these years, she comes to me for money."

Lally squeezed her hand. "I know, Miss Olivia. That child has some nerve."

Olivia blew her nose into a handkerchief. "Of course, I'm going to give it to her. I can't let her go to prison, but she has to know how this hurts me. And does she care? Does she act like she cares? No." She shook her head and sniffed. "I don't know what to do, Lally. All my hard work to protect her and she still doesn't understand. It's like her father influenced her despite my best efforts."

"Maybe you could explain to her what she needed protecting against?"

"And tell her what a monster her father really is? I told Harlow he was dead. I'm not sure what came over me. I should have done it years ago after—" Olivia stilled, realizing how much she'd just revealed. "Thank the dear sainted Elizabeth Taylor that Augie wasn't awake to see that nonsense."

Lally made a derisive noise. "That child sleep through a hurricane if you let him."

Olivia smiled a tiny bit as the doorbell rang. Her smile faded. "If she's come back to try to talk me into telling her who her father is again or to get out of coming to breakfast, I swear I will let her go to jail."

"No, you won't." Lally got up. "I'll take care of this. You get some of that breakfast into you." A few minutes later, she returned. "You have a visitor, Miss Olivia. He says it's real important, so I put him in the library."

"He?"

"Says his name is Fenton Welch. Looks fae to me."

"Elektos," she muttered as she pushed up from the table. They were the only ones bold enough to call at this hour. She went into the library and took the chair across from her visitor, glaring at the cypher fae who'd had the bad luck to call on her on this particular morning.

She should have had Lally toss him out. The woman took a strange joy in telling people to leave, but continuing to refuse the Elektos wouldn't keep them from her door. They were a stubborn lot. At least they'd sent one of their less intimidating members. The slender, freckled fae in spectacles looked about as threatening as your average accountant. A suitable image considering his freckles were actually tiny numbers. Legend said if you could add up a cypher's freckles and get their total, that cypher would be forever in your power. But she also knew not to touch him. She wasn't about to give up her account and password information that easily. "What do you want at this uncivilized hour, Elektos?"

"I want to know the whereabouts of Augustine Robelais."

She shrugged and sat back. "He's a free man. Comes and goes as he pleases. Hasn't been here in months."

"He was seen in the Quarter last night celebrating *Nokturnos*."

She kept her mouth shut and just stared at him. Years of watching her agent negotiate contract terms and movie deals had taught her that the first one to speak usually lost.

He pushed his glasses up. "I have the authority to search this house, Ms. Goodwin. You've got fae bloodlines and as you reside in a Haven city, you receive the same protection and must abide by the same rules as every other fae within city limits."

She tapped her cane impatiently on the library's loblolly pine floor. "I was born here, you idiot. I retired here because it's my home, not because I needed the protection of the Elektos." She stifled a laugh at the thought of this bureaucrat trying to protect her from anything greater than a paper cut.

He canted his head to the side, looking up through his lenses at her. Like she was a child that needed things explained to her. The nerve. "Be that as it may, you enjoy our protection whether you actively seek it or not. Now I will ask you one more time, where is Augustine?"

"I have no idea." Not a lie. She really didn't know where he was and frankly, she preferred it that way.

Then the sound of boots thudding down her stairs pulled a sigh from her throat.

The fae across from her arched a brow. "No idea, Ms. Goodwin?"

"I don't monitor his coming and going, peckerhead."

Augustine's voice rang out. "Livie, where are you?"

"In the library. With *company*," she called back. Damn bothersome company.

Augie sauntered around the corner, the look on his face telegraphing his understanding of her inflection. He shifted his gaze to the newcomer and leaned heavily against the door frame. His horns were gone. He must have sawed them off after he'd come home last night. "I knew we'd come to this sooner or later."

"This is…" She frowned at her visitor before introducing him. "Fartus Wanker—"

"Fenton Welch," the man corrected sternly.

She waved his comment away with an impatient hand. "Fenton, Fartus, whatever your name is, you're not taking Augustine away from me. I need him. I'm an old, old woman and he's my caretaker. Without him, I'd take the wrong pills and drink drain cleaner by mistake and there'd be no one to call the doctor when I fall and break my hip. Then my death would be on your head." It wasn't like Harlow was going to take care of her in her dotage. All that child wanted was the name of the man most likely to kill her. And money.

"Ms. Goodwin, I don't think—"

"Refreshments?" Lally walked in with a tray of house recipe Bloody Marys. So much for being alone. At least the drink
would make Olivia feel better, especially since the house recipe
was heavy on the vodka and spice.

Fenton gave Lally the eye, then cleared his throat. "Ms.
Goodwin, I'm not here to take Augustine away, although con-
sidering his recent actions that would certainly be within the
Elektos's rights."

"You're not?" She took a Bloody Mary off the tray Lally held
out and swallowed a healthy portion. Vodka was so restorative.
Especially when accompanied by a large dose of good, local hot
sauce.

"No." Fenton helped himself to a drink also, but after the
first sip, he coughed and set it down. Lightweight.

She patted the cushion next to her. "Augie, come here." He
walked over and settled his lanky form onto the divan with a
dancer's grace. Somehow he made the bulk of muscle he carried
seem easy.

Augustine stared at the Elektos, looking unconvinced
Fenton wasn't about to cuff him. "What do you want with me
then?"

Fenton put his hands together. "We've had some terrible
news. Our current Guardian, Khell, was found dead this morning. Throat slit. Never had a chance to fight back."

Augustine swore softly under his breath. Olivia grabbed his
hand, her heart cold in her chest. "That poor boy. And just
married, too."

"That is a damn shame." Augustine stroked the back of Olivia's hand with his thumb. Always such a comfort. "Slitting his
throat would take away his best defense." Khell was part wysper
and they had a scream that could kill vampires. "Good chance
it was vamps."

Fenton nodded, obviously surprised by Augustine's knowledge. "We think so, too. Their numbers have been increasing in our city with alarming speed and with last night's festivities it was easy for them to blend in. Can I ask how you know this?"

"I hear things. And while I'm very sorry about Khell, this news changes nothing. Like I've told you before, I am not interested in becoming Guardian." He crossed his hands through the air. "Not now, not ever."

Olivia nodded. "Khell's murder proves how dangerous the job is. You can't force Augie to do this."

Fenton sat a little taller in his chair, the light in his pale eyes suddenly stern. "No, I can't force him." He looked at Augustine. "But if you don't take this job, the Elektos will have no reason not to prosecute you for your crimes against fae society. Namely admitting a mortal not only to the fae plane, but to the Claustrum, a place you will become very familiar with should you turn us down again. In fact, the chance that you'll accept is the only reason you haven't been arrested so far."

A muscle in Augustine's jaw twitched and the light in his eyes went hard and icy. An image of eighteen-year-old Augie flashed before her eyes, more anger than sense and nerves like tripwires. A sudden sense of dread drifted through her.

His voice came out a low growl. "There are other candidates."

"Yes, but none with your... background."

Augustine snorted. "What is that supposed to mean?"

Fenton inched back in his seat, but otherwise held his position. "We know what you're capable of, Augustine. That you killed a man when you were eight without even knowing what your powers were. How you earned your way with underground fights until no one would oppose you any longer." Fenton paused. "We need that kind of fae for our next Guardian."

Olivia stiffened. She'd known what Augustine was capable of, but never in such black-and-white terms.

Augustine's face was steel and stone. "So you want a fae with a record? There are a lot of us out there."

"No." Fenton held Augustine's gaze. "We want a fae who will be as much of a threat to our enemies as our enemies are to us."

"And one," Augustine added, "that you won't mourn too much when the job kills him."

Chapter Seven

The anger arrowing through Augustine's spine felt like it was about to split him open. It shattered the calmness he'd worked so hard for and made his muscles itch with the memory of physical violence. He tried to contain his temper, tried to push it back down, but that was not something he'd had to do in a very long time and he was out of practice. The struggle paralyzed him for a long, long moment.

"You can't do that," Olivia whispered, her voice rough with emotion. "You cannot take him from me. He and Lally are all I have."

"He's made his own choices, Ms. Goodwin. Now he must make one more." Fenton stood. "You have a day to think it over, Augustine. Twenty-four hours." He tipped his head at Olivia, who still sat motionless. "I'll see myself out."

As the cypher left, Augustine bent his head into his fists. He hated to lose control around Livie. He'd made her afraid a few times in their early days, before he'd mastered his temper and his instinct to lash out. It wasn't something he wanted to do again. "I should never have helped Chrysabelle. Never should have taken her to the Claustrum. I knew it would come back to bite me on the ass. Damn Mortalis. He never should have sent her to me. I could kill him for—"

"Augustine." Her quiet voice interrupted him. "Maybe you should take the job."

He looked at Olivia. The library's overhead light emphasized the lines on her face and for the first time, she seemed her age. "After all your protest? It's a death sentence, Livie, you know that. That's the second Guardian we've lost in three months. And how long was it before that? Two years? Besides, it would mean leaving you."

"Just because the Guardianship comes with a house doesn't mean you have to live there." Her eyes were bright with unshed tears.

"Livie..." He took her hand again. "I just need to work out a way around this."

"I don't think this is something you can charm your way out of." She pulled her hand away, blinking hard and scowling. "I know about the Claustrum, Augustine. I don't want you in that place. You think being Guardian is a death sentence? What kind of life will you have in that hellhole? A worse one, that's what kind. If being locked in that place can even be considered a life." She inhaled deeply. "I don't want you—or anyone I love—ending up in prison. No matter what plane it's on."

He took her hands in his and pulled her attention to him. Her heartbeat thumped in his ears. "Livie, Livie, I'm not going to let that happen, I promise. Look, I've got twenty-four hours to figure something out, and I will. It's going to be all right. Even if I have to go away again for a while."

"That's not an answer." She gave him a short, unconvinced look, but already her pulse had dropped a few beats. "And I don't like you being gone."

"I don't, either."

A couple of breaths passed between them before she spoke again. "Promise me you'll at least think about taking the job?"

"Livie." He sighed. "I'll think about it." It was a lie, one that hurt to tell, but if it made her feel better, that was all that mattered.

"Promise," she insisted.

He nodded, unable to refuse her. "Promise." There went the lie, but thinking about something and acting on it were two very different things.

His answer calmed her. She blew out a sigh, collapsing in on herself a little. "Did you find Dulcinea? Maybe you should talk to her about this."

"I saw her last night. Not sure what good talking to her about this would do. She's not going to want me to take the job, I can tell you that much." None of their crew had ever had a great relationship with the Elektos. The years hadn't changed that, either. At least for those who were still alive.

"Let her read your cards." Livie turned her gaze on him, something desperate in her eyes. "Let her read your cards and tell you what they say about this situation."

Augustine laughed. "Livie, she only does that to goof on tourists and line her pockets. It's a performance, not a prediction. You can tell the future better than she can."

She made a grumpy noise. "I can tell the present much better. Suss out lies and truths. That's my thing. Dulcinea *can* read those cards when she wants to." Livie pressed to her feet, her fingers tight around the crystal top of her cane. "You go back to her this afternoon and see what she says."

From the doorway, Lally clucked her tongue. "We'd be awful sad for you to leave again. And life on the run ain't no way to live."

"Fine." Defeated, he raised his hands. "If it makes you feel better, I'll go see Dulcinea." He stood, walking out of the library alongside Livie.

"Good. And thank you." She stopped in front of the big hall mirror. "Now go wash up for lunch."

"Breakfast for me."

"Lazybones."

He winked at Lally, tipping his head toward Olivia. "You

two sure like to boss me around." But he understood. Being away from this place he considered home and these women he considered family had left him empty and out of sorts. Dulcinea would have no solution, but for their sake, he would ask what she thought.

Lally stopped him with a hand on his arm. "Mr. Augustine, I see you cut your horns."

He nodded. "It was time."

Her eyes took on a funny light. "You still have 'em?"

"They're in my trash. Why?"

"You mind if I have them? As a memento?" She smiled a little. "They're a curiosity."

"Sure."

She nodded. "All right, then. Thank you. I'll collect them next time I'm upstairs."

He waited until just before sunset to return to Jackson Square. He hoped to find Dulcinea there spinning tales for the tourists and that's exactly where she was. The oil lamp on her table painted her with a mysterious light as dusk fell. Giselle was gone, probably didn't like the rowdy crowd that emerged with the evening. He sat on the steps on the far side of the square and slightly behind Dulcinea, knowing she'd kick out her paying customer again if she saw him. He wasn't about to keep her from earning.

For February, the night came on cool and clear; the sky above sparked with stars. Most of the tourists were drifting toward Bourbon by now, ready to suck down drinks, dance in the street and flash each other for cheap beads, but the square was almost empty. That would change in a few weeks when Mardi Gras came. There'd be more tourists than any one street could handle and they'd clog the city with their drunken, happy selves. At least they left a lot of plastic behind.

If he couldn't find any security jobs right away, maybe he'd pick up a few shifts bouncing at one of the clubs, get a little of that plastic for himself. They always needed extra help during Mardi Gras. For all that he enjoyed Livie's generosity, he liked making his own cash even more.

He pulled rolling papers and a pouch of *nequam* out of his pocket and twisted himself a cigarette while he waited. The reddish brown smoke drifted upward, filling the air with the scent of burnt fruit and his brain with a subtle calm. His mind drifted to Angel, the woman who'd run from him on *Nokturnos*. He checked the women that passed, even though he knew he wouldn't be able to recognize her since he hadn't seen her face. That evening felt so unfinished. All he wanted was a few more minutes with her. To talk her into staying.

He was about halfway through the cigarette when Dulcinea's customer got up and left. He took one more drag, ground out the cherry and tucked the rest into his pouch for later.

He stood, then hesitated. A new group of people were loping past her table. A split second later, he knew they weren't looking to have their fortune told or get drunk on Bourbon Street. At least not drunk on alcohol. Their eyes held the kind of wicked intent he'd seen a few times before.

Vampires.

Dulcinea knew it, too. She pointed at them. "Get out of my city, bloodsuckers."

A big male led the crew, a jagged scar running from cheek to lip. He gave a sign and the pack shifted direction. Dulce pulled a blade, causing them to laugh as they surrounded her. One caught a handful of Dulcinea's dreads in his fist and yanked her toward him. "It's our city now, fae."

With a curse, she slashed at him, but he let go and danced out of reach.

Augustine grabbed the dagger from his boot and bolted toward them with a low growl. Dulce was stronger and faster than a human, but not as strong and fast as a fae with cleaner bloodlines.

He vaulted over her table and went feetfirst into the chest of the nearest one. A small female. She held on, raking her nails down his ankle, ripping through his jeans and scratching the leather of his boots. Augustine kicked her away as he flung his blade into her chest. The big male howled in sorrow, reaching for her, but she went to ash before he touched her. He whipped around to glare rage at Augustine, baring his fangs and cursing.

As the head vamp started forward, another male tore past Dulcinea, trying to grab her again, but she stabbed him, doing some damage but missing his heart. He sliced his nails across her face, cutting three gouges into her cheek before he fell and went to ash.

She hadn't missed his heart after all.

The big, scarred male yelled for retreat and the pack backed away, but he kept his gaze on Augustine. "This will be settled, fae."

Augustine laughed, standing his ground. "Go suck yourself, leech."

"Go after them, Augustine," Dulcinea urged. She started to sway. "Don't let them get away."

"In a sec. You don't look so hot." Her cheek was still oozing blood. "He might have had poison on his nails. You're not healing right."

She huffed. "I'm fine. If there was poison, I'd feel it. Now seriously, go finish them." Except that her cheek was turning black, an unsettling sight against her gray skin. She reached out for her table as her lids fluttered.

"Like hell, you're hurt and I'm not leaving you." He grabbed her arm as he righted her chair and helped her into it, then he crouched to take a closer look at her cheek. Besides the skin retaining its normal color, the edges of the cuts should be pulling together by now, the bleeding done with. It wasn't. "Dulce, this isn't healing like it should."

She nodded, wincing even as she did it. "My face feels like it's on fire." She worked her jaw, testing her cheek. "Damn, that hurts. I still think you should go after them."

"Getting this cleaned up is more important than chasing those leeches. Trust me, they're not coming back here tonight."

"What about tomorrow night? Or the day after? Khell's dead, you know. Vamps slit his throat to keep him from using his scream. His dirty lieutenants aren't going to snuff those buggers." She hoisted a black messenger bag from under the table and fished around in it until she pulled out a small first aid kit.

"This is going to need more than a Band-Aid."

She gave Augustine a look as she popped open the box and took out a brown glass bottle and some cotton wool. She wet the wool with liquid from the bottle and started dabbing at her cheek. "A little help?"

He took the wool from her and cleaned her face. The green liquid smelled bitter. As he worked, the cuts began to heal and her color returned to normal. "What is this stuff?"

"Tincture of jewelweed. Neutralizes most plant- and insect-based poisons. I take it it's working?"

"Like a charm." Her cheek was almost back to normal. He wiped off the last of the blood and pushed to his feet. "When did you go all earth mother on me?"

"I didn't make it. I bought it off Giselle's sister down at the farmers' market. Now that I know it works, I like Zara even better. Giselle can still suck it." She put the first aid kit away and stood. "What are you doing down here anyway? I thought you'd be having some big dinner with Livie tonight."

"Not exactly." He filled her in on the demands the Elektos had made. "Livie made me promise to let you read my cards. She thinks you can find an answer for me."

"I don't need cards to tell you what to do." She wound a slim dread around her finger. "You should take the job. It would solve all your problems." She dropped the dread and raised her hand before he could speak. "But I know you. I know you're going to do everything you can to get out of this." With a sigh, she took her seat.

"The job would only create more problems." He righted the little folding stool on the other side of the table and sat. "I know you're not in the mood, but will you read my cards anyway? Since I promised Livie."

Her mouth was a hard, thin line, which translated as "I'm only tolerating you right now." Breathing deeply, she gathered her cards from where they were scattered over her table, neatened the deck and set it in front of him. "Cut the stack."

He picked up half the cards and set them beside the other half.

She rejoined the two piles, shuffled them and fanned them out on the black velvet draping. "Pick one and I'll give you your answer."

He grinned. "The down-and-dirty version, eh?"

She didn't smile back. "Pick one."

Damn. He'd seen Dulcinea angry before, but not at him. Subdued, he tapped a card near the end of the right side. "This one."

She pulled the card and flipped it over directly in front of him. "The hanged man."

"That's cheery." He snorted. "So there it is then. If I take the Guardianship, I end up dead. Good enough for me." He started to get up.

"Sit down." Dulcinea's glare put him back in his seat. Then she continued. "The hanged man is a card of decisive surrender. It represents martyrdom and sacrifice to the greater good."

She stared at him, her oddly colored eyes piercing even in the weak glow of her oil lamp and the flickering streetlights. "This is a card you should meditate on to help you break bad habits and old behaviors. To learn to leave behind *things* that restrict you from following the path you're meant to travel."

He sprang from the stool like he'd been bitten. "Did Olivia put you up to that? I didn't think you'd play those kinds of games with me, Dulcinea."

She narrowed her gaze and shook her head. "You picked the card. I simply told you what it means."

"I'm out of here." He flipped up the collar of his long coat and strode off. He needed the walk, to think and to cool down. He'd never yelled at Olivia and he didn't want tonight to be the first time, but it was wrong of her to try to force his hand like this. And for Dulcinea to go along with it? He was shocked, really. She wasn't what anyone would consider a team player by any means.

He lost himself in the streets, moving on instinct and muscle memory. There was no good solution for the problem at hand. No clear path that would lead him out of this mess. He'd have to leave. Again.

Maybe for good.

The bitterness of that thought sank into him, blinding him to the people he passed. All he saw was everything he loved in life being taken away. He thought about his half brother, living fat in Paradise City. Even if Mortalis did work for a vampire, he had a cushy life. Hell, he'd always had a cushy life, something Augustine hadn't known anything about until Livie had taken him in.

He stumbled over a root protruding through the cracked sidewalk, catching himself on the tree's massive trunk. Behind him, footsteps scraped to a sudden stop. He turned, but there was no one there. He listened. Nothing. Not a heartbeat, not a breath. If the Elektos was having him followed, they could go screw themselves.

He broke into a jog, eager to get home, however much longer that word would apply. He approached Livie's house and jumped over the block wall surrounding the property. The lights were on downstairs, so she was still up. Probably waiting for him, but he was in no mood to talk. Tomorrow morning would be soon enough.

With practiced ease, he scaled the trellis on the side of the house, then vaulted onto the second-story porch. From there, he climbed the gutters to the attic and the big window he never locked for this very reason. Once inside, he cranked up some blues, a sign he was home but wanted to be left alone. He collapsed onto the bed, folding his arms over his face. His head hurt from trying to come up with something, anything, that would get him out of this mess.

Exhausted, he drifted off.

The low whine of bluesy horns lifted Olivia's head from her tablet. Augustine was home. And unhappy, by the sounds of his musical selection. Did that mean things hadn't gone the way he'd wanted with Dulcinea? She'd have to wait to find out. When he listened to blues, it meant he was in a pensive mood.

Let him think. They could talk before breakfast. Before Harlow arrived. Olivia reread the last line of the book on her display, *The Mother-Daughter Dilemma*, but it had no solution on how to handle her relationship with Harlow. That child. How many times could one person break your heart? Tomorrow Harlow would suffer through breakfast so she could get her money, then she'd disappear again. Agreeing not to discuss her father would only make Harlow hate Olivia even more, but Olivia saw no other way. Protecting Harlow was all that mattered. All that had ever mattered since that horrible night.

With a shudder, she tapped off the tablet's power and got to her feet, picking up her cane from where it rested against the couch before walking out into the hall to stare up the steps.

She sighed, the tiniest niggle of guilt creeping into her bones. Maybe she should have pushed Augustine harder to become more independent, but she wasn't the boy's mother. As much as she acted like it. Or wished she could have been. Perhaps indulgent aunt was a better description.

He lived here rent-free, worry-free, responsibility-free. And all because she allowed it. Was that any different than paying Harlow to spend time with her? The niggle turned into a genuine pang and she shook her head, disgusted with herself. She'd failed Harlow; would she fail Augustine, too? Sweet St. Elizabeth, that boy needed some sense talked into him. Tough love, they used to call it. She tapped her cane on the floor. "Augie!"

No response. "Augustine, come down here. We need to talk."

Still nothing. Her mouth bunched in frustration. She hadn't taken those stairs in years thanks to the house's elevator, and she certainly wasn't going to start now. Fae hearing was excellent. He could hear her, even over those whining horns. If he wanted to behave like a child, so be it. "I'm going outside to sit on the porch, Augustine. If you know what's good for you, you'll come out there and join me." They did some of their best talking out there. No reason they couldn't work this thing out tonight.

Otherwise, she'd ream him a new one in the morning before Harlow arrived. The position of Guardian was potentially fraught with danger, that was true, but then what part of life wasn't? People keeled over from heart attacks while doing nothing. Better to face one's fears and stare death in the eyes than have it creep up on you in your seniority.

She stormed out of the house, slamming the big leaded-glass door so hard she cringed and waited for the crack of glass, but it never came. Exhaling her relief, she took her place in one of the rattan rockers, easing her weary bones onto the cushions. If only every aspect of life was this easy. Sit, rock, let your thoughts drift. That was part of the life she'd envisioned when she'd left Hollywood to return to New Orleans's welcoming embrace. That and having Harlow here with her, going to school at Tulane, living at home, the two of them happy. As they should always have been.

Instead, Harlow had ignored Olivia's pleas to move here, ignored the promises of school paid for, of a new car, of providing anything Harlow needed to be happy. Except the one thing Olivia could never, ever give her—her father's name.

Then Olivia had met Augustine. He'd scared the daylights out of her at first, but she couldn't help but feel pity for him. For what he'd been through. How he'd kept himself alive. That boy had *needed* her. His mother had done such a job on that child. Torn the boy down until he felt as worthless and *wrong* as his mother had led him to believe, and then she'd kicked him out.

Who put a not-yet-fourteen-year-old child on the street?

Olivia shook her head, the ache of memories building tears in her eyes. Yes, he'd filled a part of the hole left by Harlow, but if she hadn't taken him in, he'd be dead, like a few of the others he'd run with. She knew that like she knew the sky was blue and the grass was green.

And then the one thought she never let herself have reared its head. Had someone adopted Harlow the way she'd adopted Augie? Had some other woman become the mother to Harlow that Olivia had never been?

She sniffed. Foolish old woman, that's what she was. Harlow was as stubborn as Augie. Maybe more. At least Augustine still spoke to his mother on occasion. Harlow wouldn't even answer the phone.

Now she was getting maudlin and she hadn't even been drinking. Not her first mistake of the night, that was for sure.

She twisted her cane in her hand, trying to focus on the evening's soothing sounds. Instead, she heard a soft thump, followed by something shaking one of the bushes at the darkest corner of the yard. She clutched her cane tighter. Augie would be down in a moment. It was probably just a coon falling out of one of the trees. Or an armadillo. The bush moved again, followed this time by a very human-sounding grunt.

"Who's there? I've got a gun." Which was unfortunately in the drawer of her nightstand. *Damn it, Augustine, get your lazy bones down here.*

There seemed to be some faint whispering. Or maybe it was just the breeze. Her age blunted the sensory advantage her narrow fae bloodlines had once given her.

Suddenly, a girl burst forth into the glow of the porch lights. Her hair was disheveled, her makeup tear-tracked and her lip bleeding.

"How did you get in the gate?" Olivia asked.

The girl let out a sob. "Help me, please, my boyfriend's following me and he's trying to hurt me and—"

From outside the wall, an angry male voice cut her off. "Jenny? Are you in there?"

"Oh my." Olivia got to her feet and went down the porch stairs toward the girl. "That will not do." She stopped beside the girl and brandished her cane like a weapon. "Go home or I'll call the cops, son. Leave Jenny alone. You're done for the night."

Quite unexpectedly, the girl whipped around to look at her. "Hey, aren't you Olivia Goodwin?"

"Yes, I am, but—"

"Then in that case..." The girl grinned, revealing fangs. "You're the one who's done for the night."

Olivia jerked back but Jenny grabbed her, slapping a hand over Olivia's mouth and pulling her close against her body. Olivia dug her heels in as the girl dragged her toward the dark corner. More thumps, the sound of more vampires coming over the wall. Olivia tried to yell, but Jenny's hand just clamped down harder. Using every ounce of fae strength she could muster, Olivia bit into the girl's fleshy palm.

The girl snatched her hand away. Olivia screamed, adrenaline fueling her stage-trained, fae-powered vocal chords to new decibels. It only served as a signal for the rest of the vampires to attack. Hands grabbed her and the weight of many bodies took her to the ground hard, knocking her teeth together and cutting off her cries.

Teeth sank into her. Stabs of pain erupted again and again as fangs pierced her skin. She tried to yell, to shout, to whisper but the only thing she could manage was a bubbling sound. A metallic taste followed it.

Then a corporeal heaviness tugged at her, dragging her down like she was underwater. Dark shapes bobbed in and out of her field of vision, blocking the stars above her until nothing remained but blackness.

Far, far away, she heard the front door slam and a familiar male voice bellowing her name.

Poor Augie, he sounded like he was in pain...

"Livie!" Augustine attacked, barely aware that the desperate howl cracking the night's quiet came from his own throat. Insensate with rage, he moved in a whirlwind of shadow and smoke, tearing through the snarling mass of vampires like a ravenous animal. Like the beast he'd once been. He ripped out a throat as he slid into another and destroyed the leech from the inside out.

Mere moments and the vampires were gone, some ash, but

a handful got over the wall. One injured enough to be help-
less but not enough to go to ash lay prone near the edge of the
garden.

Exhausted by the reality of his dear Livie torn and bloody
before him, Augustine dropped to her side and cradled her body
in his arms, whispering her name through his sobs. "Livie, hold
on, I've got you, I'm here, stay with me—"

"They were…after…me…" she gasped.

"Oh, Livie, no. They were after me. This is my fault."

She tried to shake her head. "Get the mirror," she breathed.
"The mirror."

The words cut into him, raising instant scars. There was no
time for pretending she had any other hope. "Okay." He nodded. For her. He understood as well as she that death was coming for her and getting to the fae plane was her only escape.

"Don't leave me yet," he begged even as he eased her to the
ground and got to his feet. He raced into the foyer, yanked the
massive wall mirror off its hooks and hauled it back outside.

He set it down, then gently lifted her. She was feather light
and utterly still. Panic gnawed his gut. "Livie, Livie, talk to me."

"Still here," she mouthed, blood tinting her lips crimson.
What little pulse he could hear was weak and thready. "Vampires," she added. "For me."

"I know who did this. They'll pay. You have my word." Relief
flooded him that she was still alive. "Let the mirror take you.
I'll find you, wherever you end up. I promise." Then he shifted
her tenderly onto the glass.

Her eyes fluttered open and a faraway smile touched her lips.
"Tell Harlow…I love her."

"I will." Something inside him cracked. The old darkness tried to claw its way out, desperate to run free. To find
vengeance.

"My boy..." Her lids began to close again. "Love you."

"I love you, too," he choked out. The ground beneath him seemed to give way, but it wasn't the ground that had disappeared, it was his control. The cracks widened, dropping him into a darkness blacker than the night.

"Don't be afraid..." She exhaled, sinking down against the mirror.

"Hang on, Livie. Hang on." He waited, but there was no inhale, no rise of her chest. The faint echo of her pulse went silent, replaced by the crashing sound of Augustine's world.

Olivia Goodwin was dead.

Chapter Eight

A strong, trembling hand gripped Augustine's shoulder. Lally slid to the ground beside him, her bathrobe bunching up around her knees. "Oh no, Miss Olivia, oh no, oh no..." Her voice trailed off in a whisper.

He couldn't answer. Couldn't breathe. Couldn't make sense of what had just happened because it was too awful to be real. He looked at Lally. Her cheeks were wet, her mouth open as if she labored for each draw of air. He understood. She fumbled in her pocket, drew out a cell phone.

A soft moan broke through Lally's quiet sobbing. Augustine started to reach for Livie, thinking some miracle had occurred, then the black rage of reality boiled up inside him. The moan had come from the remaining vampire. The leech was dragging himself toward the wall with his one good arm.

Trying to get away.

Augustine got up, eyes focused on his prey across the garden. "Call nine-one-one, then call the Elektos," he told Lally.

Sniffling, she nodded, her fingers already touching the numbers on the screen.

He leaped across Olivia and landed crouched over the vampire. "Move again and you'll regret it."

The vampire barely glanced at Augustine and kept crab-walking toward the wall. Augustine whipped the dagger from his boot and drove into the vampire's shoulder. The monster hissed, baring his fangs. Augustine put the weight of his body on the blade and drove it deeper into the wound. More hissing.

He leaned in. "You think that's bad? Have you ever been possessed by a shadeux fae? Or burned by a smokesinger?" He paused. "Can you imagine what a mix of those two could do to you?"

The vamp stopped moving, the determination in his eyes replaced by resolution. Maybe he knew he was about to die. "You're the fae who killed our leader's girl."

"And now you've killed mine." The realization of who these vampires were tore new wounds into Augustine. These were the vampires from Jackson Square. The ones he'd refused to go after. They really had been after him. Over the sound of Lally's brokenhearted weeping, sirens whined in the distance. "Who's your leader and where can I find him?"

The vampire had the audacity to laugh. "I'm not telling you anything."

Augustine raised his hand so the vamp could see it, then channeled his shadeux blood, letting his hand go translucent. The vamp's eyes widened just before Augustine plunged his hand into the leech's chest and grabbed hold of his dead heart. Then he applied a little smokesinger heat. The sirens were louder now. "You feel that burning inside you? That's what it feels like right before you go up in flames. Name and location."

Defiance sparked in the fringe's eyes. The wound in his shoulder had already begun to knit closed. "Never."

The sirens stopped, replaced by slamming car doors, but the lights stayed on, bathing the house and yard in alternating washes of red and blue. Augustine squeezed the vampire's heart a little harder, applied a little more heat. Defiance switched to fear. "Last chance. Tell me and I'll dump you outside parish boundaries alive." A complete lie. "Refuse and you're ash."

"That's enough, Augustine." Fenton Welch stood over him,

a bolt stick in his hand, the end glowing blue with a charge. Behind him, cops and fae he didn't recognize swarmed the yard. One led Lally back toward the house.

Fenton's glasses reflected the flashing lights from the cop cars, making it hard to see his eyes. Augustine shook his head. "It's enough when I say it's enough."

Fenton tapped the shaft of the bolt stick into his palm. "That's Guardian business. And seeing as we don't have a Guardian, the prisoner becomes the property of the Elektos. Now get your hand out of his chest and let me do my job."

Augustine didn't move. "I need to know who their leader is and where to find him."

"We'll get that information from him and then we—the Elektos—will deal with it." Fenton nodded toward the police officers standing between them and Olivia's body. "Talk to the cops. Tell them what happened here so they can get out of our way. The longer they're here, the less we accomplish."

Augustine hesitated. Could he slip into the vampire and make it over the wall? He'd never possessed a vampire before. How long could he keep the leech from exploding into ash? Long enough to get information out of him?

Fenton lowered his voice. "Don't make me take you into custody, Augustine. Not tonight."

"Like you could." Lally's soft sobbing started up again. Augustine glanced at her. She stood near the house, shoulders shaking, head down. He slid his hand out of the vamp's chest and stood. He wasn't about to leave her alone.

The vampire got one hand on the ground and pushed like he was going to get up. Fenton jammed the bolt stick into his chest. A blue flash and a crack like bottled lightning and the vamp convulsed once, then lay still.

Fenton turned to the team he'd brought with him, two males who appeared to be some kind of goblin fae with their squat muscular bodies and dusty skin. "Guz, Rat, get this vamp contained and back to headquarters."

They grunted and got to work. Fenton nodded at Augustine. "Talk to the cops."

Augustine walked away, too numb with unspent rage to do anything else. Two police officers met him at the porch steps. Human cops. Yeah, they'd be helpful. He put a hand up. "I don't want to talk. Not now."

"Understood," the first officer started. "I know your... kind has their methods of dealing with situations like this, but if you could just answer a few questions so we can turn this over to your people officially, that would be very helpful."

Is that how things worked in New Orleans? The police completely washed their hands of othernatural business? Or is that how the Elektos had set it up? Anger gave him the strength to speak words he'd never imagined himself saying. "Olivia Goodwin was killed by a pack of fringe vampires. What else do you need to know?"

"Can you tell us specifically what happened?"

Augustine took a breath and prayed for patience. "I was in my upstairs apartment—"

"You live here?"

"Yes."

"Are you related to Ms. Goodwin?"

"No."

"You rent a room from her?"

"No." What little patience he had was fast disappearing.

"What's your relationship with Ms. Goodwin?"

"We're friends."

The second officer pulled a face, like he was imaging exactly what kind of *friends* they might be. A muscle in Augustine's jaw twitched, causing his teeth to grind together.

The first officer kept going. "In exchange for this friendship, you live here for free?"

Augustine's hands balled into fists. "She's like a *mother* to me. She took me in when I had nowhere else to go." He bit back the fresh pain his memories unleashed. She'd done more than take him in, she'd rescued him. Kept him alive. Shown him there was more to life than getting by on brute force and hoping not to get caught.

The first officer scribbled something on his tablet, then his stylus paused midair. "Do you have any idea why these vampires would come after her? They had to jump the wall to get to her. If they wanted an easy meal, there are a whole lot of drunk tourists in the Quarter they could have gone after."

Augustine teetered on the edge of a very dangerous cliff. "Vampires don't need a reason. They're monsters."

The officer stared at him a second too long. "I suppose you're right. Thank you for your time. Don't leave the city for the next few days in case we need to talk to you again."

He frowned. "Are you saying I'm a suspect?"

"I'm saying don't go anywhere." The officer tapped off the screen of his tablet and tucked it back into his utility belt before making eye contact again. "Your juvenile record doesn't put you high on our list, but it does put you on it."

"That record was sealed."

The cop shrugged. "Nothing's sealed anymore. Not in this country." Then he and his partner walked away.

Seething, Augustine turned to the scene in Olivia's front yard. They had her on a gurney now. Covered in a white sheet. She looked so small. His stomach pitched like he was about to lose his dinner. He made his way to the porch and sank down onto the steps. Lally sat behind him in Olivia's rocker, the cross, key and locket on the end of her gold chain clasped in her hands like a rosary.

"Mr. Augustine." Her voice was a rasp of pain. "What we gonna do?"

He shook his head, unable to speak. He had no answers. How could he? He was the reason Olivia was dead. He was the one to blame.

The cops were talking to Fenton now, exchanging information maybe. The first officer glanced toward the porch, then Fenton did the same thing, shaking his head like the cops had nothing to worry about it. Damn it, did they really think he was involved in this?

Other than the fact he'd led those undead murderers right to Olivia's doorstep. He dropped his head into his hands and, for the first time since he'd lived under Olivia's roof, felt as worthless as his real mother had told him he was.

She couldn't be gone. She couldn't. If there was any justice in the world, anything fair or right or good, then Olivia couldn't be gone.

The urge to explode scratched at him like it had in the old days. *That* Augustine would punish this city. Make it hurt the way he was hurting now. Tear it apart until he found what he was looking for. He raised his eyes enough to watch the cops. They thought they knew about him based on his juvenile record. They knew nothing. The mayhem he'd authored then was nothing compared to the kind of hell he could raise now.

And if they kept him from finding the person behind this vampire invasion, they would discover just how much.

The buzz of Harlow's LMD woke her. She fumbled for it, opening her eyes enough to find the snooze on her alarm and tap it. She'd been up late, searching obituaries for any mention of any man who might possibly be her father. Given that she had no name, didn't know his age or where he was from, the search had been pointless. And also somehow completely necessary.

This breakfast with her mother felt like premeditated torture, but she'd decided enough was enough. If her mother was willing to give her the money to pay her fine, the least Harlow could do was be a little more communicative. It certainly couldn't make things worse. And maybe, at some point, her mother would realize that Harlow's desire to know her father wasn't so she could replace Olivia. She just wanted to know the human side of herself. To find that missing piece of her puzzle. Olivia couldn't fault her for that, could she? Especially now that the man was dead, what harm could there be in at least sharing his name?

She punched the holovision remote and searched through the channels until she came to a local station. Weather, the thing she'd been looking for, scrolled across the bottom. She yawned, satisfied that at least it wasn't snowing like it was at home.

Flipping the covers back, she put her feet on the floor and got up. She tugged her T-shirt down as she walked to the bathroom, the anchorman's drone barely registering as she cranked on the shower.

Until the man said her mother's name.

She stopped, hands in her duffel bag as she searched for clean clothes, and turned toward the holovision.

"Hollywood legend and beloved local Olivia Goodwin was murdered last night in an apparent mugging gone bad. Police have no suspects at this time but—"

Harlow slumped to her knees, the man's voice fading as the ringing in her ears took over. That couldn't be right. She'd just seen her mother. Just talked to her. A pit opened up inside her, a dark place that bubbled with guilt and regret. Then a new noise broke through the ringing in her ears, a strangled keening sound that Harlow suddenly realized was coming from her own throat.

Her mother was dead. And so was any chance Harlow was ever going to have to fix things between them.

A day passed before Augustine could surface from the grief and guilt suffocating him. That second morning came bitter and gray, the oddly warm weather they'd been enjoying replaced by the kind February usually brought. The afternoon added a drizzle. Augustine couldn't help but think New Orleans was mourning Olivia right along with him and Lally. He stood at the big leaded window in his attic apartment, staring out through the rain-streaked glass at the sprawl of the Garden District but not really seeing anything. His head was too full of memories. The past was all that made sense, really, because the reality of what had happened was too horrific to believe.

Sleep had mostly eluded him the last two nights, coming in short, restless spans that dissolved into nightmares. Visions of Olivia's broken body in his arms. His mother screaming at him. Fingers pointing, accusing. He'd woken up drenched in cold sweat several times only to realize the nightmares weren't his imaginations but the worst of his memories.

On top of it all, Olivia was gone. His sweet, wonderful Olivia. And he was to blame.

He scrubbed a hand over his face, eyes gritty with lack of sleep and the abundance of sorrow. How on earth was he going to get through this? Muffled noises and the scent of coffee filtered up from the main floor, reminding him he wasn't alone.

Somewhere below, Lally was hurting just as much as he was.

Moving like he was trapped in amber, he pulled clothes onto his body and lumbered down the back stairs to the kitchen so he wouldn't have to pass the gilt-framed hall mirror, now leaning against the foyer wall, waiting to be cleaned and rehung.

Lally stood at the sink scrubbing out her gumbo pot. She greeted him when he came in but didn't make eye contact. "Afternoon, Mr. Augustine."

"Afternoon." The fact that neither of them had added "good" underscored the rottenness of the day. He poured a cup of coffee, then slumped into one of the kitchen chairs. "You doing okay?"

"I suppose so. I called Miss Olivia's lawyer. Got...things started. He's going to take care of notifying people and letting the papers know and all that. Funeral be in two days." Her voice was soft as she kept scrubbing.

"That's good, Lally. Thank you." How she'd found the strength, he had no idea, but if she hadn't been a strong woman, she never would have lasted around Olivia.

She rinsed the pot and put it on the rack to dry. "You want breakfast? Or lunch?"

"Nothing." He rubbed at his eyes. "No appetite."

"Me neither." Her hands went still and her voice grew weaker. "I can't believe Miss Olivia's gone." She bent her head and her shoulders began to shake.

He leaped from his chair to comfort her, pulling her into his arms and letting her bury her head against his chest. His own eyes burned, but he was long out of tears. "I know. I feel the same way."

After a minute or two, she sighed deeply and pulled back to lean against the sink, patting at her eyes with a handkerchief from her apron pocket. "Mr. Augustine—"

"Please, just call me Augustine. Or Augie. I'm not your boss, Lally."

She nodded, but he wasn't really sure she was agreeing. "Can I ask you a question?"

"Only if you promise to stop calling me Mr. Augustine."

The tiniest fragment of a smile lightened her eyes. "Okay."

"Ask away."

"You know I don't know much about your kind, other than what I've learned from Miss Olivia." As far as he knew, Lally was one hundred percent human. "Why did Miss Olivia have you bring that mirror out?"

He went back to his coffee, taking a sip before he answered. The hot liquid tasted muddy and flat. "Fae can travel through mirrors. We can go to other places in this world, or we can go to places on the fae plane." He blew out a long breath. "I guess Livie thought she could escape this world before it was too late."

Lally thought for a moment. "But she didn't? Is that what you're saying?"

"Her body would have vanished if she'd made it through. So, no." He swallowed, trying to erase the ashy disappointment coating his mouth. "She didn't make it."

She hugged her arms around her waist. "Do your people believe in the afterlife? Do you have souls like humans?"

"Yes on both accounts." Although his mother would probably argue the last one.

"Well, then, Miss Olivia had a fair bit of fae blood in her and we know she was a fighter. Seems to me maybe a part of her would have gotten through, don't you think?"

He narrowed his eyes. "You think her soul made it through?" He'd never heard of such a thing.

"Don't know. But maybe you could go and have a look around." She glanced up at the kitchen clock. "That man gave you twenty-four hours to make your decision about taking his job offer, but no one came round yesterday so I'm guessing they gave you one more day on account of what happened. Means they'll be coming soon and that don't give you much time to do a lot of searching."

"It gives me almost no time. The fae plane is a big place. If she did make it, she could be anywhere."

Lally's face dropped. "I understand."

He hated to squelch Lally's hopes by saying there was no point, but he had doubts about the possibilities. Serious doubts. If such a thing were possible, it seemed he would have heard about it being done before, but then his knowledge of all things fae had a lot of holes in it. "It wouldn't hurt to take a look, I suppose."

A tentative smile curled her mouth. "Thank you, Mr. Aug— I mean, Augie."

He stood slowly, Lally's optimism causing hope to well up in him. Allowing some of his sorrow to be replaced by something he had no right feeling was an uncomfortable sensation. "I don't like leaving you here alone knowing the Elektos could be on their way. Don't let them in until I get back, okay?"

"Absolutely." She adjusted the gold chain she always wore. "I ain't letting anyone in this house until you get back. Now you shoo. See if you can find Miss Olivia and bring her back here. Or at least let her know we miss her."

"I need something of hers. Something with..." His voice dropped. "Something with blood on it would be best."

"Her cane." Lally nodded. "It's in the front hall by the mirror."

"I'll have to run upstairs. I need a mirror to take with me so I can return, too."

"Wait." She dug into her purse on the counter, pulling out a cosmetic mirror and holding it toward him. "Will this do?"

He flipped it open. Silver backed. "This'll work." He clicked it shut and tucked it in his jeans pocket, then hesitated. "I should take two so I can leave one behind."

"Why's that?"

"If she made it, the only way she can get off the fae plane is with a mirror."

"Hang on." She went to her room and returned with a small mirror framed in carved wood dark with age. "Here."

"You sure this isn't valuable?"

"It is. That's why I want Miss Olivia to have it."

Together, they walked out into the hall. Livie's cane rested near the door. Flecks of dried blood covered the crystal finial. He tucked the framed mirror beneath his arm, then picked up the cane and stood before the mirror with it. The reflection staring back at him made it clear just how deeply Livie's death had affected him. Grief was its own special kind of ugly.

Lally hesitated, then backed up a little. "You mind if I'm here? If I see you...go through?"

"No." He glanced at her, trying to determine if she had some greater plan in mind. "Just don't try to follow me. Under any circumstances."

"I—I wouldn't even know how."

By touching him as he passed through, that's how, but he wasn't about to share that information. Not that Lally was the type to act on something like that. "Good. Okay. I'm going through."

He held the cane in one hand, then focused on the glass, realizing there were droplets of blood on it, too. That was good. Blood was a powerful magic of its own kind. It should help tune the mirror to Livie's path. Which made him think that maybe Livie *had* made it—but no. Her body hadn't even wavered like she was trying to cross through. Still, he'd told Lally he would go. He let the blood speak to him, trying to picture whatever part of the fae plane Livie might have made it to, then he let his fingers graze the glass and a second later, the magic pulled him through.

The world before him was a sprawling gray field capped with an infinite gray sky. Foggy drifts obscured the mountainous horizon with more gray. Wind moaned in the distance, a lonely, eerie sound that drew goose bumps over his skin as it came closer to tug at his clothes and ruffle his hair.

What little hope he'd allowed into his heart vanished completely, torn away by the wind. He knew this place, the horrors that resided here. If this wretched plane was where Livie had been pulled through to, there was no chance of getting her out and even less chance she'd survive long enough for him to find her.

He turned, dreading what lay behind him but needing to see it anyway.

The great black rock formation towered over him, its entrance carved into the center where slivers of jagged stone along the edges guarded the gates leading in. *In* almost exclusively, because few who ever entered came out.

The mirror had brought him to the Claustrum.

Chapter Nine

He couldn't bear to think of Livie here or anywhere near here. The Claustrum was a hellish prison where the fae incarcerated those of their kind too destructive and too criminal to be let loose on the mortal plane. The creatures caged in this place were monstrosities, some twisted variations on the various fae lines, some the rare remainders of lines now bred out of existence. The raptor fae, the one he'd brought the human Chrysabelle here to see, was a milder example but still not a creature anyone would want to run into alone.

Why would the mirror bring him here? There was only one answer that made sense. And that would be because it was the last place Livie had traveled. For some reason, if Livie had gotten through, this was where she'd ended up. The how and why of that made no sense to him, but mirrors were just tools of transport, not capable of deception.

He held Livie's cane up as the air buffeted him. "Olivia Goodwin!" The wind ripped her name away, carrying it off into the grayness surrounding him. Again he shouted for her. "Livie! Are you here? It's me, Augustine."

But his only response was the whine and cry of the wind squealing through the Claustrum's craggy spires. There were other parts of the plane he could investigate; the Grand City, the Valley of Focus, Alucinor Forest... all a thousand times better than this place but searching them meant months of work, not hours.

He set the framed mirror on the ground so that it was protected by a few rocks, then rested the cane in front of it, the idea of time swirling through his head. Maybe that's exactly what he needed—or what Livie needed. Maybe a transition from one life to another took time. Maybe she was still finding her way through this plane.

It was better than thinking he'd never see her again, even if he knew deep down he was telling himself a lie. In a way, trying to fill the hole in his heart with false hope only heightened the ache of his loss. He already hurt so much the only thing he could think of that might take the pain away was finding the person responsible for bringing these vampires into the city and making them pay. The Augustine who'd once run the streets of New Orleans would have no trouble wiping those vampire vermin—and their benefactor—from his city in Livie's name. Or making his home the safe haven it was meant to be.

He still could, but not without breaking laws and creating the kind of havoc that would taint any chance of finding this traitor. There was only one way to do what he needed to and stay above the law.

Accept the Guardianship. If he reverted to his old ways without the Elektos behind him, they'd call him a threat and he'd become the hunted once again, exactly what Olivia had tried to keep him from. No, he had to do this in such a way that the driving need for revenge in his gut had some kind of authority behind it. He couldn't be the loose cannon he'd once been. The kid who'd just as soon cut someone as look at them.

He closed his eyes at the thought. That's not who he was anymore. Not who Livie had taught him to be. That part of him was a product of his mother. A product of rebellion. Maybe if his mother had raised him differently, raised him to embrace his true heritage, that past wouldn't exist. But it did. And he was about to call on those skills once again.

If only he had someone to talk to, someone to comfort him and reassure him that the decision he was about to make was the right one, but that person had always been Livie.

There *was* one other person, someone he felt obligated to inform about his decision, but talking to her had rarely ended in him feeling better about anything. Maybe this time would be different. Just like maybe Livie was here somewhere on the fae plane. He almost laughed at how easily he stacked one lie on top of another. Even so, he pulled Lally's mirror from his pocket and left the fae realm behind in search of the impossible.

A room service tray sat near the door, the barely touched food gone cold, but Harlow didn't care. The butler could clean up when she left. Until then, no one else was getting in. She sat on the floor, her back against the bed, her knees pulled to her chest. At her side, the roll of toilet paper she'd been using to blow her nose and wipe her eyes after the tissues had run out. She'd kept the news on hour after hour, watching, praying for some new story that would tell her the report of her mother's death had been wrong. For the reprieve that would give her time to make things right.

But of course, it never came.

Her LMD buzzed. She dug it out from under a pile of used tissues. Not a number she recognized. She accepted the call anyway. "Hello?" Her voice rasped, raw from crying.

"Harlow Goodwin?"

Not a voice she recognized, either. "Yes. Who is this?"

"Lionel Cuthridge. I'm your mother's attorney. I'm afraid I have some bad news."

"I already know what it is." She bit back a sob. This meant her mother really was dead.

"I thought you might have heard. I am very sorry for you loss. Your mother was loved by everyone who knew her."

Not everyone, Harlow thought. *Not by her awful daughter. Not enough.* The darkness inside her tried to swallow her again. She thought about letting it.

He went on. "There is the estate to be handled, the will to be read. Unpleasant things to think about at this time, I know, but necessary nonetheless."

She made a soft noise that he seemed to understand as his cue to continue.

"I know you live in Boston, so we can certainly adjust things until you're able to travel to Louisiana—"

"I'm already here," she whispered, hoping he didn't ask why.

"I see. Well, that's good then. Are you staying at your mother's? I wasn't aware—"

"No."

He hesitated. "There is plenty of room there, if you wish to. I'm sure I'm not out of line suggesting that, but it would make things easier. You are her heir, after all."

Harlow rubbed at her eyes. That hadn't occurred to her, but he was right. And her cash wasn't going to last forever. "I can move out of my hotel and go over there this afternoon."

"Very good. And this number is the best way to reach you for further correspondence then?"

"Correspondence?"

"The information concerning the execution of the trust, those sorts of things. As you are a beneficiary of her trust, I need to be able to reach you. Eulalie Hughes, your mother's housekeeper—"

"I know who she is."

"Eulalie will be handling most of the funeral arrangements, so you won't need to deal with that unless you wish to help." He paused. "You'll be at the house then?"

"By this afternoon, yes." A beneficiary of the trust. She went still. Was there a chance her mother had left her the information Harlow had been trying to get all her life? Might she be about to find out who her father was? There was no reason for her mother to take that secret to her grave, was there?

Another hope sprang up in Harlow, this one heavy with the weight of shame. Beneficiary meant her mother had left something to Harlow despite their differences. Maybe more than the information about her father. Maybe...money. Enough that she might not have to go to prison after all? The thought that her mother had loved her enough to take care of her even after death brought new tears.

She fought them down, struggling to accept the inevitable. These legal things had to be taken care of. She was her mother's heir. It was her responsibility, no matter how great her sorrow. Still, she was glad her mother's housekeeper was willing to handle the rest. Harlow wasn't sure she could get through planning her mother's funeral.

"I'll speak with you soon, then, Ms. Goodwin."

"Thank you, Mr. Cuthridge." Now to pull herself together. She got to her feet and took a long look at herself in the bathroom mirror. Her eyes were puffy and her nose red. She looked like hell. In general, more than she could fix in a few hours with a hot shower and some makeup. What did it matter? She was moving into her mother's estate. Wasn't like she was going to run into anyone she knew.

Augustine had long ago learned that coming and going via mirror required discretion. Appearing in the middle of a street or a crowded room tended to cause accidents and panic. To that end, he now stood in the back corner of the Ursuline Convent's gardens, deep in the shade of the trees and almost within arm's reach of the high wall surrounding the two-block compound. The main building loomed before him, an austere stucco rectangle that was as plain as it was large. Standing here, in this tranquil place, it was hard to imagine the Quarter was just beyond. Harder still to think that the woman who'd made his life so miserable called this peaceful place home.

The sound of singing came from deep within the building, children's voices by the lightness and purity of the notes. The convent had returned to its original use after the Great War, reopening as a convent and an orphanage and helping to bring peace and comfort after so much turmoil.

Behind him were the nun's apartments, but at this time in the afternoon, he imagined most of them would be in the main building with the children, finishing up lessons on math and history and spelling.

The woman he was looking for would probably be in one of the smaller outbuildings. He headed for the nearest, adjacent apartments, hugging the wall and the shadows to hide himself. Curls of steam and the perfumey scent of laundry soap drifted from a partially open transom window. The main door was open, too; the second, screened one left closed. He eased through it, expecting it to creak, but it didn't. A woman bent over to lift a laundry basket of sheets, her graying hair pulled back in a low bun, her unadorned face lined with age but unable to hide that she'd once been beautiful. Even with the covenant gone, he imagined she had no trouble passing as human.

He cleared his throat to announce himself.

She hefted the tub onto a table and turned, fingers still gripping the handles. Her gaze shifted over him, pausing where his horns would be, then settling on his face. Her mouth was thinner than he remembered, but her eyes carried the same disappointment tinged with disgust.

"Hello, Mother."

She turned back to the sheets, dumping them onto the table. "I don't have any money, if that's what you're—"

"Have I ever asked you for money before? No and that's not why I'm here now." He sighed and leaned against one of the dryers. Nothing changed. She still expected the worst from him. His news would go over big, then.

She separated one of the sheets out. "Saw on the news this morning that woman you were shacked up with was murdered."

He took a deep breath, reminding himself that he'd chosen to come here. "I was not *shacked up* with Olivia, Mama. We were friends. There was nothing untoward about our relationship."

"You didn't do it, did you? The murder? Are you seeking asylum?" She found the corners of the fabric, pulling them together. "At best, the archbishop could give you absolution."

His mouth fell open. "Are you serious? You think I did it?"

She shrugged, her back to him as she folded, her work more important than her son. "I know what you're capable of."

They both did, but that didn't give her the right to accuse him. "Holy hell. You're unbelievable, you know that?" He stared at the condensation beading on the ceiling, imagining that water could cool the irritation building in his bones.

She turned to glare at him. "Watch your language. This is sacred ground."

He pushed off the dryer and shoved the screen door open. "I should have known not to come here. No matter how many years go by, you never change."

"What did you come here for? What do you want from me?"

He squared himself toward her and stood his ground. "I don't want anything from you. I came to let you know I'm accepting the Guardianship of the city."

"Hmph. Like it matters to me. I don't know why you haven't done it sooner, you love showing off your fae blood so much."

"I never accepted it *because* of you." Finally she faced him for more than a few seconds. "Because I was trying to respect your wishes that I not flaunt my fae side. But you're right. None of my efforts have ever mattered to you."

"I suppose that means you'll be growing your horns back?" She crossed her arms over her chest.

"Yes, it does. I know that disappoints you, but it's not like they're the only thing that designates me as fae. Horns or not, my skin will always give me away. I'm fae, Mama. And unlike you, I'm too fae to pass for human. No matter what you'd rather I was, I will never be anything else."

If his words made any difference, it didn't show. The sour expression on her face remained the same. "And now you're going to be the big fae in charge, huh? Am I supposed to be proud? Because I'm not."

He shook his head. "I can't do this. You're my mother and I know that means something, but I'm not sure why I care." He pushed through the door.

"That's right, leave. Just like your father."

The screen door slammed shut behind him.

"At least you know he'll be proud of you!" she shouted after him.

But he kept walking.

Lally was in the kitchen when he came through the back door. The table was covered with casserole dishes and cake plates, all full. Her brown eyes held questions, making him sorry he had no answers. "Did you find her?"

"No, but that doesn't mean anything. It might take time for

her to fully transition." The lie slipped so easily from his mouth it almost tasted real.

"Well, that's something." She wiped her hands on her apron, tipping her head at the table. "Neighbors been coming by, bringing food. Dining room table's full of flowers, too. News carried the story this morning."

"I heard. What did they say?"

"Mugging gone bad."

"I figured it would be something like that. The Elektos has as much to lose as the tourism board if word gets out that vampires killed one of the city's best-known residents." He tapped the lid of a crystal cake plate. "Mrs. Chalmers's coconut cake?"

"You want some? I'll cut you a slice."

"No, not right now. Has Welch been here?"

"Not yet, but I'm sure—"

The doorbell rang. Augustine held a hand up for her to stay. "I'll get it. I'm sure that's him."

"Augustine?"

He hesitated. "Yes?"

"You going to take that job?"

He took a deep breath. "I have to, don't I? It's the only way to make this city safe again. And to properly avenge Livie. You know what I was like in the old days. I do that again without some kind of sanction and I'll be the one they're after."

"I suppose so. Miss Olivia would like that. You taking the job, I mean. It would make her proud." Lally smiled, but the small movement of her mouth didn't reach her eyes.

"My mother definitely doesn't feel that way."

Lally's eyebrows rose a tiny bit, her mouth pursing. "You saw her?"

He nodded. "That's where I came from."

Lally reached over to give his arm a squeeze. "I know it's hard for you having a mother like that, but the way she is toward you? That's her burden to bear, not yours. Miss Olivia loved you like a son and somewhere, right now, she's smiling down on you for what you're about to do."

"I hope so, because there's no turning back." He slipped into the hall and headed for the front door. The shape on the other side of the leaded glass was definitely not Fenton's. Shorter. More feminine. Why had they sent someone else? That didn't seem like a good sign.

He opened the door. The woman on the other side was younger than he'd expected for an Elektos, a good head shorter than him, and looked more like a junior accountant than an Elektos enforcer. She seemed vaguely familiar, but then so did a lot of women. Her hair, a deep purply red that was almost black, was twisted up in a clip that turned the ends into a spiky plumage and she wore a slouchy hoodie with black leggings and scuffed-up ankle boots. Her eyes were covered with oversized sunglasses too dark to see through. Forget junior accountant, she looked like an off-duty Goth librarian. Which would have been kind of hot if he hadn't been in mourning.

A rolling duffel bag sat beside her on the porch, a laptop visible in one unzipped pocket. He realized a second later that she was wearing thin, flesh-colored gloves. Not that unusual, depending on what kind of fae she was. Maybe cypher, like Fenton. "I suppose you're here to find out my decision." At least they hadn't sent that proper old fart again. Augustine definitely preferred this mysterious female. "I appreciate you giving me the extra day. That was unexpected and very kind."

She scrunched up her face. "Decision? What? No. Who are you?"

"Augustine. I live here." He frowned. Not Elektos then. "Who are *you*?"

"You live here?" She let go of the rolling bag to push her sunglasses onto her head, revealing a sprinkling of freckles across her heart-shaped face and amber eyes as bright as Livie's despite the dark circles beneath them. "Harlow Goodwin. Olivia's daughter. I'm here for the reading of the will."

Chapter Ten

Harlow looked at the...*man* in front of her. Six fingers, pale gray skin, obviously muscled in that unattractive way of his kind...obviously fae, too, but at least he didn't have horns. That would have been too much of a freakish coincidence with Charlie. The memory of him almost lightened her overwhelming sadness, but she stopped it in time. All she deserved to feel right now was grief and guilt. "The lawyer didn't say anything about anyone living in the house. Other than the housekeeper, who I already knew about."

He stared at her, hard, his eyes rounding suddenly. "You."

"Me what?"

"*Sturka*," he muttered. "This is not good. You're Olivia's daughter?"

"Yes, that's what I'm trying to tell you."

"You don't recognize me, do you?"

"Should I?" But already a vague, sickly familiar sense was welling up inside her. She tried to ignore that this man in front of her might be—

"Charlie, but I had horns then." His finger went from pointing at himself to pointing at her. "And you're Angel."

Her stomach flipped and the pleasure she'd tried to suppress hit her hard. She swallowed it down. If this was the universe's way of punishing her for being a horrible daughter, there was nothing she could do but take it. "Why are you...how is this... oh, this is not good." The man—no, the fae—she'd kissed and run from was standing in front of her. In her mother's house. "What are you doing here? Where are your horns? You said they were real."

"They are real. I sawed them off." His frown grew. "I find it hard to believe your mother never mentioned me."

"She was good at keeping secrets." She frowned back. If Olivia hadn't mentioned him, maybe it was because she knew Harlow wouldn't approve of the relationship. "Please, in the name of all that's holy, don't tell me you're her...boy toy, because I will vomit."

"No. Hell's bells, is that what you think? Olivia and I were very good friends. Like mother and son. Nothing more. Damn."

"That's a relief." But only a small one. Knowing her mother had a substitute child only added to her sense of shame. "Maybe you could go back to your own place now. Let me deal with all of...this."

"My own place?" He smirked like he had all the answers. Cocky piece of work, this one, but then he'd been that way the night of *Nokturnos*. "I've lived here for almost twenty years. I'm sure your mother must have said *something* about me."

"My mother and I haven't been on the best of terms for a long time. I'm sure she must have said something about *that*." Not that it was any of his business. Just like it wasn't any of hers as to why her mother had invited this annoyingly charming man to live with her. Maybe he was like a butler. Granted, Olivia had been up in years, but that didn't mean she couldn't hire a handsome guy to wait on her, right? As odd as the thought was, Harlow clung to it. And as the butler, he could certainly provide her with a few answers. "Are you going to let me in?"

He stepped out of the way, opening the door wide and sweeping his hand toward the interior in an overly dramatic gesture that almost got her to smile. "By all means, come on in, Miss Goodwin."

"Harlow is fine." Even without having previously spent time with him, she could tell his type. Probably spent his days polishing his pickup lines and spent his nights pillaging the local female talent, hoping to never run into the same one as he cut a swath through the bar scene. At least New Orleans had a steady influx of tourists. That high turnover must make things a little easier on a guy like him. She smirked, knowing she'd figured him out. "No wonder you love New Orleans."

"What's that?"

Had she said that out loud? Living alone and working from home had given her the bad habit of talking to herself. "Just that you must love the city. It's so . . . fun."

He looked unconvinced of her opinion. "I was born here. I can't imagine living anywhere else." He closed the door, then held a hand out. "Can I take your bag? I assume you're staying here for the funeral and everything."

Was he really that nice or was he playing her? "I'll hold on to it." She'd never been inside the house, but it was certainly big enough. Ridiculously so. Although the décor was oddly restrained, considering what she knew of her mother's taste. The house carried the strange scent of smoke mixed with citrus. Incense maybe? "Tell me again why you live here?"

"I live here because your mother wanted me here." His words almost sounded like a challenge.

She started to answer him when Eulalie came out from a room at the end of the hall. She glanced at Harlow, then smiled, her eyes full of sorrow. "Miss Harlow. I'm so glad you're back, but I'm sorry it's under these circumstances."

"Hello, Eulalie."

"Call me Lally. Everyone does." Her smile faded. "You have my deepest sympathies, child. I loved your mama dearly. I'm so glad you're going to stay here with us."

"Thank you." Harlow wasn't sure how else to respond. Being

called "child" only underlined the thinness of her relationship with her mother and freshen the pain of losing her. Then to be suddenly thrust into Olivia's world, surrounded by her mother's things and her friends...tears threatened, but Harlow fought them. She would not break down in front of Augustine.

Staying here was probably not the best idea after all. Especially with him being here. She'd spent too much money on that damn suite, so she'd have to find a cheap place now. Or hack her way in. A couple of clicks and she could have a paid-for room almost anywhere. *If* she wasn't being monitored, which she was sure she was. "I think I should probably stay at a hotel."

"Nonsense!" Lally held up her hands. "We'll have none of that now. There's plenty of space here. I'll just go fix up that big guest room on the second floor that overlooks the pool." She headed for the stairs that dominated the foyer. One foot on a tread, she stopped. "Unless you'd rather stay in your mama's room?"

"What? No." Harlow blinked hard at the very idea. "A guest room is fine." It was hard enough being in her mother's home, but sleeping in her bed? Unthinkable.

"I'll bring her bag along later, Lally," Augustine called up the steps.

"Thank you, child," Lally called back. Good to know that was a general term and not specifically meant for her.

"A pool, huh? This is quite the place." Harlow took another look around, trying to imagine her mother in this house and picturing her happy. At least Harlow hoped Olivia had been happy here.

"It sure is." Augustine turned to her. "You want to see the grounds? Or tour the house? See what you're about to inherit?" At the last word, a cloud of melancholy came over him.

Probably because he just realized he wouldn't be living here anymore. Hopefully because he was also sad. Harlow ached with the pain of her mother's death, but it was impossible not to be grateful about the possibility of finding out who her father had been. What if she had step-brothers and sisters? A tiny spark of joy lit inside her at the idea.

And then there was the potential inheritance. Even if there was no cash, selling this place would allow her to pay her fine. If there was any left over, she'd finally be able to hire a private investigator to track her father down, something she could probably do herself if she had his name.

Maybe she'd even have enough left to buy a house, a place with enough space for a dedicated server room. Then she could turn her small penetration-testing business into a real force to be reckoned with. Take on bigger companies, develop more complicated hacks. Go completely legit. She got lost in the dream, an easy way to brunt the grief.

"Hello? Anyone home?" Augustine peered at her like she'd zoned out. Which she had.

"Sorry, I'm just tired from...everything." She shook her head. He must think she was a total flake. Not that she cared. "If it's okay, I'd rather see the house later."

"Look, things don't have to be weird between us just because of *Nokturnos*."

She snorted like she hadn't even thought about it. "No, of course not." Oh yeah, things were weird.

The doorbell chimed.

She looked toward the front of the house, thrilled that someone had chosen that moment to interrupt. "I imagine you've had a lot of visitors. I'm sure my mother was pretty popular." Especially if she took in random strangers.

"She was well loved in this city, but I don't think that's anyone here to pay their condolences. Not yet." Augustine's expression changed into something more solemn and serious. "If you'll excuse me."

"Sure. I'll just…" But he was already opening the door.

She ducked into what looked like a library, staying just inside the doors, where she could see who it was and hear what they had to say about her mother. But Augustine was right. The visitor, a tall, thin man with glasses, didn't seem to have come about Olivia.

Augustine spoke first. "Fenton. Thank you for the extra time."

"Of course. Have you made your decision?"

Augustine didn't invite him in. "Yes. I accept."

The man's brows lifted a little and he nodded. "Very good. Not what I expected, but a welcome response."

"Did you really think I'd let the right to avenge Livie's death fall to someone else? Hell, no."

"I understand." The man nodded, his hands coming together in front of him. He wore flesh-colored gloves like she did. Was he fae? "It's a shame it took something like this to bring you to this decision."

"It's a shame I have to accept this position." Augustine sighed heavily. "I want it to be official immediately. I need to talk to the vampire."

Vampire? An icy shiver shook Harlow. Was that who had mugged her mother? She knew vampires existed, but to find they were here, in this city, set her nerves on edge. She wasn't one of those who'd welcomed the breaking of the covenant with open arms. Not when it meant people now automatically assumed she was fae.

The man, definitely also fae, continued. "We can perform the ceremony tonight. Seven o'clock at the Prime's home."

"I know it. I'll be there."

The man relaxed, looking very relieved. "Thank you."

Augustine snorted. "Like I had a choice." Then he shut the door.

Harlow sidled over to one of the bookcases, pretending to

peruse the volumes as Augustine came in, and putting a little distance between them. She had a thousand questions to ask about the vampires, but wasn't sure she wanted the answers. Instead, she tapped one of the books' spines. "I guess my mother wasn't much on technology. There's a fortune in books here."

"She was fine with technology. Read on a tablet just like everyone else, but she liked the feel of paper books, too. Liked the way they smelled, the way they felt in her hand. Liked to think about all the people who might have read the book before her."

Harlow nodded. "That sounds like her. She was very sentimental."

He perched on the back of one couch. "And you're not?"

"Not like her. I prefer to live in the present. I like simplicity. Practicality."

"Is kissing a stranger practical?"

She ignored his question, but couldn't escape the heat it raised on her skin. "I like the conveniences of modern technology." She waved her hand through the air, hoping to focus him on a different subject. "This place is beautiful, but it also seems like it's stuck in the past."

"This house?"

"This house, this city...all of it."

His incredulous look said he wasn't impressed with her opinion. Again. "I understand you're new here, but this city is all about history and tradition. We live and breathe it. That's why people come here, you know. That charm. That sense of gentler times when people knew their neighbors and actually spoke to each other. Which we still do here."

She nodded like she understood, but what he'd just described sounded horrifying. "I suppose."

Silence stretched between them like barbed wire until Augustine spoke. "What's with the gloves? What kind are you?"

"What kind?" She knew what he was asking, but even talking about it put her in defense mode.

"What kind of fae? I know you're part haerbinger because that's what Livie was, but are you another kind or did the line just come through you so strong you don't like skin-to-skin contact? I'm guessing that's what it is based on the way you pulled away from me after our kiss."

"You ask a lot of questions." And he kept bringing up what had happened between them. So much for it not being weird. She tucked her hands into the pouch of her hoodie. She had zero interest in answering his questions.

He shrugged. "Just curious. I know it's rare for a particular line to strengthen in a single individual unless combined with another fae line that causes it to magnify." He tapped his chest. "I'm one of those. Part smokesinger and human mixed with a whole lot of shadeux."

She didn't have any idea what he was talking about so she just nodded. "I'm not any of those things. Really I'm barely fae at all. My father is human." Then the lie she fell back on popped into her head. "I just don't like germs." She wiggled her fingers at him. "Total germaphobe."

He laughed, his sudden smile lighting up his face in a way that reminded her of the night of *Nokturnos*. And of the smokiness that perfumed him. And of the way his kiss had left some of that smokiness dancing on her tongue. The sudden intensity of the desire that memory built in her made her squirm.

He nodded like he'd suddenly figured her out. "No wonder you like things modern. You're gonna hate New Orleans then. History tends to make things a little grimy around the edges. And Bourbon Street? Well, you saw for yourself that it's not exactly clean and tidy, although they try. You might like a plantation tour, though. Or the aquarium."

"I don't plan on doing any touristy things." She'd done

enough of that already. "I just came to take care of my mother's estate, then I'll be leaving."

His brows shot up. "What was *Nokturnos* all about then? You sure looked like you'd planned for it."

"I didn't. It was a whim. And obviously a bad one. Can we please let that drop?"

He held his hands up. "Got it. But really, if you want to do a tour or visit one of the museums—"

"No. None of it. I just want to take care of my mother's estate and go home."

His smile morphed into confusion. "You're in New Orleans and you're not the least bit interested in seeing what else this great city has to offer?"

"All that charming, grimy history?" She raised her brows in disbelief. After how it had worked out the first time? "I'll pass."

He slid off the couch and back to his feet. "Fine, but that's just weird."

She'd had enough weird.

The housekeeper came in. "Room's ready for you. I can take you up there unless you'd like something to eat? There's plenty of food in the house."

Before Harlow could answer, Augustine jerked his thumb in her direction. "Lally, get this, she doesn't want to go to the Quarter or the aquarium or do a tour or *anything*."

Lally tipped her head to one side. "Augustine, her mama just died. Let the poor child mourn." She held her hands out to Harlow. "Look at her. All pale and tired. You can see she's grieving."

Harlow cleared her throat. Pale and tired was the general tech geek appearance; grieving for two parents had only multiplied it. "I'm fine, really. Just want to get things taken care of, get the house up for sale and get home."

Lally paled. "What?"

Augustine swiveled to look at her like she'd just announced

she planned to murder someone. He shook his head like he didn't understand. "You're selling this place?"

"I don't see that I have much choice. Did you think I was going to live here?"

Lally put a hand to her mouth, then tried to compose herself. "I don't know what I thought was going to happen, but I guess that's that then. It's your right, being the heir and all. I just... I should go start dinner."

"Lally, wait," Augustine said. "You won't have to look for another job or a place to stay. You can come with me to the Guardian's residence."

"I can't leave this house." She looked at Harlow. "You wouldn't understand."

"That's for damn sure." He shot Harlow a look. "You might be Olivia's blood and you might have her eyes, but you sure don't act like her."

"I'm okay with that," Harlow shot back. "She wasn't exactly a model parent."

He laughed as he walked out. "You really have no idea. No damn idea."

The only thing that superseded the knowledge that Harlow was the captivating woman he'd kissed the night of *Nokturnos* was the news that she intended to sell the house like it meant nothing. It stuck in his throat like a fish bone, but for the sake of the ritual that was about to begin, he would find a way to swallow it down. There would be time to deal with Harlow after the Guardian ceremony was over.

The black-robed Elektos formed a circle around him in the living room of the Prime, Hugo Loudreux. As Prime, he was the head of the Elektos, voted into power by the rest of the council.

The Elektos as a whole chose and approved the Guardian, who then appointed his own lieutenants. The Guardian's power was autonomous, his only charge to protect the city and her citizens.

In theory, the Guardian and the Elektos were to work hand in hand. But Loudreux had a reputation for forcing his will. Maybe that had worked with past Guardians, but he'd find Augustine to be harder to bend.

Somewhere else in the house, Augustine's half sister Blu stood watch, her position as Loudreux's personal bodyguard still not enough to grant her access to this ritual. He'd often wondered how she could work for Loudreux and now he was about to do the same thing. Almost. The Guardianship allowed him more independence. At least that's how he planned to move forward.

The furniture had been pushed to the walls, and the rug rolled up to expose the wood floors. Augustine stood in his bare feet, Hugo directly in front of him. Loudreux's dislike for him was easily readable in the man's eyes, but finding someone to agree to be Guardian wasn't always an easy task, so Augustine doubted the cypher fae would argue against him. After all, Hugo knew Augustine had been asked before and he had to have been the one who'd sent Fenton to the house. But how difficult Loudreux made Augustine's job as Guardian remained to be seen.

Tall, slender and covered with the tiny freckle-like numbers that distinguished cypher fae, Hugo stared into Augustine's eyes. Just because he and Fenton were both cypher fae didn't mean they were related, but Augustine wondered if there was a connection. Hugo got things under way by lifting his open palm in Augustine's direction. "Augustine Robelais, do you come here of your own free will, without coercion or promise of monetary gain?"

It was so odd to hear his last name spoken aloud. It was the one thing other than blood that linked him to his mother. "I do."

"You agree to protect this city and her people, othernatural and human alike?"

"I do." His mother should like that part about protecting humans.

"You further agree to abide by the wishes of the Elektos and to uphold the law as we see fit?"

Augustine paused before he answered, causing the faces of the surrounding Elektos to crease with tension. "I'll take it on a case-by-case basis."

The assembled Elektos dissolved into discord. Hugo held up his hand. "Silence." Then he returned to Augustine. "It is your job to do as we say."

One of the Elektos made a small dismissive noise. Another shook his head like he couldn't believe Hugo was pushing this issue.

The vibe flowing off the rest of them was very interesting. Augustine decided to test it. "It's the Guardian's job to protect the city and the people who live in it from all forms of menace, natural and othernatural." That creed was drilled into every fae who lived in a Haven city. "Nothing about being the Elektos's hired stooge."

One of the Elektos, Salander Meer, a saboteur fae with the ability to decay things at will, spoke up. "I dislike your belief that the position of Guardian is one of *stooge*, Augustine, and hope that we can persuade you otherwise, but I respect your adherence to the original purpose of the role." He shifted his gaze to Hugo. "His refusal to answer this question to your satisfaction will not prevent me from voting him in."

Augustine wanted to smile, but didn't. It was good to know Salander was on his side. Saboteur fae were much better allies than enemies.

A few of the other Elektos nodded, causing Hugo to grimace. He surveyed the circle of fae. "Are you all in agreement in this?"

Yanna Quinn, ignus fae and granddaughter of one of the most famous Guardians, stepped forward, her flame-red hair done up in elaborate braids. "Loudreux, you know how we feel about this."

Polite, but restrained. Enough to tell Augustine that Hugo might be Prime, but that didn't make him popular. How had he been voted into power if he was so disliked? Or perhaps the position had changed him. Augustine vowed not to let that happen to him.

Hugo lifted his hands in slight surrender. "So be it then. His actions are upon your heads." He stepped back, unhappiness warping his face like a fun-house mirror. "Augustine Robelais, do you accept the Guardianship of the Haven city of New Orleans understanding that it is a position you hold until death and that relinquishing the Guardianship can only be accomplished in death?"

Surprisingly, the tightness in Augustine's chest relaxed. "I do." Perhaps from knowing that he was doing something that would make Olivia proud. Or perhaps it was knowing he'd now be free to avenge her brutal murder.

Hugo turned, looking at the Elektos. "All those in favor of Augustine Robelais becoming the next Guardian?"

To a person, they answered, "Aye."

Hugo dropped his hands. "None opposed?"

Faces twisting strangely, two different Elektos suddenly cleared their throats and muttered, "Nay." So much for unanimous.

With a deep inhale, Hugo continued. "Let the record show three opposed."

Augustine knew he was only supposed to speak when spoken to, but screw that. "I thought cyphers could count better than that."

Hugo slanted his eyes at Augustine. "I oppose, but I also

know the life span of most Guardians is short, so why should I stand in the way of this appointment?"

"Good to know." Augustine gave him the same cold, calculating look right back. "But I'm not most Guardians."

"We'll see." Hugo held out his hand. "Bring me the brand."

Augustine watched as Yanna walked forward with a metal rod, one end tipped with a fleur-de-lis that looked like it had been edged in silver. She wore gloves to hold it, but he would have known it was iron by the smell of it and the way it lifted the small hairs on the back of his neck.

Hugo pulled on gloves, affirming the rod was indeed iron. "All those who serve bear the mark of their city, Guardians included."

"Fine." No way was he letting Hugo at him with that thing. He hooked his thumbs in his front pockets to keep his hands from going around Loudreux's neck. "I choose Yanna to administer it."

She looked at him with complete understanding and before Hugo could say anything, responded. "I accept."

"That's, that's not protocol," Hugo sputtered.

"Does anyone object if Elektos Quinn does the brand," Augustine asked the assembly.

Fenton answered first. "It's perfectly acceptable. Go on, Yanna."

Branding iron in hand, she stepped closer to Augustine. "If you could remove your shirt. The brand goes over the heart."

He unbuttoned the shirt Lally had pressed for him, his gaze on the branding rod. "Iron so that the mark is permanent." Fae skin would heal away anything else.

"The silver is what remains." She nodded, even though it hadn't been a question. "Are you afraid," she whispered.

"No." He dropped his shirt to the floor.

She held the rod in both hands, brand at eye level, and focused on it. Tiny flames engulfed her irises and the brand glowed red hot under her gaze. "I mark you as one who serves, Guardian of the city of New Orleans." She reversed her grip, aimed the iron at him and pressed it to his chest.

The pain registered a second after the first sizzle of flesh, searing sharp and causing him to tense, but she was already removing the brand. The relief must have shown on his face. She leaned in and spoke softly. "It'll hurt more once your adrenaline wears off." Louder she announced, "You now belong to the city of New Orleans. Serve her people in all you do and her people will never forsake you."

The rest of the Elektos, save Hugo, clapped, and a few of them came up to shake his hand and extend offers of assistance for whatever he might need. A cork popped and glasses were filled.

Yanna, who'd disappeared after her announcement, returned with a small pot of ointment and a bit of gauze. "Keep a little of this salve on it for the next few days."

He glanced down at his chest. The skin was puffed and red and burned with pain, but very clearly there remained a silver fleur-de-lis imbedded in his skin. "Have you ever done that before?"

She raised a brow as she gently dabbed at the blood, then smoothed some of the ointment over the brand. "Are you saying my technique lacks finesse?"

"Not at all. But I sensed Loudreux wasn't happy with you doing it."

She peeked over her shoulder at Hugo, who was talking with the two other Elektos who'd opposed Augustine's nomination. "Loudreux is often unhappy with how the council goes, but one who's risen to such a rank through fear and intimidation cannot expect to be universally loved."

Augustine's mouth opened slightly at her frank statement. It confirmed everything he'd thought.

"I have said too much." She smiled wryly, letting him know she'd said exactly what she meant to. "But you are Guardian now and you'll soon learn more than you ever hoped to know." Her smile flattened. "I am deeply sorry about Olivia. She was a lovely woman and a great friend to this city and all fae."

"Thank you." He picked his shirt up and pulled it on. "When can I question the prisoner?"

"Straight to it then." She nodded. "I admire that." She crooked her finger at someone, calling them over.

Fenton joined them. "Congratulations."

Yanna put her hand on Fenton's shoulder. "Augustine wants to question the prisoner. Can you take care of getting him outfitted?"

"Of course." Fenton tapped his fingers against his other hand. "I'm afraid the Guardian's estate won't be ready for a few more days. Khell's widow is—"

"I don't want to run her out of there. I'm sure I can stay at Olivia's a while longer."

"Good." Fenton nodded. "That's very understanding of you." He held out a folded slip of paper. "This is the address of the Guardian's house if you want to go by and take a look." He smiled. "Don't be surprised if it takes you a few tries; the house is very heavily warded and you won't be tuned into it until you actually take up residence there."

Augustine took the paper and tucked it into his jeans pocket. "Like I said, I don't need to move just yet, but thanks."

"As you wish. Now, if you'll come with me, we can take care of the rest." He tipped his head to Yanna. "If you'll excuse us?"

"Of course." She leaned up like she was going to kiss Augustine's cheek. Instead she whispered into his ear. "I'll be in your contacts list. Call if you need me. Otherwise, trust no one." And then, with a sly smile, she was gone.

Head thick with questions, chest throbbing with pain,

Augustine followed Fenton out and down the hall to see what new madness awaited him. They went into what must have been Loudreux's study. A thick black leather roll lay on the coffee table. Fenton picked it up and handed it to Augustine. "Your weapons."

"Such as?" The roll only weighed a few pounds but it was nearly the length of his leg and the thickness of his thigh.

Fenton shrugged. "Take it home. Follow the inscriptions. Do it *tonight*. And feel free to wear them. We have an understanding with the NOPD."

"An understanding?"

"Yes. Our Guardian and his lieutenants may carry whatever weapons they see fit. The NOPD has quickly come to realize bullets do little to stop most othernatural criminals." Apparently done with that explanation, he checked his watch. "Meet me tomorrow morning at Lafayette Cemetery Number One, six a.m. in front of the Miller crypt."

"The cemetery doesn't open that early."

Fenton smiled. "Will that be a problem for you?"

If this was a test, it was an exceedingly simple one. "No."

"Very good. After you meet with the prisoner, we can take care of everything else."

"Such as?"

"Some details." He waved a hand. "Nothing that can't be discussed in the morning."

Augustine wondered if these details Fenton didn't want to talk about were going to make him regret taking this job. Even if they did, he was in this for Livie. That's what mattered. Resolved to the course he'd chosen, he swung the roll's strap over his shoulder. "See you at six."

Chapter Eleven

Gloves off, Harlow sat on the guest room bed, laptop before her, fingers flying over the keys. She had no idea what the password was for the house's Wi-Fi, but not knowing a password hadn't stopped her in years. Once in a computer system, she flowed through it like she was one of the tiny info packets, except she was able to control where the packet went, what it saw and how it interacted with other packets.

She wasn't a hacker. She *was* the hack. Pretty cool, but she'd give up the gift of reading emotions in a heartbeat. Once in a while it came in handy, but the reward was rarely worth what she had to endure to get it.

Worse, she hated being considered fae. She preferred to think of herself as a normal human being with mad computer skills, which was pretty easy to manage when you lived your life online.

Except here in her mother's house, she couldn't deny what she was. Everyone here knew her mother had been fae, so there was no way Harlow could say she wasn't.

No way she could deny that the kind of fae she'd inherited from her mother was something…a little dark. A little devious. Something that pushed her to do things she knew she shouldn't.

Like hacking into her bank account and changing the balance so her rent payment wouldn't bounce. Since her conviction, the risk level on such a simple adjustment was massive. Something she shouldn't even be attempting, but if she didn't and her rent didn't get paid, her landlord wouldn't hesitate to change the locks. Or worse, put her stuff out on the street. She couldn't bear that. Not with everything else going on. And anyway, she'd have some money soon, either from her inheritance or the sale of this house. Maybe enough that she wouldn't need to rent anymore. She nodded as her fingers flew over the keyboard. She could do this without leaving a trail. She'd only been caught the first time because she'd been set up. That much she was sure of.

The account appeared before her and with a few more keystrokes, she postdated a deposit that added just enough to cover her rent. The wrongness of it made her stomach sick. But this was about self-preservation. Life would be so much easier once she had some money and her fine paid off. Then her freedom would be ensured, and she could focus on getting her own place, her own business, her own fortress of solitude where she'd never have to personally interact with anyone ever again if she so desired.

Which she didn't. Unless it was someone with information about her father.

Before she logged off, she opened the app that monitored the webcams in her apartment. Her place wasn't in a great section of town and after her first break-in right after she'd moved there, she'd set up cameras that were programmed to record continuously and store all data for up to a month. If someone broke in again while she was gone—whether it was to the grocery store or a con—she'd have great evidence of them in action and she felt pretty confident that her videos would give the police enough to catch the perpetrators. Overkill? Probably. But she had too much computer equipment that she still owed money on not to protect it with more than the standard security system.

Everything seemed exactly the way she'd left it. Neat, tidy and all in its place. Although her apartment looked smaller than she remembered. Smaller than this room, actually. Not that it mattered. She didn't need a lot of space to be happy. Just servers and—

A knock on the door interrupted her.

"Yes?" She powered her laptop down and shut it, sliding the lock into place.

"Miss Harlow, supper be ready soon."

In response to Lally, her stomach grumbled. Amazingly, her appetite was returning. She hopped off the bed and pulled her gloves back on before she opened the door. "Anything I can do to help?"

Lally gave her a dubious look, clearly still upset about Harlow selling the house. Finally, she nodded. "I guess. Come on down and you can snap beans. You know how to do that?"

Cooking for her usually meant takeout, but how hard could it be? "Oh yeah, I do that all the time."

She followed Lally down to the kitchen, where the woman handed her a big bowl of green beans and another smaller, empty bowl. "Just put the ends in there."

Harlow took the bowl. "You're mad at me, aren't you?"

Lally's back was to her. "About what?"

"Selling the house."

She turned and sighed. "House has been sold before. I manage. Have been for years."

"You seem mad."

"Child, you don't know me mad and you don't want to. Now, get those beans done if you're gonna. I got to get them in cooking."

Harlow sat at the table, staring at the bowls in front of her.

Lally shook her head. "The stem end, just snap it off, the little thin end you can leave."

"Got it." Harlow started prepping the beans, but Lally kept watching.

"Don't you want to take those gloves off?"

"No."

Lally nodded. "You got the same touch as your mother, don't you? You sense things in people? Maybe see their futures?"

"Something like that," Harlow answered. She quickly changed the subject to the real reason she'd offered to help. "So, Augustine, what's his story?" Besides being almost more male than she could bear.

Lally turned back to the stove, where she salted a big pot of simmering water. The light in the top oven showed a roasting chicken, the source of the delicious aroma filling the house. "He was a child in need of a mother and Miss Olivia was a mother in need of a child."

"She had a child. Me." The old resentment reared its head.

Lally pulled a towel off a tray of raw, flour-dusted biscuits. "True, but seems to me you weren't all that keen on her being your mother."

"I was fine with her being my mother. I wasn't so fine with her not answering my questions." How many times had she tried to explain to her mother about the hole inside? The sense that something was missing? Nothing had swayed Olivia to talk. "Being sent to boarding school wasn't high on my list of fabulous life experiences, either."

Lally nodded. "I know you have your hurts, but I also know Miss Olivia well enough to know that whatever she did, she thought she was doing the best for you. You can't blame a mother for that, child. She wanted...never mind." Lally sighed and took a glass dish of crumb-topped macaroni and cheese out of the lower oven. "You weren't exactly easy on her, now were you?"

"She wanted what? What were you about to say?" Harlow tossed a stem end into the trash bowl.

"Don't feel right talking about a woman who's dead and gone and can't defend herself."

Harlow shrugged. "I probably already know what you're about to say anyway. How she wanted to give me everything she never had, all that."

Lally nodded. "That's right. But it was more than that. She wanted to protect you."

"Protect me from what? The evils of Hollywood? I've heard that speech and I'll tell you the same thing I told her. If it was that bad, she could have moved when I was born."

Lally cocked a brow. "You know all those movies she made paid for that boarding school and all the other fancy things you had. And this house."

Harlow snapped the last bean and pushed the bowl across the table to Lally. "I know where the money came from. That's partly why I stopped taking it when I graduated." Not that there weren't a million times she'd come close to accepting it again. To say things were tight was an understatement. "And besides, most parents protect their children in person. Not by hiring an armed bodyguard."

The pure gleam of truth filled Lally's eyes. "What she wanted to protect you from, she couldn't do herself. It wasn't Hollywood, although I think that's how it started, or maybe where it started, but there was something else."

"What then?"

"I don't know, child. Miss Olivia came close to telling me a few times, but the subject made her so jumpy she never did." She picked up the beans and dumped them into the boiling water, then leaned against the counter. "I just think until you know the whole truth, you shouldn't judge her so harshly."

The conversation's uncomfortable turn brought Harlow to her feet, guilt making her too itchy to sit. "I'll be in my room until dinner's ready."

Lally lifted the chicken out of the oven and set it on the stove to rest, then slid the biscuits in to cook. "Suit yourself."

Harlow turned to go when the back door of the house opened and Augustine strolled into the kitchen.

"Smells like Sunday dinner in here." He grabbed a hunk of the crusty brown topping on the mac and cheese and shoved it in his mouth, then licked all six of his fingers. Slowly. Like he knew she was watching.

She was.

Lally swatted at him, but not with any real intent. "Everything go all right?"

"Went fine." He planted a hip against the end of the counter and tipped his head at Harlow, those stormy eyes of his taking her measure. "You want to see the house now?"

"I can wait until it's light out." Traipsing through this big house with him in the dark seemed like a bad idea. Besides, there was no point falling in love with *anything* here. She was selling the house. Had to. A stain on his shirt caught her eye, giving her a chance to happily change the subject. She pointed at his chest. "Is that blood?"

He glanced at Lally, who met his gaze, then tucked her head down and busied herself with washing a bowl. "Must have cut myself. I should change."

Harlow watched him go. That blood was fresh, his shirt still damp with it, but the shirt wasn't cut, so any injury had been to his bare skin. She knew from personal experience that fae healed quickly. That wound should have scabbed over before he'd had a chance to put his shirt back on.

For once, she didn't need to touch someone to know they were lying.

⚜

Augustine was on the second flight of steps when he heard footsteps behind him. He stopped unbuttoning his shirt and paused on the landing. "Changed your mind?"

Harlow climbed after him. "About?"

"Seeing the house?"

She made the landing and gestured farther up the steps. "Sure." The hardness in her gaze told him she was upset about something. What, he had no idea. "Let's start with your room."

"Rooms." He got moving again, wondering what had sparked this sudden desire to see where he slept. "I live on the top floor."

"You mean the attic."

He shook his head, muttering softly.

"What?"

"Nothing." He pointed at the double doors facing them on the third-floor landing. "Through there is a large gathering room with its own bar. That's original to the house." He glanced at her, watching for her expression. "Olivia used it for a lot of charity events and parties, but in the house's heyday it's where the men used to play cards and drink in between girls."

She looked in the direction he'd pointed. "In between girls?"

He barely restrained his grin. This ought to wind her up. "Up until the 1950s, this house was one of New Orleans's most popular brothels."

She grimaced. "Figures my mother would buy a house of ill repute. She loved drama."

"You don't think much of her, do you?"

"Just because we didn't get along doesn't mean I don't love my mother. I also got enough of the guilt trip from Lally. I don't need it from you, too, so do me a favor and don't start."

"I wasn't starting anything. Just commenting." Leave it to Lally to speak her mind. "Hey, I get it. My mother used to scream at me to act more human. She'd file my horns down and remind me daily what a disappointment to her I was."

Harlow paused, her gaze traveling to the top of his head. "Why did you file them down again? Not all fae have them, and you're all about being fae, so what gives?"

"Shadeux and smokesinger fae have them if the bloodlines are strong enough. Grinding mine down is just what I'm used to. Or was. When you first met me, I'd grown them out for a particular reason. I'll be growing them out again now that I'm Guardian."

"Fabulous," she whispered, going slightly green.

Was kissing him that bad? He'd been sure she'd liked it a little bit. "What? Don't think you can take the reminder of that kiss every time you look at me?"

"Actually, no." She stepped back, maybe to put space between them, but her foot didn't quite find the tread. Her hand shot out toward the railing but Augustine caught her first, his hand latching on to her forearm, just as he had that night.

He made sure she was stable, then immediately let her go. Now was not the time to play cute. "It's not a big deal. It was *Nokturnos*. Everyone kisses a stranger."

She nodded without making eye contact. "I suppose so." She looked like she wanted to disappear. Or at least change the topic. Which she did. "So, ah, your mother, you said she *used to* scream at you. Did she pass away, too?"

"No. Still alive. Lives on the other side of the French Quarter and wants nothing to do with me." Just like Harlow didn't want anything to do with him, either. What was it about him that inspired such animosity?

"I'm sure it's hard on both of you. I should go—"

He stepped around her, blocking her way. "You think it's hard on my mother having a son like me? How do you know what kind of son I am?"

"I just meant—" Frustration brought her head up. "You didn't have any problem moving in here, did you? Letting my mother take care of you. Don't you think that had anything to do with your relationship with your own mother? With *my* relationship with Olivia? Having you around must have made it easier to ignore my questions about who my father was." She jabbed a finger at him, but didn't come close enough to touch. "I don't think you have any idea what it was like growing up with a mother like—"

"Olivia? Let me guess." Dark, swirling heat built along his bones. "Olivia treated you like dirt, right? Probably threatened to give you over to an orphanage all the time, told you how you were an abomination, how she wished you'd never been born, slapped you silly when she found you trying to figure out what abilities you were born with—"

"You know she wasn't like that." Harlow's voice was soft, her eyes flashing with irritation, reminding him very much of the woman she claimed had ruined her life.

He glared right back. "Yeah, I do know she wasn't like that, but my mother was, so whatever bad feelings you have toward Olivia, keep them to yourself because I don't have time for it."

"Just because she wasn't as bad as your mother doesn't mean things with her weren't hard. She told me my father was dead. No lead-up, no easing into it, just 'He's dead.' Hitting me in the face with a hammer would have been less of a blow."

He paused, as if considering her words. "I still take offense to you running her down. She was the closest thing I had to a real mother, and the only woman who ever cared enough about me to make sure I was fed and safe and had a place to rest my head."

Her eyes went liquid, but the hard set of her mouth said she was fighting back the tears with everything she had. "You've already lied to me," she rasped, her finger aimed at his chest. "Why should I believe anything you say?"

"What have I lied about?"

"That blood on your shirt is fresh and you acted like you

didn't know about it, but you do." She pointed at the wound. "I'm barely fae and even I heal too fast to leave that kind of mark."

He pulled his partially unbuttoned shirt open to reveal the brand. She cringed a little when she saw it. "Of course, I know about the blood. I volunteered for the mark that caused it. This brand designates me the Guardian of the city. New Orleans is a Haven city, meaning that as of this evening I am personally responsible for the well-being of every fae, othernatural and human within these parish borders. That included you, as difficult as that might be to believe. Anything else you want to know?"

She looked like she might be sick. She swallowed before answering. "No, but you've helped me realize something."

"And that is?"

"You need to go." She shook her head, eyes shining with unshed tears. "I can't be in this house with you." A muscle in her jaw twitched and her words came out thick with emotion. "You're not a bad guy, you're really not, but you're a constant reminder of everything I never had. Of everything I'll never get a chance to have." She turned away and headed downstairs. "I'm sorry, but the moment this house is legally mine, I want you out."

Chapter Twelve

Augustine couldn't remember a time in his life when he'd had to set an alarm. The annoying buzz in his ear made him hope he'd never have to do it again. Normally, he'd be coming home at this hour, not waking up and heading out. Life as Guardian was going to take some getting used to. He smacked the old folding travel clock scrounged from one of the guest bedrooms, silencing the alarm, and pushed himself upright.

His chest still throbbed from the brand. He reached for the pot of salve Yanna had given him. The pain had made falling sleep last night difficult. That and the guilt over the upset he'd caused Harlow. He rubbed some of the ointment over the fleur-de-lis. He shouldn't have started up with her, but she vibrated with acrimony anytime anyone said a word about being fae or Olivia and he couldn't abide it.

Livie hadn't even been eulogized yet. He closed his eyes and groaned, realizing Lally had been left to take care of all the arrangements. Tipping his head back, he swore he'd do whatever she needed him to as soon as he got back from meeting Fenton.

He lumbered into the bathroom, hoping a hot shower would wake him up enough to function until he could get some coffee. It did, reminding him halfway through that he hadn't done a thing with the weapons roll. Rinsing off, he snagged a towel, wrapped it around his waist and hustled back to the sitting area at the far end of the attic. He grabbed the roll and unfurled it onto the sofa where he'd tossed it last night.

The thickness was mostly because the leather was well padded, but there were still a fair number of weapons inside. Including one that looked like it had seen better days. A banged-up, tarnished hilt held a rough gray stone in its pommel, which was all that was visible, but beneath the leather, the blade's length matched the roll's. Unquestionably a sword. The size of its compartment within the roll also meant it was probably stored in its own carrying sheath.

He unzipped the compartment and took the weapon out. He'd been right. Black leather encased the blade, a black-buckled strap hanging down. So far, the sheath was a lot nicer than the weapon. He fitted his palm to the hilt and drew the weapon out. A real clunker. The dinged, warped blade was pitted with nicks and gouges. He gave the weighty thing a halfhearted swing. Little chance this blade could cut through anything.

A slip of paper stuck out of the top of the sheath. He set the sword down and pulled out the paper.

Hold firmly to the sword's hilt, then read these words: Peto hoc gladio per Guardianus scriptor rectus.

Why not. He picked the sword up, wrapping his fingers around the hilt and applying pressure, then held it out before him. "*Peto hoc gladio per Guardianus scriptor rectus.*"

Pain shot through his hand like his palm had been set on fire. He opened his fingers and dropped the blade onto the sofa. Pinpricks of blood covered his skin. He looked at the sword's hilt in time to see tiny, blood-covered, needle-thin prongs disappearing into the metal. They vanished so thoroughly there was no way of telling they'd been there.

The entire sword changed. The blade gleamed with fresh polish, all signs of age and wear gone. The hilt was no longer tarnished, but wire-wrapped and burnished to a soft shine.

The tiny cuts had already healed, but he wiped the blood off on the towel. Then he picked up the sword again, this time by the pommel. The stone it held was no longer a rough gray, but a gleaming black cabochon. When he stared into it, it seemed to...stare back.

And now the weapon weighed almost nothing. He swung it in a figure eight, unreasonably pleased with the way it sang through the air.

Fae magic. That was the only explanation. He'd ask Fenton when he saw him, but Augustine had a feeling that the sword was also now tuned to him in some way. He grabbed another blade, a small dagger, and exchanged it with the one he normally carried there. Whatever else remained in the weapon roll would have to wait. Being late for his first official day as Guardian would only firm up Loudreux's belief that he wasn't fit for the job.

He dressed quickly, strapping the sword on under his black leather duster so it sat low on his hips, then went out through his bedroom window so he wouldn't wake Harlow or Lally, although Lally was probably already up.

The gray, drizzly day showed no signs of breaking. He turned his collar up against the damp and started toward the cemetery. On the empty street in the still-dark hour, his only company was the patter of rain and the rustle of leaves.

A few blocks and he turned onto Prytania, stopping when he reached the cemetery gates. He glanced both ways. A few of the prep cooks stood outside of the Commander's Palace restaurant at the end of the block, but they were busy talking to each other. Satisfied he wasn't being watched, he pressed his fingertips together and called upon his magic. As he eased his fingers apart, sooty lines danced between them. Using mental direction, he guided the smoke into the lock.

The soft heat of the magic work warmed his bones as the

form solidified into a key. At last, he snapped his fingers away to break the connection and turned the key.

The gate creaked open, announcing his presence. He started to cringe, then remembered he was Guardian. He could do as he pleased. Hell, he could have leaped the gates without a care for someone seeing him. The realization lightened his steps. He removed the key, shut the gate and relocked it, then crushed the key in his hand, returning it to smoke that drifted away to blend into the gray sky.

Lafayette Cemetery Number One was a popular tourist destination. Why had Fenton wanted to meet here? He picked his way through the rows of grave sites looking for the Miller crypt. At last, one row away from the very back corner, he found it by way of the cypher in front of it.

Fenton sat on the crypt's crumbling steps, sipping coffee. Guz and Rat, the goblin fae who'd been with him the night of Livie's murder, stood a few crypts away. Bodyguards, maybe.

"Morning. How's the brand?"

"Almost healed."

"How did you enter the cemetery?"

Augustine glanced back toward the gates. "Smoke key." Was this a test?

Fenton nodded. "Good enough, but slow. If you were being chased, how would you have come in?"

"Same way, I guess. Or over the wall. I could jump that."

"And your pursuers would have seen you." Fenton shook his head. "What about coming through the wall?"

Augustine smirked. "I'm not a ghost."

Fenton frowned. "No, you're a self-taught fae. Which is fine, but there is so much more you can do." He tapped his finger on his chin. "You're part shadeux, part smokesinger. Your half form should render you ephemeral enough to pass through walls. Is that not the case?"

Augustine shrugged. "I have no idea. I never tried."

"It should be doable," Fenton said. "No matter. I know your education has a few holes. We'll work on that. Now, on to the crypt."

"Good. I was beginning to wonder why we were here." The crypt was in worse shape than most of the others, the grass and weeds around it robust with abandon. In places, the plaster had fallen away to reveal the brick beneath. Nothing about this mausoleum made it seem like anything special. Was he supposed to know the Miller family? He didn't.

Fenton stood and turned toward the crypt's stone door. "Why don't I show you?" On one side of the dull marble door was a rusted metal sconce designed to hold flowers. Fenton grabbed it and twisted.

Augustine expected it to come off in Fenton's hand. Instead, the door swung back so quietly there was no way the hinges weren't oiled regularly.

Augustine shook his head. "You have got to be kidding me."

Fenton twisted the sconce again and the door shut. "You try it."

Augustine climbed to the second step, grabbed the sconce and turned it. The door opened.

"Do you know why that's possible?" Fenton asked.

"Fae magic?" There was a lot of that going around. And a lot he didn't know, apparently.

"Yes, but it's not like any fae could walk up and do that."

"Is this another shadeux/smokesinger thing?"

"No." Fenton undid two buttons and pulled the neck of his shirt to the side. He bore the same silver fleur-de-lis brand that had been seared into Augustine's chest last night. "This mark does more than just show you're the Guardian. All of us who serve bear it and the magic imbued in it is what grants us access to the most secret places."

"Us? How many is that exactly?"

Fenton went up the steps and through the door. "It's a fluid number, but as many as there needs to be."

"Oh good, straight answers. I love those."

Fenton looked back at Augustine from the murky depths of the tomb. "Coming?"

Augustine entered the crypt. Cobwebs and caskets lined the walls, filling the crypt's shelves. "I'd ask what we're doing in here, but I'm sure you're about to tell me."

"Watch and learn." Fenton reached for another sconce, this one with a candle stub in it, and twisted as he had the first one. The door slid shut, leaving them with only the light filtering in from the cracked stained-glass window on the back wall. Fenton turned to face it. Augustine mimicked his actions.

A panel in the floor in front of the window slid back beneath the casket on the right side. "Stay close to the door when you enter or you'll fall down the stairs when this opens."

Stairs? But there they were, descending into where, he had no idea. They were hewn from the same marble as the crypt's door, the center of each tread eroded as though they'd been heavily traveled. Soft light emanated from whatever was down below.

"Follow me." Fenton headed down without waiting.

"To where exactly?" This felt like a lot of information.

"The Pelcrum. Our headquarters. We have much to do." Fenton paused. "And you wanted to speak to the prisoner, didn't you?"

"Yes."

"Then let's go." And down he went again.

Augustine followed, still perplexed. "How does this place even exist with the water table so high?"

"Through the power of complicated and ancient fae magic." Fenton stopped when he got to solid flooring and waited for Augustine. "Have you heard of weaver fae?"

"Sure, they're who build the charm and protection spells around fae houses, and who set the counter-spell to the witch's curse so that vampires forget they can daywalk in New Orleans the second they leave parish boundaries." Beyond Fenton was a long hall, all stone, with a couple of doors on the sides and one larger one at the end. Gas lanterns, like the ones used throughout the city, lit the way. "They're our good witches."

"Interesting you should mention witches." He lifted a finger. "Remind me to speak about that later. As for the weavers, you're exactly right. And New Orleans was privileged to be the home of one of the most powerful weavers ever born, Shavara." He held his hand out toward the hall behind him. "She built the Pelcrum. With the help of a few other powerful fae. This is how New Orleans came to be a Haven city. The first, actually. She's also the one who was able to mitigate the curse on the city."

"Amazing." Augustine felt like he was getting part of the education he'd missed out on. He moved his coat to the side to reveal the blade strapped to his hip. "She have anything to do with the sword you gave me?"

"Absolutely. That original spell was created by her, too." Fenton smiled. "That sword is bound to you now. In anyone else's hand, it will revert to the state you found it in."

"Was it Khell's before me?"

Fenton's smile faded. "Yes."

Time to change the subject. "So you—we—keep prisoners down here?"

"Prisoners we don't intend to release, yes. We keep some other things down here as well."

"I'm sure the vampire loved being hauled through the cemetery." Vampires couldn't tolerate sacred ground, be it a church or a cemetery.

"We did it as quickly as possible, but no, he wasn't a fan. I'm sure he's recovered by now, though." Fenton glanced down the hall. "Are you ready?"

"Since the night you took him into custody." The memory brought with it grief and anger. "I know you did that to force me into the Guardianship."

"I did it to keep you from digging a deeper hole than you were already in. You would have killed that vampire, correct?"

"Damn straight."

"Which would have prevented us from interrogating him and finding out why these vampires are flooding our city like rats. And caused you to be arrested." Fenton's face held an odd sadness. "I did what I thought necessary for both of us. Now, on to that prisoner."

They went through the first door on the left and into a large room. On each side were cells. Phosphorescent paint coated the ceiling, giving the place an ambient glow.

Fenton pointed toward the end. "Very last cell. He's all yours. Your brand will allow you to open the cell if you wish to conduct your interrogation more *personally*. Just turn the handle and you'll be in."

"Good to know. Any protocol I need to follow?"

"You're the Guardian. Interrogate as you see fit. But within reason. The Prime wants him alive until this whole thing is resolved."

"Loudreux is not my boss."

"No, but working with him will make your life a lot easier than working against him. Trust me." Fenton pulled the door open and made a move to leave. "Come through the door at the very end of the hall when you're done and we'll finish up the rest of your orientation."

"Great, thanks." Augustine strode toward the cell, fresh anger and determination driving him. Screw what Hugo wanted. Once this leech gave up his boss's location, Augustine would take great pleasure in making the vampire who'd taken Livie's life his first official kill.

He stopped in front of the cell Fenton had indicated, but couldn't see anyone inside. The cell looked like it hadn't been cleaned in ages. He peered closer, cold realization settling in at what he was seeing. He uttered a vile curse. "Fenton!"

The cypher came running back in. "What?"

Augustine turned to him, fists clenched, barely able to control his rage. "There is nothing in this cell but *ash*."

Harlow's desperate need for coffee boosted her courage to walk into the kitchen even though that probably meant running into Augustine, but he was nowhere in sight. Probably still in bed. And happily, there was a fresh pot at the ready. Today was looking up. She set her LMD on the table and made a beeline for the coffeemaker. "Augustine always sleep this late?"

"He'll be here when he's ready." Lally sat at the table, paging through a newspaper. "You want breakfast?"

"Not yet, I'm—" Harlow stopped. "Is that a *paper* newspaper?"

Lally looked up over the edge of her glasses. "Yes, child. Haven't you seen one of these before?"

"Yes, but not in a long time. I mean, I knew they'd made a resurgence since the price of electricity skyrocketed, but it doesn't take that long to get your news online."

"I like to linger. Read the whole story. Look at the ads. And I always recycle them—I can't be paying no fine. I guess I'm what you call old-school. Although your mama used to read her news online."

At the mention of her mother, Harlow went back to getting coffee. She grabbed the biggest mug she could find, then filled it and added three heaping spoons of sugar and a large glug of creamer. "You could watch the holovision. Get your news that way."

Lally didn't look up this time. "Too much holovision bothers my eyes. And that *still* uses electricity. Your mother never cared, but that bill belongs to you now and I don't want to be running up something I haven't got permission to."

So there it was. "You can watch the holovision whenever you want for as long as you're here. When the house sells, there'll be plenty of money to pay whatever bills are left." Harlow sipped her coffee. And grimaced.

"Something wrong?"

Of course, now Lally was looking at her. "Coffee's just... different than I'm used to."

"It's the chicory. It's how we drink it here." She set her paper down. "I've got some plain coffee. Your mama used to keep it for finicky visitors. You want me make some of that?"

"No, this is fine." She forced a smile and took another sip, desperate not to be considered finicky in the eyes of this woman who was clearly judging her for her treatment of Olivia. Maybe she'd add more sugar. Right after she changed the subject. "Augustine said this place used to be a whorehouse."

At the word, Lally's brows shot up. "Many, many years ago, this building housed a brothel, yes." She folded her newspaper and smoothed a hand over the crease. "In the way back, all those places were out in Storyville 'cept for this one." Her fingers crept to the chain around her neck. "The place here catered to the fae. All the girls were fae, all the customers fae, and the magic that kept this place hidden from human eyes and human law was fae."

"That's why it lasted so long." Harlow shivered with the implications. "Was it built by the fae, too?"

"Yes." Lally picked up her paper. "And a lot of folks know the history of this place since the covenant broke. Not many humans want to buy a place thick with so much powerful magic and old fae history. Some think that old song 'House of the Rising Sun' was written 'bout this house. And some say it's haunted." She looked toward the center of the house. "Some days, I think it is."

Harlow sat back, unwilling to be intimidated. Haunted didn't scare her nearly as much as the fact that she was steeping in fae juju. "Is that so?"

Lally was nose deep in her paper again. "Yes, that is exactly so. There is history here you can't even imagine."

Too bad there wasn't a clue about who her father had been. "What do you think a place like this is worth?"

"I don't know much about real estate."

Harlow pushed. "Guess. You've lived here long enough to know what these big houses go for."

With a sigh, Lally set her paper down again. "I don't know. A house this size, with all that's on this land, maybe five, six million."

Harlow nodded, barely able to hide the surprise bubbling up inside her. "Then I'll put it on the market for half that and no one should mind what kind of place this used to be." Coffee mug in hand, she stood and headed to the library.

Three million. That would pay her fine and leave enough to hire a really good private investigator, buy a nice little house, a great big security system and set her up perfectly with servers to ramp up her business. She let out the breath she suddenly realized she'd been holding only to realize what this really meant. She was trading Olivia's legacy for her own freedom. Her troubles—and prison—were about to be behind her. But at what cost?

Chapter Thirteen

Fenton shook his head, his eyes glazed with panic. "I-I don't know how that could be. He must have killed himself."

"A vampire that kills himself without the aid of sunlight?" Augustine slammed his fist against the bars, the clang ringing out over his fiercely beating heart. Someone had robbed him of his chance to avenge Livie. "I want a list of everyone who had access to him."

Fenton jerked back. "Are you suggesting that one of those who serve did this?"

Augustine leaned in. "That's exactly what I'm suggesting."

He wrung his hands together. "I don't know..."

"Listen to me." Augustine stabbed a finger toward the cell's ash-coated interior. "This vampire could have led me to his boss, who would have then led me to whoever's responsible for letting these leeches into our city in the first place."

"Maybe. You don't know that's what's happening."

"Yes, I do." Dulcinea was rarely wrong. Maybe she could help him with this. "Someone is making plastic bringing these bloodsuckers into our town, someone high enough up on the food chain that they feel untouchable."

Fenton paled. "Surely you're not saying one of the Elektos..."

"No. I don't think someone in your position would risk their reputation and rank for plastic." Augustine paced away from the cell, the acrid tang of ash filling his nose. "My guess is it's one of Khell's lieutenants." A plan began to form in his head.

"I assume the vampire was searched before he was locked up. Where are his personal things?"

"I'll get them for you. And speaking of lieutenants, that's one of the things I was going to go over with you today."

"Khell's lieutenants?"

"Yes. You need to meet with them, have them get you up to speed on what they know about this vampire issue. See if there's anything else you need to be read in on. Basic Guardian business."

Augustine thought for a moment. "Those lieutenants, they were all put in place by Khell?"

"Not all. Some were appointed by the Guardian before him. Maybe one even older than that."

"Do I have to keep them all?"

Fenton shook his head. "As Guardian, you may appoint and dismiss whomever you like."

Augustine stuck his hand into his coat pocket, only to remember he'd left the address Fenton had given him in his jeans. "Give me the address of the Guardian's house again, then get me the vampire's things. I have an errand to do. I'll be back as soon as I can. In the meantime, set something up with the lieutenants. Don't tell them anything about my suspicions."

"As you wish," Fenton said. "I'll take care of everything. The vampire's belongings are in the strong room." A hint of a smile played on his lips.

"You think this is amusing?"

The smile turned into horror. "Hell, no." He stood a little straighter. "I'm just proud that I was right about you. You may not have had a proper fae education, but you have the heart and you have the courage and you have street smarts. In some ways, that's worth more than a proper fae education. Follow me to the war room. I have something else to give you before I get the vamp's things."

A war room? "It can wait."

"No, it can't." Fenton walked out into the main hall.

Augustine gritted his teeth, but followed anyway. Fenton went through the door at the very end. The interior of the room reminded Augustine of a medieval library, the walls lined with shelves, each one filled with leather-bound, gilt-embossed volumes. Another book, the largest of the bunch, sat open on a podium. "What are all these?"

"Records and such." Fenton nodded at the separate one. "That's our Codex." Then he shut the door and walked to the center table, a massive circle of wood inlaid with an enormous fleur-de-lis. Twelve chairs encompassed it, and near the edge, a metal box sat waiting. He opened it and pulled out a black rectangle half the size of a plastic bill and slightly thicker than several stacked together. He handed it to Augustine. "Your Life Management Device. I'm assuming you don't already have one; if you do, you'll need to carry this one as well."

"No, I don't have one, but I know what an LMD is. Basically." He'd never thought one worth the expense, although Livie had offered to get him one years ago. The device didn't feel very sturdy. It flexed in his fingers.

Fenton pointed to it. "That LMD is your phone, your navigation, your connection to any Elektos assistance you might need. It also carries your identification, your credit—which as Guardian is fairly unlimited. It's everything you need to function as Guardian. Don't lose it. Although if you do, it can be destroyed remotely."

"That's what Yanna meant about being in my contacts."

"Yes."

Augustine stared at the thing. "Knowing what an LMD is and knowing how to work one is a very different thing."

"It's intuitive. Play with it and it will come to you. In order to access it, you just have to press your index finger to the screen. Only your fingerprint can unlock it."

"And it's already been programmed. Meaning you already had a set of my prints."

Fenton raised one brow. "That really shouldn't surprise you at this stage of the game." He then took a matching LMD from his pocket, tapped the screen a few times, then put it away. "I just sent you the address to the Guardian's house."

The LMD in Augustine's hand vibrated and the screen lit up. He pressed his finger to it as Fenton had directed. A window popped open with an address on it. In the window was another tiny square that looked like a map. He held it out so Fenton could see it. "And if I touch that little square?"

"Satnav will direct you to the house. On the back of the LMD is a com cell that will act as your earpiece. It's not like the old ones that had to be implanted. Just peel it off and stick it behind your ear. It should last indefinitely. If something happens to it, we'll get you another one. Although not everyone adjusts to the voice in their head. If you choose not to use it, that's all right, too."

Augustine flipped the LMD over. He scraped a tiny flesh-colored—in his case a pale gray—dot off the back with his fingernail. "This thing?"

"Yes. And if you need me, I'm in your contacts list. All the Elektos are."

"Crazy." He pinched the dot between his fingers, finally flattening it against his skin. Then he shoved the LMD into his pocket and readied to go. "I'll try not to break it."

"If you do, we'll get you another. Once you get to the Guardian's house, you'll find the LMD will also unlock and start your car."

Augustine paused. "My car?"

"It's in the garage at the Guardian's house. I know you're not going to live there just yet but please use the vehicle. It will make your job and your life easier. Mirrors are wonderful for transport, but suddenly appearing in a place can sometimes have unconsidered consequences. And Augustine, watch the parking tickets." Fenton made an odd face. "We paid the fines you had accumulated, by the way, so your license is no longer suspended and you're cleared to drive."

Augustine smirked. It had been a while since he'd driven, but man, it had been fun. Livie had some nice cars. "What can I say? I've never been much on obeying rules."

"We know. That willingness to flout convention to get whatever you want is part of why we chose you for Guardian. Provided what you want is in line with the role of the Guardian, we have no problem with that." He shut the metal box. "I'll be right back."

Augustine paced, too impatient to sit. Fortunately, Fenton wasn't gone long. He returned with a brown paper bag, the top folded over.

He handed the bag to Augustine. "Not much in there, I'm afraid. A leather jacket, two knives, his belt and some random things from his pockets: pack of smokes, keys, about three grand in plastic, a flask of blood, that sort of thing."

"That's a lot of walking-around money. I guess he didn't trust his hotel."

Fenton nodded. "I'm sure you're right. Keep the cash. Consider it a starting bonus."

"Thanks." He tucked the bag under his arm, hoping his plan would work. Either way, he was about to shake things up. "I'll be in touch."

"Augustine, there is much to be done yet—"

"I know, the lieutenants, but I can't imagine anything more important than finding out who murdered Khell and Olivia and stopping whoever is responsible for letting these vampires into our city."

"I agree, but I'm speaking about fae protocols. At some point in the very near future, you must meet with Evander Vincent."

"The coven leader? The hell why?" Giselle's father was a fourth-level grand wizard and not someone high up on Augustine's list of people to hang out with.

"Because since the treaty between the fae and witches, it's been our custom that any new officials must make themselves known to the other party. When Evander took his position, he came to us. When Loudreux became Prime, he went to Evander, just as Khell did after his swearing in as Guardian. Now, it's your turn. It's little more than a courtesy but those courtesies are how we keep peace." He shrugged. "The voodoo practitioners are not so organized that they have one main leader, and as we have no formal agreements with them, all that needs to be done is send out a few notices to the higher-ups in that religion, let them know we've chosen a new Guardian. It's just good politics."

"And the treaty between us and the witches is why the witches agree to the regulations placed on them."

Fenton nodded. "It was that or be banished from New Orleans." He sighed. "I worry what will happen when Evander passes on. His daughters strike me as the types who would turn their backs on the past in exchange for power. Well, not Zara perhaps, but Giselle for sure."

"I know a bit about Giselle. All I know about the other one is she sells stuff at the farmers' market."

"Zara's a green witch, lives here in the Garden District in their mother's old house, keeps to herself, seems more interested in her plants than people. She supplies the coven with most of their herbs. She's never caused problems before, but sometimes the quiet ones are more dangerous."

"I'll remember that. I would have pegged Giselle for the troublemaker, but maybe she doesn't like getting her hands dirty. Certainly suits what I know about her." Augustine adjusted the bag slightly. "I'll make the meeting with Evander happen. I just need to take care of this vampire issue first."

"I understand. Be safe," Fenton added as Augustine left.

Augustine nodded, but he was done being safe. Since Livie, he'd cleaned up his act and changed the way he lived, careful not to get involved, not to take on too much responsibility, not to upset his cleverly crafted life. Fat lot of good that had done him. The time to return to dangerous living had arrived.

The com cell took some getting used to. He could see why some people ditched the thing. Having a voice in his head wasn't just intrusive; it made him feel borderline mental. But without the walking directions from the satnav, he might not have made it to the Guardian's house. There was nothing difficult about finding the place, but even as he approached it, he had a hard time seeing it. Like it slipped out of his field of vision every time he looked directly at it. A powerful urge to keep walking pushed his feet forward, a sure sign of the ward used to protect the house.

He was almost to the next property when he forced himself to backtrack. By focusing on the house next door, he was able to go through the gate and walk up the porch steps. Once on the porch, the strong magic faded, perhaps as a courtesy to visitors who really intended to be there.

He rang the bell and waited. The house was nice by Garden District standards, but not showy or overdone. It looked like conservative money, where as Livie's looked like old money. *Grand* old money. Nothing about this place felt like home. He couldn't imagine himself living here, but he would have to.

His hand went for the bell again just as the door opened. A pretty igneous fae answered the door, her face pale except for the dark circles under her eyes. Beatrice. Khell's widow, and based on her reputation, not a woman to be trifled with.

Which was backed up by the fact that her free hand held a ball of fire. Ignus fae could melt stone if they were mad enough. Skin and bone had no chance. Her gaze scoured him. "What is it?"

Not the greeting he'd expected, but he understood grief made formalities less important. She'd probably had her fill of formalities these past few days. He held his hands up. "I'm Augustine, the new Guardian. I just wanted to—"

"They said I could have a week." Her face screwed into an angry half sob and the fire in her palm shot higher. "I'm doing the best I can. It's only been a few days. We just had the funeral. You can't expect me to—"

"I don't expect you to move. Nope. Not even a little bit. And I didn't know about the funeral or I would have been there. Look, I'm not here to kick you out. I swear."

"You're not?" She stopped sniffling. The flames died down.

"No. I wanted to introduce myself. See how you're doing."

That seemed to satisfy her, since she lost the fireball. He'd give her the real reason as soon as he sussed her out a little more. "I'm...okay. The funeral was small. Just family. Your...lady friend was murdered, too, wasn't she?"

"Yes. Most likely by the same vampires who killed Khell."

She averted her gaze to the floor, perhaps to hide tears. "I already told the Elektos everything I know. Which isn't much. Khell tried to protect me from the work he did, thought it would be better if I didn't have information that could be used against him."

He wasn't sure how much he believed her, but then maybe she'd chosen to keep her distance from Khell's work on purpose. It didn't mean she wasn't capable of filling the position he had in mind for her. "I understand his thinking." Didn't like it, but understood it. "But I'm not here to get information out of you."

She pushed a strand of hair out of her eyes and looked up at him again. "What are you here about then?"

"I'm here to ask you to stay."

Confusion colored her dark eyes. "Stay where? Here?"

"Eventually I'll have to move in, but yes, you can stay in the house. From the size of it, I'm assuming it has enough bedrooms."

"Five actually." She crossed her arms and flames danced in her eyes. "I was Khell's wife. I don't automatically come with the Guardianship, so if you think you're going to move in here and get some kind of side benefit—"

"Nope. Again, not what I was going for." He shook his head. "Roommate situation only."

She nodded, looking only slightly convinced. "And you're doing this out of the goodness of your heart because?"

He looked around. No one in sight, but he wasn't keen on having this conversation outside. "Can I come in?"

"It's your place, I can't stop you." She moved out of the way to let him pass.

Empty and partially packed boxes littered the rooms he could see. The house was nice inside. The dark wood, muted greens and gold were simple, but elegant. Reserved New Orleans at its best, which suited the house of the fae chosen to protect the city. He closed the door. "Beatrice, I know you're still grieving because I am, too. And I know Khell was a good man."

"The best," she whispered, dipping her head.

"The thing is . . . I'm not a hundred percent convinced about the loyalty of all of his lieutenants."

She went very still. "Go on."

It was too soon to ask her if she had any suspicions. She needed to trust him first. "I need people around me I feel confident in. People who are doing the job for more than just the perks that come with it." He let that sink in. "Maybe even for personal reasons. Like revenge."

She rubbed her fingers together. "Revenge is a powerful motivator."

"I know. That's why I'm here."

Beatrice's eyes went bright with understanding. "Are you asking me what I think you're asking me?"

"Yes," Augustine answered. "I want you to be one of my new lieutenants."

The doorbell rang, knocking Harlow out of her daydreams of what it would have been like to meet her father. She sat up, wondering if she should get it, but heard Lally coming down the hall from the kitchen. Harlow stayed on the couch as Lally went past the library doors.

Lally opened the front door. "Morning. What can I do for you?"

"Are you Lally Hughes?"

"Yes, sir."

"This is for you. Is Augustine Robelais here?"

"No, but he'll be back soon." Harlow had assumed he was sleeping in. For him to be up and out of the house already... She hadn't pegged him as a morning person.

"Can you make sure he gets this?"

"I certainly will."

"Thank you. Have a good day."

The door closed and Lally meandered into view, holding two ivory envelopes. She tucked one under her arm and opened the other, pulling out a letter and standing in the library doorway as she read. "Well, I'll be."

"What is it?"

She lifted her eyes from the paper to look straight at Harlow. "It's from Lionel Cuthridge?"

"My mother's attorney." She'd wondered when he'd be in touch again. "If that's for me—"

"It's not." Lally held up the creamy sheet of paper. "Seems he wants Augustine and me there for the reading of the will, too."

Harlow nodded. "I'm sure my mother left you both something. You especially. I know how much she loved you." Olivia loved giving gifts. Her will was probably an endless list of people she'd had the briefest acquaintance with being left some small memento. She sighed. No doubt the reading of the will would take forever. All she wanted was her father's name. Maybe the lawyer would start with her. Her LMD vibrated. She snatched it off the cushion beside her and unlocked it. A text from Cuthridge with the location of his office. Once again, she prayed Olivia had included the information about her father in these final documents.

But what if it didn't? What if Olivia's will was just her last grand gesture to her friends? Harlow hadn't been anything close to friendly with her mother in a long, long time.

Lally lingered. "I guess we'll know more this afternoon. We're supposed to be at Mr. Cuthridge's at three o'clock." She tucked the letter back into the envelope. "I'll go start some breakfast."

Harlow just nodded. Suddenly she didn't have much of an appetite.

Chapter Fourteen

With Beatrice's assertive yes still ringing in his ears, Augustine's confidence grew. He jogged down the back steps of the Guardian house and toward the detached garage. His plan was gelling. Now if he could just get Harlow to be helpful, but that was going to be an uphill battle. She didn't seem like she'd want to help him do anything but move out.

The alarm panel lit as he tapped in the code Beatrice had given him. The garage door slid up. As it rose, he went very still, his mouth slightly open. Fenton had said there was a car, but *car* didn't do this machine justice. There, in the darkness of the old wooden building, sat a Tesla Thrun. More muscle than car, the sleek black beauty had lines like a showgirl and was the automotive equivalent of a ninja on steroids. No doubt the vehicle had probably been upgraded with some kind of special Guardian package, too. Bulletproofed and all that.

Hell's bells on Christmas morning. He ran his hand over the hood as he walked to the driver's door. The windows were so darkly tinted he couldn't see in. He grabbed the handle and pulled, but the car was locked. He dug his LMD out and brought the screen to life. Fenton had said the LMD would unlock the vehicle. One of the screen icons was shaped like a car. He tapped it.

And was rewarded with the soft snick of the door unlocking. Unable to stop smiling, he tossed the bag holding the vampire's belongings into the back, then slid into the driver's seat and closed the door. Every outside noise immediately went silent in the Thrun's vaultlike interior, so quiet that his own heartbeat thumped audibly in his ears, the soundtrack to this very interesting new episode of his life. He adjusted the mirrors, figured out where some of the other controls were, then looked around for a way to start the beast, which was the only word that seemed to adequately describe the engine he knew was under the hood.

A fingerprint recognition pad sat next to the steering column. He pressed his thumb into it and the dashboard screen lit as the head-up display flickered to life on the windshield.

Great. More technology to learn. Jet fighters probably had simpler controls. He did the first thing that came to mind. "Engine on."

A soft, feline purr greeted him.

He smiled as he eased the shift out of park and rolled the car into the driveway, then punched the button to shut the garage door and took off.

Five minutes later, he was home, slightly disappointed the drive hadn't taken longer. He pulled through the rear gates and parked in front of the detached garage that held Livie's Bentley and Aston Martin, then grabbed the vampire's stuff and went into the house through the back door.

Lally was in the kitchen reading the cookbook he'd given her for Christmas. Looking up, she smiled. "Everything go okay this morning?"

"It did." Except for someone murdering his only suspect, but she didn't need that worry.

She stood, looking out the window. "That's quite a car you came home in." Her gaze shifted to him. "I didn't think you were allowed to drive after that last ticket."

"The Elektos took care of that." He grinned. "I'll take you for a spin later, if you want. It's a fun ride."

"I'm sure it is, but I'll take your word for it considering how you got all those tickets." She glanced at his waist. "I see you're a little more armed than usual, too."

"Elektos issued and NOPD approved."

"How about that." Her smile widened. "I saved you a plate from breakfast. You want me to warm it up?"

"Yes, I'm starving." He set the bag on the floor, then poured himself a cup of coffee. "I haven't been much help with planning things for Livie. I'm sorry about that. Tell me what you need done and I'll do it."

Lally squeezed his arm. "You're doing what you need to and things here are all taken care of. She told me a long time ago what she wanted done and I've been following that. Her ashes will be delivered sometime this afternoon and then tomorrow, the house will be open from three to six so people can pay their respects. After that, we'll have the processional to the cemetery to put the urn in the crypt. Except..."

"Except what?"

She pulled a foil-covered plate from the refrigerator. "Except Miss Olivia wants her ashes spread on the fae plane."

"That's not a problem. I can do that."

"Yes, child, but for her to be interred in the Catholic cemetery, the ashes have to stay in the urn. Spreading them ain't allowed." She popped the plate into the convection oven. "People have to think she's in there, so you're going to have to be sly about getting those ashes out."

He sipped his coffee. "I'll figure it out. For Livie, anything."

Lally smiled. "I knew you'd take care of it. Miss Olivia must've known, too. Thank you. Oh, and the florist will be coming by tonight to set things up in the parlor for the service tomorrow."

He kissed her cheek. "Thank you for taking care of all this."

"It's my honor." She brushed it off with a wave of her hand, but her eyes held gratitude for his appreciation.

"Is Harlow helping you with any of this?"

"That child didn't even know how to snap beans."

"I'll take that as a no then. Is she around?"

Lally raised her brows. "She's got enough to do grieving. You're not going to cause more trouble, are you?"

"Not more than I already have." He picked up the bag of the vampire's things. "In fact, I'm going to be extra nice because I need her help on something."

Giving him a look like she wished him luck, she tipped her head toward the front of the house. "In the library. Looking a little nervous. Don't be gone too long. Your food'll be ready in a few minutes."

Already heading toward the library, he stopped. "What's she got to be nervous about?" Had she mentioned *Nokturnos*? What had happened had been consensual.

Lally peeked into the oven. "Messenger came by earlier, dropped off that envelope on the table for you. I got one too so I'm pretty sure yours says the same thing. Miss Olivia's lawyer wants us at his office at three o'clock for the reading of the will."

He tucked the paper bag under his arm, tore open the envelope and pulled out the letter inside. He skimmed it for the pertinent parts. "Yep, that's what mine says. You think Harlow's afraid of what Livie might have left us?"

"More like worried about what her mother might not have left her. Told me earlier she plans on selling this house for half of what it's worth so no one will worry about the history or how soaked in fae magic it is."

He frowned. "Nothing I can do about that, but you know you have a place with me. And Khell's widow, if things work out the way I think they will."

"I ain't going to leave this house." She glanced at him. "Child, you're going to have to explain that last bit."

"Trust me, it's nothing weird. First I need to talk to Harlow, regardless of what kind of mood she's in, and see if she'll help me."

"*Bonne chance*," Lally muttered.

Leaving the envelope on the table, he walked to the library. Harlow was on one of the couches, nose in a book, hair in a messy twist that made her look like she'd just gotten out of bed. And not from sleeping. *Down, boy.* He knocked on the wood trim around the open pocket doors. "Can I interrupt?"

She put the book down and shot him a bemused look. "Can I stop you?"

"Nope, but thanks for asking." He pulled his LMD from his back pocket before taking a seat on the adjacent couch, adjusting the sword as he perched on the edge to be a little closer. All this paraphernalia was going to take some getting used to. "This is about your mother. I need your help."

Harlow's amusement was palpable as she set the book aside and sat up. "You need *my* help. This should be good." She glanced at his LMD, then the sword. "If I say no are you going to run me through?"

"I'm being serious." He looked at her gloved hands. "Despite your whole germaphobe thing, I know you wear those gloves because of the reason I originally guessed. The same reason you pulled away when I kissed you the night of *Nokturnos*." Her cheeks colored, setting her freckles on fire and telling him he was on the right track. "There's some kind of transfer with skin-on-skin contact, but it's more than that, isn't it? You inherited a bigger dose of your mother's gifts than you care to admit."

She opened her mouth to protest, but he kept talking, unwilling to stop until she knew what he was after. "I'm hoping that's the case, because..." He opened the bag and set it in front of her. "I need someone who can read these things and give me a clue as to where I can find the vampire that killed your mother. This stuff belonged to one of the members of his crew."

The muscles in her jaw tightened. "Please stop talking about what happened the night of *Nokturnos*. I've put that behind me and you should too."

Based on the way she reacted when he brought it up, he doubted her success at putting that kiss behind her. He certainly wasn't about to.

"Instead why don't we talk about how I was told my mother was mugged, but that's the second time I've heard the word *vampire* used. Was she mugged by a vampire?"

"Not just one. A pack of them." He wasn't in the mood to explain that night in detail. Telling Harlow he'd been the reason her mother had gotten killed would only lower his chances of getting her help. "That's why I'm hoping the stuff in this bag will lead me to the pack's leader."

Her mouth closed and her gaze shifted to the bag. "You are being serious, aren't you?"

"Absolutely."

She studied him, like she was searching for some kind of answer. "How did you survive before my mother took you in?"

"You don't want to know."

"Yes, I do. I think you can tell me that much."

His narrowed his gaze. "I survived however I could."

"What does that mean?"

He snorted. He'd forgotten he was talking to a woman who'd had the benefit of Olivia's fortune growing up.

"I'm serious. What did you do?"

"Hard things. Stealing. Gambling." He paused. "Fighting."

"Killing?"

"If it meant staying alive."

She dropped her gaze to stare at the bag. Her hands curled

into balls. "I can't do what you're asking." She slid forward, pulled the edge of the paper back and peered in a little deeper.

Her answer didn't satisfy him. "Have you ever tried to read an object?"

"I've never *tried* to read anything. I just touch people and their emotions overwhelm me." A faraway look filled her eyes and her heartbeat jumped up a notch, making him guess she was thinking about their kiss. What had she felt from him? How much he'd enjoyed it? Why would that scare her off? "That's why I wear the gloves. I hate being… invaded like that."

"I can imagine it's pretty upsetting. Do you just get emotions or do you get pictures?"

She sat back. Her hand strayed to the book she'd been reading, her thumb rubbing the cover. "Emotions, pictures, scents, sounds, it's a whole freaking sensory overload." She shuddered like it was too much to bear. "I hate being fae. I hate not being *normal.*"

In that moment, she sounded very much like his mother. His skin prickled with memories, but he swallowed down the unintended hurt. "Normal is relative. What's normal to the fly and what's normal to the spider are two very different things."

"Fabulous. Is that fae philosophy? Which one are you? The spider or the fly?"

"In the case of these vampires, I'd like to be the web. So what do you say? Will you read these things?"

The pulse at her throat ticked.

"All I'm asking you to do is try." As Guardian, he could probably order her to do it, but his position wouldn't hold any sway with someone who didn't even want her fae abilities. "Look, these vampires are still out there, roaming the streets of this city. It's only a matter of time before they kill again. Or worse, come back here to finish what they started."

Her eyes rounded. "You think they're going to come back here? How much danger are we in?"

"None, so long as I find them first." Maybe he could get Fenton to send a weaver over and ward the house. It couldn't hurt and as Guardian, it was certainly within his power to have it done.

She wrapped her arms around herself. "I'll think about it."

"I need you to try now. I know you had a difficult relationship with your mother, I know you don't like me, but try to see past that." He bent his head a moment and tried to maintain his cool. He had no patience for her stubbornness. Not when so much was at stake.

Finally, he looked at her again. He had to tell her the truth and hoped she understood how important this was to him. "Your mother wasn't mugged. I killed the gang leader's girl-friend. They followed me back here." The words burned his throat as the confession left his mouth. "I'm the reason they went after her. Revenge." Anger and revulsion swirled through him in equal measures. "I'm asking for your help so I can make this right."

She stiffened, pain etching her face. Her jaw worked as she seemed to be searching for something to say.

He understood that pain. "I can't bring her back, but I can rid the city of the vampires and the person responsible for them being here."

That seemed to loosen her vocal chords. "How could you? You live here scot-free on my mother's dime, eating her food, using her electricity, taking full advantage of the comfortable life she provides, and then you lead monsters to her door and let them kill her?"

He bit back the words he really wanted to say. "I didn't *let* them—"

"You didn't stop them, either." She jumped to her feet, eyes shining with tears. "Just one more reason to hate all things fae." She nudged the bag with her foot. "I'll try to read this stuff, but it's not for you. It's for my mother, understand?"

"Loud and clear." A worse reaction than he'd expected, but if it helped him get a lead on the vamp boss, he'd bear it.

She shook with anger or grief, he couldn't tell. "I can't be in this house with you a minute longer than necessary. Not now that I know you're responsible for my mother's death. I need you out of here as soon as we get back from the lawyer's."

He sat back, nodding slowly and keeping his voice calm just like he used to when his mother yelled at him. Except with her it never worked. "I am very sorry to have upset you. Trust me when I tell you my responsibility in this will be a burden I carry the rest of my life."

Her glare sharpened. "I am not my mother. You can't charm me into forgiving this."

He held his hands up. There was only so much he could take. "I'll get out of your house as soon as I can." Beatrice would just have to deal with him being there earlier than anticipated. Good thing he'd already spoken to her.

She grabbed the bag and upended it onto the coffee table. Chest heaving, she ripped one glove off and planted her hand squarely on the vampire's leather jacket. "There. Happy? I can't sense a damn—"

Her eyes rolled back in her head and she jerked hard like she'd grabbed a live wire. A second later, she collapsed onto the couch behind her.

"Lally!" Augustine flew to Harlow's side, his fingers pressing her neck for a pulse even though he could hear it pounding. He shook her gently. "Harlow, are you all right?"

Lally ran in. "What happened?"

"I don't know. She grabbed that leather jacket to see if she could read anything off it and then she passed out."

"I'll call the doctor."

As Lally rushed toward the door, Harlow let out a soft

breathy sigh followed by a moan. A faint sheen of sweat covered her brow.

"Wait, I think she's coming to. Get a cold cloth maybe." With a nod, Lally left.

Harlow moaned again, this time lifting her hand to her head. "What happened?"

He sat back to give her space. And to avoid being in striking distance. "You touched the jacket and had some kind of seizure."

She blinked a few times like she was trying to focus. "My head is killing me."

"Did you get some kind of read off it? Is that what happened?"

She put her hand over her eyes and slowly rolled her head back and forth. "I have no idea. The last thing I remember is..." She moved her hand and her gaze locked on him. Anger suffused her amber eyes with an uncomfortable darkness. "You telling me how you were responsible for my mother's death."

"You have to know I feel awful about that, Harlow. I would give anything to undo what happened. Anything. My own life. It's why I agreed to be the Guardian. To make things right." He sighed. "That's why I need your help."

Lally came in with a damp cloth. "Here, child, put this on your forehead."

Harlow accepted it, but just held it as she pushed herself up to sit. She squeezed the washcloth while she stared at the jacket on the coffee table. He stayed quiet, waiting for her to speak next.

When she did, it was without looking at him and in a frighteningly even tone. "What do you think happened when I touched that jacket?"

"I have no idea. I don't have any haerbinger blood; I don't know what it's like to get visions and feel things that belong to someone else."

Lally cleared her throat softly. "But we know someone who does."

He and Harlow looked at her at the same time.

Lally answered without either of them having to ask. "Dulcinea."

Augustine left Harlow to rest and went to find Dulcinea. On a drizzly, gray day like this there was no certain place she might be. Tourists would be keeping dry, so there'd be little business for her in Jackson Square. For as long as he'd known her, she'd never had a physical address. Even after they'd both left the street life behind—he to move into Livie's and Dulcinea to start her fortune-telling business—her home base had remained a mystery. He had a sneaking suspicion that most nights she turned into a cat and holed up in someone's garden.

Parking was a lost cause, but then he remembered money wasn't an issue anymore. He drove into the nearest parking garage, flashing the credit screen from his LMD for the attendant at the gate. The man scanned the bar code and motioned him forward without a hitch. Augustine let out the breath he'd been holding. Damn, that was nice. Being flush would take some getting used to.

He found her at Stella's telling fortunes at a back booth and sipping an Abita. The place was crowded with tourists avoiding the weather, turning it into a sauna of beer fumes and stale bodies. He wished his fae senses had an off button.

She grinned widely the moment he walked into her field of vision. "Gussie!"

"Hey, Dulce." He let the nickname slide since he was about to ask her two big questions. "You have a minute?"

"For you I have lots of them." She looked at the patron across from her, jerked her thumb toward the exit and said, "Scram or I'll put a hex on you."

Wide-eyed, the balding and slightly inebriated tourist scooted out of the booth as fast as he could. Augustine took his spot. "Since when do you put hexes on people?"

"Since never, but you know tourists. Witch, fae fortune-teller, voodoo priestess...eh, we're all the same." She drained her Abita. "How's life as my favorite Guardian? I'm digging the new blade."

"Thanks. Being Guardian is good, I guess. That's part of why I'm here."

She poked his chest. "How's the brand healing up?"

He stared at her. "How do you know about that?"

Shrugging, she gave him a typical Dulcinea grin. "I know lots of stuff."

"I hope that's true, because I have a situation I need help with." He explained what had happened with Harlow, skipping the part about the *Nokturnos* kiss. "What's it sound like to you?"

Dulcinea twisted so that her back was against the outside wall and her feet flat on the booth seat. She wiggled her fingers at the bartender, then pointed to her empty bottle. "She wears gloves all the time?"

"All the time."

"How long has she worn them?"

"I don't know but judging by how she talks, I'd say most of her life."

Dulcinea rapped her fingers slowly on the tabletop as she thought. "Sounds like a combination of things. One, she never learned to use her abilities, and two, she's deprived herself of touch for so long that even the slightest bit creates a much greater impression now. She's made things worse for herself, not better."

That might explain a little about why she'd reacted so

strongly to his kiss. "Do you think she's capable of seeing something from the jacket?"

"I do, but you're never going to get it out of her if it's so overwhelming it blanks her out. My guess is there's probably a time frame to her reading objects. Too many days go by and the piece loses whatever was connected to it." The bartender dropped off a fresh beer and picked up the empty. Dulce twisted again, this time to face Augustine. "I know you need that information, but she's going to be gun-shy about trying it again. If she'll even consider it."

"I don't think she will. Not without some kind of serious persuasion. All she really wants is me out of her mother's house." He shrugged. "It's fine. It's not my house and she's got every right to kick me out. Besides, I have a place to go, so it's not a big deal." He sighed, thinking how much he'd screwed things up. "But yeah, I need that info. You have any suggestions?"

"Actually, I do. Let me be the buffer."

"In what way?"

"I put my hands on the jacket, then she puts her hands on me. It's pretty clear we share the haerbinger gene and you know how like-kind fae can sometimes magnify each other's powers."

"But don't they usually have to be related for that to work?"

"Not always." She raised her brows. "What do you think? Will she go for that?"

He honestly had no idea. "It's worth a shot. You willing to come back to the house with me right now?"

She held her hands up and looked around the bar. "And give all this up?" She laughed. "You know I'm in."

He laughed, too. "Thanks, Dulce. I owe you."

"Yeah, you do." She took a long swig from her beer.

"You're right, which probably means it's not a great time to ask my second question, but I'm going to anyway."

She slouched in the seat, eyes twinkling with curiosity.

"Feeling frisky, is that it? I know rainy days were made for getting naked and sweaty, but I think it's better if we left that part of our relationship in the past."

He held his hands up. "Agreed. We're much better as friends." Some things weren't meant to be repeated. "I was going to ask if you would help me with this Guardianship."

She wiggled back to an upright position. "When have I not helped you? What do you need?"

He looked her straight in the eyes, mustered all the sincerity he could so she would understand exactly how much he wanted this. Then, for added insurance, rested his hand over the top of hers knowing the contact would let her feel how serious he was. "I want you to be one of my lieutenants."

Her mouth dropped open.

It wasn't a no, so he kept going. "You can live in the Guardian's house with me and Beatrice, she's Khell's widow—she's going to be one of my lieutenants, too—I've already worked it out. I need people I can trust. People that want to clean things up as much as I do, who love this city and want the best for it. And I know you feel that way because—"

"I think you've forgotten one thing." She slipped her hand out from under his.

"What's that?"

She picked at the label on her beer bottle. "I'm a remnant of indiscriminate origin. I have no idea what my bloodlines are except that they're fae *and* varcolai."

"So?"

"So the Elektos aren't going to like you putting a remnant in a position of power. Especially not one with my record."

"Screw the Elektos. I have final say on who's a lieutenant and who's not. And I say you're in. If you want to be." He'd ask Fenton about expunging her record, too. She'd like that.

She smiled, nodding slowly. "All right then. I'm down. Do I

get a sword, too? I could totally rock a sword. Or one of those stun sticks? Oh, what about a company car?"

"Maybe to some of it." He laughed. "I actually don't know. They *did* give me a vehicle to use." He paused for effect. "It came with the job."

"Not Khell's old ride." Her gaze moved toward the door like she expected it to be parked out front.

"The very same one."

Her fingers stilled, a strip of label in between them. "The Tesla?"

He sat back and grinned.

Her eyes widened in shock. "Holy cats. I want to drive it."

"I wasn't under the impression you had a license."

"I don't, but I'm a lieutenant now. The law can't touch me." She threw her head back and cackled, then gave him a wink as she slid out of the booth. "C'mon, let's go see little Miss Repressed Abilities about this jacket so we can start staking some vampire ass."

Chapter Fifteen

Harlow woke to find her hand still tingling with pins and needles. She checked the clock. She'd slept for about an hour, but the nap hadn't done much toward helping her make a decision about trying to read the jacket again. Knowing what might lie ahead of her, she got up, went into the bathroom and splashed some cold water on her face.

But finding the nerve to do what needed to be done was going to take more than cold water. She clenched and unclenched her fist trying to work out the numbness as she walked a path into the carpet of her room. She never should have agreed to touch the jacket but Augustine was after her mother's killer. That wasn't something she'd stand in the way of.

Usually when it came to touch, she put up her personal firewall and went on the defensive, but this time, right before she'd touched the leather she'd decided to treat it like a system she was trying to hack, opening herself up in a way she'd never done before.

Bad idea.

She'd never expected to take such a surge. It had shaken her, hard. More than that, the split second of information she'd received before she'd passed out had jolted her heart, caused her brain to go nova and made her feel like she was dying.

And she was going to have to do it again.

Because no matter how she felt about Augustine, which wasn't all that clear, or how damaged her relationship with

Olivia had been, her mother was still her mother. And maybe it was petty, but Harlow wanted the bastard who'd murdered her mother to pay, even if she had to use Augustine to do it.

If the killer had been a corporation, she would have hacked in and deleted his client files or locked up accounts or created some other kind of havoc, but this was something so physical that it would take a brute like Augustine.

Someone who wasn't afraid to get dirty or spill blood. Someone who could take charge and do unspeakable things.

She stopped pacing to sit on the bed, fanning at the sudden warmth creeping over her skin. As if the idea of Augustine doing such things was somehow...attractive. Or maybe it was Augustine himself. No *freaking* way. Why did her stupid fae side have to get all worked up over him? That's what had gotten her into trouble during *Nokturnos*. If only she'd picked a human guy to kiss. There must be some weird fae connection thing that made her feel that way. Like-attracting-like kind of thing. That was the only reasonable explanation for the way he...drew her to him. Or maybe it was none of that and what she was feeling was just animalistic bloodlust born out of her desire for revenge.

She liked that better, actually. Because there was nothing appealing about her mother's feckless house companion, no matter how good a kisser he was. Except that he wasn't really all that feckless since he'd taken on the Guardianship and pledged to protect everyone in the city.

Like a freaking superhero.

She glanced down at her tablet, where the latest issue of *The Dagger* had recently been delivered. It was currently her favorite graphic novel and not just because the Dagger was a total badass who took no prisoners as he defended Mecropolis, but also because the Dagger's sidekick, Perl, was a computer whiz and unnaturally beautiful in the way only chicks in comics could be.

"Snap out of it," she told herself. "You are not Perl and Augustine is not the Dagger." Even if he had started wearing a sword on his hip. As far as she was concerned Augustine was barely a butter knife. She looked at the tablet's dark screen, her face reflecting back at her. Maybe she had been living alone too long. Maybe online friends *really* weren't a substitute for real-life friends.

She sat on the edge of the bed and put her head into her hands. At least the headache was almost gone. "Just go downstairs and do it. Read the jacket, find out where the vampires are and tell Augustine." It would hurt again, but so what, right? What was a little pain for that kind of information?

Maybe too much to bear, that's what. Especially when that small inner voice reminded her she didn't like uncomfortable things. Like confrontation. Or pain. She inhaled, on the verge of melting because she *was* a coward. It's why she hid herself away. Why she'd been too afraid to face the abilities she'd been born with except for the ones that made her life easier, and why she'd been too afraid to fix things with her mother. And now too afraid to endure the pain that might provide the answers to who killed her mother.

But unlocking this new side of her ability was terrifying. She didn't *want* to know how to access such things. Or imagine what it might do to her. All that chaotic force flowing into her, scrambling her circuits. People were dark and messy and full of emotions, not clean and simple like her precious computers.

A knock on her door startled her.

"Harlow?" Augustine's voice.

"Yes?"

"Can I talk to you?"

She hesitated, but they'd have to have this conversation sooner or later. "Yes. Come in."

He opened the door, concern in his eyes. "You okay?"

"I'm fine." She looked away. She didn't want his pity. Or to see her reflection in his eyes. In that magnetic storm of gray-green, she looked small and useless. "I know you want me to read the jacket again."

He held his hands up. "I do, but that whole thing did not go the way I thought it would. I'm sorry you got hurt."

Not the response she'd expected. "Thanks."

He shifted, staring at her like he was trying to see into her head. "Do you remember anything?"

"Just the pain." Which was mostly true. She'd seen something, she knew that much, but those images were gone, pushed out of her head by the intense rush of pain that had followed.

"That's what I was afraid of. Maybe…" He ran a hand through his hair, revealing the stump of one growing horn.

What would she feel if she wrapped her naked fingers around that? "You want me to try again right now, don't you?"

He looked up. "Yes, but before you say no, hear me out. I have a friend who thinks she can help."

"The one Lally mentioned?"

"Yes. Dulcinea."

"How's she going to help?"

"She's got some haerbinger in her just like you and your mom, enough that she thinks she can act as a buffer."

Harlow frowned. "In what way?"

"She'll touch the jacket, then you touch her." He shrugged. "I have no idea if it will work. You might not get anything."

"Except what I pick up from your friend." She shook her head. "No. I don't want her baggage in my head. Anyone I touch, I get information from. I can't deal with it." Can't. Wouldn't. It was all the same.

He nodded like he understood, but there was no way he could really know what that intense surge felt like. "Can you just come down and talk to her?"

She looked at the clock. "We need to be at the lawyer's office soon."

His expression hardened. "And then you want me out. I know. And I'll go, but first, how about some help finding the vampire that killed Olivia." He took a breath and softened his tone. "Please."

"I want that vampire to pay just as much as you do." If only her cowardice weren't making her so reluctant, but she wasn't made of the same kind of stuff he was. "I'll talk to your friend. *Talk.* No promises of more."

He lifted his head a little, like he was surprised she hadn't fought him harder. "Thank you." He turned to go, then paused, his hand on the door frame. "Whether you like it or not, I'm coming to the services tomorrow."

She tucked her LMD into her pocket, then pulled her gloves on. "Of course you can come. I never said you couldn't."

That erased some of the tension in his face. "Thank you." But the tone of his voice made it clear that the words were a struggle to get out. So what. She wasn't going to feel guilty about making him move out. Especially now that she knew his role in her mother's death. At least not *that* guilty. "Dulcinea and I will be in the library when you're ready."

She listened to his descending footsteps, her own feet frozen to the spot. She was never going to be ready, but he wouldn't be pushing if time wasn't of the essence. Inhaling deeply and cursing her fae bloodlines, she forced herself down the steps to the library.

The woman waiting with Augustine gave off the kind of in-your-face fae vibe Harlow had worked her whole life to hide. It was as if the woman wanted everyone within visual range to immediately understand that not only was she fae, but she was proud of it and how dare anyone think differently. Harlow didn't go into the library more than a few steps, her level of discomfort clicking higher.

Augustine stood. "Harlow, this is my friend Dulcinea."

Dulcinea wiggled her fingers. At least she had the usual five. "Hey. I hear you've got some real gifts, huh? But you're not sure what to do with them."

Harlow stiffened. "I know exactly what to do with them—keep them hidden. But I want my mother's killer found as much as Augustine does, so I've agreed to try to help."

Dulcinea made a face as she looked at Augustine. "A fae who doesn't like being fae? Bizarro."

The conversation made Harlow's skin itch. "I'm barely fae. A tiny percentage from my mother."

Dulcinea laughed and pointed at Harlow's hands. "Babe, if it was a tiny percentage, you wouldn't be wearing those gloves. You pass as human pretty well, though. If not for your hair and eye color, it would be pretty hard to tell. Why not dye your hair and wear colored contacts if you hate being fae so much?"

Augustine rubbed his forehead. "Dulce, leave it be. That's none of your business."

A shot of pleasure ran through Harlow at Augustine's defense, but not enough to override the intrusion of Dulcinea's question or make Harlow dislike him any less. "He's right. It isn't any of your business, but I'll tell you why. I like the color of my hair." She tousled her shaggy mop for emphasis. "As for contacts, I stare at computer screens all day, every day. They're not practical or comfortable. Anything else?"

Dulcinea sat back down, a ghost of a smile playing on her mouth. "All right then."

Harlow put her hands on her hips and turned her gaze to Augustine. "Can we do this?"

Looking somewhat dumbfounded by her outburst, he nodded. "Sure, but I didn't think you wanted to."

"I don't, but this isn't just some parlor game for the sake of seeing what I can do. This is about my mother. It's important." The sooner she did this, the sooner it would be over. She looked at the small crystal clock on the closest table. "And I need to get ready for the lawyer."

He gestured to Dulcinea. "You know more about this than I do. What do we need to do?"

"Not much." Dulcinea scooted forward so she could reach the leather jacket still splayed over the coffee table. "I'll put my hands on the jacket, then Harlow, you put your hands on me and do whatever you did the last time. I should be able to control the influx of information so that you don't have the same reaction."

Harlow wasn't convinced. "Have you ever done this before?"

"No, but in theory fae powers can be chained like this."

Harlow pulled back a little. "In theory?"

Dulcinea sighed, her patience clearly wearing thin, not that Harlow cared. "It's been done."

Augustine nodded, looking hopeful, as he sat back down.

Dulcinea tipped her head at Harlow. "Just not with such a thinly blooded fae like you and a remnant like me."

"What's a remnant?"

Dulcinea shook her head. "You really don't know much about othernaturals, do you? A remnant is someone who's a part varcolai—that's shifter—*and* part fae and part human. Or maybe just fae and varcolai. Basically it would be like a person's mother was half human, half wolf varcolai and their dad was human with a quarter cypher fae in him. That kind of thing."

Harlow felt a certain satisfaction. "So you're a mutt."

Dulcinea's eyes did a weird glowy thing. "You want to see if I bite?"

Harlow ground her back teeth together. "You want to read this jacket yourself? See what information you can get without me?"

Augustine's heavy sigh cut through the tension. "Dulce, enough, okay? Harlow, please, I need this help from you."

"Fine." Harlow took the chair next to the couch Dulcinea sat on. "Do you have enough control to prevent your own emotions from spilling into me, too? Because I'd prefer not to have anything *extra* in my head."

Dulcinea held up her hands. "I'll do what I can, but that might be stretching me a little thin. Although, I *can* guarantee you won't get the same shock you did the first time. I have enough control over *my* abilities to prevent that." Her lips bunched to one side. "And so would you, probably, if you practiced with them instead of pretending they didn't exist."

A retort danced on Harlow's tongue but she held it back, satisfied that the great and powerful Dulcinea wasn't that great and powerful.

"Are we ready then?" Augustine looked at Harlow, his eyes filled with hope and pain.

The guilt he must be feeling... but she shook off feeling sorry for him. He'd earned that pain. "Yes. I'm ready."

Dulcinea pushed her sleeve up so that her arm was bare, then she put her hands on the jacket. "Let's do this."

Harlow stripped her gloves. "Are you sure you can't get anything off the jacket?" Maybe she wouldn't have to do this again after all.

Dulcinea shook her head. "I can't read objects. Just people. And even then..." Dulcinea tilted her hand back and forth to indicate her skills weren't all that hot. Amazing how her bluster disappeared in the face of reality. "This is all you."

With a resigned sigh, Harlow reached out and slowly wrapped her fingers around Dulcinea's forearm.

The visions hit a second later. More pins and needles but without the same intense pain. They hurt, but she could bear it, at least for a little while.

This time, they also weren't the blurred mess of information they had been before. Instead they came in shadowy screenshots, pixilated images and snippets of scent and sound. Not much more readable than the first try. She concentrated harder as she realized some of the input was coming from her surroundings. She closed her eyes in an effort to narrow her focus to only what was in her head.

Nothing made sense at first. Then slowly she began to separate a few things. The scent of sweat and the image of gray skin on gray skin had to be from Dulcinea. Revolted, she pushed that aside and tried to pull something useful from the onslaught, but some of the images went by so quickly they were gone before she could interpret them.

They sped by, each one as fragmented as the next, none of them lasting long enough for her to latch on to.

Her frustration built until at last something clean enough to read came through. A woman's name. She yanked her hands off Dulcinea's arm and gasped for breath. Her heart thumped like it might explode. "Helen. Does that mean anything? I saw the name Helen."

Dulcinea looked at Augustine. "Was that the female you killed?"

He shook his head, so grateful for what Harlow had done but telling her wouldn't do any good. "I don't know her name. Still, it seems familiar." Instead, he leaned toward her. "Harlow, are you okay? Your heart sounds like it might explode."

Her eyes widened slightly. "I forgot you could hear that." She put a hand to her chest. "I'm fine."

He wasn't so sure. She was breathing openmouthed, but obviously didn't want to be fussed over. He tried to think why the name should mean something. "What else did you see?

Anything you remember could be useful, even if you think it's not."

She slouched in the chair and stared at the ceiling like she was trying to recall what had just happened. "All I remember is a jumble of bits and pieces, nothing really clear until that name came across."

"How did it look?" he asked.

She scrolled a finger through the air. "Fancy. Like calligraphy. White on black. Maybe fabric." She nodded. "Something that moved like...like it was blowing in the wind? It seemed familiar, but I don't know why. It's not like I know this town well enough to recognize anything. Except that...it smelled like the French Quarter. Maybe."

The first nudge of an idea straightened him. "Are you sure it was Helen? Maybe it was Helene?"

Dulcinea's eyes widened. She had to be thinking the same thing he was.

Harlow closed her eyes for a moment, then opened them and looked at him. "Yes, that's it. Helene."

Anticipation zipped through him. "Hot damn. I know where the vampires are," he answered. "Hotel St. Helene."

Chapter Sixteen

The phone rang but Augustine ignored it. Lally would answer it and he was too amped up with this new information to talk about anything else. He caught Dulcinea's gaze. "Beatrice will want in on this. Those vamps killed Khell and she wants blood just as much as we do."

"I'm sure she does," Dulcinea answered. "And Beatrice is a lot more lethal than she looks. You know how vampires feel about fire."

"So long as she doesn't ignite them before I find out who's behind all this."

Harlow pulled her feet onto the chair and wrapped her arms around her knees. Her pulse was slowly winding down, putting Augustine's mind at ease that the stress of the read had been too much for her. He needed her help, but not at the cost of her health. No matter what she thought of him, she was still Olivia's daughter. That was reason enough to protect her. Not because he was having any kind of feelings for this amber-eyed hellion who just wanted him gone. No, it was all because of Olivia. For her sake, he'd do whatever it meant to keep Harlow from harm.

She looked at him. "You're just going to go after them? Three against how many ever there are?"

He nodded. "Pretty much. You have a better idea?"

"I could...go with you." She hugged her knees tighter, reminding Augustine of a scared little girl. Maybe that's all Harlow really was. He felt sorry for her, not pity exactly, but the kind of sorry that lay heavy on his heart for taking her mother away from her. Despite the distance between Harlow and Livie, Harlow had obviously loved her mother to some extent. Your mother was your mother, no matter what.

"Absolutely not."

She stopped hugging her knees to drop her feet to the floor. "I could be a lookout or *something.*" The words were almost a whisper. "She was *my* mother."

Before he could say anything, Lally came in. "That phone call was from Miss Olivia's lawyer. He said if we wanted to come in early, we could since he had another appointment cancel."

"Fine with me." He looked at Harlow. "You okay with that?"

"I can be ready in a few minutes." She seemed subdued since the reading. Had something else come through that she wasn't sharing? At least the call had given her something else to focus on besides accompanying them on the raid.

He turned to Dulcinea. "Will you stay and keep an eye on the house? They're supposed to deliver Livie's urn this afternoon." He couldn't bring himself to say ashes. It just seemed so...final.

"Of course." Dulcinea smiled at Lally. "Any chance I can raid the fridge?"

Lally's joy at the opportunity to unload some food was obvious. "I'd be happy if you would. People've brought so much food I'm out of room."

Dulcinea rubbed her hands together gleefully. "Oh, I'll make you some room, don't you worry."

Harlow stood, her face still not registering much readable emotion. What else had she seen? "Ten minutes and I'll be back down." She left, moving like she was walking through mud.

Lally disappeared after her, leaving him and Dulcinea alone.

She leaned over, her voice low. "I think your little fae got more than she bargained for."

Harlow wasn't his, but correcting Dulcinea would do zero good. He frowned instead. That was exactly what he'd been afraid of. "Like what?"

"I couldn't read anything that came through—it whipped by so fast my fingers are still tingling—but I could certainly feel it. There was a lot of energy flowing through me. A lot." Dulcinea bit her lip. "I can't be sure some of my own stuff didn't leak through."

"Like what?"

"Like I might have been thinking about something you and I did a long time ago—"

"Dulce, why would you do that?"

She threw her hands up. "I was worried she might get a whiff of it, so I was trying really hard not to think about it, which turned into me thinking about it." She raised her brows a tiny bit. "Sorry."

"Damn it. That's not going to help." Augustine sighed. There was nothing he could do about it now—except hope the fallout didn't come back to bite him. "What's done is done. We got what we need and she won't have to do it again. That's probably all she cares about anyway. Besides getting me out of this house."

He stood and Dulcinea got up with him. She hitched her thumb toward the back of the house. "I'm off to the kitchen. When you get back, I can help you pack up your stuff if you want."

"Thanks. For everything."

"You got it." She waved as she walked out, and his mind shifted to what Livie had left in her will for him and Lally. He really hoped it wasn't much. Taking anything from her when he was responsible for her death seemed very, very wrong.

A half hour later, the three of them sat in Lionel Cuthridge's office, Lally in the middle, Harlow and him in the side chairs.

Lionel adjusted his glasses, a sheaf of official papers before him. He glanced over his frames at Lally. "I'll start with you, Miss Hughes."

She nodded stiffly, her small purse clutched on her lap, her mouth a thin, tense line.

"Let me see now," Mr. Cuthridge began. "Yes, here it is. To Eulalie Hughes, my dearest friend and most abiding companion, I bequeath the sum of two million dollars and the case of Macallan in the wine vault."

Harlow glanced over, surprise plain on her face.

Lally's expression froze as she leaned forward. "I don't believe I heard you right."

Mr. Cuthridge glanced up from the papers. "Miss Goodwin has left you two million dollars and if I may say so, a case of very fine Scotch whisky."

Augustine barely heard the jump of her pulse over the thud of his own. He could only pray Livie hadn't been remotely that generous with him. She wouldn't be, would she? She'd already done so much for him and they weren't blood relatives. Not that that had ever stopped him from thinking of Olivia as family. Lally had been with her longer, too. That had to come into play, didn't it?

"Two million." Lally breathed the words out like a prayer. "I can't accept that. It's too much."

Mr. Cuthridge smiled. "You may do whatever you like with the money, but you do have to accept it. It's what Miss Goodwin wanted you to have."

She turned to Augustine. "What do I do?"

He reached out and squeezed her hand. "You take it. It's what Livie wanted."

Lally nodded, as if she was suddenly coming to her senses. "I can't believe Miss Olivia did that. Except that I can." Her eyes welled up. "That woman. God bless her soul."

Mr. Cuthridge continued. "Now, on to Harlow Goodwin and Augustine Robelais." More shuffling of papers. "Here we are. I, Olivia Goodwin, do hereby bequeath to my daughter, Harlow Goodwin, half of my current estate to include—"

Harlow's mouth dropped open.

Mr. Cuthridge continued. "All monetary assets such as stocks and bonds, accrued interest, film and television residuals, and to include all and any other sources as handled by my trust which shall be purposed for maintaining the Garden District property. In addition, I hereby bequeath the other half of my current estate to Augustine Robelais, also to include all listed monetary assets. These details are laid out in the trust."

Augustine went cold.

"In addition, Harlow shall not be permitted to sell the Garden District property to anyone but Augustine and Augustine shall not be permitted to sell the Garden District property to anyone but Harlow. Nor shall they be permitted to sell the Garden District property jointly and divide the profit or loss.

"Furthermore, the funds generated by the estate, including royalties, investments and other incomes, are to be administered by the executor of the trust for the sole purpose of maintaining the Garden District property and satisfying the expenses generated by said property."

Harlow paled. "There's nothing else? No letter? No envelope of information? No paperwork? Nothing about who my father might be? Can you check again? Maybe you missed something."

Cuthridge shook his head. "I'm sorry, there is only what I read."

Her shoulders slumped forward. "That's it then. Not a word about my father and half the house. And he gets the other half? And neither of us can sell it unless we own the whole thing? And on top of that, all the money in the trust is so the house can be taken care of?"

"That's exactly what this means, Miss Goodwin." Mr.

Cuthridge turned to Augustine. "Do you have any questions about the meaning of this decree?"

He sat back, his disappointment at being included in Livie's will not great enough to keep him from smiling. Guilt overwhelmed him, but he had no questions. He knew exactly what Livie had done. How she must have laughed when she'd finalized this plan, knowing what trouble she would cause. "That was perfectly clear to me." Beside him Lally covered her mouth with her hand.

Harlow stood, trembling slightly. "I need to sell that house." She looked at Augustine. "You have to sell me your half so I can sell it outright. Please." She pointed at Mr. Cuthridge. "I can do that, right? Sell the whole thing if he sells me his half?"

"Yes," Mr. Cuthridge answered. "That would be perfectly allowable."

Augustine raised a finger. "Now I do have a question. What's the house worth?"

Mr. Cuthridge thought a moment. "I'm not a Realtor, you understand, but current market value seems to me to be around twelve and a half million dollars."

"Thank you." Augustine steepled his fingers and smiled at Harlow. Clearly, Livie had wanted her daughter here in New Orleans. He could at least hold up that end of her machinations. "I'll give you a deal. You can buy my half for five million."

"Five mil—are you out of your mind? I don't have that kind of money."

Neither did he, something Livie had no doubt planned on. Augustine stood and offered Lally his hand to help her up. "Then you don't have my half of the house, either."

Disappointment weighing her down, Harlow slumped in the backseat of her mother's Bentley while Lally and Augustine chattered on about how wonderful Olivia was. Harlow wanted to beg them to be quiet, but she wasn't sure what else might come out of her mouth, so she tried to ignore them. How could Olivia not have at least provided the name of the man who'd fathered her? A name. Was that so much to ask? Apparently, it was. Now, not only did she still have a gaping hole in her heart, but she also couldn't touch any of her mother's money, *and* Olivia had only left her half the house. What was she going to do with half a house?

Not much, that's what.

She would never know who her father was, never pay her fine off, never keep herself from going to prison. Her dreams were dying. Forget that, they were dead. As dead as her...she couldn't stop the word *mother* from popping into her head and immediately felt awful about it. She was the worst daughter ever. In truth, undeserving of the half of the house she was getting. Not that she cared that much about the house. She'd give it up for her father's name.

Her gaze went back to the driver's seat. Augustine probably did deserve his half. He'd kept Olivia company, watched over her, been the dutiful child Harlow hadn't been. Except for leading the vampires back to the house, something she was sure he hadn't done intentionally, he'd been exactly what Olivia had needed. A substitute for Harlow.

Which made her despise him and appreciate him at the same time. She was happy he'd been there for her mother, but without him in the picture, Olivia would still be alive. Maybe that wasn't fair. And maybe it was. While he'd never have knowingly led trouble to her mother's door, the fact remained that he had.

He'd caused her mother's death. Caused this rift in Harlow's reality. And now he was being rewarded for it.

And she was going to prison.

She tucked her head against the side of the leather seat. All she wanted to do was go home to her little apartment, disappear into her computers and forget any of this had happened until the date came for her to turn herself in. Her professional reputation would be ruined and she'd probably be in debt for the rest of her life, but what could she do about it? Hacking had gotten her into this mess in the first place. They were watching her now. Anything more than a minor account tweak and they'd probably haul her back to court and charge her with something new.

Maybe Augustine would get killed in the line of duty and she'd become sole heir.

Shocked at herself, she squeezed her eyes closed and wished the universe would ignore the horrible thought that had just passed through her brain. She didn't mean it, not even a little bit.

She needed a change of scenery. Some space between her and Augustine until she could return home, because if he owned half the house there was no way he was going to leave it. Sitting in the library reading her mother's dusty old books or playing her RPGs wasn't going to cut it, because both of those things meant she was still in the house. With him. And that was the last place she wanted to be right now.

Lally looked back at Harlow. "You have any special requests for dinner? I'm sure Dulcinea's done a good job on what's in the fridge, but there's no way she'll have eaten the whole ham. I could—"

"I'm not going to be around for dinner."

Lally's brows went up. "You going somewhere, Miss Harlow?"

"Down to the French Quarter. I just need to get out for a while." As much as she hated crowds, it seemed like the perfect place to get lost.

Augustine looked at her through the rearview mirror. "I can drive you."

Like hell. She was trying to get away from him, not get closer. "I have a car. I can drive myself there."

Lally smiled softly. "I understand not wanting to be in the house, child. With the florists coming this evening and all..." She nodded approvingly. "You go on down to the Quarter and have some fun. Forget all this mess for a while."

"It's not safe," Augustine mumbled.

"Neither is going on that raid," Harlow shot back. She should at least be allowed to observe.

"It's fine." Lally put her hand on Augustine's shoulder. "There's lots of crowds and she's a grown woman. She knows not to go off with a stranger."

"You sure about that?" Augustine met Harlow's eyes in the rearview mirror and gave her a knowing look. She turned away, feeling heat rise in her face. Too bad he wasn't still a stranger.

Lally tapped him lightly on the shoulder. "She can look after herself."

"Thank you." Harlow pointed the comment in Lally's direction. Augustine could crash and burn for all she cared. Which she didn't.

Dulcinea greeted them at the door with the announcement that Olivia's ashes had been delivered. The news hit Harlow with a sense of finality that almost doubled her over. She held on to the kitchen counter to keep from crumbling to her knees.

That's how it had been these last few days. The pain came in waves, hitting her when she least expected it. Drinking a cup of coffee. Brushing her hair. Hearing that what was left of her mother now fit into a small, ceramic vase. What Harlow craved was a way to quell the storm. To escape.

Which is exactly what she did. Within half an hour, she'd left her car in a parking garage and hit Bourbon Street, happy to be anywhere but her mother's home, even if it was the dirty, smelly chaos of this constant street party. The crowd was different than the night of *Nokturnos*. No masks, of course, but also the people around her were almost exclusively human. Her people, she thought. Still frightening, but a drink or two would fix that and it was still better than being surrounded by the crazy fae who wanted to pull her into their world and make her into a bigger freak than she already was.

A sign advertised frozen hurricanes. She'd yet to try one of those, so she aimed toward the blinking neon with the goal of lifting her mental state and forgetting, at least for a couple hours, what these last few days had dumped on her.

Hurricane in hand, which tasted more like a fruit punch slushy than anything alcoholic, she ducked off Bourbon to wander the rest of the Quarter she'd yet to see. She studied the tourists as they went by, most so happy they bordered on oblivion. How did you get to that place in your life? How did you find that kind of happiness? Head filled with unanswerable questions, she window-shopped, staring at pretty things she'd never be able to afford and had no reason to buy. What good was a black studded messenger bag in prison?

The food aromas wafting from a small café reminded her that she hadn't had much to eat, but the drink, which was almost gone, had taken the edge off her hunger. Inhaling the drink had been her plan from the beginning. Get buzzed, enjoy the blur, then waste more time walking off the buzz until she was clearheaded enough to drive home.

As she turned a corner, music greeted her. A raucous mix of a man's gravelly voice accompanied by horns and other instruments. The earthy, joyous sounds pulled her along. She sucked down the last of the slush, dropped the cup in a bin and followed the bluesy rasp. Her path took her past a big white church and out into an open square.

The music came from a group in the corner closest to her, the men dressed in suits and ties and playing like they couldn't imagine anything better to do with their time. She smiled as she listened, nodding her head along. At the start of the next song, she dug a single from her pocket and dropped it into the open instrument case in front of the group. Judging from the pile of plastic already in there, they were doing okay.

A flash of envy hit her. What a simple life. Play some music, make some money, have no cares. But that was the alcohol, wasn't it? No one's life was carefree.

She wandered farther down the square. All along the fenced, landscaped center were rows of vendors. Colorful paintings, jewelry, T-shirts. Nothing she could imagine buying, but interesting to look at.

"Tell your fortune?"

"Hmm?" Harlow looked to see where the voice was coming from. The woman smiling back at her appeared too sophisticated to be reading palms. Her silky black hair was swept into a high ponytail and her elegant ivory sweater and pants seemed out of place for the square—the whole city, actually—but somehow perfect for her. "No, thanks. I'm fine."

The woman nodded at Harlow's gloves as if she understood the desire not to be touched. "I don't read palms." She overturned a tall silver cup about the size of a toothbrush holder, spilling a rainbow of crystals and cut gems onto her creamy velvet tablecloth. "I read stones. Much more accurate."

"Wow." Harlow moved closer, drawn to the rich colors and sharp facets. The stones sparkled with inner fire.

"Sit," the woman offered. "It's just for fun."

Harlow suddenly wanted to sit even though she knew it was the alcohol making the decision. She didn't care. She was tired of caring. "How much does this fun cost?"

"Less than a fancy dinner." The woman smiled and tapped a small ivory placard with the prices neatly printed in simple black font.

Compelled for no real reason except maybe the alcohol, Harlow pulled a few shiny plastic bills from her wad of ill-gotten cash and handed them over as she took a seat. "Why not, right? I came down here to do touristy things and have some fun. This is both of those."

The bills were already off the table, although Harlow hadn't seen the woman touch them. She scooped the crystals back into their silver cup. "I am Giselle, mistress of the crystals and keeper of the light. And you are?"

"Harlow, mistress of the interwebs and keeper of the servers." She laughed. The hurricane had made her more clever than usual. "Harlow's kind of a weird name, I know. My mother was in love with all the old movie actresses."

Giselle's expression stayed true. "It's a beautiful name. Now, please, don't tell me anything more about yourself. I prefer to let the crystals speak to me unaided." She put the silver container in front of Harlow. "Cover this with your hand and think to yourself one question you'd like to have answered. Don't tell me what it is."

"Is this going to work with the glove on?"

"You may take it off if you like, but psychic energy is not constrained by fabric."

"Cool." Harlow left her glove on and placed her hand over the container's opening. Her head was a little fuzzy, so she closed her eyes to help her think. Questions, questions, questions. What did she want to know? So many things. Too many things to put into one question. Would she ever find out who her father was? Could she find a way to stay out of jail? Would she ever get the other half of the house from Augustine? Would she ever kiss him again? *Whoa.* Scratch that. Not something she cared about *at all*. What she needed to know was if there was any chance of her paying that fine. Or would her hacking get her into trouble again? Finally, a question that encompassed several thoughts. *What's coming next?*

She opened her eyes as she took her hand off the cup. "Okay, I thought of something."

Giselle picked up the cup. "Very good." She whispered a few words over it, then tipped the container out, spilling the stones across the velvet. They twinkled like an alien sky. She stared at them intently, not saying anything for almost a minute.

"What is it? Bad news?" Harlow laughed. "Go ahead, I can take—"

"Quiet," Giselle snipped. She raised her eyes to Harlow, her voice a little softer. "I must have quiet."

Harlow made her best *whatever* face, but Giselle was back to studying the stones. They *were* pretty. And probably expensive.

Giselle pointed to the first cluster, where one long purple crystal touched another long clear shard. "You don't like the situation you're in."

Well, that was generic. Harlow popped her head to one side. "Who does?"

Giselle breathed out, slowly and controlled. Her fingers moved to the next cluster. Three tiny faceted green gems lay in a row almost parallel to a polished stick of something black. "You feel like someone else is responsible for your trouble."

"Doesn't everyone?" What a waste of plastic. Even through the soft boozy fog, she realized the woman in front of her was a con artist. A convincing one, but a scammer nonetheless. "I could tell fortunes like this."

Frustration marred Giselle's model good looks and darkened her brown eyes. "A recent disappointment has caused you to reconsider your future."

Harlow paused. That was pretty dead-on. Then she forced herself to laugh. No way was she getting sucked in by this nonsense. "Okay, I guess I should have realized sooner that this was just another tourist trap—"

"A parent is about to put you in danger," Giselle snapped.

Harlow froze as a new wave of grief hit her. "That's not funny."

"It's not meant to amuse you. I tell only what the crystals reveal." With a satisfied air, she moved on to the next grouping, two rough crystals, a pale yellow round and a muddy orange oval. "You will see a foe in a new light and be forced to make a choice."

Harlow pushed up from the chair, wobbling slightly. "I don't have enemies." Unless you counted the CCU. And the client who had set her up in the first place. And maybe Augustine a tiny bit. "None of what you said makes sense."

Giselle crossed her arms and sat back. "I do not conjecture. I only read."

"Whatever, it's all garbage you made up." Harlow shook her head, almost loosening the clip holding up her hair. "None of it will come true."

"Everything I read comes true." Giselle lifted one shoulder. "You will see."

"No, I won't. There's no way one of my parents can hurt me. You know how I know?" Harlow backed away, bumping into someone. She'd come here to forget. So much for that. "Both my parents are dead."

Chapter Seventeen

Giselle watched her customer rush off and disappear down Pirates Alley alongside St. Louis Cathedral. Something was odd about that girl Harlow. No fae ever sat at her table, tourist or otherwise. They just didn't mix with witches, as a rule. Sure, there was the occasional tourist with such a slight percentage of fae blood they were unaware of it, but this girl had gloves on. That meant she knew what she carried in her veins and she either feared it or didn't know how to control it enough to manage casual contact.

Both, most likely.

Odder still was the one thing the crystals had spelled out but Giselle hadn't spoken of. A sense of coming power, like something important was about to happen and this girl was a part of it. Almost in the midst of it. And not just something in her life, but something bigger, something with roots that sank deep into the city's foundations.

It unsettled her enough that she scooped up the crystals and funneled them back into the silver cup, then screwed the lid on and tucked them into her bag. What she'd read might be nothing, but it might also be something her father should know about. Pulling out her LMD, she scrolled through the incoming information, but there was no word from him yet.

Every othernatural in the city was waiting to see who the next Guardian would be, the witches included. If the Elektos hadn't done so already, they would soon appoint a new Guardian and when that fae came to meet with her father, she was sure he'd at least text her to let her know who it was.

She'd rather meet the new Guardian herself. That way she could charm him and get him on her side, determine how pliable he would be, how much she could bend him to give the witches more freedom. Help him see that the time had come for the constraints on her people to be loosened.

Her father was not a young man. His years crept over him a little more every day, but like most men he was stubborn, refusing to abdicate the leadership position to her. Eventually her father would have no choice and if this new Guardian was smart, he would understand that and realize how important getting Evander's daughter on his side was. She smiled. Perhaps it wouldn't matter after her father's death.

With him gone, and the power of the younger witches behind her, she might find a way to rid the city of the fae and their Guardian once and for all.

And then, just as New Orleans had belonged to the witches at its founding, so would the city again. She was tired of being regulated by the fae, of having to license her spells and register each year as a practicing witch. Just because her great-great-grandmother of centuries past had put a curse on the city? Foolishness.

But all in good time. All in good time.

Augustine took a good look around the main hall of the Pelcrum. Seems he'd beaten Fenton here, but Fenton wasn't driving a Thrun, either. At least not that Augustine knew. Maybe there were too many tourists hanging around and Fenton was waiting for them to clear out before he came down.

Either way, Augustine wasn't wasting the opportunity to

investigate. He started with the holding cells, walking directly to the one the vampire had died in. The cell was still open. He crouched and sifted a handful of ash through his fingers, impatient to get to the Hotel Helene, but going in alone, without any real idea of what to expect, could turn ugly fast. He needed more backup and until Fenton brought in the other lieutenants he wouldn't know who else he could trust.

Something gleamed on the floor farther back in the cell. He brushed the ash away and pulled out a tarnished silver cross. No markings or decoration on either side. He sniffed it, pulling back at the bitter tang of dark magic that shot through the acridness of the ash. Had this been what had killed the vampire?

"Augustine?" Fenton's voice rang out.

Augustine stood, slipping the cross into his pocket. Until he knew who he could trust, this evidence stayed with him. "In here." He went to meet Fenton in the hall. "Thanks for coming on such short notice. We need to talk about the lieutenants."

"I assumed that's what you'd called me here for." Fenton pointed ahead. "Let's go to the war room then."

When they were seated at the big round table, Augustine laid out part of what he knew. "I have a lead on where the vamps are holed up, but I don't want to go in alone." He raised a hand. "I've chosen two new lieutenants, but obviously, that's not going to be enough."

"Who are they?"

"Dulcinea and Beatrice."

Fenton's brows rose. "The changeling and Khell's widow? They're both powerful enough."

"And loyal. I trust Dulcinea with my life and Beatrice has very good reasons to want these leeches cleaned out of our city. Right now, I don't know who else to trust." Especially since Yanna had told him not to trust anyone—and she was Elektos.

"Your choices are fine with me, but they will need to take

the brand before they can be officially recognized." He looked down at the table, a slight shadow of disappointment darkening his face. "You can trust me."

Augustine let a few seconds slip by. "I believe that, but put yourself in my position. Look how much has been thrown at me in such a short time. The facts are that someone on the inside is letting vamps into this city and those vampires have already killed Khell, Olivia and a handful of tourists." He sighed. "I have no reason not to trust you, Fenton. But I can't be the same person I used to be. I have to think about every decision I make now because it affects so many more people than just me."

Fenton nodded. "I understand and I applaud that thinking." He rested his forearm on the table between them, unbuttoned his cuff and rolled up his sleeve. Two faint puncture marks.

Augustine frowned. It took a lot to scar a fae, but caustic vampire saliva could do it if the fae was young. "You were bitten?"

"I was attacked when I was a kid. A pack of vampires very much like the ones running loose in our city now. They were vicious, hunting us out of sport and for the misguided belief that they might gain some of our powers."

There was no other reason for vampires to hunt fae since the leeches hated the taste of fae blood.

Fenton's chin dropped, his gaze fixed on the scars. "They killed my little sister in front of me and would have killed me, too, if not for some other fae that heard her screams and came running."

Augustine swallowed. Cypher fae were some of the most vulnerable of their kind. "I'm really sorry."

Fenton shoved his glasses back on his nose, then rolled his sleeve down and buttoned his cuff, a hardness in his eyes Augustine had never seen before. "You have to know you can trust me."

"You're right. I have to start somewhere." Augustine tapped

the table. It was good to have another ally, even if it was an unlikely source. Did he trust Fenton a hundred percent? No, but after Fenton's story, Augustine thought the cypher was a safe bet. He reached into his pocket and pulled out the silver cross, then pushed it across the table to Fenton. "I found this in the vampire's ashes."

Fenton picked it up and examined it, then just as Augustine had done, he sniffed it. His lip curled. "Dark magic. Black magic."

"Exactly." He pointed at the cross. "Someone used that to kill the vampire in that cell before I could talk to him. Someone with access to this place, so that leads me to my next question. Who else can we trust? Which of the lieutenants?"

Fenton set the cross down, then pulled out his LMD and tapped the screen, scrolling through some icons until he came to the one he wanted. He tapped it and a list appeared on his screen. "There are seven lieutenants. There are only three I'm willing to vouch for." He counted them off on his fingers. "Khell's cousin, Dreich. Like Khell, he's got enough wysper in him to channel the scream that kills vampires, but not enough that he's mute. He and Khell were raised like brothers. He's chomping at the bit to find these vampires and exact his revenge."

"Finding the person responsible for letting these vampires into the city is more important. We need to cut them off entirely. Think Dreich would share his ideas on who might be behind this?"

"I'm sure he would." Fenton continued. "Then there's Sydra, who is half dryad, half saboteur. Because of her dryad side, she can only decay natural things, but that dryad side is what also makes her completely trustworthy." Fenton canted his head as if to say there was no question about her loyalty.

"Agreed." Dryads were a type of fae who were anchored to their place of birth. If they were removed from it, or something happened to their home, they would die. "She's not going to do anything to hurt the city. Another good one to talk to."

Fenton held up a third finger. "Last one is Cylo. He's an ethos fae—"

"That's a mimic, right? Aren't they a little rare?"

"Yes. Good job." Fenton's smile carried an edge of sympathy.

"I'm not a complete novice."

"No, you're certainly not. Anyway, Cy is an ethos, but his real talent lies in his true form. He's a brute. Enormous. About six eight, neck like a tree trunk with a body to match and a will to fight that doesn't quit. Fortunately for us, he's also exceptionally loyal."

Augustine had a slow, sinking feeling. He whistled low. "This Cy, is he really good with knives? Like blindfolded circus freak good?"

"Yes, do you know him?"

"Sort of." Augustine glanced at the ceiling. "I accidentally slept with his girlfriend once. *Ex*-girlfriend now, so hopefully he won't hold that against me anymore, but damn, that's not going to be a fun meeting."

"Accidentally?" Fenton held up a hand. "Don't explain. If he decides to quit, we'll make do."

"That's our team then. Let's call them in and see where they stand. I want to hit that hotel as soon as possible."

Fenton leaned back. "If the vampires are keeping the same kind of schedule here as most mortals do, that means they're staying out late and sleeping through most of the day, much like they normally would."

Augustine nodded. "Old habits die hard."

Fenton traced the grain of the wood in the table. "The best time to hit them would be right before daybreak. It would give us time to get everyone on the same page and map out a plan."

"I hate waiting, but I also don't want to waste a trip and tip them off." Augustine wanted to make this a decisive strike. "Sounds like a plan."

"Good. I'll arrange things on this end, you take care of Dulcinea and Beatrice. The goal will be to meet at the hotel at dawn. I'll make sure Dreich, Sydra and Cy know we want the leader captured alive for questioning."

"Excellent. Will you be there?"

"No. Elektos rarely engage in these kinds of hands-on missions—"

"I figured. The Elektos are more the paper-pushing, number-crunching, rule-making politicos."

Fenton shrugged. "We are. But I will make sure the other three lieutenants understand what needs to be done. They'll be there, ready to go." He looked at Augustine. "There's still the matter of meeting with Evander. We can't put it off much longer. He'll know there's a new Guardian soon, if he doesn't already, and we risk an imagined slight if you don't go see him soon."

"I'll go now." It wasn't what he wanted to do, but he understood his new position came with some unpleasant but necessary chores. "Unless you have a better idea."

"Let me set it up." Fenton punched in a number on his LMD. "Evander, please." A few seconds ticked by. "Evander, how are you. Fenton Welch here." He nodded. "I figured you'd heard. Yes, it was, very unfortunate." A short pause. "We do as a matter of fact and he'd like to stop in and see you. Right now, actually. You are? Wonderful. He'll be by shortly." Then he tapped the screen to end the call, tapped it a few more times and set the LMD down. "It's all set. I've sent the address to you."

"Can I question him about the magic on the cross?"

Fenton nodded. "Absolutely, just don't expect much of an answer. The coven is a very closed circle. They protect their own just like we do ours. But good luck."

"I figured as much." Augustine stayed seated. "One question. What happens to the lieutenants I no longer want? If they bear the brand, they have access to the Pelcrum. How secure can this place be if that's true?"

"If you decide not to reinstate them, they will be moved to other positions or retired. It happens." Fenton cringed slightly. "Some occasionally choose to have their brands removed."

"That sounds unpleasant."

"It is. As far as the Pelcrum goes, they've been sworn to secrecy. If any of them is found to have revealed this place or even spoken of it in a way that puts us at danger, they will have their tongue cut out before being imprisoned in the Claustrum."

Augustine raised his brows. "That's medieval."

"Perhaps, but that's how we've kept this place safe."

"How many retired, still-branded lieutenants are out there?"

"In other words, how many other people have access to the Pelcrum outside of current staff?" Fenton nodded as if he understood. "Twelve, I believe. But we keep a very close eye on them. Only five of those still live in New Orleans; two of them are in ill health and one is currently away on an extended stay."

"If it turns out that one of these lieutenants, retired or otherwise, is behind these vampires getting access to the city?"

Fenton's expression hardened. "They will spend the rest of their lives in the Claustrum, just as any other traitor would."

As that sank in, Augustine's mind turned to Olivia. "Are you coming to the house tomorrow for the funeral?"

"Yes, of course." Fenton straightened a little. "Tomorrow will be a hard day for you. If there is anything I can do to help, please let me know."

If anyone could help get Livie's ashes out of the cemetery, it was the man in front of him. "Actually, there is one thing…"

Giselle thanked the goddess that she'd been in the right place at the right time. She'd stopped by to see her father only to learn the new Guardian was on his way over.

Her father sat in his office, record books strewn about his desk, shelves overflowing with catalogued ingredients, scrying bowls and ancient grimoires. At least his shirt was clean. Not pressed, but clean.

"Aren't you going to straighten up before he gets here? I thought Cormier kept things up better than this." Her apartment in the French Quarter was pristine without the help of a butler or any other live-in help.

"This is a workingman's office, Giselle. I like things the way they are." Which meant Evander probably didn't let Cormier touch a thing.

Which was the problem. Nothing ever changed, nothing ever improved. "You know computers can keep track of all this information very easily. You could create spreadsheets to see what spells are the most requested, which coven members haven't paid their dues, whose licenses are coming up for renewal next. Think how much simpler your life would be."

He sighed and looked over the rim of his glasses at her. "We've been over this. Computers can be hacked. I don't want the world knowing our business. Why would people come to us for help if they could whip up a love potion from a recipe online?" He glared at her. "No. This is the way we do things. This will always be the way we do things."

Not after she became coven leader. "Did you invite Zara?"

"No, and I didn't invite you," her father answered. "Besides, your sister isn't interested in such things."

"She's not interested in much, is she?" Zara didn't live that far away, choosing to remain in their late mother's Garden District home nearby. Zara rarely left the house except to sell her handmade soaps and tinctures at the farmers' market, but her garden provided the coven with the bulk of the plant materials used in their spells. In that respect Zara wasn't totally useless. Nor was she much competition.

"Leave your sister alone. She's happy in her life. You should take a lesson from her."

Giselle planted her hands on the edge of her father's desk and leaned in. "What lesson would that be? To be less ambitious? To never want more for myself than a pretty garden? Forgive me for following in your footsteps, Father. I thought that's what you wanted. I know you wish I'd been a boy."

He rubbed his forehead. "Giselle, that's not what I—"

The doorbell's chime interrupted him. She spun away from her father, already knowing the lie he was about to repeat, and walked toward the front of the house. The Guardian had arrived. "I'll get it."

She met Cormier in the hall. "I *said* I'll get it." She shooed her father's butler away and opened the door, letting a long second pass as she took in the man across from her. Then she forced a smile. "Hello there. I didn't expect *you*."

The fae across from her tipped his head in greeting. "Giselle. If I may call you that." There was too much mystery in his eyes. What was he hiding? "I'm Augustine Robelais, but you probably already know that. I'm here to see your father, something I'm sure you also know."

Her smile broadened, but she caught herself before it became obviously faked. "I only know that you are a friend of one of the other readers who work in the square." Hellfire. Dulcinea's friend. This was an unexpected twist. "Come in, Mr. Robelais."

"Please, call me Augustine." He entered, his eyes on her and not his surroundings, unlike most people who saw her father's home for the first time. Evander's collection of antiques was astonishing not only for sheer volume but also for quality. If only they knew what power came from such aged objects.

"That's very kind of you." He reeked of power himself, a heavy, smoky metal scent that announced his virility like a blaring trumpet. She'd never been this close to him before, but it explained a lot about his reputation as a heartbreaker. And the way that ratty Dulcinea fawned over him. He probably wasn't even aware he gave off such a magnetic aura.

She held out her hands. "May I take your coat?"

"Sure." He slipped off the long leather coat he wore, revealing a gorgeous sword strapped to his hip. The sword had magic. That much she could discern. The fae and their weavers. Such a bothersome bunch.

"My father is in his study. If you'll just follow me."

But Augustine didn't move except to come closer to her. "I understand you've been saying unkind things about my friend, Dulcinea."

She backed up, feigning intimidation. "I would never do anything of the sort."

He grabbed her wrist, his grip firm but not unbreakable. "I can tell when you're lying. I can feel it through your skin, little witch."

A tremor of real panic trilled through her. She was supposed to be charming him, wooing him to her side. This was not going as planned. She swallowed her pride for the sake of the game. "I may have said something about her to a tourist out of anger. She sometimes steals my customers away, you understand. I apologize. It won't happen again."

He released her. "Thank you. I appreciate your honesty."

She rubbed her wrist, all for show. "You didn't give me much of a choice, did you?"

He winked at her. "I can't actually tell if you're lying or not. That ability isn't in my wheelhouse." He pointed down the hall. "I assume that second heartbeat I hear is your father. I'll announce myself."

The nerve. She stood there, her swallowed pride bubbling back up as anger. How dare he trick her? How dare he? She was next in line to be coven leader. An honest-to-goddess descendant of Aurela La Voisin, the grand witch who'd put the original curse on New Orleans after her heart was broken by a fae. Probably a fae just like Augustine. Giselle charged after him as he entered her father's office.

"This is the new Guardian," she spat out before he could say anything. "Augustine Robelais."

Her father stood and extended his hand. "Good to meet you, Augustine."

Augustine shook Evander's hand. "I appreciate you meeting with me on such short notice, but my time is at a premium these days."

Evander nodded. "It usually is for every Guardian when they take over, especially in a case where the previous Guardian has met an untimely death. You have my sympathies."

"I didn't know Khell well, but thank you." Augustine glanced at Giselle before looking back to Evander. "A dear friend of mine, Olivia Goodwin, was also murdered. We believe by the same vampires."

Her father looked genuinely shocked. "I'd heard of Ms. Goodwin's passing, but the news said it was a mugging. I had no idea vampires were involved. Again, my sympathies."

Giselle nodded. "I told you there was more to it."

Evander gestured toward her. "My daughter always thinks there is more afoot than there truly is. In this instance, it seems she was right."

Augustine turned to her. "You're always in the Quarter. Have you seen a lot of vampires? Do you know anything about the pack that's in the city now?"

"I'm always in the Quarter because I live and work there." She caught her father's disapproving frown in her peripheral vision.

For his sake, she tried for a more demure tone. "I haven't seen many vampires. One or two, but not enough to call a pack."

Augustine narrowed his eyes and rested his hand on the hilt of the weapon on his hip. "You're not lying again, are you?"

She swallowed, sneaking a peek at her father. If he frowned any harder, he'd sprain a muscle. "Of course not. Why would I do that," she asked. Perhaps she should tell him about some of the fae who came to see her secretly, who used her services because they had business they wished to keep hidden. Guardian or not, he had no idea what really went on in his city.

Evander rapped his knuckles on his desktop. "What's this about my daughter lying to you?"

"Nothing serious," Augustine answered. "Just a little self-protection."

Evander gave her the glare she knew meant trouble. "I am sorry about it, nonetheless." He came out from behind his desk. "Giselle, get us some wine, please." He gestured toward Augustine. "We'll have a glass together, toast your new position."

"Thanks, but I'll pass," Augustine said. "Really, I can't stay long."

She hesitated. This should be good.

Evander looked askance at Augustine. "It's traditional to share a drink at this first meeting. It shows trust, among other things. I'll assume you weren't informed of that and give you the opportunity to answer again."

The fae held up his hands. "You're right, I wasn't informed, but there's no one to blame for that. We've just been preoccupied with these deaths and getting our affairs in order. I'm sure you can understand the chaos our house has been in." He nodded to Giselle. "I'd be happy to share a drink with you and your father."

She smiled sweetly, because he'd just stepped in it again. "I'll be right back." She strode away while her father informed

Augustine that the only person he needed to share a drink with was the coven leader, not his daughter.

She came back with three glasses anyway, the stems laced between her fingers, the neck of the bottle firmly in her other hand. "Daddy?" She held out the bottle to him. "Would you care to open?"

It was a chance for him to show off, a little gift from her and something that would please him.

As predicted, he smiled and took the bottle. Augustine shifted, his body tense. He was either ready to leave or worried that her father was slightly unhinged. Evander was perfectly sane, just a stickler for diplomacy, and having Augustine be unsure of Evander could work to her advantage, especially if she offered herself as a go-between.

Bottle stripped of its foil seal, Evander spoke the opening spell and the cork wriggled free of its own accord.

Augustine clapped. "That's a handy trick."

Giselle almost laughed, but held back. The fae had already insulted her father enough.

Evander chucked the cork into the trash with more force than necessary. "It's not a *trick*, Mr. Robelais. We are wizards and witches, not magicians."

Proud that her father had at least stood up for them on that front, Giselle took the bottle from him and poured a few ounces into each glass. What a lucky, lucky turn of events that she'd gotten to be here for this.

Augustine let out a frustrated sigh as he widened his stance into something a little more defensive. "I didn't mean to imply anything by my wording. I'm not a diplomat. I'm not even a decent fae ambassador. In fact, I'm barely a member of fae society. Up until Olivia was killed, I had refused the Guardianship on more than one occasion."

He took a deep breath. "I am here because I was told it was

the right thing to do. To extend you the courtesy of meeting me on your own ground. I get that the treaty between our people is important, but you're going to have to cut me some slack. All I care about right now is getting these monsters out of our city and protecting the people that live here—all of them, witch, fae, varcolai or human—so if I don't use the proper words or step left when I should step right, get over it. It's not what I'm about."

A glass of wine in each hand, Giselle popped her jaw to one side and waited for Mount Evander to explode. His eyes were bulging out of his head a tad, a sure sign her father was about to blow.

Evander slowly closed his mouth, reached out and took one of the glasses from Giselle. He lifted it. "The Elektos are lucky to have you. Forgive me for placing such importance on the trivial. If I can help you in any way with eliminating these vampires, I am happy to do it."

Looking relieved, Augustine took the second glass from Giselle and clinked it against Evander's. "Much obliged."

Then the two men drank, leaving her out of the toast and feeling very much like she'd somehow arrived late to the very party she'd planned.

Augustine set his glass down after the first sip. "There is something I'd like to talk to you about." He cleared his throat. "Alone."

Evander waved a hand at Giselle. "Close the door on your way out, my dear."

Dumbstruck with anger and humiliation, she did as her father asked. She stood in the hall for a moment, staring at the closed door. If the rest of the coven could see how her father had welcomed this fae into his bosom as if the Guardian were the new salvation of the city, they would charge him with treason. Well, some of them anyway. And right now, Evander was in there probably giving away the last scrap of freedom the witches had. What the hell was her father thinking? What new regulation would the fae heap on them now? There wasn't much left.

She stormed out of the house, not caring if the slamming door disrupted her father's precious meeting.

The only thoughts that brought her comfort were knowing he would not be coven leader forever and fantasizing about that day.

Chapter Eighteen

Augustine had no idea if Evander could be trusted or not. Giselle couldn't, that was plain, but a child didn't always follow in a parent's footsteps. Augustine and his own mother were proof that the apple sometimes fell very far from the tree, but there was only one way to find out. He tugged the small silver cross from his pocket and tossed it onto Evander's desk. It landed with a tinny clink. "What can you tell me about that?"

Evander picked it up and flipped it over, then looked at Augustine. "I assume this is of some import or you wouldn't have wanted to discuss this alone."

"It's very important."

He turned it in his fingers, finally bringing it to his nose. "Smells of dark magic and ash."

Information Augustine already knew. "Elaborate on the magic part."

Evander set the cross down to take another sip of his wine. "The smell of the magic tells me whatever spell was attached to it has been used up. There's no way to tell what the spell was now." He swirled the wine in his glass. "No vampire could tolerate this symbol, but to also cast this piece in silver..." He shrugged. "Combine that with the scent of ash and the kind of magic involved and I'm guessing this was a murder weapon. Or it at least played some part in the death of a vampire, yes?"

"It played some part, but I can't comment more than that." Augustine wasn't about to reveal that it might also be connected to whoever was behind letting the vampires into the city. There was every chance Evander was connected to that. No reason to give away evidence the wizard might use to protect himself. But he'd confirm what Evander had already figured out.

Evander returned his glass to the desk. "Then what can I help you with?"

"Can you tell me who created that spell?"

Again, he shrugged. "In theory, each witch's magic has a signature, but identifying it isn't so easy. Can you look at a fingerprint and tell who it belongs to? Not without some time and effort. It's the same thing with magic."

"But it is possible."

He passed a hand through the air. "In *theory*."

Augustine shook his head and sat back. "I need a different answer."

"Can you leave the cross with me? I could run some tests on it, see if I can narrow things down."

"No."

Evander put a finger on the cross and pushed it back toward Augustine. "So someone murdered a vampire. I'm not sure I understand your eagerness to track this person down. Isn't death your endgame for the vampires in the city? Or were you going to shuttle them to the parish line and see them safely on their way?"

Death was his endgame for whoever was allowing these leeches into the city. Augustine snagged the cross and tucked it into his pocket. "It's more complicated than that."

"It always is. I'm sorry I can't do more."

There had to be another way. "Actually, you can. Give me a list of your people who practice this kind of magic."

Evander touched his chest. "Mr. Robelais, none of the members of my coven practice any form of the dark arts. It's forbidden by the treaty."

Augustine's patience was gone. He stood and leaned over Evander's desk. "All that tells me is your daughter isn't the only liar in the family."

Evander snorted, indignant. "I will not be spoken to this way."

"Lie to me, hamper any aspect of my investigation, do one tiny thing to aid the person responsible for these leeches and I'll speak to you any damn way I please."

Evander hauled his bulk to his feet. "You're putting the treaty on very shaky ground, son."

The urge to press a blade against the wizard's neck made Augustine's fingers itch. Instead, he slammed his fist onto the desk, making the mess covering it jump. Evander's flinching was a bonus. "You think I care about that treaty? That benefits you and your coven, not my people. That treaty *allows* you to stay here. If you're not interested in maintaining it, I'd be happy to let the Elektos know the coven is moving out."

Evander huffed, suddenly out of words.

Augustine straightened. "I thought so." He pointed at the wizard. "Until you provide me with a list of witches most likely to be responsible for that dark magic, every one of your coven members will be considered a suspect." He headed for the door. "You have twenty-four hours to deliver that list or I'm going to start revoking licenses."

He paused at the door. "Giselle's first."

Dawn was an hour off, but Augustine sat on the second level of the parking garage across from the Hotel St. Helene, smoking a *nequam* cigarette and waiting for the rest of his lieutenants. He'd left the house earlier than necessary, but he was eager to get this raid under way. Granted, capturing Olivia's killer was just the first step in finding whoever was responsible for bringing the vampires into the city, but it might also make things a little easier between him and Harlow. She'd come home last night still in a mood and had retreated to her room without a word to him or Lally. Just stomped up the steps and slammed her door. He got it, he really did, but he couldn't erase the kiss they'd shared or do anything to change Livie's will.

Nor would he go against what Olivia had been trying to accomplish. Sooner or later, Harlow would calm down. He hoped.

He peered through the louvered window, watching the street below and the hotel's entrance. The Quarter was grumbling awake around him, but the parking garage was still quiet.

Except for footsteps.

He turned. Dulcinea and Beatrice headed toward him. Dulcinea had a to-go cup in each hand. She held one up and smiled. "Coffee, boss?"

He ground out the cigarette and walked forward to take the coffee from her. "You're a mind reader."

"Fortune-teller," she corrected him. "And I knew we'd have bad fortune if you didn't have your morning brew."

He took a sip, then smiled. "How are you doing, Beatrice?" As far as he knew, she'd never been on the front lines like this before.

Her face was serious. "I'm armed and ready to kill some vamps." She patted the bolt stick hanging from her belt. "This was Khell's. Thought it might come in handy."

"You know how to use that?"

"My father was a Claustrum warden." She gave him a sly look as she opened her palm and produced a fireball. "And if that fails, I'll toast a few."

"All right then." More footsteps brought the other three lieutenants. Dreich and Sydra were in front with the hulking Cy bringing up the rear. Augustine said a silent prayer that the ethos fae had learned to forgive and forget. He'd already spoken to Beatrice about handling Cy if it came to that since she said she'd gotten to know him through Khell.

"Here comes the rest of our crew." He downed a little more caffeine, then set his cup on a nearby hood.

Beatrice took a few steps toward the incoming group. Their expressions warmed as they saw her. Dreich gave her a hug and Cy patted her on the back with his meaty paw. The tension that had been as thick as the *nequam* smoke vanished.

He waited until the small talk passed, then began. "Thank you for coming. I understand Fenton filled you in, but if you have any questions, feel free to ask me."

Cy rolled his thick shoulders, his voice low and gravelly. "Just tell us where you want us, boss." Dreich nodded, looking committed and ready to get the job done. Sydra patted the slim, folded crossbow hanging from her hip.

Augustine took Cy's answer to mean the big man wasn't holding the past against him. Excellent. Whatever Fenton had said had done the job. Augustine relaxed a little. His team seemed like a good group. One he'd extend some trust to until given a reason not to. "Dulcinea, what did you find out?"

"I talked to the guy I know who works on the housekeeping staff here. The joint is small, only sixteen rooms and three floors, so he knew right away who I was looking for. The third floor holds two big suites and they've been rented out for the last three weeks. He's not sure how many are in the group, but he thinks eight, maybe as many as twelve."

"That's since the night at Olivia's?" He'd killed at least four that night.

"Yes."

"Decent odds," Augustine said. "What about the hours they keep?"

"No real pattern. They come and go in groups, but someone's always on the floor, standing guard by the elevator."

Cy spoke up. "They're taking shifts to guard the sleepers."

Augustine nodded. "I agree. They know how vulnerable they are when they're in daysleep—"

"Like they're dead," Sydra interjected.

"Easy to kill like that," Dreich added. "Real easy. And just because they're in New Orleans doesn't mean they can go without it."

Augustine thought for a moment. "We just have to take the guard down without rousing the others. They must have some kind of alarm system in place."

Dulcinea rummaged in the bag hanging off her shoulder. "I scored two master keys so we can get into those suites quietly."

"Nicely done." Sydra smiled. "How'd you manage that?"

Dulcinea wiggled her fingers. "Don't ask, don't tell." She grinned. "I also got this." She pulled out a black short-sleeved collared shirt and held it up. The breast was embroidered with the hotel's name, the word *staff* underneath.

Augustine raised his brows. The shirt looked like a kid's large. "Well, we're not putting Cy in that."

"I'll do it." Beatrice reached for the shirt.

Augustine held up a hand. "I appreciate the enthusiasm, but whoever wears this is going to be the first person in. They're going to have to kill the guard without waking the others. I'm not sure you have the experience for that."

Sydra held her hand out. "Give it to me."

Augustine raised a brow. "What about your crossbow? That's not standard company issue."

She grinned. "I won't give the vamps time for questions."

Augustine nodded. "All right then. Sydra, you take the elevator up. Beatrice, you and Cy take the courtyard in back, make sure we have no escapees. Dreich will stay here to watch the front of the building and Dulcinea will come with me up the stairs. As soon as the guard is subdued, she and Sydra can take one suite and I'll take the other." He held up a hand. "Remember, we need the leader alive."

"How will we know him?" Dreich asked.

"He's got a scar on his left side." Augustine drew his finger across his cheek to illustrate. "If he's not there, we need at least one alive for questioning. Got it?"

"Got it," they answered.

He nodded at Beatrice. "You and Cy have five minutes to get into position. Then the rest of us are moving."

As Cy and Beatrice hustled off, Augustine went back to the louvered window to watch their progress. Behind him, Sydra changed into the uniform shirt so he kept his eyes on the street below. Already the activity level in the Quarter had picked up.

Dreich came to stand beside him. "Thank you for giving Beatrice a shot at this. She really needed something to do."

"I didn't give her the job out of pity, I did it because I need people around me I can trust." Augustine watched Cy and Beatrice cross the street at the corner.

"Agreed. I'm glad you feel like you can trust the rest of us. I'm assuming someone vouched for us?"

Augustine looked at Dreich, trying to determine if there was something deeper behind his question. "Fenton told me you, Cy and Sydra were the best of Khell's lieutenants and that you were loyal. I trust him, so that's how you ended up here."

Curiosity twisted Dreich's face. "You think one of the other lieutenants is involved in this vampire thing?"

Dreich was Khell's cousin, so he had probably been privy to whatever Khell had known. Maybe he had some insight to offer. "Do *you* think it's possible? Anyone you'd suspect?"

He shrugged. "I don't know. It's a pretty ballsy move. One there's no coming back from."

"Agreed." Augustine pushed a little more. "Which one of the remaining lieutenants fits that description best?"

He shook his head. "I don't want to put anyone's neck on the chopping block, man. I'm not pointing fingers without proof. It could be one of the Elektos for all I know."

Augustine cocked his brow. "Are you saying you think that?"

Dreich blew out a long, slow breath like he was choosing his words. "I'm saying I wouldn't rule it out."

"If you had to pick one, who would it be?"

"I want to find Khell's killer just as much as you do, but these are hard questions you're asking me to answer." Dreich rubbed the back of his neck. "This is not a game I want to play. There are members of the Elektos who don't follow anyone's rules but their own."

Augustine didn't need to hear Loudreux's name to guess that's who Dreich was referring to, but he still wanted it confirmed. Maybe Dreich would be willing to talk with less company. He gave Sydra the sign to go. "Wait outside until Dulce and I get there."

"Will do." She gave a little salute and jogged off.

He looked at Dreich again. "There are no secrets between Dulcinea and me. Who in the Elektos do you think could be involved? If you want to help find Khell's killer, this is your chance. Because if I have to do it on my own and I find out you knew something and didn't step up, it will not go easy for you. Understand?"

Dreich bristled, wavering slightly in the way of a wysper. "You think I would hold back? I loved Khell like a brother. How dare you accuse me of—"

"Whoa, now." Dulcinea started to put a hand on Dreich's shoulder, then apparently thought better of it. "Augustine's just doing his job as Guardian. The same as Khell would have done."

Dreich swallowed, gaze flicking from her to Augustine. He nodded, calming down some. "Petrick Hayden."

Augustine didn't know the man. "Why?"

Dreich shrugged. "There's something sketchy about him. He's been around the longest of the lieutenants. He's just... odd. And don't ask me how, man, you just have to meet the guy. Maybe he's working a back-end deal so he can retire. And as long as we're talking about that, you might want to look into Loudreux, too."

Augustine stared at Dreich, surprised he'd actually named Hugo. "The Prime? Bold statement adding him to your list of suspects."

Dreich frowned. "Khell thought there was corruption among the Elektos, so he started digging into a few things. Then he ends up dead. Coincidence? I don't think so, man."

"This is good information." Augustine softened his expression. "Next time, don't make me work so hard for it." He checked the time. "Dulcinea, we're on. Dreich, the front's all yours."

As Augustine started for the first floor, she fell into step behind him. "You okay?"

"Fine, why?"

"Really? After that information?" She glanced back toward Dreich's position in the parking garage. "You're not ready to storm Loudreux's and interrogate him?"

"One raid at a time." As they crossed the street to the hotel's entrance, Augustine pulled out his LMD and shot Fenton a quick text.

"What about Petrick then? I don't know the man. I'm assuming you don't, either."

"No, but he and Hugo are both worth investigating. Petrick first." Augustine held up the LMD. "I've already told Fenton to pull whatever info he has on the man." He stuck the device back in his pocket as they approached Sydra. "Let's go clean out this nest, shall we?"

The lobby was small and the desk clerk sleepy. Sydra went ahead of them into the elevator while he and Dulcinea zipped toward the stairs. Sydra held the elevator until they were in the stairwell, then let the doors close. He and Dulcinea jogged the three flights, stopping outside the third-floor door. A few seconds later, the elevator chimed. Then came the swoosh of the opening doors. A few seconds after that, some more muted sounds. One a gasp cut off mid-voice, one the dull thunk of metal on bone.

The door handle turned and Sydra peeked in. Gray ash dusted her black hotel shirt. She nodded to Augustine. He nodded back, then he and Dulcinea slipped out. Ash coated the floor, crunching softly underfoot. The foyer between the two suites was smaller and darker than he'd expected.

As if reading his mind, Sydra pointed to the light fixture. The bulbs were gone. He nodded. Old habits died hard. The vampires still craved the darkness they were used to. Or they were expecting company and had hoped for the element of surprise. Except that fae saw about as well at night as they did during the day.

He pointed toward the suite on the right, motioning again for Sydra and Dulcinea to take the left one.

They moved into position and readied their weapons. Augustine eased his sword from its sheath, marveling at how light the fae blade was. This was going to be fun. He looked at his teammates and held up his master key in the other hand. Dulcinea waved hers back at him. He mouthed the words, "One, two, three." On three, they each waved the keys in front of the locks.

As soon as the lock clicked open, Augustine pushed the door open and stepped into...more darkness, but this time it was utterly black. Fae eyes needed a sliver of light and the vamps had done a good job of eliminating most of it. He could see enough to make out furniture shapes, but not much else. Had they painted over the windows? They didn't need the darkness, so they must have done it for advantage. Damn it. Were they expecting the raid?

If only these leeches had pulses, he'd be able to tell how many he was up against. They could certainly hear his if they were awake.

As best he could tell, the living room was empty. The soft thud like something shutting came from the room ahead of him. Then a zipping sound. He snuck toward the bedroom, sword at the ready. The door was ajar. He crouched outside it, listening.

Someone—had to be a vampire by the smell—passed by the door. He coasted his fingers up the wall and found a light panel. He tapped it and reared back to kick in the door, the crystal chandelier flaming to life as the wood exploded into the room.

A male vampire stood in the middle of the room, suitcase in hand. He made eye contact, hissed and darted toward the balcony window, which had indeed been painted black.

"Not so fast, bloodsucker." Augustine threw his sword like a javelin, catching the vampire in the back.

He dropped the suitcase and arched in pain as he clawed for the blade, mewling like a wounded animal. Augustine tackled him to the ground. The vampire twisted, unable to turn onto his back because of the sword, but enough to get a swipe at Augustine, cutting his cheek.

Augustine punched him in the face. "Where's your leader?"

The vampire spit out a fang. "Go to hell, faery." He yanked one leg up, planted his foot on Augustine's chest and shoved him off.

As he fell back, Augustine reached for the dagger strapped to his thigh—another of his new weapons—and the vampire reached for the suitcase. Augustine flipped to his feet, but the vampire was in no hurry to bolt. With a queer smile, the vamp wrapped one arm around the suitcase, then lifted the circular amulet around his neck to his mouth, put it between his teeth and bit down.

Augustine had no idea what that was supposed to—

The vamp got out half a laugh before bursting into flames. Augustine shielded himself with his hands, but the fire was quick, taking the vampire and the suitcase to ash in seconds. The fae blade clattered to the floor unharmed. "*Sturka.*" The amulet had been the vampire version of a suicide pill. If there were any other vamps in the suite, they would have attacked by now. This one must have been alone.

His cheek stung where the vamp had sliced him. Maybe Dulcinea and Sydra had had better luck. He loped through the suite and started across the foyer to the other one, but the women were on their way out.

Sydra collapsed her bow as she shook her head. "No one in there and the place is picked clean."

Augustine muttered a curse and punched the wall. "One vampire. Must have been the one sent to clean things up, but when he realized he was caught, he incinerated himself and anything that might have helped us find the rest of them."

Dulcinea looked stricken. "You think someone tipped them off that we were coming?"

He did, but he didn't want to reveal that in front of Sydra. "No. I think they got spooked by the episode at Olivia's. Figured it was time to change venues." His hands itched to break something. Or someone.

"What now, boss?" Sydra asked.

Dulcinea answered as she dug into her hip purse. "Now we clean up those scratches on his face before they scar over." She pulled out the stuff she'd used before, wet a cotton ball and went to work on him.

He put his hands on his hips while she cleaned him up. He stared at the ash coating the foyer floor. Somewhere out there, the person responsible for letting a horde of murderous vampires into their city was still roaming the streets. He'd let the citizens of New Orleans down. "Done?"

Dulcinea stepped back. "Good as new."

"Great. Now, I can go home while the rest of you go back to whatever sources you have and see if you can find anything that will bring this dead end back to life." He sighed deeply. "In the meantime, I have a friend to bury."

Sydra hit the panel for the elevator as Dulcinea gave his hand a little squeeze. "We'll get them, boss. We'll get them."

Chapter Nineteen

Harlow looked at the woman in the cheval mirror and frowned. It *was* her reflection, but she looked like an imposter. The plain black dress, the reserved makeup, the hair blown out and let loose... none of it seemed like her, but she knew if her mother could see her, she'd have been pleased. The outfit was a small concession to make on such a dreadful day, but dressing up didn't mean she was over what her mother had done. Not a word about her father and half the house. The house wasn't nearly as important as her father, but Olivia's slight would take time to get over.

She shook her head, trying to let her anger go as she slipped into a pair of simple black heels she'd found in the back of her mother's closet. The last time Harlow had worn heels, she'd just graduated from college and was on her way to her first—and last—job interview. She'd learned pretty quickly that no one was going to pay her what she could earn doing gray work, the kind of backdoor security stuff that meant keeping her identity hidden. Which was fine with her. Most of the people who hired her didn't know she was female or fae. With her computer skills, they didn't care.

She navigated her way to the dresser, testing her stability. Some women, like her mother, could walk in heels as if they'd been born to it. She was not one of those women. Not like her mother in a lot of ways, actually. Not as beautiful, not as charming, not as easily the center of attention. There was a reason her mother had risen to such stardom. All the things that Harlow was not.

She added a pair of diamond studs and a slim diamond bracelet—both gifts from her mother on various birthdays— and a pair of short black gloves. Considering today's event and how far south they were, no one would question the gloves, so if people noticed them, she wasn't concerned. Not that she cared anyway.

She pushed her sleeve back to check her watch. Twenty minutes and people would start arriving. As if the crowd wasn't bad enough, there would be the questions about how she was doing, the condolences, the remembrances of a woman she felt so disconnected to and yet was still grieving for. A shudder ran through her. The afternoon would be a tedious exercise in pretending while trying to maintain control, but she would get through it and in a day or two, she'd go home, put this all behind her and prepare for the horrific reality of life behind bars.

Her mother's decision to split ownership of the house had changed nothing. Harlow still had a fine to pay and since she couldn't, she still had to face jail time. Once that was served, she'd still be broke and would go right back to living job to job, getting ahead only enough to slip under again with the next bill. She sighed. It was her own fault for expecting her mother's estate to provide a windfall. She'd gotten exactly what she deserved.

Nothing. Except more complications.

"Harlow?" The biggest—and most fascinating—of those complications called her name from the other side of the door. "You doing okay?"

"Yes." Augustine sounded genuinely concerned, but if he really wanted to be nice to her, he'd sell her his half of the house for a dollar and let her get on with her life. She could always tell him about the fine, play on his sympathies, but the fewer people who knew about that embarrassment, the better. "I'll be down shortly."

She waited until she was sure he'd be downstairs giving last-minute instructions to the caterers or whatever it was that needed doing, then she headed into the fray. It wasn't possible to dread these next few hours any more than she already did. She picked her way down the steps slowly, partly because of her reluctance and partly because of her heels. The last thing she needed was an injury from a fall that would keep her here longer than she could afford.

The soft buzz of preparations rose up to meet her as she descended. Servers in white shirts and black bow ties sailed past with silver trays of finger foods. She stopped on the bottom step to let one go past.

A long, low whistle brought her head around.

Augustine stood in the dining room looking at her with a slightly confused expression. Like he didn't quite recognize her.

"What?" She knew what she looked like. She didn't need him pointing it out. Being judged made her want to run back to her room.

He blinked a few times and shook his head. "You look... beautiful. Like the pictures of your mom from her movie days. Like the woman I met on Bourbon Street. Without the mask, of course."

She pressed her tongue to the roof of her mouth to keep from calling him a liar, because his eyes held no guile. He actually meant what he said. She swallowed the sharp words and managed to say, "Thank you," instead.

And then, as if remembering who he was and who she was, he nodded and lost the mesmerized expression in favor of something much more aloof. "You're welcome. You really do clean up nice. Not that you were dirty before. I mean—you know what I mean, right?"

She smiled. It was rare a man got tongue-tied around her. "You clean up nice, too." He did. Not that she'd ever seen him looking remotely shabby, but what man didn't look nice in a dark suit and tie with a crisp white shirt? His horns had grown enough to be noticeable through his hair. To remind her with every glance he was the man who'd kissed her senseless on the streets of the French Quarter. "How did your raid on the hotel go this morning? Did you catch them?"

A sudden darkness crossed his face and he looked away. She could have sworn she saw a shimmer of heat around him. "It was a bust. But I will get them. I swear it."

"That's too bad." She still thought she should have gone, but something about his earnestness dissolved most of her anger. Today of all days, there should be peace between them. "Is there anything else I can read for you? Like I did with the jacket?"

When he faced her, his eyes held surprise. "I appreciate that. I really do. Why don't we talk about it after we get through today?"

"Okay." Relieved that her offer of help hadn't turned into anything immediate, she pointed at his throat. "Your tie's a little crooked."

He reached for it, then came around to the hall mirror to adjust it. "Thanks."

She walked down the last step and stood beside him at the mirror. "I see you rehung it." Until today, the mirror had been leaning against the foyer wall. She pointed to the black cloth draping the top of the frame. "Is that some sort of New Orleans tradition?"

He nodded, tie now straightened. "It's a fae tradition."

She turned her gaze to the small table in front of the mirror, which now held a portrait of Olivia, also draped in black. "I don't know anything about those sorts of things."

She could feel his eyes on her, but refused to look at him when he spoke. To be sucked in by that hypnotic gaze of his. "I didn't, either, until I hooked up with my crew. I learned some more when your mother took me in. I still don't know as much as I should."

That brought her head up. "*My* mother taught you about fae stuff?"

He nodded solemnly. "Some of the history, yes. She wasn't as versed in it as some are, but she knew enough people to get answers for things she didn't know."

"I guess your own mother didn't teach you much." Even as she said the words, she knew she had no right to broach that subject with him.

"The only thing she taught me was to be ashamed of what I was. Just like her."

A prickly silence strung out between them.

Finally, Harlow broke it. "Olivia…always wanted me to embrace being fae." She shook her head. "I never understood that. And then, after things changed—"

"You mean after the covenant was broken?"

She nodded. "When humans suddenly realized that all these nightmare creatures were real and living among them, when they could see the othernaturals for what they really were, I was so happy that I'd distanced myself from her."

"Because of the way she came out?"

Harlow remembered the online articles, the pictures, the exposés. "Entertainment news was filled with stories about what stars were othernaturals." She exhaled hard. "The joy those rags took in revealing that Olivia Goodwin, beloved 'vampire queen,' was actually fae was disgusting."

"I remember that. Your mother didn't think it was disgusting.

She really enjoyed the press. And the bump in royalties from the new interest in her work."

Harlow laughed and glanced at the ceiling. "Of course she did. Meanwhile, I was praying no one would link us." But then, how would they? She'd been living under a screen name for years by then. She turned away from the photo, her throat thick with emotion. "This is really hard for me to say, but I'm glad you were here for her. I'm glad she had someone who . . . who . . . was everything I wasn't."

She started to walk away but he put his hand on her shoulder, the warmth seeping through to her skin comforting in a way she hadn't expected. "I can't believe I forgot to tell you this, but her last words to me were 'Tell Harlow I love her.' I'm sorry I'm just telling you this now, but it's true. She did love you. Deeply."

Harlow just shook her head, unable to speak for a moment until the wave of pain in her chest subsided. "Thanks for letting me know."

The doorbell rang, cutting off further conversation. Lally came out from the back of the house, dressed in a black skirt suit. "Don't you two look nice." She pointed toward the parlor. "If y'all want a minute with Miss Olivia before the crowds come, I can hold them off. Or you can wait until we leave for the cemetery to have some last words."

Augustine stepped out of Harlow's way. "Why don't you go ahead? I've had lots of time alone with her."

She balked. "No, I'm good."

He raised a brow. "You sure?"

"Yes. I can wait until we get through all these people." A little sigh and she looked at Lally. "Go ahead, let them in."

Augustine leaned down. "You really do look beautiful. And I know you're dreading dealing with all these people, but I'm happy to handle them. Just stay next to me and I'll do the heavy lifting." He reached into his suit pocket and took out his LMD.

"In fact, why don't we exchange numbers? That way if you can't find me and you need me, I'm just a call away. You can do that, right? I'm really not that great with that thing yet."

She pulled her own from her pocket as she narrowed her eyes at him. The last time he'd been this chivalrous, they'd been up against a wall in the Quarter, his mouth moments from hers. If he thought that was going to happen again... She exhaled hard. "Why are you being so nice to me? I don't mean to sound cynical, but what's up?"

After unlocking his device, he handed it to her. "Nothing's up. And you do sound cynical." His brows knit together. "I'm being nice because I have no reason not to. Today is going to be a tough day for both of us and facing it as a team will make it easier."

She opened her mouth but realized she had nothing to say. The idea of the two of them as a team was not something she'd contemplated. Ever. But it wasn't completely unpalatable. She nodded, then with both LMDs in one hand, tugged a glove off with her teeth. She tucked it under her arm. "This will just take a second."

He nodded and looked toward the front door. She took the opportunity to do more than dupe their contact info. With her bare fingers on his LMD, she pushed her way into the GPS circuitry and added a little something extra.

"People are coming in now."

She handed his LMD back. "All done. Thank you for offering your number. That was nice." She slipped her glove back on and took a deep breath.

The first couple was done talking to Lally, who looked back at Harlow with sympathetic eyes.

Augustine cupped her elbow. "We should go into the parlor."

Even his touch reminded her of that night, the way he'd gotten her out of the crowd when she'd started to freak out. She let him guide her until she faced the baby grand piano, the sight of her mother's urn erasing all other thoughts. The top of the piano had been covered with a colorful fringed shawl and on top of that was another large portrait of Olivia, flanked by enormous sprays of spring-hued flowers. At the side of the portrait was a milky glass urn with all the colors of the rainbow swirled through it.

Her mother was in there. The thought struck her with such clarity that she stopped as if rooted to the spot. "It's so...final. And bright."

Augustine stopped beside her. "In that regard, it's very Olivia."

Harlow nodded. "Yes, that much I know about her." The whole room was done up in flowers and greenery and the seating had been rearranged to allow more space around the piano. "She probably would have loved this."

Augustine smiled sadly. "That's a safe bet. According to Lally, she planned all of this, right down to the urn."

Harlow shook her head, almost amused by it all. "She always had a plan, didn't she?"

The couple that had been at the door entered the room and she could hear more people coming in behind them. Her heartbeat kicked up a notch as the panic of being around so many people in *this* situation settled over her.

As if sensing her distress, Augustine put his hand on the small of her back and directed her to a nearby chair, then he set off to face the fray. She sat there, watching him steer people away from her or into the dining room for food and a new realization began to take the place of the panic.

This place and these people, Augustine and Lally, weren't so bad after all. They'd loved her mother and her mother had loved them. Olivia had loved this city, too, despite its wear around the edges and unrepentantly shady past. Enough so that she'd given up Hollywood and made a home here.

A home Olivia had mistakenly thought she could persuade Harlow to live in while she attended Tulane. Instead, Harlow had run in the other direction and gone to MIT. Olivia's bitter disappointment had resulted in package after package of New Orleans–themed goodies.

A little half smile curved her mouth as she remembered the King cakes. Olivia had kept sending them every Mardi Gras season, even after Harlow had graduated. She'd never admitted it to her mother, but they were one of her deepest guilty pleasures.

Maybe the time had come for Harlow to make a new plan of her own. Two years of jail time—maybe less for good behavior—and she'd be free to make a new start. Half of this house was hers and that was ten times more space than she had in her cramped apartment. And with Augustine and Lally here, she wouldn't have to worry the house wasn't being taken care of while she was incarcerated.

She looked over at the photo of her mother. Olivia was smiling like she knew what Harlow was going to do. Maybe she did. Maybe that's what the fortune-teller had been talking about when she'd said a parent was going to put her in danger and she'd see an enemy in a new light. Living here would definitely qualify as dangerous. She'd be outside of her comfort zone, forced to interact with living breathing people, not just avatars and screen names.

And if Augustine was the enemy, then yes, she was certainly seeing him in a new light. He wore the role of Guardian well. Almost as well as that suit.

With a deep breath, Harlow stood and went to join him. If she was going to live here, she might as well try to figure out what else her mother had been so in love with.

⚜

When the black-gloved hand reached out from beside him to welcome someone, Augustine almost jerked back in shock. Instead, he met Harlow's amber gaze and raised his brows in question. She gave him a shrug that seemed resigned but not unhappy. More like she was prepared to deal with whatever the day held. She stayed with him for a while, eventually leaving his side to show some new people where the food was set up in the dining room.

A few minutes later, Lally came in and pulled him aside. "What did you do to that child?"

"Who? Harlow?" Now what?

"Yes. She came into the kitchen and thanked me for everything I've done for her mama and for being such a good friend to her and for all the work I'd put into making this day everything Miss Olivia wanted it to be. Made me downright weepy." She pursed her lips. "You throw some kind of fae spell over her?"

"No, I swear." He held his hands up to show they were empty. "She does seem like she's had a change of heart, though." It gave him hope for…something he wasn't ready to put a name to yet.

Lally waggled her head. "Maybe all this death has given her a little come-to-Jesus moment and she's realized life's too short to be angry over what you can't change."

"Let's hope you're right." He glanced over Lally's brown curls. "Speaking of what you can't change…"

His half brother, Mortalis, walked through the archway leading into the great room. At his side was the comarré Chrysabelle, the woman Augustine had escorted to the fae plane and the reason he'd been forced to run from the Elektos.

Lally turned to look in the same direction. "Be kind, Augustine. Your brother's here to pay his respects, not cause you more grief."

"Let's hope you're right." He walked toward the other fae. "Mortalis. Chrysabelle."

The comarré spoke first as she embraced him in a quick hug. "I'm deeply sorry for your loss. Olivia was a truly amazing woman and I feel honored I was able to know her in the small way I did."

"Thank you." He looked at Mortalis. "Are you here because she wanted to come or are you here out of choice?"

"Choice. But also to accompany Chrysabelle." Mortalis shifted uncomfortably and made Augustine question how much he'd really wanted to come. "I know what Olivia meant to you and to the city. She was a good woman. Damn shame." Chrysabelle nudged him gently with her elbow. "Also, I'm... proud of you for taking the Guardianship."

Lost for words, Augustine stared at the fae across from him. Something was in the air today. They shared a father, but that's where the connection ended. There wasn't enough relationship between them to consider it a relationship. It was the same between Augustine and Blu, although she didn't seem to have much use for Mortalis, either, and they were full-blooded siblings.

"Say thank you, Augustine," Chrysabelle said quietly.

He nodded at his brother. "Thank you. That means a lot coming from you."

Mortalis returned the nod. "I know it wasn't under the best circumstances."

"That's for sure."

Mortalis, dressed in full fae leathers as per his usual, rested his hand on the dagger hilt protruding from his belt. "If you need me for anything, you know where to find me."

"That's unexpected. But appreciated." An offer of help? There was no more shock left in Augustine's system. He smiled at Chrysabelle. "I have a feeling you played a big part in this."

"A little." She smiled sadly. "I really did want to pay my respects."

"How did everything turn out for you after…" There were too many ears here for him to mention the Claustrum. "Our adventure?"

"Very well."

He glanced down at her flat belly. "And the baby?"

"With his father."

"Malcolm, right?"

She nodded. "Yes, and Malcolm and I are now married."

Augustine raised his brows. "That's pretty unusual for a vampire."

"So is having a kid," Mortalis added.

Chrysabelle laughed. "Oh, Uncle Morty, you love babysitting little Rafe."

"This might officially go down as the weirdest conversation I've ever had," Augustine said with a laugh. "Babysitting? Really?"

Chrysabelle patted Mortalis's shoulder. "He needs the practice."

Mortalis smiled suddenly. "Nyssa and I are about to have one of our own."

The smile was almost as shocking as the news, but Augustine did his best not to overreact. "Does this have anything to do with your new attitude toward me?"

Mortalis lifted one shoulder. "Maybe."

"Having a child changes everything," Chrysabelle added.

Apparently. "Rafe, huh?"

"Raphael," she said. "But Rafe suits him. He seems to know he's the only vampire-comarré hybrid in existence. He's…quite a handful at times."

Mortalis snorted. "He's exactly what Malcolm deserves."

"Maybe I'll get to meet the little terror someday. Like when my nephew is born." Augustine reached out and shook his brother's hand. "I really appreciate you coming. Both of you.

I need to talk to some more of the guests but please don't leave without saying goodbye."

"We won't," Chrysabelle assured him. She gave him another hug and a kiss on the cheek.

"Is Blu here?" Mortalis asked as they parted.

"Not yet, but I'm sure Loudreux will come, so it's only a matter of time." He'd kind of expected Loudreux to be the first to arrive since he was Prime, but so far he'd yet to show. If Loudreux didn't come, his half sister Blu most likely wouldn't be allowed to, either, unless she'd been given the day off.

The crowd in the house was almost overwhelming. He looked around for Harlow, but she wasn't anywhere he could see. He pushed through the crowd, finally finding her standing alone near the stairs. The house was too crowded to pick out her pulse, but she almost looked like she was cowering. "You okay?"

She straightened a bit and did a little shrug/nod thing that did nothing to reassure him. "There's a lot of people here."

"And there's a lot more to come." He grabbed a glass of water from a passing server and put it in her hands.

She took a sip. "That fae you were talking to looked a lot like you. Especially now that your horns are coming back in."

He looked toward where he'd been standing. She must have seen him with Mortalis. "He's my half brother."

"And the blonde with the crazy gold tattoos?"

Was that a hint of jealousy in Harlow's amber eyes? More like his own delusions. "Her name's Chrysabelle. She's a comarré."

"She's very pretty."

"She's very married." He let that sink in, casually adding, "To a vampire," without much thought.

Harlow's face went pale. "Why would anyone marry one of those monsters?" Horror clouded her eyes. "They killed my mother."

Damn it, that had not been the right thing to say. "Not that kind of vampire."

She glared at him. "There are other kinds? As in the kind that don't kill people?"

"It's complicated." Also not the best answer he'd ever given.

She set the water on the hall table and wrapped her arms around herself, the diamonds at her wrist twinkling before they slid beneath one glove. "What isn't complicated in this place? I thought I could do this. I don't know."

She was retreating fast and he wasn't sure how to stop it. "It's okay, it really is. You *can* do this. I'm here for you, Harlow." He tapped his chest. "Whatever you need, I'm here."

Her gaze went right through him. "People keep coming in."

He looked toward the door. Fenton was entering with a few people behind him. One of them was Evander. That was interesting. And unexpected, but perhaps the wizard was attempting to stay in the fae's good graces. Augustine returned his attention to Harlow. "I'll handle it. Why don't you take a break? Go up to your room for a little bit and get some peace."

She nodded, but something in her eyes said she was already a million miles away.

Chapter Twenty

M iss Harlow? It's time."

"Thank you, Lally." Harlow sat on the edge of the bed. She'd waited in her room until the last possible second. Now, judging by the quiet that had settled in, the throng of people who'd come to her mother's memorial had moved outside to follow the horse and buggy to the cemetery.

The break from the crowd had been a good thing and although trepidation still filled her, she wasn't going to miss this last chance to see her mother off. She slipped shoes on—her own flats this time for the walk to the cemetery—and headed down the steps to find Augustine.

Wearing an overcoat now, he stood in the foyer. She'd expected there to be some people still inside, but the space was wonderfully empty. He'd seen her near meltdown and hadn't judged her. In fact, he'd been kind and understanding. Amazing how a little shared emotion had changed things between them. He smiled when he saw her. "Feel better?"

She nodded. "Where did everyone go?"

"Some are outside still talking, but the rest went home. I know the crowd overwhelmed you, but I can't remember the last time so many people showed up to a memorial. There must have been over five hundred people through here. Livie would have loved it."

Harlow twisted her toe into the floor. "She would have, I'm sure. I, on the other hand, almost needed medicating."

"You did fine. Your mother liked her privacy, too, you know. You're probably more like her than you realize."

"I doubt that."

He took a coat off the hall rack and held it out to her. "It's turned a little cool now that the sun's going down. Even with your long sleeves, you'll want this."

She slid her arms into the coat. Her mother's perfume clung to it. "It *is* nice that so many people wanted to see her off. You said a lot of those people went home?"

"Livie wanted the interment to be private, so from here out it's really just us."

"You, me and Lally?"

He nodded. "And a few of her close friends and neighbors. Maybe twenty people, tops."

"Okay." She relaxed, exhaling softly.

"Easier to handle."

"Yes."

"Good. I'm guessing you've never seen or been part of a jazz funeral before, but it's pretty simple. We follow the buggy while the band plays some hymns, then after the interment, they'll play something happy as they leave and that's about it. Kind of the abbreviated version, but that's what Livie wanted."

"How far of a walk is it?"

"Couple of blocks. Not far from the Guardian's house, actually. You ready?"

She nodded, feeling slightly ill at ease again. She'd gone from thinking there was no way she could ever live here to thinking there was definitely a way if she had Augustine around to explain things. But she'd assumed that he'd be staying here, forgetting that he'd eventually move into the Guardian's house, taking Lally with him. Very soon, Harlow would be forced to head home to face the consequences of her hacking before she could come back here. If that was still what she wanted in two years. Actually, it might be all she had left after time served. Augustine would still look after the house, wouldn't he, seeing as it was half his?

Mind rushing with new concerns, she walked with him to the door and down the steps. The small group of people had left a space between them and the buggy. Lally was already there waiting. She held a hand out as if to say, "Right here, next to me."

Harlow took the spot, then Augustine fell into place beside her. The buggy driver nodded to the band in front and they began to play what sounded like "Nearer My God to Thee" and they were off, slowly.

Her mother's urn sat strapped onto some sort of flat platform at the back of the buggy and high enough that it could be seen. The multicolored glass urn almost glowed with the rays of the setting sun glinting off it. Augustine was right. Olivia would have loved this. It almost felt like she was there in some way.

When they arrived at the cemetery, two police officers stood at the gates, nodding as the small party of mourners went in. They assembled around a crypt where a man with a Layman Brothers Funeral Home badge stood waiting in a black suit. He took the urn from the buggy driver, said a few words, then went into the crypt. When he came back out, he thanked everyone for coming.

The band assembled behind them broke into "When the Saints Come Marching In." The mourners began to file out, but neither Lally nor Augustine moved, so Harlow stayed right where she was.

As distance muted the music, Augustine looked at her. "You want to go in? You can."

"Into the crypt?"

Lally unpinned the red carnation from her coat. "It's all right, child. Ain't no boogeyman in there." She walked up the steps and into the crypt, returning a minute later without the carnation.

"I don't have a flower—"

Augustine held out a long-stemmed red rose to her. She hadn't seen him holding it. Maybe he'd pulled it from the spray on the buggy when they came in. She took it and went inside.

The urn was set into a niche in the wall. There were other urns, and some caskets, too, but she forced her mind to blank them out and concentrate on the only one that mattered. She set her flower beside Lally's carnation. "I'm sorry," she whispered. "I really wish things had been different between us. I do love you. And I will...try to be more like the person—the fae— you wanted me to be. Someday." Her mother would understand what she meant.

She stepped back outside. A sharply dressed man approached the crypt. Augustine put Lally behind him and moved to stand in the man's path. "Can I help you?"

The man stopped, his gaze coming to rest on Harlow for a moment before he answered. "I'd like to speak to Harlow."

The small hairs on the back of her neck stood at attention for no reason she could name other than the way Augustine was acting. If he thought the man was dangerous, she was happy to go along with that. He stayed where he was, blocking the man's path. "Who are you and what's your business with her?"

The man had a high, sloped forehead and when he smiled, his eyes crinkled in a way that shouldn't have seemed threatening, but gave her a strange vibe. "That's between Harlow and me."

She came down the steps but kept some distance between her and the man. "What's your name?" Was he a creditor? A CCU agent? Could they have tracked her here? Of course they could have. Damn it. Her fine wasn't due for at least three more weeks.

"My name is Joseph Branzino." He held the smile while he looked at Harlow. "I'm your father."

"I don't like this." Augustine paced the kitchen while Lally cleaned up the few remaining things the caterers had left behind. The way that man had laid claim to Harlow didn't sit right. "I don't like him, I don't like how readily she agreed to talk to him, I don't like how he just showed up."

Lally sighed heavily, shaking her head. "I don't like it, either. And I know Miss Olivia didn't like him, but that's Harlow's father. Of course she's going to talk to him. Child's been trying to find out who he was for years. Miss Olivia told her he was dead, for land's sake."

"How do we know that's her father? Did Livie ever tell you the man's name?"

"Never." She sank a pot into hot water. "Miss Olivia never talked about him except to say he was bad, bad news. Poison, she called him. You think he's making it up? That he ain't really her father?"

"Maybe. Harlow's set to inherit a lot of property."

"Man looks like he has plenty of his own, but I see your point." Lally set the kettle on for tea.

"I'm not okay with this."

"I don't feel that good about it myself." She pulled cups from one of the cabinets. "But what can we do? If Harlow wants to talk to him, who are we to say she can't?"

"She can talk to him. But I don't have to like him. Especially not if Livie thought he was poison. In fact—" A knock at the back door kept Augustine from going on. He opened it. "Fenton. Come in."

Leather doctor-style bag in hand, the Elektos walked into the kitchen. "What's going on? You seem agitated."

"A man showed up at the cemetery claiming to be Harlow's biological father." He looked at the bag. "Are those the ashes?"

Fenton nodded. "Yes. I replaced the liner bag with another filled with wood ash. It won't hold up if it's checked, but I can't imagine that happening."

Augustine shrugged. "And if they do? So what. Livie wanted her ashes spread on the fae plane and that's all that matters to me. If they say we can't keep her urn in the cemetery, we'll bring it home."

Fenton looked toward the interior of the house. "This man who claims to be Harlow's father, you think he's not?"

"I think it's bloody convenient he showed up now. And apparently, Olivia never liked him, either."

Lally worried a lace-edged handkerchief. "Even though I believe the child should talk to him if she wants to, I agree with Augustine. The man's timing makes a person wonder."

Augustine ran a hand through his hair. "Harlow's vulnerable right now. The thought of getting a crack at a relationship with the one parent who's been kept from her all these years might be more than she can resist."

Fenton pulled out a chair and sat. "What do you know about him? Is he fae? Do you at least have a name?"

"Joseph Branzino. And yes, he's fae, but I don't know what kind. He's hiding it somehow, but I can still tell."

Fenton took out his LMD and started tapping on it. He expanded something, then turned the screen around so Augustine could see it. "This the man talking to Harlow?"

"That's him."

Fenton started reading from the copy beneath the picture. "Says here he's a businessman from Chicago. Imports and exports."

The kettle whistled. Lally removed it from the fire and added the hot water to the teapot. "I told you he had money."

Fenton tapped the screen dark, tucked the LMD away and stood. "The info online is suspiciously tidy. Let me dig a little deeper with our resources and see what I can find out. Also, I couldn't find anything unusual about Petrick Hayden, but I'll continue to dig."

"Good. I'll come by in the morning and we can talk about this more." Augustine nodded at the bag on the table. "And thanks for helping me with Olivia."

"It's what we do." Fenton tipped his head at Lally. "Ms. Hughes."

As he left, Lally brought the teapot to the table. "You going to take those ashes to the fae plane now?"

"Not yet." Augustine stared toward the library. He wanted to barge in, see what was going on. Make sure everything was okay. "Not while there's the slightest chance Harlow's in danger."

Her father was *alive*. Every nerve in Harlow's body pinged with energy. She was nervous and scared and excited and incredulous all at the same time. Hell, she was that and more. Sitting still took a lot of effort. She wanted to stand, to pace, to expend some of what was coursing through her. But more than that, she wanted answers. Fortunately, the man across from her seemed interested in providing them. "Why did you wait so long to contact me?"

Joseph's smile went sad. "Olivia made me promise. When I saw that she'd passed on—may she rest in peace—I no longer felt obliged to that promise."

That made sense, didn't it? "I see." She had so many questions, but she also had doubt. "I don't mean to sound...that is, how do I know..." She bit her lip. "It's just that I have no way of knowing if you're really my father."

He nodded. "I understand that. If I were in your position, I'm sure I'd have doubts, too." He touched his chest. "It's my own fault we're starting at zero. I should have pushed your mother more to let me be a part of your life, but..." He shrugged. "Your mother was a very stubborn woman."

Harlow smiled. "She was that. She told me you were dead."

He snorted softly. "That sounds like her." He shook his head. "Look, I'd be happy to submit to a blood test, if that would make you more comfortable."

"That's very kind of you," she said. But it would never happen. Determining paternity would mean testing her blood, too, and that would reveal just how much fae she had in her, something she preferred not to know. "Why do you think my mother refused to tell me anything about you? She talked about you like you were...not a good person." That was putting it mildly.

His head dropped. "After you were born, I lost my head a little. I tried to get custody of you. Sole custody. It turned into something very ugly. I'm not surprised your mother wouldn't tell you about me. She was probably afraid she'd lose you to me."

"Why didn't you try to contact me?"

"Like I said, it got ugly. There were...documents restricting what I could do." He waved his hands like he was trying to make the past go away. "I would do anything to make it possible for us to be family now. To make up for all the years I've missed out on."

She liked the sound of that, even if she didn't totally believe a man like this would let documents keep him from doing anything. Maybe it was something he wasn't ready to talk about. She could understand that, but he had better be ready to talk about *some* things. "Can I ask you something personal?"

He slid forward on the couch, inching closer. "Sure, sweetheart. Ask me anything you like."

She licked her lips. His answer could end this conversation very quickly. "You're human, right?"

For a nanosecond, he looked shocked, but his expression smoothed out, going right back to the calm demeanor he'd had the whole time. He shrugged like it was nothing to be concerned with. "Of course, I'm human." He laughed. "I have a little fae in me, but not enough to matter." He tipped his head and sat back. "And not nearly as much as your mother, I might add, although she liked to hide it."

She'd expected him to deny or embrace, but this casualness threw her. And destroyed the belief she'd always had that her biological father was completely human. How much fae did he have? Was there any way he could be behind the strength of her abilities? How much more fae was Olivia than she'd let on?

Nothing she'd wanted to believe had turned out to be true. Her spirits sank a little.

"You okay?"

"I'm fine." Disappointed, but it was better knowing.

His suit fabric had an expensive sheen to it and the lines looked like it had been cut for him. Which it probably had. He adjusted his jacket. "Can I ask you a question?"

She ran her thumbnail down the seam of her leggings. "Sure. Fair is fair."

His laugh came out low and throaty. "Funny. I say that all the time."

"You do?"

He held his hands out like he was holding dinner plates. "Fair is fair. That's my thing."

She sat back, realizing a second later she was smiling along with him. Maybe it was okay that her father had a little fae in him, especially when it didn't seem like it was keeping him from being normal. Her *father*. The word got more comfortable by the minute. "What did you want to ask me?"

He spiraled a finger in the air, gesturing to the room around him. "This house. I'm guessing it's yours now. You need any money for the upkeep? I know a place like this can't be cheap and I'd be happy to help you out."

"Are you serious?" A tiny spark of hope flared to life inside her like a phoenix rising from the ashes.

"That's what a father does, you know?" He smiled sheepishly. "I've known about you all your life. No matter what you think of me, to me you'll always be my little girl."

An overwhelming rush of new emotion swept through her. She did her best to tamp down her excitement and focus on getting to know this man before she became indebted to him. "Do I have brothers and sisters?"

"Three brothers, but one is deceased—may he rest in peace." Joseph crossed himself. "I'd be happy for you to meet them when you're ready. As for daughters, you're my one and only."

She sat quietly, trying to process everything. His only daughter. Surely he'd want to keep her from prison, wouldn't he? She shook her head. That was a crass thought, born out of her own desperation. She would *not* ask him for money.

"Something wrong, sweetheart?"

She forced a little smile. "This is a lot for me to take in."

He picked up his hat from the cushion next to him. "I should go, give you time to think and all that." He stood. "Maybe I could come see you tomorrow? Or I could take you out to dinner? Whatever you like."

"Sure." She had so many more questions. So much more to discuss. With her *father*. The word made her giddy.

He pulled a card from his pocket. "Here's my number. You can call or text me with whatever you'd like to do. Even if... you don't want me to come around anymore."

She stood and took the card. It was thick white stock with engraved black lettering. A pretty fancy card considering most people exchanged info electronically these days. His business must really be successful. How could Olivia have thought he was such a bad guy? Because he wanted custody of his daughter? Because he'd *wanted* to be a father? "About the house..."

"Yeah?"

"I don't own it. Not all of it. And even if I did, I wouldn't be keeping it. I'd sell it in a heartbeat." Well, maybe not a heartbeat, but for some unnamed reason she didn't want him to think she cared about this place too much.

"What do you mean not all of it?"

"Olivia's will left me exactly half. The other half went to Augustine, the fae who was with me at the cemetery. Supposedly, the estate can pretty much run itself with my mother's investments. But your offer was very generous and kind, considering you hardly know me."

"Half the freaking house?" His face took on a cruel twist. "What was your mother playing at?"

Harlow held the card with both hands. Olivia loved her games. "I have a feeling, but it's fine, really. Things have a way of working themselves out."

"Can you buy the other half off this chump, Augustine?"

Her father's assessment of Augustine rankled more than expected. "Mr. Branzino, Augustine isn't a chump. He's been very nice to me—"

Branzino snorted. "Sweetheart, you're a beautiful woman who stands between him and the other half of this place. I can't imagine he'd be anything *but* nice to you."

"I..." The idea that Augustine might think her beautiful had thrown her more than Branzino's idea that Augustine was playing her. Imagine if Branzino knew they'd already kissed. And that she'd liked it, despite not wanting to. "I don't think—"

"What's he want for his half? How much does he want for you to buy him out?"

"We haven't discussed it. Well, not exactly."

"But he gave you a price, am I right?"

She felt a little ill as she nodded. Maybe her father's assessment wasn't that far off. "He did. Five million."

Branzino whistled. "The boy's got a pair, I'll give him that." He buttoned his overcoat. "Tell him you'll give him two. He says no, you go as high as four. When he says yes, you call me and I'll take care of it."

"Take care of it?" She stared at him, knowing what he was saying but not really comprehending. "You mean give me the money?"

He winked at her. "For my baby girl? You betcha."

Chapter Twenty-one

As soon as Augustine heard the front door close, he raced to the foyer. Harlow stood there, her back against the door, looking a little dazed. He tried to judge her mood. "You okay?"

She nodded, eyes still not focused on him. "Yeah, I'm good, but I have a lot to think about."

"Like whether or not he's really your father?"

Finally, she made eye contact. "I'm pretty sure he's my father."

Augustine snorted derisively. "On what grounds? How conveniently he timed his appearance?"

She raised her hand. "Enough, okay? I have a lot in my head right now and I don't need your opinion mucking it all up."

He stepped back. "Excuse me for caring. You run hot and cold, you know that? Makes it really hard to be friends with you when I don't know—"

"I'm not my mother. I don't need you to be friends with me. And I don't need you to protect me."

His expression softened. "I know what it's like to wonder about your father."

"Do you? Then you know what that hole inside of your heart feels like, that hole that can't be filled because the piece that fits there is missing. I've lived with that all my life and that's long enough."

"I guess I understand that. I never knew my father—still don't—but I can't say it's had that much effect on me. Maybe because he didn't care enough about me to make the effort, either, so—"

"Olivia kept my father away from me with a court order because he wanted custody of me. He *wanted* to be my father and she wouldn't let him." She pushed off the door and strode past him, clomping up the steps like she was on a mission. The slam of her bedroom door followed.

"Damn it," he muttered. Branzino must have done something to upset her. That was the only explanation he could come up with for Harlow's reaction.

"What's the racket?" Lally came out from the kitchen, a tea towel slung over her shoulder.

With a final glance upstairs, he shook his head. "I'm not sure things went so well with Harlow and her"—he made air quotes—"father."

"Uh-uh." She shook her head. "I do *not* like that man and I do not like all this chaos in this house. It ain't healthy." She pointed upstairs. "And that child got enough on her plate with her mother being dead. If her daddy's going to come out of nowhere and cause trouble, I might have to have a talk with him myself."

Augustine bit back a smile. "Hold on, there, Lally. I know you mean well, but until we know exactly who this Branzino character is, I don't think either one of us should confront him."

"Maybe you're right." She frowned as she spoke.

"I know. It's hard to wrap your head around me being the reasonable one, isn't it?"

"It is." She laughed. "Miss Olivia would never believe it."

"Speaking of which... now that our visitor is gone, I'll go take care of her final wish."

Lally's smile evened out. "I'll fetch the bag for you."

"I'll go grab my return mirror and change."

"Don't change." Lally's gaze traveled the length of him. "You look so nice in your suit. Seems fitting you wear it for this one last thing, don't you think?"

"I suppose so."

"Good. I'll bring you the ashes and the same mirror you borrowed last time." She went back to the kitchen, returning shortly. "Here you go." Her hand stayed on the purple satin bag holding Olivia's ashes a second longer than necessary. "If you see her... you tell her I took care of everything just like she wanted, okay?"

"I will. And I'll tell her how beautifully you did it, too." He tucked the mirror into his suit pocket and held on to the satin bag with his other hand, wrapping the gold drawstring around his palm. "Back soon."

She nodded and stepped back.

He faced the mirror and just like the last time, filled his being with thoughts of Olivia, mentally urging the mirror to take him to wherever she was. The pull of the magic caught him and on a blink, he opened his eyes to see the gray plane of the Claustrum. Again.

The wind howled, tearing past him in a quick burst that scoured his face and hands with grit. He squinted as his suit jacket flew out behind him like a sail. This was no kind of weather to scatter ashes in.

He questioned going back, but then, as if something greater understood his purpose, the wind died away. A few slim gusts raced past, but nothing as harsh as the first.

"Livie, if you're here, and I hope you're not, I also hope you can find a way out. There are so many better places your soul could roam."

He raised the bag of ashes. "For you, Olivia Goodwin. May you find your peace, wherever that is."

Working the knotted cord loose, he opened the bag, got the wind against his back and shook the contents out.

The ashes drifted down, then a breeze caught them and

whirled them into a cyclone. The wind picked up, whipping the cyclone faster and higher. His mouth opened. The spinning mass began to take on a very recognizable shape.

"Livie?" He breathed the word out on a whisper. The ashes spun faster, tighter, higher and as they did, the faint scent of lemon verbena wafted toward him. It *was* Livie. Somehow. He yelled her name and the ash golem reached out for him.

He moved toward her, his hand out to take hers.

Her lips moved. "Augie..." But the sound was so faint he questioned whether it was a voice or the wind whining in his ears.

Before he reached her, another howling gust shoved against him, pushing him back and filling his eyes with grit. It ripped the bag from his hand. He grabbed at it, but it belonged to the wind now. He coughed, blinking hard. Then the wind disappeared and the ash figure was gone. He twisted, searching the plane for her. Nothing.

In the relentless gray around him, it was impossible to even tell where the ashes had fallen.

He'd had some hope before, a tiny, foolish amount that had clung despite all reason, but now not even that remained. Olivia was truly gone. The truth pressed on him heavier than anything he'd felt before.

A slip of air brushed past his cheek so light it could almost be a caress. He scowled and turned away from it, bitter at the plane for its sour magic.

"Damn this place." He pulled out his borrowed mirror and slipped home to stand on ground he could trust.

"Deliver the list."

Giselle refused to move. Her father had lost his mind. She glanced once at the envelope he held out to her, then shook her head. "He asked you for it, not me. If you don't want to go yourself, send a messenger. Surely he can't expect to have you at his beck and call."

Evander raised his hands skyward. "I told him at the memorial you would be by with it later. It's later. You need to take it."

Her cheek spasmed from clenching her jaw shut. There was no way out of this. Continuing to refuse would anger her father to the point where she'd spend more energy getting back into his good graces than she cared to waste. She snatched the list from his hand. "You owe me."

He shook his head. "You foolish girl. Without that list, he will pull your license. If you can't practice, how will you live?"

She thought of her private clients, the elite of New Orleans who paid dearly for her spells and detailed readings. She needed that business to survive. "He wouldn't do that to me."

"To you and every other member of the coven until he gets what he wants. He promised as much. Starting with you."

"Bastard."

"Watch your language, girl. You're still my daughter and you still represent me and the New Orleans Circle. Be careful you don't do anything to harm our reputation."

"You think I could harm our reputation? Spare me, Daddy. You think the tourists that come here seeking us out for the spells and potions do that because they respect us?" She laughed. "We're a sideshow to them. A strange band of misfits who hug trees and worship flowers and dance skyclad under the full moon.

"And do you know why they think that?" She slapped a hand on his desk. "Because that's all the fae will let us be. They've castrated us like dogs. We had power, but we've become too afraid to use it and now so few of us remember how to call up that kind of strength, we have no choice but to limp along under the weight of the fae thumb."

An angry cloud shadowed his face. "And what? You'd change all that if given the chance? How, you stupid girl? The fae are greater than we are."

"Only because you let them. You and the last few wizards before you." Her heart pounded. She'd thought this way many times, but had never spoken the words to her father, although she was sure none of this was a shock to him.

"You don't understand a thing." Her father's face went ruddy with rage. "He's got evidence that black magic was used to murder a vampire. I can only presume it was the vampire arrested in connection to the last Guardian's murder. I am trying to protect us. I am already working angles you can't imagine. Stop fighting me."

An image of a charm she'd recently bespelled filled her head. She shoved it away, then stepped back, raising the list. "Is my name on this list?"

He heaved out a sigh. "Are you listening to me, girl? I just said I am trying to protect us. No, not your name, nor mine nor your sister's. Will you ever trust me? I know what I'm doing."

She nodded, thankful that her father was willing to do that much. "I will deliver this for you. And I apologize if I am… enthusiastic about returning to the old ways. I see so much potential for us, but as long as the fae collar us with their regulations, we'll never get there."

His face softened at her words, exactly her desired effect. "Giselle, Giselle." He shook his head and sat heavily in his chair. "Your mother…"

She held very still, afraid the slightest thing might keep him from going further.

He looked out the window. "You're so much like her. She felt the same way. Pushed me to break the treaty with the fae, to find some way to allow us more freedom." He paused, swallowing down something painful.

Giselle had an idea of what that was. "She didn't kill herself because of you," she said softly. That was a burden they'd all dealt with, but her father most of all.

He laughed once, short and sharp. "She didn't kill herself at all."

"What?"

"Not intentionally, anyway." He shook himself as if an old memory had gotten stuck. "She was performing the *ruina vox.*" He wiped a hand over his mouth. "She lost control of it and the spell turned inward. The only thing she destroyed was herself."

Giselle reached for the chair beside her and fell into it. All these years she'd thought her mother weak for committing suicide. And all these years it had been a lie. "Why tell everyone she killed herself then?"

The sadness on his face was instantly replaced with anger. "Tell the world she was killed performing chaos magic? That she'd intended to destroy the fae with it? How would that be better?" He shook his head as the anger faded. "I did what was necessary to protect the coven, but mostly you and Zara."

"You did what you did to protect the status quo." She stood, newly energized. "You made her out to be weak and incapable of dealing with life. At least she died trying to make a difference."

"Giselle—"

"Save it." She headed for the door. "I've had more than enough conversation for one day."

She slammed his office door and left the house before he could come after her. Not that he would. His world was too comfortable and didn't require her assistance. She glanced at the list in her hand. Except for the fact that he'd kept her off the list, she was just another member of the circle to him. One that needed to be controlled. Had he also controlled her mother that way? Was that why she'd struck out on her own? Why they'd divorced?

Giselle pulled her coat tighter against the evening air. The sidewalks were almost empty. She got her bearings and headed for Augustine's. What else was her father lying about? Were there details of the treaty she didn't know? Did Augustine really have proof of black magic being used or was that Evander's way of getting her to do as he wished?

Zara would have to be told the truth about their mother, although Giselle couldn't predict how her sister would react. Perhaps plant a tree in her mother's memory. That is, *another* tree. Although, to be fair, Zara did live in their mother's house, which is where she'd died. Had she performed the *ruina vox* in the house or in the garden? A spell that big needed space. Had to be the garden.

Giselle almost stopped walking. Did Zara already know the story about their mother's suicide was a lie? Zara was a green witch, and a very powerful one. If the garden had secrets to tell, Zara was powerful enough to find them out. But why would she not share that information? She must not know. Zara wasn't the kind to keep something like that hidden, even if it meant protecting their father.

Augustine's house was up ahead. Enough lights shone from inside that someone had to be home. She opened the gate and walked up the steps to the double glass doors. Even in the porch light they sparkled. She pushed the doorbell.

He didn't keep her waiting long. "Giselle. What is it?"

His sharp response almost made her snap, but his suit reminded her today had not been an easy day for him. She almost let it slide. "Weren't you expecting me? I have the list you asked for." She dug the envelope out of her coat pocket and offered it to him.

"Yes, I was. Just…a lot going on." He took the list, then opened the door a little wider. "Come in."

She hadn't expected the invite. "I was just going to drop that off."

"These names don't tell me anything about the person. I need to go over this with you and ask questions."

Sighing and not caring what he thought, she stepped inside. "For the record, I'm against this."

He frowned. "Going over the list? Or coming in? Afraid someone will see you fraternizing with the enemy?"

She almost said yes, then caught herself. "I'm against you asking for a list of coven members who *might* be performing prohibited types of magic and I'm against my father agreeing to it."

"True to type, then." He walked down the hall, crooking his finger for her to follow.

She followed. "What's that supposed to mean?" The room they went in was a library about three times the size of her father's, but there was no way the books in here held the kind of power her father's did.

Augustine slid the pocket doors shut after she entered. "It means it's what I expected of you. You're the rebellious daughter. You clearly don't like the rules the Elektos have imposed on your people. I'd have been far more surprised if you'd thought the list was a good idea." He sat and tore the envelope open, then slipped the paper out and started reading.

She sat on the couch opposite him, looking around the room while she waited. From the books to the paintings to the objets d'art, the place dripped in valuables. A glass case against one wall caught her eye. It was illuminated from above and the book within seemed to glow in that way of old books made of onionskin paper. Augustine was still reading, so she got up to take a closer look.

The glass reflected her face back at her, the shock in her eyes plainly visible. "Is this real?"

"Yes."

The voice came from directly beside her and she jumped. Augustine was no longer on the couch but right next to her. Damn his fae quietness. She turned, using the move to put a little distance between them. Her finger tapped the glass. "You're telling me this is a genuine Gutenberg Bible?"

He nodded. "Livie loved books and this was one of her favorites."

"They're extremely rare. And very expensive." A million dollars? Maybe more? She wasn't sure about the amount, just that it was very high. But nothing compared to the power in such a thing.

"I think she loved it more for its rareness and content than its value." He held the list up, the paper folded the way it had been in the envelope. "The New Orleans Circle is nearly five hundred members with what, twice as many novices waiting to be confirmed? There are *twenty-nine* people on this list." His gray-green eyes darkened. "I'm sure your father told you what I would do if I didn't get this list."

"He did, but you got the list." She crossed her arms. "And making good on that threat? Not really a road you want to go down. Pulling licenses makes for a good scare tactic, but in reality it will only create enemies. And it won't stop any of us from practicing." She tipped her head and smiled sweetly. "You don't want to be *that* Guardian, do you?"

He stepped into her personal space, his gaze pinning her to the spot. "I'm already *that* Guardian. If I don't get the corrected list by nine tomorrow morning, your license will be revoked by one minute after. Am I clear?"

She snatched the paper from his hand. "Clearly insane." She marched away from him, glad she'd kept her coat on.

He followed her into the hall. "I have murderers to find. Maybe you don't get that."

She spun to face him. "You have vampires to find. We're witches. There's a difference. Or maybe *you* don't get *that*."

He opened his mouth to say something, then abruptly turned to look at the big mirror hanging on the wall beside them. "Do you smell that?"

"What?"

He moved toward the gaudy gold mirror. "Lemon verbena. Her scent." His fingers traced the outside edges of the frame.

"Who?"

"Olivia Goodwin." But he was focused on the mirror, staring into it like he could see beyond the glass.

She held her tongue and took a closer look. Something was off about the mirror. The glass wavered like it had a watery depth to it. Like you could stick your hand into it almost. Something shadowy darted through the main field of vision. She jerked back. "What magic is this? Who bespelled this glass?"

He looked at her. "Why? Tell me what you see."

The desperate longing in his eyes almost undid her. "I can't see anything, but I can tell that this mirror is more than it seems. Like something is trying to get out." Telling him more would only lead to questions she couldn't answer. "Is this mirror a portal to somewhere? This is gray magic at best. You shouldn't play with it."

Annoyance erased the longing. "I'm not playing. I am trying to help a friend." He ran his hands over the nubs of his horns. "Out. Please. I have work to do. I'll see you tomorrow morning."

She backed toward the door, sketching a sarcastic bow. "As you wish, Guardian."

But her insolence was lost on him. He was already leaning into the glass and whispering something she couldn't quite hear.

Whatever that mirror was, it was important to Augustine. She put her hand on the doorknob. Something he wouldn't want damaged or destroyed. The kind of thing that might make a valuable bargaining chip. She stored that away and smiled as she walked out of the house.

He'd better think twice before revoking her license. Glass was very fragile. A mirror that large could be broken so easily.

Chapter Twenty-two

Harlow dragged herself out of bed, the seductive scent of coffee too much for her to ignore, and pulled some clothes on. Not even eight o'clock yet. After her late night, she'd expected to sleep longer, but the excitement of finally knowing who her father was wouldn't let her rest.

She'd worked well into the early morning, scouring the Web for information on Joseph Branzino and hardly finding much more than when she hadn't known her father's name. For someone with her skills, that could mean only two things. One, he was one of those very rare people who truly had no interest in social media or publicity and had managed to maintain a nearly infinitesimal online presence. Or, two, his lack of online presence was carefully cultivated by a team of erasers, which seemed much more plausible.

Considering Branzino's claim of being a businessman, she chose to believe the latter. It made sense. Very wealthy people often hired erasers to protect them from the kinds of electronic mischief so blatant online these days. It had been worse before the Great War, when electricity was less expensive and connectivity almost an innate right.

But even consciously believing that was a little tricky. She'd done some erasing work herself. Whoever he'd hired was good. As good as she was. And she was *really* good. She'd yet to meet an eraser better than her, one that didn't leave some tiny trace of info, some little footprint that led her to a back door somewhere. An overseas bank account. A dummy corporation. *Something.*

Branzino had none of that. The best she could unearth was the names of his two sons.

Sons.

Her half brothers. She stopped in the middle of the stairs on her way down to the kitchen. Was it possible one of her half brothers had the same computer ability she did? That would explain so much. She started moving again, hitting the floor with new questions.

If one of her half brothers was as computer-savvy as she was, what exactly was Branzino hiding? Nothing, she told herself. Because that's what she wanted it to be. Even though she'd been wrong about thinking her father was human, too. That revelation had scoured away part of her dream about who her father was. She wasn't ready to let any more of that dream go yet.

"Morning." She sailed past Augustine and Lally on her way to the coffeepot.

"You're chipper this morning." Augustine slid the creamer toward her spot at the table.

"Sarcasm isn't pretty on you, *Augie.*" She took the first sip black just to get herself started.

He grinned. "Did you just call me pretty, *Harley?*"

Lally laughed and set a big bowl of grits on the table. "Y'all sure you wouldn't rather eat in the dining room?"

"I'm fine here." Harlow looked at Augustine. He *was* pretty, but that didn't give him leeway to give her a nickname. "Don't call me Harley."

"I'll try to remember that, Harley." His eyes glittered with the kind of impudence that told her she shouldn't have said anything. He gave her one last look before turning to Lally. "Are we in your way if we eat breakfast in here?"

"Lands, no." She added another plate of scrambled eggs and

sausages, which Augustine wasted no time digging into. "I like having you in here," Lally added. "It's cozy."

Harlow sat. Before she could reach for the grits, Augustine picked up the bowl and held them out to her. "Thanks." She took a small spoonful, wishing it was hash browns. "Did my mother always eat in the dining room?"

"Usually." Lally took her seat at the end of the table. "Your mama was real traditional about that kind of stuff, but not so much that she didn't usually ask me to join her."

Harlow nodded. "It's nice to know that she broke the rules sometimes. I wish she'd done that for me." She pretended not to notice the look Lally exchanged with Augustine.

"Have you decided to stay in New Orleans?" Augustine asked.

"I don't know." Now would be a good time to talk to him about Branzino's offer, since he was in a good mood. "I have a lot of bills to pay at home and I need to get back there soon."

He nodded, chewing. "Can't you work here?"

"I could, but I have some obligations there I have to take care of." She could work from anywhere, if she didn't have time to serve. In fact, she'd found a few new job requests in her inbox after her search for info on Branzino.

"So go home, take care of these obligations and come back." He got up for more coffee. "Move in here and let the estate take care of your bills."

If he only knew just how big a bill she had hanging over her. "I have to go home one way or the other. I can't leave all my stuff there." Not that her stuff was worth much. Other than the rest of her computer equipment and her collectables, the other things in her apartment—furniture and odds and ends—were easily replaced. Or in a house like this, no longer necessary.

Augustine nodded. "I have to run out this morning, but we can talk about it more when I get back." The doorbell chimed.

"I'll get that, Lally," he said. "It's for me anyway. And ahead of schedule. I like that. Maybe I can get back from my errand a little earlier than expected." He set his cup down and went to the door.

She went back to eating, but a moment later, Augustine called for her, his voice edged with dislike. "Harlow, it's for you."

She excused herself and left the kitchen. Branzino stood in the doorway. She walked toward him, wondering what, if anything, he'd said to Augustine.

Branzino smiled at her. "Morning, sweetheart. Sorry to bother you so early, but I couldn't stop thinking about you." He shrugged. "I was hoping we could talk some more." He held his hat in his hands. "If you want me to leave, just say so—"

"No, no, come in. We can go in the library again." After last night's search, she had questions that needed answering before she made any life-changing decisions. He might be willing to give her the money she needed, but with what strings? "You want some coffee?"

"Sure, that would be nice. Black." He lifted his hat toward the library doors. "I'll just wait for you in there."

Augustine moved out of the way as Branzino passed. He clearly wasn't happy, but what could he say? This *was* half her house.

She went back to the kitchen for the coffee, Augustine hot on her heels.

"I don't like that guy," he hissed.

She poured a new cup. "You don't have to like him. He's not your family, he's mine."

Lally interrupted. "What's going on? Who was at the door?"

"Branzino. Again." Augustine sat back down at the table and stabbed a fork into his eggs.

Lally made a disapproving noise, but Harlow took the coffee and left before the discussion went any further. Who cared what they thought? This man was too important to ignore until she had more information.

He stood near one of the windows when she went in. She nudged the doors shut with her elbow, then brought his coffee to him.

He took it with a smile. "Nice collection of goods you got in here."

She had more important things to discuss. "Yes, Olivia was a big collector. Why don't we sit?"

"Sure, sure." He gestured for her to go ahead of him to the seating area. "How are you this morning?"

"Fine." She sat in one of the high-backed chairs. No one could sit by her that way. She let him drink a little of his coffee and make small talk a few more minutes. She needed him comfortable. Finally, she smiled to look as lighthearted as possible and asked the first question. "Tell me about my half brothers. What are they like? What do they do?"

"They work for me in the business. Michael does mostly... hands-on kinds of things. Works with the product, as it were. Teddy, he's my youngest, he's more of an office guy."

There was her opening. "An office guy? Like an accountant?"

"Not exactly, although he's good with numbers. He takes care of all our computer stuff. Inventory lists, stuff like that."

"He must be really good at it."

A flicker of something crossed Branzino's face. "What makes you say that?"

She laughed, more out of nervousness than anything else. "I tried to find out a little more about you last night, but your online presence isn't just clean, it's almost nonexistent. For someone running a business, that's a rare thing these days. Even for the ordinary user, there's usually some kind of social media presence. Something."

His jaw flexed. "I'm a private person. And I'm wealthy. I don't like people knowing more about me than necessary."

"I understand that." She nodded for emphasis. "I really do."

As if sensing she was about to ask more questions, he spoke quickly. "How's it going with the house? Did you come to terms with Augustine? It's not as though he needs to live here, is it? I understand he's the city's new Guardian. Odd thing, these Haven cities, but people seem to like them. Too many rules for me." He smiled. "I like my freedom."

"I haven't had a chance to talk to him about it. In truth, I'm not sure what I want to do yet."

He made a face. "You would stay here and share what's rightfully yours? Or would you run home with nothing to show for your inheritance? You have bills to pay. No house of your own. I'm offering you a new start. A way to keep your freedom."

How did he know so much about her? A tiny vibration of fear worked along her spine, the same feeling she got when she was hacking her way into a system rife with security bots. "Like I said, I don't know yet. But I've been alone all my life. I'm used to making decisions on my own and I'll figure this one out, too."

He stood and paced toward the door. "That's just it. You're not alone anymore. You have me to help you. You can lean on me. Rely on me." He turned to walk back and thumped his chest. "I am not a man who makes promises lightly."

"But I don't know what kind of man you are, and I feel like you're rushing me to make this decision." She wasn't about to be bullied into anything by anyone, family or otherwise.

"I'm your father. Don't penalize me because your mother wouldn't let me into your life." His tone grew dangerously low. "And this decision is an easy one. Buy the fae out and then I'll pay you whatever you want for the house." He bent forward, standing over her in a way that made her skin itch. "Your money issues will be over for the rest of your life and the house won't have to leave the family."

"You want to buy the house?" This was new information.

He straightened and adjusted his tie. Then, like it was an afterthought, he smiled. "Something like that, yes. I've given it some thought and I feel that it's time to diversify my investments. This house would make a wonderful bed-and-breakfast, don't you think? It would stay in your name, of course. That would allow the company to pay you a wage and make it worth your while."

"That's…interesting." Why would an importer/exporter from Chicago want to own a B&B in New Orleans? And leave it in her name?

"When I say a wage, I mean the kind of money that would allow you to pursue whatever it is your heart desires. You're my daughter. I want to spoil you. To make up for all the years we've missed. But for that to happen, I need your answer on all this."

"That's very generous, but it's still a big decision. I need to think."

"About what?"

She sensed his impatience like a new perfume had entered the air. "About what it all means. About whether or not I'm ready to enter into that kind of arrangement with someone I just met. Even if we are family. I'd rather we take some time and get to know each other."

He put his hands on the arms of her chair and leaned in very close. "We can get to know each other while we make this happen."

She pushed back into the chair as far as she could go. "You're scaring me."

"Am I?" He didn't move. "I have that effect on a lot of people. It's probably one of the reasons people rarely refuse me." He licked his lips. With a forked tongue.

She jerked away but the chair kept her from retreating. "I don't like this."

"Neither do I. I want to move forward on this decision. I need your answer. Do you accept my offer? There is so much I can offer you as part of my family. Everything you've ever dreamed of—"

"Get away from me." Her voice came out a whisper. What the hell kind of fae had a forked tongue? No wonder her mother had kept this man away from her.

He stood up and laughed. "You'll see. Your life will be better than you could have imagined."

"No." She ground the word out, her anger the only thing keeping her from fainting out of sheer terror.

His laughter died. "What did you say?"

She swallowed. "I said no. I'm not taking your offer." As much as she needed the money, there was no way she could be indebted to this man. This *fae*.

He grabbed a handful of her sweatshirt and yanked her out of the chair. With one foot, he shoved the chair back so there was nothing for her feet to touch. It toppled over with a soft thud. "I don't think you understand what's going on here. We're fae and fae stick together, but more than that, you're my daughter. A Branzino. *Family.* That means you do as I say without question, just like your brothers, because you know I've got the best interests of the family in mind. Always." He pulled her closer in until his scent filled her nose. He smelled like... pool water. "Got it?"

She was trembling, but anger kept her from backing down. "Or what? You're going to hurt me? I have a hard time believing that's in my best interest."

"You got steel in that spine, kid. I'll give you that." He threw her into the couch. "Just means it's going to hurt like hell when it breaks." He shucked his coat like he was preparing to fight.

Her legs almost refused to work but she rolled off the couch, pushed to her feet and ran for the door. He caught her in two steps, his big hand tangling in her hair. He yanked her back. She hit the floor and cried out in pain before the impact took her breath. "You're hurting me."

"Because you're making me." He crouched over her. "Now, you're going to go out there and have your little discussion with Augustine and then we're going to get this deal under way. Do you understand?"

She was about to scream for Augustine when the library door flew open and he charged in.

"Get the hell off her!" Augustine shoved Branzino away, knocking over a side table and breaking a lamp.

She scrambled to her feet. Branzino punched Augustine, pushing him back. She grabbed a small marble figurine and chucked it at Branzino, catching him in the shoulder. He reached back, giving Augustine an opening. He landed a fist across Branzino's jaw. A second punch caught the man in the ribs.

Branzino howled and bent as if trying to catch his breath. Augustine tackled him, knocking them both into one of the bookcases before they went down.

She edged around the couch to see Augustine lift Branzino's chin with a short blade, his other hand and one knee pinning the man to the library floor. "Your time here is done. *Done.* Come back and I'll make sure you regret it. Now apologize to Harlow."

Branzino's eyes almost glowed with hatred. He kept his gaze fixed on Augustine. "You're the one who should apologize. This is *family* business."

Augustine shoved the blade higher, lifting Branzino's chin. "I said apologize."

Branzino's nostrils flared before he spoke in a halted, begrudged tone. "I'm sorry."

Holding the blade in place, Augustine pulled Branzino to his feet. "Harlow, get his coat."

She nodded, unable to say anything, and ran for the coat. She held it up like a piece of old fish.

"Awesome. Thanks. Walk with us to the door." He pushed Branzino into the hall.

Without being asked, Harlow went ahead of them and opened the front door. Her heart pounded as Augustine shoved Branzino onto the porch, then took the coat from Harlow's arms and tossed it at him. "Get the hell out of New Orleans."

"Or what?" Branzino slipped his coat on, stiff with rage.

"Or I'll remove you."

"That's my daughter. I have a right to—"

"You have no right. Come at her again and I will kill you."

"You wouldn't da—"

Augustine slammed the door. His twisted expression smoothed out the second he faced her. "Are you okay?"

She nodded, on the verge of an angry, scared, ugly cry and feeling like she was about to burst open like a water balloon.

"That never should have happened. I'm really sorry it did." He looked toward the porch. Through the double glass doors, Branzino's blurry figure got smaller and smaller as he stormed toward the street and his waiting car. "I know he's your father and all, so if I overstepped my bounds—"

"No." That word she could manage. She put her hand over her mouth, her body shaking with adrenaline and raw emotion. A small sob escaped.

Augustine's arms wrapped around her. She leaned against him, surprised by her lack of resistance about being close to someone, but this wasn't just anyone. This was Augustine. The man who'd just come to her rescue. She got her breath under control, her forehead pressed into his hard chest. "I thought he was going to kill me."

"Not on my watch." He rubbed her back. "Are you sure you're not hurt?"

"Maybe a couple of bruises, but I'm fine." She pulled away a little so she could see his face. "Thanks to you."

He rested his hands on her shoulders. The heat coming off him radiated through her. It was strangely comforting. "Did he give you any reason to think he might come back?"

"I don't know. My mother was right about him. To think how I fought her..." A moment passed before she looked at him again. Then she lifted a shaky finger to point at his lip. "You're bleeding."

"Better me than you." He swiped at it with the back of one hand before putting it back on her shoulder. "Just a flesh wound. What did he want? If you don't mind me asking."

She turned her head to look into the library. Shards of glass speckled the carpet from the broken lamp. "He wanted to give me the money to buy out your share of the house, then he was going to pay me off and turn this place into a bed-and-breakfast."

"What's going on out here?" Lally asked from behind her.

"Just a little disagreement," Augustine answered. He took his hands off Harlow. "There's some broken glass in the library."

"Augustine!" Lally exclaimed. "Did you run that man out of here?"

Harlow smiled and shook her head. "Don't yell at him, Lally. He was protecting me. My father got a little rough." She grimaced. "Ugh. I don't like calling him that. Not after..." She waved her hand toward the library. "That business."

Lally frowned. "I knew that man had bad intentions." She headed back to the kitchen. "Don't you children touch that glass. I'll take care of it."

Harlow tugged at her sweatshirt, smoothing it over her leggings. "Thanks again. I don't know what I would have done if you hadn't been here."

Augustine glanced at the mess before bringing his gaze back to her. "I know you want to go home, but I'd feel better if you stayed here a few more days, just to make sure he doesn't try anything else. That way, if he does, I'll be here. Unless there's someone at home?"

Lally came back with a dustpan and brush. Harlow bit at her lip in an attempt to slow the answer trying to get out of her mouth. Augustine and Lally would find out about her sentence sooner or later. After what had just happened, sooner seemed the best option. "Branzino knew a lot about me. A lot. And there's no one at home. I live alone."

Lally looked up from where she bent by the glass. "That's it. You're staying here."

Harlow sighed. "I can't." Time to tell them the truth.

"Sure you can, child. Augustine and I will help you with whatever you need."

The best Harlow could manage was a half smile. "What I need no one can help me with. In about three weeks, I have to report to the Massachusetts Correctional Institution for Women."

Augustine looked like he'd just been slapped. "What on earth for?"

She rubbed her hands over her face, unable to look at either of them at that moment. The answer stuck in her throat. "I was convicted of some cyber-crimes." When neither of them said anything, she glanced up. "Crimes I didn't knowingly commit." She sighed, looking away again. "It's a long story."

Lally just shook her head.

Augustine held a hand up. "I need to make sure Branzino's gone, but when I get back, I want to hear this story. All of it."

"There's nothing you can do," Harlow assured him.

"Don't be so sure. As Guardian I have deep pockets and endless resources. We'll figure something out later, okay?"

She nodded like she was agreeing, but there was no way his

budget as Guardian included shelling out nearly a million dollars to pay her fine. She wasn't even a citizen of this city. So unless he could come up with eight hundred and fifty thousand dollars out of his own pocket, there really wasn't much to talk about.

Chapter Twenty-three

With Harlow's bombshell heavy on his mind, Augustine left her in Lally's capable hands and slipped out the back door to do a quick perimeter check. As he walked the grounds, he called the Guardian house and asked Dulcinea if she was available to stand watch. She was, so he told her he'd be over to pick her up shortly. She and Harlow might not get along the greatest, but he wasn't leaving Harlow and Lally alone while he got back to searching for the traitor behind the vampire influx.

He called Fenton next.

"Morning, Augustine. I was just about to call you. There's been another tourist murdered."

"Damn it. I assume vampires."

"Yes. I'm handling it, but we've got to make headway on this."

"Agreed. Unfortunately, I'm going to be late getting to the Pelcrum this morning. Any news on Branzino?"

"Not really. He's a virtual dead end. His online information is so clean that it must be purposeful. There is very little in his name and only slightly more in the name of his company. I imagine we'll find more in time, but it's going to take a concerted effort by someone more talented than I."

Augustine swore. "I don't know if it matters. He was here this morning. He got rough with Harlow so I threw him out of the house and threatened him if he came back."

Fenton made a disgusted noise. "It would still be good to

know who we're dealing with. If this Branzino is the kind of man to retaliate." Fenton paused. "May I ask what the altercation was about? Seems odd that a man trying to create a relationship with the daughter he's never known would fight with her."

"Agreed, but he wanted more from Harlow than just a relationship. He wanted to give her the money to buy out my half of the house, then compensate her further so he could use the place as a B-and-B but keep it in her name. Does that make any sense to you? Why would a businessman from Chicago want to open a B-and-B here?"

After a moment of silence, Fenton spoke. "Branzino is fae, correct?"

"Yes, but no idea what kind. I think he's using some kind of enchantment to pass as human." Just like Augustine's father had done with his mother.

"It's not unheard-of. That could mean he's hiding a very unsettling bloodline." Fenton continued. "And yes, Branzino's plan for the house does make sense. Any fae with a criminal record is prohibited from owning land or property within a Haven city's limits. If he keeps the house in Harlow's name, he bypasses that. If indeed he has a criminal record."

"It wouldn't surprise me. Just like it wouldn't surprise me that he's trying to gain a foothold in New Orleans." Augustine had walked the entire property and now stood in the front yard near the gate. Giselle walked toward him, dark sunglasses hiding her eyes.

"That gives me another idea about how I might find out more about him," Fenton said. "Let me do some more searching and then get back to you. What's your next plan for going after the vampires?"

"I need to go. I'll call you later and fill you in." Augustine hung up, then checked the time. One minute to nine. "Punctual. That's good." He opened the gate for her. "You have it?"

She didn't come into the yard, just pulled an envelope from her coat and handed it over. "I'm sure you'll be happy with this list of names. It's much more inclusive."

"Excellent." It definitely felt thicker than the first one. "Then come in and we'll go over it."

"I can't right now. My sister's not feeling well and I need to check in on her." Giselle pushed her sunglasses onto her head. "Give me a day or two, all right?"

After Harlow's experience this morning, he wasn't in the mood to add to her stress by bringing another stranger into the house. "Fine. I'll be in touch." He let the gate swing shut behind him.

"Thanks." She pulled her sunglasses back down, turned and walked the way she'd come. He jogged back into the house and opened the envelope.

Name after name filled the pages until he got the distinct feeling all she'd done was list every member of the New Orleans Circle. "That witch." She'd played him.

"Augustine?"

He looked up. Harlow stood at the end of the hall. "Do you need me?" Giselle and the witches could wait.

She walked toward him, something in her gloved hand gleaming softly. "Lally found this when she was cleaning up the library." She held her hand out. In her palm was the small silver cross he'd been meaning to ask her about, waiting until the time was right to broach the subject of her doing another reading. "Is this yours?"

"Sort of." He took it.

"Did my mother give it to you?"

"No." He turned it in his fingers. "It's evidence, actually."

"Of what?"

"Of whoever else is involved in bringing vampires into the city."

"And who's responsible for killing my mother?"

"Yes."

Her eyes widened a little. "What have you learned from it?"

"Nothing. That's the problem." He looked at her, then back at the cross, shifting uncomfortably. He needed her for this, but he wasn't interested in putting her through another reading right after her father had almost beaten the daylights out of her.

She balled her hands into fists. "That's what you wanted to talk to me about, isn't it? You want me to read it. See if I can pick anything up like I did with the jacket."

"Yes, but I can't ask you to do that, not after everything you've just been through with your fath—"

"Don't call him that."

"Sorry. With Branzino." He took a breath. "Maybe this isn't the best time."

"Screw Branzino." Her chin quivered. "I've got enough to deal with without worrying about him."

"I appreciate that, but you're still shaking." He tucked the cross into the pocket of his jeans. "It can wait." He moved toward the stairs.

She stepped into his path. "I'm shaking, I'm not falling apart. And this can't wait. Not if it's going to lead you to whoever killed my mother."

He stared at her hard, assessing her current state. He'd known her for a short time, but he couldn't imagine her looking any more determined than she did right now. "You're absolutely sure about this? Even knowing what happened last time."

"Yes, I'm sure and yes, even with what happened last time, but I also don't plan on doing this without Dulcinea's help again." She lifted her chin slightly. "How soon can you get her over here?"

"I'm leaving right now to get her." He smiled, then impulsively grabbed her shoulders and kissed her cheek. "Thank you."

As Augustine ran out of the house, Harlow put a hand to her cheek, trembling for a brand-new reason. The quick skin-to-skin contact had caused a lightning flare of emotion to zip through her. She grabbed the stair newel and sat on the steps, trying to get her breathing under control.

The things she'd felt from Augustine weren't immediately definable as individual emotions, but as she calmed, the tangled threads winding through her began to make sense. He cared about her, but he was struggling to keep his feelings platonic. Odd that such a thing would make her feel better, but after Branzino's insistence that Augustine was only being nice to sway her for financial gain, it did.

Augustine was also worried about her. Actually, the vibe she got from him was that he was worried about her leaving. Worried that if she did, he wouldn't be able to look after her. Which wasn't his job, but she was willing to let that slide.

But mostly, he was proud of her. For agreeing to stay, for offering to help, for finding strength after Branzino's attack.

That pride brought a stinging heat to her eyes. She'd never felt that from anyone. Oh, she knew her mother had probably been proud of her in the way that all mothers were proud of their children, but at some point, she'd begun to doubt that. Olivia had no good reason to be proud of Harlow, so why should she be? Harlow had done nothing to earn her mother's pride. In fact, she'd done a lot to destroy it.

But Augustine's pride was so genuine it sang through her body like white light, searching out the dark, ugly places and making them...less ugly.

It was a lot to live up to. Too much, maybe.

She bent her head to her knees, her breath at last regulating even as her spirits sank. This was why she didn't like being around people, why she shied away from contact of any kind. To know what a person expected of you was crippling.

Maybe offering to read that cross had been a mistake. What if she failed? What would Augustine think of her then?

The pressure built in her skull like steam she had no way of releasing. She raised her head. What would her mother do in a situation like this? She had no idea, but she knew who would. "Lally?"

A moment later, the housekeeper came out from the parlor with a feather duster in one hand. "What can I do for you, Miss Harlow?" She frowned. "Are you all right, child? You look shaken up. You still fretting over that business with that man?"

She loved how Lally called Branzino *that man*. "No, not really, it's just that plus everything else, I guess."

Lally nodded. "You sure have had a time of it."

"I was wondering, what would my mother do to calm herself down when she got stressed?"

Lally tapped the feather duster against her leg. "Well, your mama wasn't a big one for letting stress get to her."

"Say when she called or emailed me and I didn't answer." Harlow smiled sadly. "I did that a lot."

Lally nodded. "Yes, child, you did. Lots of times after that, she and I would go sit out on the porch and have a mint julep. You ever had one of those?" She grinned. "The way I make 'em, one makes you forget your troubles and two will bring you a brand-new kind of happy. Your mama loved them."

Harlow smiled. "I've never had one, but it sounds like just the thing." She sighed. "Too bad it's too early."

"Too early for what?" Lally asked.

"For a drink."

This time Lally laughed. "You got a lot to learn, Miss Harlow. This is New Orleans. Ain't no such thing as too early for a drink in this town."

Augustine parked the Thrun in the side garage near the back of the house, then he and Dulcinea jumped out and walked toward the rear porch. On the way over, he'd filled her in on the morning's events.

Laughter rang out. He rounded the corner to see Lally and Harlow in the big wicker chairs, a silver pitcher and two glasses on the little table between them. Even without the smell of bourbon and the mint sprigs floating on top of the ice cubes, Augustine would have guessed they were drinking juleps. The drink had been Livie's favorite when she'd needed to lighten her mood. He hadn't guessed Harlow shared that love.

"I see brunch is being served Olivia-style this morning," Dulcinea said.

Augustine took the porch steps two at a time. Harlow's cheeks glowed with the flush of good bourbon, but her lids looked a little heavy. He guessed also from the bourbon. "Everything okay?"

"It is now." She raised her glass. "We're de-stressing."

"I see that." Her words had the roundness of someone on the edge of a good buzz. "Lally, you have anything to add?"

"Just what the child said. We're getting calm the same way Miss Olivia liked to."

"Calm is good. Comatose is not." A cord of anger began to

knot in Augustine's gut. "Harlow, I need you clearheaded to be able to read this cross. Are you going to be able to do that?"

She waved him off. "Sure. I'm fine. Better 'an fine. I'm a brand-new kind of happy." Then she looked at Lally and burst into laughter.

Dulcinea raised her brows. "Oh, that's a new kind of happy all right." She pulled Augustine into the house. "You better get some of that alcohol out of her system before she attempts to read anything. She can barely control her powers sober."

"Agreed." He stared out the kitchen window, listening to Harlow laugh. He soaked up the sound, wondering how long it had been since she'd felt like this. And how long it would be until she felt this again without the help of alcohol. She'd seemed unhappy since she'd arrived, which was understandable considering the circumstances, but especially since she'd revealed the fate that awaited her when she returned to Boston. What wasn't understandable was how he felt responsible for a small part of her unhappiness.

Like maybe if he hadn't been such a big part of Livie's life, she would have tried harder to reconnect with Harlow. He knew deep down Harlow blamed him for some of that. Even if she wasn't consciously aware of it, those feelings of resentment would surface someday.

Dulcinea put her hand on his arm. "Hey, I know you're anxious to get on with chasing these vamps—we all are—but considering the last couple of days, I'm more shocked this little cocktail party didn't happen sooner."

He looked away from the window. "You're right."

"Judging by the sound of what's going on out there, Harlow's not much of a drinker." Dulcinea moved toward the door. "How about I help her upstairs, get her to lie down for a bit? A little nap might help."

"I'll help her." After all Olivia had done for him, he could look after Harlow. Showing her he wasn't such a bad guy was just a side bonus. Like being close to her, even if she was half out of her head.

Dulcinea made a funny little noise as he opened the door.

He paused, already regretting that he was about to dig further into whatever nonsense she was cooking. "What?"

"You're *so* gentlemanly." She waggled her brows suggestively. "It's very sweet."

"Stop reading into what's not there." He scowled. "I'm the Guardian. It's my job to take care of people."

"Especially if those people are super-cute and kinda tipsy." She snickered.

With a sigh, he left Dulce behind to squat by Harlow's chair. "Hey, how about we get you upstairs for a little nap before you read that cross for me? Make sure you're in good shape for it."

Harlow sucked down the last of her mint julep, then plunked the glass onto the table. "Those are really, really good. Lally is a mean mix-alog...misholist...mixologist." Her eyelids had gone from heavy to drooping, but her face held a sad sweetness unlike anything he'd seen there before.

"Yes, she is." His traces of remaining anger dissolved. Harlow's indulging might have cost him some time, but pushing her wasn't healthy. She was already dealing with so much. "What do you think? You want to catch some shut-eye before we do some work?"

"Sure." She yawned and tipped her head back like she might go to sleep right there, but at the last second raised her hand to him. "Help me up."

He stood and took her hand. Her glove was damp with the condensation off the glass. He pulled her to her feet. She sagged against him, so he hooked his arm around her waist and held her upright.

"You're tall," she muttered. "And you smell like barbecue."

Lally laughed. "She's right. You do. Y'always smell like you been working the smoker at Quinton's Rib Shack."

"It's my smokesinger blood—can we talk about what I smell like later and maybe get her someplace to lay down?"

Lally threw her hands up. "All right, all right."

But Dulcinea already had the door open. "You need help?"

"No, I got her." He scooped Harlow into his arms and carried her into the house.

When they hit the steps, her head lolled back and she smiled at him, eyes dreamy and half closed. "No one's ever carried me before."

"I'm taking you up to your room." And trying not to think about the body filling his arms. Warm, soft, curvy. There was no way her baggy clothes could hide her shape now. If not for *Nokturnos,* when he'd first held her against him, and the little black dress she'd worn to the memorial, he would have been more surprised, but now...now his brain couldn't help but connect how she looked in that dress to how she felt in his arms.

He pushed her door open with his foot and carried her to the bed.

As he set her down, she reached up and wrapped her fingers around the nub of one of his horns. "I've wanted to touch these ever since they started peeking through your hair."

He swallowed hard. "You already touched them during *Nokturnos.*" Even though her hands were gloved, the sensation made his lids drop to half-mast and a little groan escape his throat. She had no idea what she was doing. No idea how the feathery touch of her fabric-encased fingers shot sparks into his blood and raised pleasure bumps over his skin. He tried to pull away but her grip tightened possessively. His body constricted in response.

"Yeah, but I didn't know that was you then." She laughed softly. "What are these things for anyway?"

Shaking his head only caused more friction. "They, um, they…" He inhaled, hoping to clear his head, but succeeded only in filling his lungs with her sweet bourbony, minty perfume. "I…you should probably…stop."

Instead, her other hand latched on to the second protruding root. She grinned like she'd just won something. "Are they handles, Augie?"

Hell's bells, she was killing him. His entire body went taut under her touch. "Harlow, I need to…" What had he been about to say? His brain was short-circuiting.

She pulled his face closer, her expression deadly serious. "You scare me, you know."

"I scare you?" *Breathe.*

She rocked her hands up and down, making him nod. "Yes. You're so fae and just like Dagger, all take charge and protective and it's sexy but I am not going to fall for you." Her amber eyes practically glowed with sincerity. "Do you understand? I don't like being fae and I don't wanna be your sidekick."

He nodded under his own power this time. "Absolutely." He had no clue what was going on, but her drunken confessions were certainly entertaining. He wanted to ask who Dagger was, but thought better of it.

"Good." She rubbed the pad of her thumb over the tip of one horn. "Hmm…pointy."

"How about you get some sleep?" He tried to ease back, but bourbon had apparently kicked her fae strength into overdrive.

"Okay." She tugged him toward her and the next thing he felt was her warm mouth pressed against his, her lips as sweet as the mint juleps that had gotten them into this mess.

He jerked back in shock, expecting her to protest, but her hands fell away. Her eyes were closed. He sat on the edge of the bed trying to figure out what had just happened.

She rolled to her side and tucked one hand beneath her cheek, looking as harmless as a newborn kitten.

He shook his head, the fire she'd stoked in his body showing no signs of cooling off. His senses seemed just as slow to return.

That was the only way he could explain being afraid of a kitten.

Chapter Twenty-four

The slight throb in Harlow's head was nothing compared to the sheer embarrassment of the things she'd dreamed about. Her body was still warm from the visions her brain had produced. All that hard muscle covered in sweat-glistened gray skin and those horns. Her fingers twitched as she involuntarily gasped. In the name of all that was electric, she was wholly grateful that dreams were still private.

As it was, she planned to avoid direct eye contact with Augustine for the immediate future, not only for the dreams she'd had but for drinking herself into stupidity when she'd promised to help.

Happily, she'd made it to bed, although she couldn't quite remember how she'd gotten here. Just that those mint juleps had been delicious. And dangerous.

She tapped her LMD to life and checked the time. Almost one. Her stomach rumbled to announce she'd missed lunch. And she still hadn't read the cross for clues to help Augustine. After a quick stretch, she went downstairs to apologize for passing out.

Lally was in the kitchen cutting up a whole chicken. "There you are. You have a good nap?"

"Maybe too good." Harlow froze, realizing what she'd said. But that was silly; Lally wouldn't know what wicked things had happened in her dreams. "I mean, those mint juleps really knocked me out."

Lally whacked the cleaver down, separating a thigh and a drumstick. "You're a lightweight, child. Should've cut you off after one. If I'd a-known, I would've watered them down some." She winked. "Next time."

"I don't know if there should be a next time." No sign of Augustine. "I guess I missed lunch."

Lally pointed the cleaver at the fridge. "There's a plate of ham sandwiches and a bowl of potato salad in there waiting on Augie and Dulcinea to get back, but you don't have to wait. Help yourself."

Harlow opened the fridge and pulled the food out. "Where did they go?"

She shrugged. "Guardian business, Augie said. Should be back soon. Also said we weren't to open the door to anyone and to call him immediately if anything strange happened, but that he was posting another lieutenant to keep an eye on the house all the same."

"Like in case that man comes back." Harlow got a plate and a fork, then sat down to eat, hungrier than she'd been in a long time.

"I suppose so."

"Was Augustine upset I passed out and didn't help him?"

"Not a bit. Augie understands you needed some downtime." She put the last piece of chicken in a bowl and went to the sink to wash up. "I know he's anxious to find who's letting these vampires into the city."

"Me too, because that person is ultimately responsible for my mother's death." She ate another bite of sandwich. "When he finds them, do you think he's going to kill them?"

Lally took a carton of buttermilk out of the fridge and poured it into the bowl with the chicken and the seasonings, then mixed it with her hands. "Maybe. Can't really say." After washing up, she put the buttermilk and the chicken back into the fridge. "Does that bother you?"

"No. I think I could probably kill that person myself." She wiped her mouth with a napkin.

"Me, too, child. Heaven help me, me too."

"It does kind of bother me. That I could feel capable of taking a life."

Lally snapped the cover back on the potato salad. "Vampires aren't people. Not those that killed your mother. They're monsters who don't deserve another day on this earth."

"Did you see them?"

Her hands stayed on the container, her gaze focused on some dark memory. "No. But I saw what they did to her. Monsters." She lifted her head and looked toward the window, hiding her face from Harlow as she did. "Monsters," she repeated softly.

"What about that woman that came to the funeral, the one that's married to a vampire?"

Lally's brows went up. "Chrysabelle? That's a different situation. That vampire isn't controlled by his bloodlust the way these monsters are."

She wanted to ask more, but the back door opened and Augustine and Dulcinea came in. "Told you we wouldn't be gone long." He glanced at Harlow. "How are you feeling?"

"Good. Great." Horrible. Having him in the same room was worse than she'd imagined. His closeness made the images from her dreams seem real again. She rolled the edge of the napkin in her fingers to give herself something to do. "I can read that cross anytime."

Thankfully, Dulcinea sat next to her. She reached for a sandwich and Harlow took the opportunity to change the subject. "Where did you guys go?"

Dulcinea leaned back to show off some kind of nightstick hanging from her waist. "I had to do some stuff to officially become one of Gussie's lieutenants."

Augustine growled. "First order of business is never call me that again."

Dulcinea stuck out her tongue at him. "You're not the boss of me. Well, technically, I guess you are now. Whatevs."

"Gussie," Harlow echoed. That was so much better than Augie. She stored that away for the next time he called her Harley. "Must remember that."

"Please don't." He grabbed a sandwich and ate it leaning against the counter. "You want to do this in the library or someplace else?"

Dulcinea tipped her head. "Augustine filled me in on what happened with Branzino. I'm really sorry."

"Thanks." For once, the strange fae didn't seem interested in sparring. Harlow shrugged and glanced at Augustine. "I can handle the library. What's done is done, right?"

He swallowed a bite and nodded. "Exactly." But the look in his eyes seemed to be recalling something very different besides the fight with Branzino.

She stood, the air suddenly very close. "I'll wait for you both in there, but don't rush on my account." Without waiting for an answer, she escaped to the hall.

The small table in front of the mirror still held an arrangement of flowers from the memorial. The rest had been taken to the cemetery, but these sat beside the picture of Olivia. Harlow looked up at the black bunting draping the hall mirror. There must be some fae tradition about how long that stayed up. Not knowing only reminded her how disconnected with this world she was.

She'd never liked the idea of being different, which was

exactly what being fae was. Maybe not so much in a place like New Orleans, where people claimed their fae heritage like it was a badge of honor, but in the rest of the world, most humans still feared what they didn't understand.

In the same way that Lally had called the vampires monsters, other people referred to fae the same way. Harlow never wanted to feel that kind of animosity directed at her. She felt human. Why couldn't she just live her life that way?

She could. If her life wasn't in New Orleans.

The decision she'd thought she'd made reared its head again. Come back here after her sentence was served and deal with being fae and all that brought with it, Augustine being no small part of that, or stay in Boston and live her simple life, taking the chance that someday Branzino would come after her there.

He wouldn't, would he?

No matter how many times she answered that question no, it never rang truthful.

Her self-preservation instincts knew that returning to New Orleans after prison was the only safe answer. Could she live here without embracing her fae side? Augustine was the Guardian, not her. She wasn't required to recognize her bloodlines, was she?

If she knew more about what was acceptable and what wasn't, she might feel more comfortable, but learning about fae history and traditions just so she could ignore them seemed a crooked path.

She stared into the mirror, hating the strange color of her eyes, which identified her as something more than human. Before the covenant had been broken, no one had understood those things marked her as fae. Most just saw her as an oddity. At boarding school, her looks and her insistence that no one touch her had made her an outcast. In college, a bit of a freak.

Both of those experiences had pushed her to pursue computers as a way of supporting herself without having to be around people. Funny how her fae gifts had been both the cause of her withdrawal and the means to enable it.

The light pouring through the glass front doors flickered as a car drove past and for a second, it seemed like her image in the mirror had turned into her mother's face. She blinked, shaking her head. Just a trick of the light, she told herself.

"Everything okay?" Augustine walked out from the kitchen.

She turned away abruptly. "Yep. Just waiting on you."

He narrowed his eyes and looked at the mirror. "Did you see something in there? Something odd?"

"Other than my own face? No."

"There's nothing odd about your face."

Unwelcomed heat rose in her cheeks. She couldn't take even a hint of him being sweet to her, not after her wicked dreams. "I'll be in the library." She left him standing there and slipped into the cool, dark room that smelled of paper and leather and whatever else made up the perfume of real books.

But a new scent soon overrode the old one. Smoke. She didn't have to turn to know that Augustine had followed her in. His presence made her hyperaware of what little distance there was between them. She moved toward the wall that held a framed map of New Orleans in the 1800s, putting a couch between them.

"Harlow."

"Hmm?" She stared at the map intently, but it was impossible to see anything more than lines and squiggles with her concentration focused on the man behind her.

"Harlow, look at me."

She still didn't turn. "Do you think this is an original? Knowing my mother, probably."

He sighed. "We need to talk about this or it's just going to get weirder and that's going to make sharing a roof difficult."

"I don't know what you're talking about." A blur of movement caught her eye. He'd leaped over the couch and now stood directly beside her. She backed up, her hand on her heart. "Don't do that. You scared me."

He didn't look the least bit sorry. "You mentioned that."

"What?"

He took a step forward. "That I scare you."

"I don't remember saying that." She shuffled back.

His eyes twinkled. "I bet you don't remember kissing me, either."

"Of course I remember kissing you. I also asked you not to bring it up again. Isn't there some sort of 'What happens during *Nokturnos* stays in *Nokturnos*' kind of thing?"

"I'm not talking about *that* kiss. I'm talking about the more recent one."

Her mouth dropped open and her heart jumped into it. "What? When?" She bumped into one of the bookshelves lining the walls, unaware she'd been retreating.

"Right after I carried you up to your room and you told me how I reminded you of someone named Dagger."

She closed her eyes and groaned softly. "I am never drinking again."

"Never?" His voice was closer.

She kept her eyes shut. "I'm sorry about kissing you, I really am."

"I'm not." Then his mouth was on hers, insistent in a way she'd never felt. Not that her experience with men was so great.

Unable to resist, she kissed him back. His hands slid around her waist and he pulled her closer. Emotion began to flood her senses. The strongest was the feeling of desire, a rare silvery thread that tangled with another darker thread the color and texture of pain. The pair wound a pleasurable path through her, filling her with longing for more. And then, just as quickly as it had begun, the kiss was over and the lines of emotion unraveled, spinning out into fading wisps of sensation.

Her fingers went to her mouth, her head still registering what he'd done. "What did you do that for?"

"To see if kissing you sober had the same effect as kissing you drunk."

"I was only tipsy," she whispered, realizing the difference because now she was drunk. On him and how he'd made her feel.

He stared at her like he was waiting for an answer. "So? Did it feel the same?"

She shook her head. "I don't remember the tipsy one." But she'd remember this one, that was for damn sure. "Don't do that again."

He almost had the nerve to laugh. "Oh, I won't. Not until you ask."

"Like that's going to happen." The question was already forming in her head. Stupid, traitorous brain.

"At least now we know."

"Know what?" She really, really needed her hands to stop trembling.

"How this kissing thing makes us feel when we're sober." What was that supposed to mean? Before she could ask, he walked to the doors and called for Dulcinea, that they were ready.

Ready? She wasn't ready for anything but maybe a cold shower and the chance to disappear into Realm of Zauron for a good eight hours. Some people imagined themselves in a tropical getaway, but her happy place came from leveling up her warrior mage.

Dulcinea came in and shut the doors behind her. She approached Augustine, who now stood in the center of the seating area. "You've got the cross?"

He pulled it from his pocket and held it on his flattened palm. "Right here." Then he looked at Harlow. Not a trace of what had passed between them showed on his face or in his eyes, which could only mean that the kiss had not had the same effect on him as it had on her. "You going to join us?"

"Yeah." She could be just as nonchalant as he was. Determined to prove it, she adopted an air of bored indifference as she came around the other side of the couch. She plopped down in the chair, happy to have Dulcinea between them like before. "There's a good chance I'll get more with this than I did the jacket."

Augustine sat. "Why's that," he asked.

"The cross is metal. And I'm really good with metal. It seems to kind of be my thing." The confession stripped her bare. It was more than she'd ever said about her gifts to anyone, other than to complain about them, but after that kiss she was so wound she couldn't stop the words from coming out.

"Cool." Dulcinea nodded.

Harlow wriggled her gloved fingers. "Not so much actually."

Dulcinea nodded thoughtfully. "I guess it could suck in its own way." Since the thing with Branzino, Dulcinea had eased up on the attitude toward Harlow.

"It does." She looked at Augustine as she pulled her gloves off. "Let's do this."

He handed the cross to Dulcinea. She sandwiched it between her hands, then held them out to Harlow.

She took a breath, her nerves pinging with the unknown.

"It's okay," Dulcinea whispered. "I'll control my end as best I can."

"I know." Harlow forced a smile. The fae woman's efforts to

be friendly were not unwelcome, just something Harlow was unaccustomed to. "Thanks." Then she covered Dulcinea's hands with her own.

The images shot into her, knocking her back in the chair and breaking the contact.

"What was that?" Augustine asked.

She shook herself, trying to shed the pins and needles as she caught her breath. Augustine's kiss had thrown her. She had to get herself under control. "Too much, too fast."

"Did you get anything?"

"Just a jumbled mess. Like trying to watch the holovision when the satellite's blinking out." She took a few deep breaths. A bead of sweat trickled down her back.

He nodded, content with that explanation.

She turned to Dulcinea. "Can you hold it back any?"

"I thought I was." She shrugged one shoulder. "I'll try harder."

"Good." Harlow shook herself, ready for another go. "If it keeps coming through like that, none of it's going to make sense."

But the second try resulted in more of the same.

Frustrated, Harlow got up and stretched. "This might not work at all. The fact that it's metal might be creating too much flow."

Dulcinea dropped her hands into her lap. "What if we use Augustine?"

Harlow stopped moving. "For what? He doesn't have the right bloodlines. I don't think." Honestly, she had no real idea.

Dulcinea tipped her head at him. "Let him put his hands over mine, then you put yours over his. Like an extra buffer. You wear those gloves because you can read people, so there's no reason you shouldn't be able to read the cross through both of us, no matter what our bloodlines are." She put her hands out again.

Oh, hell no. Harlow shook her head. "I don't think—"

"That's a great idea, Dulce." Augustine stuck his hands over Dulcinea's and looked at Harlow. "Let's give it a shot. At the worst, it won't work."

Yeah, that was so not the worst that could happen. Feeling like she was about to fry her motherboard, she sat back down and gave him a long, hard look. "Do your best to keep your thoughts and feelings to yourself, okay?" Before he could answer, she looked at Dulcinea. "You work on filtering out anything you feel from him and your own stuff as best you can."

Dulcinea nodded. "Will do."

If Dulcinea suspected anything had happened between her and Augustine, she wasn't letting on. Not like what had happened meant anything. It didn't. Still, Dulcinea's seeming lack of awareness gave Harlow a small measure of comfort. "Fine. Let's try this again."

She clamped her hands over Augustine's, the warmth of his skin wicking into hers and making her want to pull back. A second later, the images began.

They were blurring and muted, like trying to read words through a flowing stream of water. She closed her eyes and concentrated the same way she did when she was trying to break into a system.

The images began to focus. A human woman's face but few details other than pale skin, dark hair and red lips. A flicker of gray skin on gray skin. The taste of ash in her mouth. A hiss. The anger of someone encroaching. The silhouette of a building she recognized as the church from the square in the French Quarter. Darkness. The tang of sweat. Money changing hands, both gray-skinned and white. More darkness. The sound of chanting. Words in Latin. Gray fingers woven through dreadlocks.

Then the human woman's face again. This time much clearer.

Harlow yanked her hands away. Her own emotions simmered barely controlled, but she would give Augustine the information he was after before she dealt with the rest of what had come through. Avenging her mother meant more to her than who he slept with. "There's a woman connected with this cross. She's got dark hair and pale skin. I recognized her from when I was down in the Quarter. She read my fortune."

"Dark hair and pale skin," Dulcinea echoed. "Did she use crystals?"

"Yes."

"Damn it. Giselle." Augustine jumped up. "Stay here, Dulcinea. Keep an eye on things."

"You got it." She stood as he left, looking back at Harlow. "You okay? You look...unsettled."

Harlow got to her feet and walked toward the door, trying not to let the residual images upset her any more than they already had. What she'd seen shouldn't matter to her, because it felt like jealousy. And that meant she cared, which she didn't, so why did she want to put her fist through something? "I'm fine. I'll be in my room the rest of the night. Don't disturb me."

"You don't seem fine. What happened?"

"Nothing" was the only answer Harlow gave as she left. There was no good way to tell Dulcinea she'd pieced these new images together with the ones that had come through last time and had seen her and Augustine in bed together. It wasn't Harlow's place and it wasn't Harlow's business.

And it shouldn't bother her, but it did. Seeing them together made her want to retreat into her online world and get as far away from this reality as she could. Something she was about to do. Losing herself in the Realm of Zauron meant she could ignore the question that kept popping up—should she return here to live when she got out of prison?

Because right now, the only answer she could come up with was no.

Chapter Twenty-five

Augustine had Fenton sending Giselle's address to his LMD before he'd left the Garden District. The car hummed with the same guttural thrum as the anger coursing in his veins. If Giselle thought she was going to keep secret her dealings with these vampires and the traitorous fae responsible for bringing them into the city, she was damn wrong. Whatever connection Harlow had found, he was going to dig until he hit bone.

He followed the directions Fenton had sent, veering off to drive down Decatur first to see if she was set up at Jackson Square. She wasn't, so he turned onto Dumaine and cut back around.

He parked the car and got out. At the far end of Orleans Avenue, the spires of St. Louis Cathedral pointed toward the sky. This area was far enough away from the heart of the Quarter that it didn't suffer from the same crowds of tourists those nearer to the river did. Most of the buildings here were residential, some shotgun-style homes, some older buildings restored and turned into apartments or larger single-family townhomes. Giselle's was one of those and easy to pick out. The two-story French Creole townhouse was stark white with black trim and a red door. The architectural personification of the witch he was about to tear apart.

"Giselle!" His fist hit the door as he yelled her name. "Open up or I'll break this door down." He pounded a few more times.

"I'm coming." Her muted voice rang out from inside. She pushed the curtain back on the front window to see who it was, then opened the door. Her slim ivory dress was trimmed in black, her hair restrained in the usual sleek ponytail. "What do you want?" Her voice was low, her gaze flicking back behind her. "I have a *client*."

He pushed his way in. "I don't care if the king of England's here, we need to talk."

She pinched her hands over her hips and stood in his way. "Come back in an hour."

He stepped into her personal space and stared down at her. "We seem to be having a failure to communicate. Get rid of your client or I will."

She sucked in a breath, her dark eyes snapping with anger, then sashayed into a back room. The house's interior matched its exterior: white walls, dark wood floors, crown moldings and crystal fixtures. Very old Louisiana money, which was exactly how Giselle must want to appear. Legitimate. A moment later she returned, an older, well-dressed gentleman in tow. The man, human, looked familiar as he glared at Augustine, but Augustine couldn't place him. He was clearly unhappy about the interruption.

Like Augustine cared. He put his hand on the hilt of his sword for emphasis.

Giselle opened the front door. "I'm very sorry, Mr. Andrulis. I'll call to reschedule as soon as I can."

"I expect as much." Mr. Andrulis shot Augustine another look before he left.

Giselle shut the door and leaned against it. "This had better be good. That man pays me a retainer."

The name finally rang a bell. "Mr. Andrulis? As in Judge Charles Andrulis?"

Giselle frowned. "I'm not answering that."

"I can't believe the judge keeps a witch on retainer."

"Many people do, but I am not confirming he is the judge." Giselle left the small front sitting room and went into the adjacent kitchen. He followed. She walked around the granite-topped breakfast bar and poured herself a cup of tea from the kettle on the stove, but didn't offer him one.

He held his hands up. "No thanks, I'm good."

"Would you like a cup? I have this blend especially made for me, but if you think you could benefit from a healthier monthly cycle, I'd be happy to share." She took another sip, her eyes twinkling over the rim of porcelain.

He rolled his shoulders uncomfortably and moved on. "I need some questions answered. Lying to me is a really bad idea, in case you were thinking about it."

She tipped her head. "Of course not."

Like he believed her. He pulled the cross out of his pocket and tossed it onto the counter between them. It landed with a clatter. "You put a spell on that cross. I want to know who you did it for."

Slowly, she set her cup down, her gaze on the silver cross the whole time. She looked like she might reach for it, but at the last second, she lifted her head. "I've never seen that before."

"You just told me you weren't going to lie to me and that's how you start? Bad idea, Giselle. *Bad* idea. Let's try again." He stabbed his finger onto the counter. "Who did you work the spell for?"

"I said I've never seen that cross before. I'm not going to be harassed in my own home. You need to leave."

"This cross was examined by a fae with the power to read metal and that fae determined the source of this spell was you." He stepped out from behind the counter so there was nothing between them. "This is your last chance to answer the question. I already know you worked this dark magic at the bequest of another fae. All I want from you is a name."

Fear tugged at her mouth. "People come to me because I guarantee them confidentiality. You're asking me to betray that. I could lose my business."

"And I'm losing my patience." He took a step toward her, grinding out the words. "Give me the name, or you won't have a business to worry about."

She swallowed and her cheek twitched. "Dell."

"Last name?"

"That's all I know. People who come for spellwork rarely give me a last name."

Augustine didn't know any fae named Dell. Maybe Fenton would. "What did this guy look like?"

She shrugged. "Like you. Like every other fae with gray skin."

He hated that whole you-all-look-alike-to-me mentality. "Horns?"

"I don't think so." Her mouth bunched to one side as her gaze went to his head. "Unless they were cut off."

He backed up and sighed. "You've been so incredibly helpful."

"Your sarcasm isn't helping." She shook her hands out, wiggling her fingers. "I'm trying, all right? Give me a little credit."

He wasn't about to give her anything. "What was the spell?"

She smirked. "None of your business."

"Did you know that as Guardian, I have the power to arrest you and hold you for twenty-four hours?"

"On what grounds?"

"Aiding a traitor. Performing an unsanctioned spell. Obstructing a murder investiga—"

Her smirk dropped. "It was a binding spell, okay? Designed so that whoever touched the cross next wouldn't be able to drop it."

"Then how did this Dell handle it?"

"It was kept wrapped in cloth." She shook her head. "And a binding spell isn't unsanctioned."

He shook his head. "Black magic is strictly forbidden by the treaty."

She scoffed. "You fae, you think everything we do is black magic. A binding spell is gray at best."

"Semantics. From now on, you record the name of any fae you do work for."

Crossing her arms, she raised her brows. "Well, that's pointless intrusion, isn't it? Anything else? Should I ask for a blood sample, too?" She snorted softly. "Not only can you not enforce that, but what's to stop them from giving me a false name? Or from going to another practitioner? Honestly."

He scooped the cross off the counter and buried it in his pocket. "You're right. I'll have to put a motion forward to the Elektos that all witches must keep transparent records of their clientele."

"What?" She dropped her arms. "You can't do that. This is our livelihood you're talking about. You'll destroy it."

He strode toward the door. "Then I suggest you start looking for an honest job." Something crashed into the wall beside the door as he was leaving, but he didn't stop to look. He was okay with Giselle being angry. Black or gray, the magic she'd worked had created a serious roadblock toward him finding who'd killed the tourists, Khell and Olivia.

She'd probably run to Evander and tell him how the new Guardian was ruining her life. Spin her story so that he came out the bad guy. His hand paused on the door handle of the Thrun.

Guess the best solution for that was to get to Evander first.

Before logging onto Realm of Zauron, Harlow opened her cam feed to check on her place.

The interior cams showed that everything looked the same. Not that there was much to see in her tiny apartment. Her desk beside the bed was tidy, the only oddity the empty space in the middle where her laptop usually sat. She tapped on the exterior camera just outside her door. Nothing there, either, but that's what she'd expected.

Satisfied, she closed the link and tapped the Realm of Zauron icon, ready to level up her warrior mage and finally get the blue sapphire armor she'd been after. She'd missed at least a dozen quests while she'd been here. Her guild probably wondered where she was. She logged in, sending them a message that she'd been gone on personal business and still would be for a while.

A knock sounded at the door. "Miss Harlow?" It was Lally. "There's a package for you. Messenger says you have to sign for it."

"Hang on, I'm coming." She left the laptop up and opened the door. "Lally, just call me Harlow. It feels odd having you call me miss."

"If that's what you want."

"I do."

Lally smiled softly. "I tried to sign for you, but the man said it had to be the person whose name is on the package."

"Thanks, I'll take care of it. Where's Dulcinea?" She didn't really want to run into more questions at the moment.

"Keeping an eye on the messenger."

"Figures. Okay, I'll be right down." She glanced back. Her gloves lay on the bed next to the laptop, but she could do this without touching anyone. Packages rarely held any significant emotion. Their contents were a different story. She headed down. The front door was open. A messenger in a brown uniform stood waiting. Dulcinea was on the porch, leaning on the railing like she might burst into action if the messenger suddenly turned into a fire-breathing dragon or something.

He had a medium-sized box tucked under his arm. "Are you Harlow Goodwin?"

"That's me."

He held out an industrial tablet. "Fingerprint in the square, signature on the line."

She used her sleeve to wipe off the touchpad before pressing her thumb to it, something she would have had to take her gloves off for anyway, then signed her name.

He handed the box over. "Have a good day."

"Thanks." Without a glance at Dulcinea, she inspected the box. The tracking label showed the package had originated in Baton Rouge. She didn't know anyone there. Maybe a friend of her mother's? How would they know her name?

Dulcinea came in behind her. "What is it?"

"No idea."

"Who's it from?"

"Again, no idea." She jogged back upstairs as Dulcinea asked yet another question, but cut her off in mid-sentence with the slam of her bedroom door. The desk held a pair of scissors. She sawed through the packing tape and opened the box.

Black tissue paper neatly covered what was inside, a single glossy black sticker embossed with a masculine *B* holding the sheets together. Her nervous system fired off a warning. She grabbed her gloves off the bed and yanked them on before slipping her finger underneath the sticker and snapping it. The tissue drifted open.

Her breath stuck in her throat as the answer to her biggest burden came into view.

Bundled stacks of brand-new plastic hundred-dollar bills. On top was a card-sized ivory envelope, an *H* written on it in gold marker.

She picked up the envelope, then slid the blade of the scissors under the envelope's flap and sliced through it. She shook the card inside out onto the bed. Ivory stock, black embossed *B* on the front.

She didn't need to see anything else to know it—and the money—was from Branzino. Was he always this relentless? If so, his actions added clarity to Olivia's position on him. Harlow stared at the card, her curiosity warring with her desire to never have anything to do with that man ever again. If this was his way of apologizing, she was going to send every single penny right back to him. Sadly. Once she figured out where to send it.

Reluctantly, she picked up the card and opened it.

Dearest Harlow,

Thank you for accepting this down payment towards our agreement. I think you'll find the sum a very handy amount. I realize you harbor some reluctance, but I can assure you this arrangement is in your best interests. My influence is far-reaching and the benefits to you far outweigh the disadvantages. You will soon learn how well I take care of my family, and you are *family. As proof of this, please log onto your webcam security system. I look forward to our next visit.*

Love,

Joseph Branzino

Her hands were trembling, but this time it was out of anger. How dare he think he was going to steamroll her into doing what he wanted. Just because she'd signed for the package didn't mean she was accepting his money. Or his damn deal.

And how did he know about her webcams? That only cemented the idea that one of her half brothers shared her computer talents. She stuck the card on top of the money and shoved the box toward the foot of the bed, then ripped off her gloves and logged back into her cam feed. After her shaking fingers messed up her first attempt at the password, she used her gift and forced her way into the site, unwilling to wait any longer.

Everything looked the same as it had a few minutes ago. She scrolled through the screens; the front door, the kitchen, all seemed exactly as they had been. Nothing unusual in the living room, either. Last she went to the bedroom/office cam.

As soon as she clicked on the screen, the camera began to move on its own. "What the..." She tapped the tracking button, but the camera didn't respond, continuing like it was on a preset course.

It pivoted to the left, showing her bed, then zoomed in closer and closer. She leaned toward the screen. Her nightstand was coming into view. There was something on it she didn't recognize.

Her anger dissolved into muscle-clenching panic.

A framed photograph. A person she couldn't quite make out.

Someone had been in her place. The person in the photograph was male. She looked closer.

A chill trickled down her spine, icing every inch of her in fear. The man smiling back at her was Branzino.

Chapter Twenty-six

Augustine was about to pull into Evander's driveway when the com cell behind his ear sent a familiar chime through his head. "Answer."

"Augustine, where are you? Can you come home? I need you to come home."

He'd never heard Harlow so panicked. "What's going on? Are you hurt? I'm in the Garden District so I'm not far." Without waiting for her answer, he shifted into reverse and spun the car around to head home. If Harlow needed him, he was there.

"I'm not hurt, I'm just really, really freaked out. How soon before you're home? I don't want to talk on the phone."

What the hell had happened? "Two-three minutes. Sit tight, okay? Don't freak out, I'm on my way."

"Okay, good. Thank you."

"Dulcinea still there?"

"She's here. I'll be in my room."

True to his word, he was bounding up the stairs two minutes later. He lifted his hand to knock, but Harlow opened the door before his knuckles touched wood. "Come in."

She was pale, her freckles exaggerated by her lack of color, and her gloved hands twitchy, moving nervously against one another, rolling the hem of her big sweatshirt, brushing hair out of her eyes that wasn't there. "Hey," he said. "Whatever it is, it's okay. I'm here. We'll figure this out."

She shut the door behind him. "It's Branzino."

Augustine went on guard. "He was here?"

"No." She walked to the bed and pointed at a box sitting near the edge. "He sent this." She pulled the flap open. "Read the card."

He dug into the tissue paper and whistled. "That's a lot of cash. How much is in there?"

"I haven't counted it, but I'm guessing two or three million." She stared at the box. "Enough to buy you out."

He unfolded the card and read it. "What's he mean about the proof and your webcam?"

She hit a button on her open laptop and the holoscreen projected above it, showing a slightly washed-out close-up of a bed. "Look at the nightstand next to the bed."

He peered closer, then stood up and looked at her. "I thought you didn't know anything about Branzino before he showed up at the cemetery."

"I didn't. That picture of him on my nightstand? Someone put it there. Recently."

"*Sturka*." Anger rose like bile in Augustine's gut. "He was in your house."

She shook her head. "Probably not him, but someone who works for him. I think he's still here. In town." She tapped another button on the keyboard and the holoscreen vanished. "Worse than that, he knew when I took delivery of the package and knew when I logged onto my system and had control of it. The second I clicked on the bedroom camera, it began to move, focusing in on that picture while I watched." She wrapped her arms around herself. "What am I going to do? How can I go home knowing he's been in my place?"

He wanted to hold her, to reassure her that he could keep her safe, but right now, Branzino had the advantage. "This *is* your home now. Stay here until you have to turn yourself in."

She hesitated like she wanted to believe that. "I guess I could.

But that messenger came right to the door. What's to stop Branzino from coming back? Or doing something worse? All my life I wanted to know my father, then he turns out to be a complete creep."

She twisted a hank of hair around her hand. "And you're moving into the Guardian house and taking Lally with you." She shook her head. "Maybe I'll turn myself in early. Get a head start on doing my time."

"I'll stay. Here." He knew that longing of wanting a father. And of being disappointed in the one you had.

She looked at him. "In the house? You can do that?"

He nodded. "If you want me to. And yes."

"That would be...good." She sank down beside the box of money, her gloved fingers pushing the flaps down.

He nodded. "Then it's settled. For as long as you need me, I'm here. And now that I'm Guardian, there's a lot I can do to increase the security of the house, too."

"Fae things?" Her nose wrinkled.

"Yes, fae things. You might not like them, or want to admit it, but they're a hell of a lot more powerful than anything humans can provide." He gestured to her laptop. "A house warded with a fae spell can't be breached without serious effort."

"Okay," she said softly.

"It would really help if we knew what kind of fae he was." Augustine looked at her. "No idea, huh?"

She frowned. "That's like asking me the current temperature on Jupiter. You know a lot more about fae stuff than I do."

"Which isn't that much. Fortunately, I have resources."

"Good." She shoved the box a little farther away. "I wish I could keep this. It's like he knows how desperately I need the money."

"For what? You own half this estate. What else could you need?"

She snorted softly. "Eight hundred and fifty thousand dollars."

His brows shot up. "That's a pretty specific amount." He grinned. "You have a gambling debt you've been hiding?"

"No." Another sigh that sounded like she was exhaling the weight of the world. "It's the amount of my fine."

"You have to do time *and* pay a fine?"

"No. One or the other."

"So pay the fine."

Her head snapped up and she gave him a look that said she thought he'd lost his mind. "Why didn't I think of that? I totally forgot about my secret Swiss bank account." Then she stilled. "Do you think there's any chance, I mean, Cuthridge said at the will reading that the estate's money was specifically to be used for the upkeep and maintenance of this place. I wonder if there's any way he could extend that to keeping one of the estate's owners out of prison."

He nodded. "It's worth talking to him about. I would think keeping one of the estate's owners out of jail would be a reasonable request for the use of funds." And if Cuthridge didn't think so, Augustine would talk to Fenton about just how deep the Guardian's pockets were. Harlow was not doing time on his watch if there was a way to prevent it.

Her mouth opened slightly and she stared into the room. "I need to see him first thing in the morning." She glanced at the box. "In the meantime, what should I do with all *this* money?"

"Send it back to Branzino."

"I don't have an address. And what if it doesn't arrive and he takes that as a sign that I'm down with his plan?"

"I'm pretty sure that's the assumption he's working under regardless of how you actually feel."

She closed her eyes for a moment. "I can't deal with this."

"Leave it to me. I'll figure something out."

She stood and backed away from the box. "Great, because I don't want it in here. Take it. Put it in your room, put it on the curb, I don't want anything to do with it."

He took hold of her shoulders. "Nothing is going to happen to you. I promise."

Her eyes gleamed with a strange glint. "I appreciate that and I'm grateful you're going to stay, but you should know that it's purely for my own selfish security reasons. Nothing else." She pulled back so that his hands came off her shoulders. "In other words, no more...kissing. Not when you're already involved with someone else."

"I told you I wouldn't do that again until you asked." He frowned. "What do you mean, involved with someone else?"

She crossed her arms. "Please. I know all about you and Dulcinea. I saw you two *together* when I was reading the cross." She challenged him with a look. "I'm not here to be another notch on your bedpost."

"I would never—Dulcinea and I, damn it, we are not involved. We are friends, nothing else, and that was a long time ago." He'd never regretted a single woman in his past until this moment. Until *this* woman. Now he regretted every one of them.

"I don't care if it was yesterday." She picked up an earpiece from the dresser and tucked it over the curve of her ear, adjusting the hair-thin mouthpiece until it sat at the edge of her lips. Lips he'd like to get close to again. "Now if you'll excuse me, I have to call Cuthridge, then I have some gronks to kill." She opened her laptop and started typing. A holoscreen popped up with an image of a dense, foggy forest. "Shut the door behind you."

He picked up the box and left, the sound of her fingers tapping on the keys fading as he closed the door. He had work to do, vampires to hunt down, Evander to visit, Fenton to update, this money to deal with and yet...all he wanted to do was stay here with Harlow and try to make her see he wasn't such a bad guy.

But he didn't know where to start.

Giselle knew Augustine would arrive at her father's before her, but such was the disadvantage of relying on public transportation. Oddly enough, when she hopped off the trolley and walked toward his house, there was no car in the driveway. None on the street, either.

Augustine had either already been here and left, which seemed unlikely considering the lengthy conversation that would ensue over this black magic accusation, or he'd been bluffing and never planned to tell Evander anything.

She'd still have to talk to her father, suss things out. She couldn't take the chance that Augustine had said anything without her being able to defend herself. Cormier answered the door.

"Is my father in?"

"No, Miss Giselle. He's out at a meeting, I believe."

"Has anyone else been by to see him today? Anyone fae?"

"No, miss. You're the first visitor today."

She nodded. That was a nice bit of news. "Thank you."

He gestured into the house. "Did you want to leave a message?"

"No." But Cormier would mention she'd been there either way. "Just tell him I haven't heard anything about the list yet. He'll know what I mean." Her father would wonder why she'd bothered to tell him such an insignificant thing, but she'd work that out later.

She headed back to the trolley stop, thinking through what her next steps might be. If Augustine had someone capable of reading that cross, then he might already know who the fae was who'd paid her for the binding spell. But why come to her about it then? Why not just go after the fae?

Was his visit a chance for her to come clean and save herself? She stood in the shade of one of the big oaks lining St. Charles. Well, she'd done that, hadn't she? She'd given up the man's name, which was without question not his real one. That was all she really knew about him, although with her skills, she could find out more if she wanted.

What if Augustine actually found the fae? And what if the fae gave up her part in bringing in the vampires? Bespelling that silver cross was one thing, but the other spell she'd created, the spell that would allow a fae to pass as human...She reminded herself that all she'd done was create the spell with the blood provided. She'd never met the fae who'd used it. Unless that fae was also Dell. And she was sure he wouldn't care if the witch he'd used got caught in the crossfire.

She shivered with sudden fear. She could not allow that to happen. Bringing in the vampires might have been the fae's idea, but she'd helped because she'd seen the potential to destroy New Orleans's Haven status and bring it back under the rule of her people.

Things had gotten out of control. She couldn't have this mess snapping back at her. The trolley was approaching. There could be no trace of her involvement, but at the same time, she had to find a way to clean this up.

There was one person who could help her. She'd end up owing him, but what was one more debt if it meant she got away clean. The trolley rolled to a stop. She stepped on, waved her pass under the reader and found a seat, a brand-new destination in mind.

⚜

Augustine took the box of money downstairs with the idea that he'd store it in the panic room hidden behind one of the library's bookcases, but when he got into the room, another thought occurred to him. If Branzino was smart enough to find his way into Harlow's security system, why wouldn't he also be smart enough to put some kind of bug in the money or the box?

He sat on the couch and took the stacks out, laying them on the coffee table as he inspected each one. With no idea what he was looking for, he hoped something would jump out at him. All counted, it was exactly eight hundred and fifty thousand dollars. The same amount Harlow needed for her fine. He tucked that info away for later and went back to his examination.

The bands wrapping the bills were all the same, no bumps or grooves that might be a hidden wire or receiver. He thumbed through the plastic bills, crisp and new and redolent of the chemicals used to recycle the plastic they were made from. Nothing seemed out of the ordinary, but that didn't make him feel any better. He wasn't exactly an expert on stacks of money.

Next, he felt inside the box, shook out the tissue and inspected the card. All of that seemed normal.

But the idea that Branzino had done *something* couldn't be shaken. There was no way Augustine was leaving this box in the house, panic room or otherwise, as long as that man was a threat. He wouldn't put Harlow under that stress.

Which meant he had to find a different place to store the money. He thought about asking Fenton, but Mortalis had once trusted the Elektos with a valuable ring and Loudreux had required a heavy favor to return it. Not that Augustine thought Fenton had the same motives, but leaving the Elektos out of this for now seemed a better option.

No, this was something he would take care of himself. He packed the money back up, folded the box flaps under each other to secure them, then left the box by the hall table and went to his room to collect a mirror. After that, he fetched a shovel from the garage. When he came back in, he gathered up the box and stood before the hall mirror.

A flicker of thought, the brief tug of magic and he was through, standing on the fae plane, facing the Claustrum. He walked toward the gates, close enough that the noise of those locked inside began to reach him. Their muted howls and moans were torn ragged by the wind, shredded into unearthly sounds that punctuated what a desperate, awful place the Claustrum was.

Choosing a point he would remember, he started digging. No one would find the box. No one would even know to look for it here. And if Branzino did have some kind of tracker on it and he followed it here, he couldn't claim Harlow had kept the money. Not to mention he'd get a nice reminder of where he belonged.

The wind licked at the sweat on Augustine's neck, curling around him and whining like a stray dog. He rammed the shovel into the hard, rocky ground again and again until he'd made a hole big enough, all the while listening over the Claustrum's noise for the soft almost-voice he'd heard the last time. The sound that had seemed very much like his name trilling over the gray plane. It never came.

He dropped the box into the hole and started shoveling in the dirt, the crunch of gravelly earth against the cardboard satisfying in a way he couldn't quite explain. At last, he stamped the dirt down and threw a few rocks over the spot to disguise it until the wind could do the rest. He wiped his hands on his jeans and stood back, looking through the Claustrum's gates into the dark maw beyond.

As Guardian, the day would come when he'd be responsible for another fae being sent here. They'd have done something to deserve it, but the idea of being in such a position gave him pause.

Power was a heady thing, but nothing he'd ever actively sought out. Sure, when he'd been running the streets, he'd felt like the king of his world, but that position had come with a very high price. Now real power had been thrust upon him. A useful tool in this new job, he knew that, but at what cost? He'd saved his own skin from the Claustrum so that... he could send others here? The irony wasn't lost on him.

He worried what the job would turn him into. How it would change him. Without Livie to temper his moods, how long before he turned back into the sharp-edged, hair-triggered rebel he'd once been? Harlow might be able to fill that role, but that would require her desire to do so, something he doubted she'd ever feel.

Would she be able to get over his part in her mother's death? Already he knew he would kill whoever was responsible for letting the vampires in, once he found them. Without compunction, without hesitation, he would take a life, and his position as Guardian meant he'd suffer no consequences for it.

If necessary, he'd kill Branzino, too, if and when the time came, although when felt much more likely than if. The man was hiding something and if Augustine had to guess, he'd say Branzino's money had come from less reputable sources than importing and exporting.

Maybe he should stop denying his own dark side and give it rein again. There was so much anger in him, suppressed for years as a kindness to Olivia, but he could easily release it. Be the Guardian everyone feared. He didn't need to be loved. His mother had taught him years ago how to live without that.

That thought brought the prickle of dark heat to his bones. Made him want to rage against all the injustices that had occurred to him.

"Livie," he whispered. "I wish you were still here." She was, in a way. Her ashes anyway, which for him made this a sacred place. "I wish you could tell me what I need to do to get through to Harlow. To get her on my side," he added, then slung the shovel over his shoulder and turned to put the Claustrum out of sight.

As he dug in his pocket for his mirror, the wind whipped up, scouring him with dirt. He scrubbed at his eyes, blinking them open only to slits.

The whirlwind of dust he'd last seen after spreading Olivia's ashes had returned. He shook his head. It was just dirt, not ashes. Not her in *any* way.

But as it began to take on her familiar shape, that became harder to believe.

"Livie?" Hope sprang up in him, only to die a few seconds later when the wind vanished and the dust fell back to the ground.

His anger clawed to be released, to hunt and destroy. He nodded, giving it some space. He'd get Dulcinea to guard the house, then he'd go into the Quarter and look for vampires.

He really, really hoped he found one.

Chapter Twenty-seven

Giselle walked the streets of Treme, returning every side glance with her own version of the evil eye. No doubt, the residents could smell the witch on her, their distrust stemming from that more than her being a stranger. Over the years, the neighborhood had become predominately ruled by the voodoo religion as the most powerful practitioners in the craft made their home here.

To hell with the neighborhood watch. She had need of their most revered resident, Father Ogun. She'd end up owing the man something for his services, but it was a necessary evil. She could not be connected to what she planned to do and these loose ends *had* to be tied up.

She knocked at his door. His house was one of the larger two-stories, painted bright yellow with white trim and square white columns on both front-facing porches. The wood around his royal blue front door was carved with runes and here and there bits of dried flowers and colorful ribbon were nailed into place.

The door opened and he nodded. "I knew you'd come."

She controlled the urge to roll her eyes. "Father Ogun, how nice to see you."

"What can I do for you, Giselle?" His brown eyes twinkled.

"Can I come in? I'm sorry for not calling ahead, but I have a matter of some urgency."

"Sure enough." He moved out of the way and let her pass.

The reek of incense hung in the air, along with something

musty. Trails of smoke curled up from his altar, revealing the source of the incense. Things covered every surface of the place. Feathers wrapped in bright thread, candles, bottles of herbs and liquids, sequined banners, carved wooden figures, a branch with a birds' nest attached. Everywhere she looked, something filled the space.

Her skin itched at the amount of clutter and for a spare moment, her lungs seemed incapable of getting enough air. She chanted a calming spell and slowly felt the claustrophobia leave her.

He sat in a big overstuffed chair draped in kente cloth, gesturing for her to take a spot on the love seat nearby. She sat on the edge, wondering immediately if the spell keeping her dress clean would be enough. Everything looked so grungy.

"What is it that has brought you into the wilds of Treme to seek me out?" His baritone seemed deeper in the confines of the space. "You are a capable sorceress in your own right, so it must not be my work."

"Actually, it is. I have an enemy who seeks to destroy me. I must get to them first, but I can't be connected with it." There was no way of knowing exactly what the fae were capable of. The more distance she put between herself and what needed to be done, the better.

He nodded slowly, then reached over the table beside his chair, took out a cigarillo from a pack and lit it up. He took three puffs before he spoke. "I see."

Inwardly, she cringed. The smoke would cling to her hair and clothes, making her smell just as bad. She reminded herself that she didn't have anyone else to turn to. Which only made her hate being here that much more. "Can you help me?"

"It's not *can*," he said. "But *will*." Another puff. "I must think on this."

"I understand that, but unfortunately, I don't have time for you to think." She tried to relax. "I'm sorry for the rush, but I'm in a bind. I need help now."

"You understand the kind of discretion you require means greater risk on my part."

She smiled sweetly. "We both know you capable of the kind of work that leaves no trace." Yes, he'd be taking a risk, but it would be a very small one. His people had no treaty with the fae, no rules to break.

He smiled back, clearly flattered, but the sharp glint in his gaze said more than flattery would be required. "The payment for such work is steep."

She nodded. "What's your price?"

"Besides my usual fee…a flesh debt. To be paid when I require it, where I require it. Without complaint or hesitation." His smile widened. "I may someday have need of the kind of work you do."

She had no doubt. A sick feeling filled her belly. A flesh debt was serious. Breaking one meant grave consequences. "Agreed."

He took a pin from a small box and handed it to her. "Any finger will do."

She pricked her thumb until blood flowed, then handed the pin back to him.

He wrapped it in tissue and returned it to the box. Should she break her bond to him, he now had her blood to use against her. A very sobering thought. He studied her, his robes flowing out around him on his chair. He plainly relished this moment of power. "Do you have blood from the person you wish to destroy?"

"No."

"Hair?"

"No." She bit back her frustration. "I don't have anything from him."

"Nothing he's touched?"

"I have the money he paid me with."

Father Ogun nodded. "That will have to work, I suppose. The rest I'll sell you."

"Thank you." She couldn't muster the politeness to force a smile. This had ended up costing her far more than she'd expected. But hiring the devil rarely came cheap.

The crowd at *Belle's* was the same group of regulars, plus the usual group of othernatural tourists. Augustine pushed through the crush to the bar and found the person he was looking for. Renny Doucette, *Belle's* most infamous bartender and one of the few gator varcolai to make a life for himself outside the swamp.

Renny smiled, showing off an impressive set of canines, and tossed a bar towel over his shoulder. He clasped Augustine's hand and gave it a hearty shake. "Augustine! So good to see you, bro." His smiled faded and he touched his heart. "I am so sorry at your loss, *mon ami.*"

"Thank you."

"Is it true what I hear? That you're the new Guardian?"

Augustine nodded. A few in the crowd cut their eyes in his direction. He lowered his voice. "I was wondering if we could have a little chat?"

"Need some information, eh?" Renny's drawl had the soft, rounded edges of the bayou. He nodded to the female bartender at the other end. "Bebe, take over, yah?" He ducked under the service bar and popped out on Augustine's side. "We can go out back."

Augustine followed him through the small kitchen and out the service doors into an alley. Renny shut the door behind them, then took a seat on a stack of crates that looked like it served as the employee break room. "What can I do you for?"

The dumpster reeked. Augustine pulled out a *nequam* cigarette and lit it up. "Had any vampires in lately?"

Renny pulled out a pack of his own smokes and fired one, taking a long draw before answering. "You're looking for them bastards that killed your *tante* and Khell, *mais* yeah?"

Olivia wasn't really his aunt, but he knew what Renny meant. "Yes."

Renny shook his head. "I've seen a few in here, but they don't hold a regular pattern. I think they know you're looking for them." He glanced down the open end of the alley. "You hang out in the Quarter long enough, though, you'll see one. They gotta feed."

"I know, they've killed some tourists, too, but I haven't seen any recently."

"Spend some time here, I promise they'll show." He exhaled a stream of smoke. "Just walking to my car last night I seen a girl stumbling down the street, drunk as the preacher at Sunday night supper." He stuck two fingers against his neck where his human skin turned to scales. "Bleeding from a bite from a you-know-what, I swear it."

Augustine's ears pricked up. "Where was she coming from?"

Renny pointed his cigarette down the alley. "Lucky Frog's, I think."

"That tourist bar on Decatur?" He flicked the ash off his smoke. "That place is blocks from here. What makes you think she was there?"

"She was carrying one of them plastic hurricane glasses. Had the logo on it and enough drink left in it to make me think it was fresh."

"Good eyes, Renny." The gator shifter grinned. Augustine ground out his cigarette. "I owe you one. And listen, you get any leeches in here, you call me. Let's go back in and I'll give you my number."

"*C'est bon.*" Renny flicked his cigarette into a puddle and opened the door. "I'm glad you took over for Khell, bro. We need someone with your skills. I ain't disrespecting Khell, but sometimes wanting a job and being skilled for it are two different things, you get me?"

"I do." A lot of people felt that way about Khell. His heart had been in it, but he hadn't been the toughest sort of man. "Renny, I have to ask. Is it hard, keeping your half-form like that?"

Renny shook his head. "It's no big thing." For a second, his eyes glittered with the red-gold only a gator varcolai could pull off. "You'd be surprised how much the ladies like it."

Augustine tapped one of his horns. "No, I wouldn't."

Renny chuckled softly as he ducked inside. "Speaking of the fairer sex, you see Dulcinea much?"

Augustine followed. "Almost every day."

Renny stopped right outside the kitchen, his face abruptly serious. "I'll call you the second a vampire steps foot in here. Hell, I'll hold 'em down until you arrive, but you gotta do one thing for me."

"What's that?"

He fished into his shirt pocket and pulled out a small envelope. "Give her this. And tell her I'm sorry." He exhaled. "I'm sorry and I want to make things up, if she just give me the chance."

"I can do that." Augustine took the note, trying hard to keep his expression neutral. Suddenly he had a pretty good idea of why Dulcinea had stopped coming to *Belle's*. Kind of crazy to think of her and Renny as a couple, but then again, this was Dulcinea.

A few minutes later, he'd left Renny with his number and was back out on the street. He walked toward Lucky Frog's, studying everyone that went past him, looking for some sign that they'd been bitten. Nothing.

When he got to Lucky Frog's, he crossed the street and hung out in a doorway, watching the patrons come and go. No sign of vampires, but he stayed, vigilant for any sign that a leech was in the area. He would have loved a smoke, but there was too great a chance the vampires would pick up the scent of the *nequam* and bolt.

At least these were fringe vamps and not nobles. Could he handle a noble on his turf? Yes. A whole pack of them? Maybe. Maybe not.

A group of human beauties walked past, all of them giving him bedroom eyes. They were exactly the kind of women he would have peeled off and followed after in different circumstances. Like not being on a vampire stakeout.

And having never met Harlow.

Hell's bells, she was a conundrum. Came off as straight as an arrow, until he discovered she had prison time hanging over her. Granted, she might have been set up, but she'd still been willing to do the crime. She had mad fae powers, but hated being fae. Seemed to do everything she could to hide how beautiful she was. Liked to kiss him drunk, didn't like to kiss him sober, but didn't like the idea of him sleeping with Dulcinea, either, no matter how many years ago that singular episode had taken place. And the wall around her... he shook his head. Just when he thought it was coming down, she slammed it back into place.

But the idea of trying to get through it... he smiled. There was something very worthwhile about giving that a go. When she allowed herself to be vulnerable with him, there was something so real about her. The kind of woman that wouldn't put up with his nonsense, but understood he wasn't perfect, either.

Now if she could just apply that to his role in getting Olivia killed...

A couple across the street caught his attention. He went into shadeux mode, the kind of wispy smoke form he'd perfected as a child as a way of hiding from his mother. Against the gray stone of the buildings and with twilight bleeding across the evening sky, he was practically invisible.

The couple had just come out of Lucky Frog's and were traipsing down the street, body movements exaggerated by alcohol. Except something about the man's seemed...too perfectly drunk. Augustine slipped in behind them.

He listened and just as he'd suspected, heard only one heartbeat. The man in front of him was a vampire. Augustine opened himself to the anger and frustration that had been festering since Livie's death as he followed the pair down a dark side street. He flexed his hands. He hadn't been in a proper fight in a long time.

Better still that this one would result in one less vampire.

Thanks to the little bug Harlow had planted on Augustine's LMD, finding him was easy. Trailing him, however, was a very different matter. He moved like a ghost, almost impossible to see and soundless in his travels.

She clung to the recess of the door, peering out as much as she dared. His dark form followed the pair of tourists into an alleyway. She slipped after them, her heart pounding in her chest so loudly she was sure he could hear it.

She slipped into the alley and crouched behind a dumpster that stank like fish. Nearly gagging, she peeked around the side. Augustine closed in on the couple. He lost the shadowy transparency he'd had, going solid so quickly she wasn't sure she'd really seen him transform.

Then he struck, knocking the man away from the woman. She cried out in confusion and stumbled toward the building.

The vampire hit the opposite wall, spun and came back

snarling, fangs bared. The woman screamed and ran. Harlow dropped behind the dumpster again, but the woman was too busy saving her own skin.

"You just cost me dinner, fae." The vampire's low growl rumbled through the alley.

Harlow positioned herself to watch.

Augustine laughed. "I'm about to cost you more than that." The vampire swung, but Augustine ducked, the air whistling above his head. He grabbed the vamp by the waist and rammed him into the wall. His reward was a grunt. The vampire went limp.

Harlow almost gasped. Had Augustine killed him? Maybe not. He shoved his forearm under the vamp's chin, pinning him to the wall with his head smashed back, then Augustine snagged his dagger from his waistband and aimed it at the vamp's heart. "How'd you get into town?"

Harlow held her breath for the answer. The vampire barely moved. "I'm not telling you squat."

She exhaled, disappointed.

"Death wish, then. Good to know." Augustine put pressure on the blade. It glinted in the dim light.

The vampire tried to retreat but had nowhere to go. "I snuck in."

Liar, she wanted to yell.

But Augustine took a different route. "Why?"

"Because we're not allowed."

"You came here because you're not supposed to?"

"Yeah, something like that."

Another lie. Anger coursed through Harlow, tempered only by Augustine's persistence. "How many are with you?"

"Just me and another male."

"You expect me to believe that story? That this is just a

weekend getaway?" Augustine dug the blade in harder. *Good.*
"Where is the rest of your gang?"

Harlow nodded, mentally urging Augustine on.

"There's no gang, I swear." The vampire's eyes widened, the
whites almost glowing. "You want some kind of payoff? I got
almost a grand on me, you can have all of it."

She slumped, fearful Augustine would take the money. She
bit her lip, praying he wouldn't.

He shook his head. She wished she could see more of his face.
"You think you can bribe me? I'm the Guardian of this city.
Your money means nothing to me. Now I'll give you one more
chance to answer my questions. There's a vampire gang in this
city. Where are they?"

"I told you, I don't know nothing about a gang."

He shoved his arm higher, scraping the vampire up the wall
and lifting his feet off the ground.

The effort pulled at the vampire's clothing, revealing a cord
around his neck. Augustine looped his sixth finger under the
slim leather and pulled it free. At the end dangled some kind of
black amulet.

It must have meant something to Augustine because he
jammed the dagger's tip into the vampire's chest hard enough
to break the skin. "Liar. Where's your leader? The one with the
scar?"

Was that who'd killed her mother?

The vampire jerked forward to head-butt Augustine, but
couldn't close the distance and succeeded only in burying the
dagger deeper. "I got nothing else to say to you."

"Then your usefulness has ended." Augustine pulled his arm
away as he ripped off the amulet and simultaneously drove the
dagger all the way home.

He backed away from the cloud of ash that exploded from

where the vampire had been. "One down... no idea how many more to go." He held the amulet up to get a better look at it. As best she could see, the medallion was a solid black circle with the letters *YB* stamped on it.

"You can come out now."

Who was he talking to?

He looked in her direction. "Harlow, I know you're there."

She stood up and brushed herself off. "How?"

He just shook his head, a little smile on his face. "Come here and take a look at this. I saw one like it on one of the vampires at the hotel we raided."

Feeling a little stupid but happy he wasn't calling her on it, she walked over to study the amulet. Maybe he was giving her a pass because of what she'd figured out about him and Dulcinea. "What's YB mean?"

"Young Bloods. It's the biggest fringe vampire gang we know of. Not much of a clue. Like finding out the needle you're looking for in the haystack is a little sharper than the others." He scratched the edge of the medallion. A waxy substance clung to the underside of his nail. He held the coin out to her. "Smell it."

She sniffed. "Kind of sweet and sort of powdery."

He nodded. "This isn't just a gang logo, it's their way out if they get caught. I've seen one in action."

"What's it do?"

"Vampire bonfire, basically."

He tucked it into his pocket. "You know what this means?"

She had a feeling. "You need me to read that, don't you?"

He hooked his arm around her shoulders. She tried to shrug it off and failed. He walked them toward the main street. "You catch on fast." His hand squeezed hard, stopping them. "Which is good, because I don't want to have this discussion again. If you ever deliberately put yourself in danger again, I will assign you a personal bodyguard. One who will stick to you like stink on a skunk."

She pulled away from him. "Like hell you will. I'm a grown woman. I don't need a bodyguard." She'd spent too many years of her life being followed around by thugs for hire. She wasn't about to repeat that now.

"And I don't need to worry about you."

"Then don't. I'm not your responsibility."

Something in his gaze darkened. "But you are. You're here because of what happened to your mother. What I caused. So until that's fixed, yes, you *are* my responsibility."

She was about to respond when he caught her gloved hand and held it. "Please, Harlow, if something happened to you... something I could have prevented..." He looked away, but the war in his eyes was plain.

Whether it was the desire to know the truth or the desire to make him suffer, she couldn't say, but the urge to make him speak pushed her. "Then what? Why do you care what happens to me?"

"I like you."

"You like Dulcinea, too."

He steeled his expression as he pulled her close. Barely an inch separated them. His smoky scent and radiating heat made her feel like she was standing in a fire. "I *like* you in a very different way than I like Dulcinea."

Despite all that heat and smoke, she shivered. Because deep down inside, she knew exactly what he meant. She liked him, too. And nothing had ever scared her quite that much.

Chapter Twenty-eight

Giselle poured rainwater over the money in her copper bowl, thankful that the plastic bills would still be usable after the scrying was done. Paying Father Ogun had been as exorbitant as expected. In front of the bowl, she placed a small mirror on a stand. Being that the man she sought was fae, the silver-backed glass should be especially effective.

Clearing her mind, she sat back and positioned her hands over the bowl. "Goddess of the bayou moon, mistress of the holy night, bring to me this man I seek, show him to me with your light. He who touched this money last, reveal his home within my glass."

The mirror fogged, then cleared. A house appeared, Garden District by the looks of it. Made sense since the affluent and important fae tended to cluster there. She jotted down the number above the door. Finding the street would take a little more work, but at least she had something to go on now.

A sense of calm filled her. This was going to work. She would be able to protect herself and no one would be the wiser. In fact, if all went according to plan, things would be tied up in a neat little bow.

She smiled, but then she remembered she'd still be in debt to Father Ogun. Her smile faltered. She sat back and lifted her chin. He might be a high priest of voodoo, but he was still a man, and she'd yet to meet a man who didn't have some weakness.

All she had to do was figure out where Father Ogun's Achilles' heel was. Then hold a knife to it.

Dulcinea was walking the perimeter when Augustine returned. "How's the night going so far?"

"Quiet," she answered. "Lally went to bed a little bit ago and Harlow hasn't come out of her room."

He forced himself not to react. "Really? How do you know she hasn't left?"

Dulcinea glanced up toward the guest room. Blue light flickered in the window. "Computer hasn't stopped. She's all hunkered down, playing some kind of game. Got a headset on and everything."

"And you've seen her up there yourself, have you?"

"Not in a while but…" The back door slammed. "What don't I know?"

"That would be Harlow going inside." She hadn't spoken to him since his confession in the alley. "She followed me. Don't know how, but she showed up."

Dulcinea groaned. "Total lieutenant fail. I'm so sorry." She glanced toward the window and shook her head. "She didn't get hurt, did she?"

"No. Fortunately. Because if she had—"

Dulcinea held her hands up. "I know, it would have been my fault." She sighed long and hard. "She's mad at me and I'm not sure why, but I get the sense she picked up a little something extra from me again on this last reading."

"I know. She figured out that you and I slept together."

"Sorry, Gussie." Dulcinea cursed softly. "She knows that was years ago, right?"

He nodded. "She knows. She just didn't seem to care."

"How was the hunting?" Dulcinea smiled. "I smell ash, so I'm thinking good."

"There's one less vampire in town, but I'm no closer to finding the nest. Although I know they're Young Bloods now." He pulled out the amulet. "I took this off the one I staked. It matches the one the vamp at the Hotel St. Helene wore, the one he bit into that lit him up like a fireball."

She took it and sniffed it, her lip curling. Varcolai had a keener sense of smell than fae; maybe that side of her would pick something up. "Totally hinky." She smelled it again. "There might be silver in this. Mixed with something else, obviously, because there's no way a vampire could wear silver next to his skin."

"That's what I figured."

She handed it back. "You going to have Harlow read this, too?"

He tucked the piece in his pocket. "Yes. She already knows I don't know how else to get information out of it and I need her help. She said she'd think about it."

"She'd probably do it if I said I thought it was a bad idea."

He snorted. "Can't blame her for being like her mother." He paused, thinking. "If they're all wearing these amulets, then they weren't made here, but she might get another location off it. Like where it's been most recently." He dug into his other pocket. "Speaking of being somewhere recently...Renny gave me this." He held out the note the gator shifter had asked him to pass on to Dulcinea.

She looked at it but didn't touch it.

Augustine pushed it into her hand. "I'm just the messenger."

"Hmph." She stuffed the note into the pocket of her long sweater coat.

"He's sweet on you."

"He's sweet on a lot a women, that's his problem. I'm sure you understand that." Her gaze shifted toward the front of the house. "I'll stay out here. You go talk to Harlow. If you need me to buffer again, just holler."

So ended the conversation about Renny. Augustine nodded. "Will do." He headed into the house, going in through the back door quietly to keep from disturbing Lally, but her light was on. He knocked softly on her door.

"Come in," she called.

He stuck his head in. She was in bed, reading. The cross, key and locket dangling from her chain gleamed against her mint-green nightgown. Her antique radio played the local gospel station quietly. "Just wanted to let you know I ran into a vampire down in the Quarter tonight." The part about Harlow being there he'd keep to himself.

She nodded thoughtfully. "He related to Miss Olivia's murder?"

"I believe he's part of the same group, yes."

She nodded again. "You kill him?"

He'd never had this kind of conversation with Lally before. There was something unsettling about those words coming out of her kind mouth. "I did."

"Mmm-hmm." Satisfaction gleamed in her eyes, a strange sight. "You have a good night then, Augie. I'm gonna sleep a little easier because of that."

He closed her door, oddly shaken by the exchange. It felt like they'd entered a period of war where hard truths and cold reality were the order of the day. If he could get Harlow to understand that, maybe couch it in terms of a real-life computer game, she could become a partner in this fight. Especially if Cuthridge could get this fine taken care of and she ended up staying here in New Orleans. He'd sure come to rely on her unique skills. And if she could track him, her skills were even more impressive.

As he walked down the hall, a familiar lemon verbena scent

floated toward him. He slowed, moving toward the mirror. "Livie," he whispered.

The surface of the mirror shimmered and for a moment, he swore he'd caught a glimpse of the Claustrum. He shook his head. He was so tired he was seeing things. He turned away.

"Augie."

He froze at the sound of Olivia's voice.

"Augie, are you there?"

He spun back toward the mirror. "Livie?" There was a shape there, a form that could be her. As he went closer and got directly in front of the mirror, she came into focus. "Livie!"

"Augie, you're there!" She reached out for him, but her image stayed flat, trapped in the mirror's glass. "I've been trying to reach you, but you never seemed to hear me. I guess I wasn't powerful enough until now."

"Trying to reach me where? In the mirror?"

"Yes, and when you were here on the fae plane."

"You mean you're really there? At the Claustrum? Why did you end up there?"

"It was the last place on my mind, I guess. I was worried about you, about what you'd do to those vampires and how the Elektos would react."

"You had nothing to worry about."

She looked at him like he was full of it. "Any unsanctioned action you take could be perceived by the Elektos as aggressive. Then Fartus will be at the door again."

"Fenton's already come back."

"And?"

"And we sorted everything out. He's not as bad as you think."

Her eyes lit with an uncertain light. "Did you take the Guardianship?"

He hesitated, but only because it seemed so odd to even be having such a conversation with her. "I did."

"Augie." Liquid rimmed her lower lids. "I am so very proud of you."

He looked away. He didn't want her pride at that moment. Not when he was the cause of all of this. "It shouldn't have taken you being attacked. They came for me."

"We never know the paths our lives are meant to take, *cher*. What's it like being Guardian? Have you staked those fanged bastards, yet?" That was Livie, forgive and forget.

"Not exactly." His gaze traveled up the steps toward Harlow's room. "There's something else I need to talk to you about. Something personal."

She smiled. "I'm a little on the dead side, *cher*. I've got no secrets anymore."

"I think you're more of a ghost."

She laughed. "That's still dead."

"Either way, I'm coming through." He slipped through the mirror and stood facing her, the fae plane oddly still for once. He reached out to her. The second their hands met, he grinned. "You're real. At least on this plane."

She pulled him in for a hug. "Good to know, because I really wasn't sure. Especially since I don't need that damn cane anymore." She let him go, the smile on her face adding some much-needed light to the dreary world around them. "Now, what did you need to talk to me about?"

"Harlow. She came for the funeral and the reading of the will—"

Livie laughed. "How'd that go over?"

"She didn't love it."

"I didn't expect her to." Livie sniffed. "I guess she hightailed it on back to Boston after that."

"Actually, she's still in New Orleans. Staying in the big guest room on the third floor."

Livie's mouth dropped. "I never would have guessed. After I

turned down her request for her father's name and the money, I didn't expect to ever see her again."

"What money?"

She looked away. "I'm not sure it's something I should share."

"If it was to pay the eight-hundred-and-fifty-thousand-dollar fine for hacking into some company's accounts, I already know about it. I'm assuming you know she's facing jail time if that fine's not paid."

Livie swallowed and nodded hard. "I do and I only said I wasn't going to give her the money out of anger. I had every intention of giving her the funds at breakfast the next morning. I'd do anything to keep her out of prison. Oh, Augie, you have to get a hold of Lionel Cuthridge; he's the lawyer you went to see about the trust and all—"

"She's already calling him so she should have an appointment with him tomorrow morning."

"Excellent. Go with her. Tell him I said to draw the funds from the account in the Caymans. He'll know that you talked to me that way. You have to keep Harlow safe, Augie."

"I will. I already promised you that, didn't I?"

Her eyes twinkled. "You did. Have I said how proud I am of you for taking the Guardianship?"

"You mentioned it."

"How's Lally? Oh, you must bring her through so we can visit."

He rolled his eyes. "You know bringing a human to the fae plane is part of what got me in trouble in the first place." He shook his head. "She's doing well, but she does miss you something awful. She did a beautiful job on your funeral. The turn-out was incredible."

She preened a little, then her face went stern. "Augustine. You're the Guardian now. If you deem it necessary to bring a human to the fae plane, who's going to stop you? Now, no more sass. Bring Lally through. Bring some bourbon, too. This place is dry as a bone."

"Livie, there's something else I need to ask you about. Someone, really."

She sat on a nearby outcropping of rock, patting the stone ledge next to her. "Who's that, *cher*?"

He stayed standing. "Joseph Branzino."

She paled, a considerable feat for a woman who was technically dead. Her hand drifted toward her throat. "I haven't heard that name in years. How . . . how do you know that name?"

"He showed up at the cemetery claiming to be Harlow's father."

"I knew this would happen when I was gone." She shook her head. "Is Harlow all right? What happened?"

"I took care of it. Is he Harlow's father?"

"Yes." Her eyes went hollow, the spark of joy that had been there dying off like the last of the summer lightning bugs. "He's also the most evil man I know."

Chapter Twenty-nine

Giselle followed the man she knew as Dell, slipping into his house under cover of the masking spell she'd used. Despite being hidden that way, she'd uncharacteristically dressed in all black. Just in case she had to make a quick getaway and disappear into the night.

He paused once in the kitchen as he unpacked the takeout dinner he'd brought home. He stared in her direction like he'd heard something. She froze, pressing herself into a dark corner and praying to the goddess he wouldn't look too closely. The masking spell wasn't exactly a cloak of invisibility.

When he went back to his dinner, she exhaled the breath she'd been holding. Rice and beans with a greasy sausage and a side of fried okra. That would do nicely. He took a beer from the fridge and as he was about to carry his meal into the other room, she used a small spell to make the doorbell ring.

He put the food down and left to answer it. She flew into action, mixing the powder Father Ogun had sold her into his dinner. It disappeared into the red beans and rice without a trace.

"Damn kids," he muttered as he returned. He picked up his food and his beer and headed for the living room, where he turned on the holovision and settled down to eat. She stayed in the kitchen where she could see him, but not too close. This wasn't some underequipped human she was dealing with. Some fae could sense things and she didn't know enough about this one to judge exactly what his abilities were.

Halfway through the basketball game, he got up for another beer. She prayed to the goddess that the alcohol would help her cause. After he finished his meal, she gave him another fifteen minutes, just to make sure the powder had taken hold.

Then she snuck into the living room and bent down from behind the sofa to whisper in his ear. "Scratch your head."

He went very still and for a second, she thought he was going to turn and ask her what the hell she was doing in his house. Then his hand drifted into his hair and scratched.

She smiled. Father Ogun's powder had been worth the price. She bent down again, this time with new instructions. "Get your tablet. You want to write a note."

He stood and walked zombie-like down the hall and into a small office. They passed a stairway with a small curved landing at the top that overlooked the foyer. She made a note of that for later.

He went through the motions of unlocking the tablet. It came to life, the soft glow of the screen illuminating his blown-out pupils. He was well under the drug's thrall. She leaned toward him, whispering what she needed him to type.

When he was done, she instructed him to leave the tablet open on his desk, then began filling his head with exactly what she needed him to do next.

"What on earth would make you get involved with that man, Livie?" Augustine stared at her in a way that made her feel small, but that feeling wasn't really his doing. It was her own disgust with herself.

"I met him on a movie set. He was one of the moneymen, so everyone treated him like a king, but I was the only one of the actresses in the film that didn't jump into his bed the second he looked at them."

She sighed, remembering. "He had a way about him, a charm so thick it made seeing what lay beneath impossible. But it wasn't the sweet talk and the gifts that got me, it was his ability to listen, the way he'd sit for hours asking me about myself and just acting as though my stories fed his soul in some kind of way." She snorted, a bitter, disillusioned noise of self-deprecation. "I had no idea how true that was."

Augie finally sat beside her. "What do you mean?"

She turned to him and took his hand, squeezing it hard because it was so good to be able to touch someone again and so good to have him near. Fear she hadn't felt in years choked her. "Branzino has barely any human blood in him at all. When he goes out in public, he uses magic to pass as human."

"Magic? What kind? Witchcraft?"

"I don't know. Could be fae. Could be witch."

"So the bulk of his bloodlines are raptor fae and raptors feed off emotion. And they read metal, right?"

She nodded. "They can touch or taste it or sometimes even sniff it and know where it's been, what it's for, how to manipulate it." She took a long breath. "I've always figured that's where Harlow got her skill with computers. All those little metal bits in there..." She shrugged.

Augustine's hand burned hot in hers. "A raptor. Damn. I can't believe it. That's why he was such a good listener. He was feeding off you." He sat back like he'd just realized something. "No wonder Harlow picks up on emotion the way she does. With your haerbinger senses and his raptor blood..." He whistled low. "I would have locked myself away from the world, too. *Sturka*."

"*Sturka*, indeed." She swallowed and clung to the easy lie. "He tried to take her from me when she was born. Claimed he could raise her better than I could. We finally came to an understanding and he agreed to leave her alone—"

"Livie, I've known you long enough to know when you're not telling me the whole truth. You can't make me believe you came to any kind of understanding with a man like that. If you got him to leave her alone, it was because you had leverage. What was it?"

Olivia's heart sank into her stomach. She dropped Augustine's hand and twined her fingers together. "I can't," she whispered. She had no desire to relive the horrors of the past.

"Livie..." Pain etched his face so deeply she realized it must be a reflection of her own. He spoke softly but with firm intent. "I might need to know this information to keep Harlow safe."

She nodded, her eyes looking forward but seeing only the past. "Harlow...was a twin."

Augustine stilled. "What? Was? Where is—"

The swell of emotion threatened to choke her. "Branzino is evil, Augie. He's probably sold himself as some businessman, but he's more than that. He's a crime lord, a kingpin. They used to call him the Shark, but he killed the last man who said it to his face. You've got to protect Harlow from him."

He interrupted her. "Nothing is going to happen to her, but you can't just tell me she was a twin and move on."

She nodded. "Early on in our courtship, such as it was, I jokingly read Branzino's palm. I did a stupid, stupid thing." Her breath came out in a ragged sigh, shredded like her insides. "It showed that his firstborn child was going to be the death of him and I told him."

"Why would you do that?"

"I didn't know how dangerous he was then and he already had a son. And obviously, that child's birth hadn't caused anything to happen to him." She covered her face with her hands, wishing she could change time.

"Okay, so if he had a kid already..."

She dropped her hands. There was no turning back now.

"That child was his nephew. He'd adopted the boy when Branzino's brother was killed in a car accident." She wrapped her arms around herself and began to rock slowly. The powdery soft scent of their little heads filled her senses with memories both beautiful and heart-wrenching.

Augustine pressed her gently. "And when Harlow was born? What happened?"

"Harlow was second. Ava Mae was first." She closed her eyes, trying not to see those sweet innocent faces and failing. "I did everything I could to keep him away. To protect my girls." A tear rolled down her cheek. "None of it mattered. I was away on a night shoot. He killed one of my security guards and broke into the house, killed the nanny I'd hired." She sobbed. The black-and-white video played in her head like a nightmare. "He smothered her in her crib."

Augustine's face froze in a mask of repulsed shock. "Are you saying he killed Harlow's twin because you predicted she would be the death of him?"

She nodded, her throat too thick with sorrow to speak.

"How do you know all this?"

She swallowed down enough of the pain to let the words out. "Security footage. He even looked up at the camera at one point, to make a point of how much he didn't care that he was being filmed." Another, smaller sob. Then her sorrow turned to anger. "He thought he was protecting himself from the police. But I knew a human prison meant nothing to him. So I told him if he ever came near Harlow, ever touched her, ever let her know he was her father, I would send that footage to every Prime in every Haven city I knew of."

She turned to look at Augustine. "I threatened him with the Claustrum, because that's exactly where he'd be sent for killing his own child."

"I should kill him right now." Augustine's anger was almost palpable. "Why didn't you send the footage anyway?"

"I was afraid. I thought he'd send his thugs to kill Harlow if I did that." Her voice came out thin and pathetic. "I wanted to. I should have."

Augustine nodded. "I understand regrets."

"Thank you." She breathed out. There was some solace in revealing the great burdens of your life. "There's nothing he won't do for money or power. If you can't kill him, you've got to keep Harlow away from him. You've got to protect Harlow from him."

"I will. I promise." He nodded. "Does Harlow know any of this?"

"No, and I don't want her to."

"Maybe she should."

"She already hates me. Imagine if she knew I let her sister be murdered?" Olivia put her head in her hands. "I only did what I thought was best."

"She doesn't hate you. And you didn't let Ava Mae get murdered. That's all on Branzino." Augie's arm wrapped her shoulders and his head came in to touch hers. "This can all be worked out. You're here and I can teach her how to access this plane and then—"

"No." Olivia sat up abruptly. "Harlow hates being fae. Can you imagine what seeing this place would do to her? I don't want her here. Give me some time to figure this out, see what I'm capable of. Maybe I'll be able to cross back over with some practice."

He gave her a curious look. "As what? A ghost?"

"It would still be better than her seeing me here." She grabbed his hand again. "Promise me you won't say a word about what I told you. And not a word about me being here, either. Not until I can better control whatever this new form is."

"Livie—"

"Promise me. I have to do this when I'm strong enough."

He sighed. "I promise, but only for a little while longer. You have to tell her soon."

She stared deep into his eyes. "I will. Now go home and make sure Cuthridge takes care of Harlow's fine, but if Branzino comes around, you use the information I gave you. Cuthridge can give you access to my safety-deposit box. You'll find copies of the footage there. Understand?"

"Understand." Augustine flipped his mirror open, the move keeping him from looking her in the eyes when he answered her. "I *am* going to tell Fenton about Branzino being a raptor. That could be vital in our investigation." He sighed. "You should know we think—Harlow and I—that he might be involved in letting the vampires into the city. And until I have reason to believe differently, I'm pursuing that angle."

"It wouldn't surprise me if he was." She forced herself not to read anything into his lack of eye contact, because as long as she was trapped in the fae plane, there was nothing she could do about it.

Unless she found a way to bring Branzino here and kill him herself.

Out of the corner of her eye, Harlow saw the bedroom door swing open and a familiar horned fae walk in. She ignored him, preferring the fantasy of Zauron to the reality of Augustine. He *liked* her. What was she supposed to do with that? How was she supposed to feel? Liking him back meant…what? That he was her boyfriend? Did people even do that anymore? Her head was a mess. Just like her heart.

He waved his hands to get her attention.

She held up a finger to indicate he should wait, then finished killing the basilisk on her screen and signed off. She pulled the earpiece out and sighed. "If you're here to yell at me about following you again, I get it. It's dangerous. Don't do it. Message received."

The way he looked at her made her feel like he was taking inventory of a very sad store. "That's not why I'm here, but before I say anything else, you need to know that what happened between Dulcinea and I was a one-time thing and it happened when we were teenagers. Years ago."

Interesting that her knowing that was so important to him. "Over and done with. Got it."

He seemed a little miffed that was the extent of her reaction. "Also, I wanted to make sure we're set for tomorrow, because I'm going with you. I got the money out of the house, too."

"Good. I called before I followed—anyway, I left a message on Cuthridge's voice mail that we need to meet and he called back to confirm for first thing." She slipped her gloves back on out of habit. "What did you do with the money if it's not here?"

"Probably better you don't know."

She nodded. "I'm okay with that. Thanks. I'll see you in the morning."

"Slow down, speedy. You think we're not going to talk about what happened tonight?"

She couldn't look at him. Couldn't. "I get it. You like me. I might...like you, too. A little. But I really don't want to talk about feelings and—"

"I meant about you following me. You never promised not to do it again."

"Oh." Heat flooded her face so fast, she knew she must be a wicked shade of embarrassed. She studied something on the opposite side of the room.

"It's nice to know you might like me, too." She could tell he was grinning without even looking at his stupid, handsome face. "Especially since we're living together."

She spun back around. "We're not living *together*. We're living in the same house. Those are two very different things."

He nodded. "Okay. Got it. Different things."

"You are so infuriating."

"So I've heard." He hesitated, leaning his hip against the footboard of the bed. "Was your case public knowledge?"

She almost wept with joy at the change of subject. "Sure, if you did the research."

"So the amount of your fine, that would be public record, too?"

"I guess. Why?"

He heaved out a long sigh and scratched his head. "I'm probably reading something into nothing. Don't worry about it."

She hopped off the bed to stand in front of him. "Tell me. If I'm going to stay here, if we're going to co-own this house together, I don't want there to be secrets between us. I've told you a lot about me. You can at least tell me whatever's rolling around in your head." She stripped off one glove and wiggled her fingers at him. "Or I can find out myself."

He looked taken aback. "You'd do that?"

She sighed and yanked the glove back on. "Actually, I wouldn't. And I suck at bluffing. Just tell me, okay?"

He straightened. "The box contained exactly eight hundred and fifty thousand."

She shrugged. "That proves that Branzino's been watching me for a while. He must have thought I'd be an easy mark with that kind of debt hanging over my head."

"Maybe." Augustine looked unconvinced. "I believe he deliberately set you up so he could swoop in and save you. Your mother's death was just—for him—a happy coincidence. The house was an unexpected bonus."

She gave that a moment to sink in, then shook her head. "But if my mother had something on him, enough to keep him away from me all these years, why set this all up while she's still alive?" The realization of her own words struck her as they left her mouth. "I think I'm going to be sick." She grabbed for the bedpost and sat down, her stomach on the verge of rebelling. It was all she could do to whisper, "He killed her."

"No, vampires killed her. I was there."

She lifted her head enough to look at him. "But you still don't know who let those vampires in, do you?"

He slowly shook his head and cursed softly. "Before your mother died, she said 'After me' and I didn't understand what she meant. I tried to explain to her I was to blame. The vampires had come after me because I'd killed the leader's girlfriend. What if she was right? What if they'd told her she was their target?" He put his hand over his eyes for a second, then dropped it and paced to the other side of the room. "If he's behind getting those vampires access to the city, if he deliberately did this to target your mother but meant for me to take the blame... it's one of the most complex murder plans I've ever encountered."

"What did you mean about the house being a bonus?"

He stopped pacing. "Any fae convicted of a felony is forbidden to own property in a Haven city. I have a feeling Branzino has a record. Owning the house through you would give him a foothold here to branch out into whatever it is he really does." He swore in a language she didn't understand. "Of course he wanted Olivia dead. He needed you to own this house so he could use it. The chaos created by the vampires was only icing on the cake. A way to distract us from his real purpose."

The world seemed to narrow down around her. "He was using me from the very beginning, wasn't he? Using me to kill my own mother." A chill swept her as her brain went a little foggy.

"You okay?" Augustine sat beside her on the bed. "You went dead white, like you were going to pass out. You're not responsible for any of this."

She nodded, mouth dry as dust. "My mother was right about him this whole time. He's no good. Not one tiny bit. And now I *know* he was my anonymous client."

"Are you sure?"

"He might have hired someone, but it was still him. I feel it. As sure as I'm breathing." Her fingers shook as she pushed hair out of her face. "No wonder I couldn't track him down. He's got his son in on this." She looked up at Augustine, feeling like she might be sick. "What kind of father tries to use his daughter like that?"

"One who doesn't deserve the title father."

"If he comes back here..." The thought caused her to shudder.

"He won't," Augustine said. "I'm going to make sure of that."

Chapter Thirty

Cuthridge nodded as he listened to Harlow explain her situation. Augustine expected the man to balk at the amount, but he didn't flinch one bit. Maybe years of being a lawyer had inured him to these kinds of things. When Harlow was done, she sat back, twisting her gloved fingers together.

Augustine spoke before Cuthridge could. "By my presence here today, I hope you understand I'm completely in favor of the estate paying this fine and securing Harlow's freedom. In fact, I believe there should be enough to cover the fine in the Cayman account."

"There is." Cuthridge cut his eyes at Augustine, a sure sign that information was not widely known. "Miss Goodwin, do you have the paperwork concerning your case?"

She dug into her purse. "I do." She handed it over.

Cuthridge perused the documents, a soft "Um-hmm" here and there. Finally, he put them down. "I'll have this taken care of immediately."

She exhaled like she'd been holding her breath. "You will? Just like that? I thought the money was only for keeping up the estate?"

"As the executor of the trust, the accounting of how the money is spent is up to me. The upkeep of the estate is very important, but taking care of the needs of the estate owners is even greater." Cuthridge smiled, softening his professorial demeanor. "I work for the trust, Miss Goodwin, and so,

in essence, I work for you. It is my job to protect you and Mr.
Robelais from these types of things whenever I can. In fact,
had this issue come to light sooner, I feel certain your mother
would have provided you with counsel beyond that which the
state did."

"You mean you?"

He laughed. "Oh no, I'm not that kind of lawyer. But I assure
you, I know some." He tucked the paperwork to the side. "I
should add, Miss Goodwin, that the trust considers this an
investment in you."

She went serious again. "Meaning?"

"Meaning there should be a return on that investment. In
plain language, I hope you will stay in New Orleans and look
after your mother's estate instead of returning to Boston. It is
not a requirement of having the fine paid, but something for
you to seriously consider."

She nodded. "I understand and I'm okay with that. I plan on
staying here."

"Very good." Cuthridge nodded, looking a bit more relaxed.
"Mr. Robelais, if I could have a moment of your time before you
leave?"

Harlow stood. "I'll give you two a minute. Thank you, Mr.
Cuthridge."

"My pleasure, Miss Goodwin." Cuthridge waited until the
door was closed to speak to Augustine. "How did you know
about the Caymans?"

"Long story short and in all confidentiality, Olivia made
it through to the fae plane. It's taken her a while to...figure
things out over there, but I spoke to her last night and she told
me to tell you this thing with Harlow needs to be taken care of
immediately."

"Of course, I'll do it today." He removed his glasses and used
his tie to wipe the lenses. "I'm very happy to hear we are not

entirely without Ms. Goodwin. I take it her daughter doesn't know?"

"Not yet and Olivia wants to keep it that way."

Cuthridge slipped his glasses back on. "I am all about confidentiality, Mr. Robelais. Tell Olivia everything will be taken care of."

"I will. And I appreciate it. I'm also going to need access to her safety-deposit box. She said you could provide that."

"I'll take care of that, too."

"Thank you." Augustine left the office, collecting Harlow as he left. On the way to the car, his com cell beeped in his head. "I have a call," he explained to her, unlocking the vehicle. She nodded as she got in and he stepped off to the side. "Answer."

"Augustine."

"Fenton. Good to hear from you. I have a few things to go over."

"Save them until you get to the address I just sent you. We have a situation."

By the sound of Fenton's voice, it wasn't anything good. "Such as?"

"Just get here."

⚜

Harlow was ecstatic that taking care of her fine had been so easy, but Augustine hadn't been in much of a mood to talk on the ride home. He'd dropped her off and sped away, something about Guardian business. She went inside, her head spinning with the sense of release and what that meant for her life now.

Like staying in New Orleans and trying to make a new start for herself. One where everything she did was aboveboard and completely legit. "Lally," she called out. "Where are you?"

"In the library, child."

Harlow ran into the room. Lally was wiping the books down with a soft cloth. Harlow couldn't keep the grin off her face. "It's done. The fine's taken care of."

"Praise the Lord, that is good news!" Lally grinned right back. "I think that calls for a big supper, don't you? Maybe cake."

Harlow nodded. "Oh, yes. Chocolate. Please?"

Lally laughed and went back to cleaning off the books. "You got it. I got a chocolate cola cake recipe my *tante* give me that is to die for."

"What's a *tante*?"

Lally smiled. "Means my aunt."

Harlow leaned against one of the built-in bookcases. "I have a lot to learn about this place."

Lally slid the book she'd finished with back onto the shelf, then turned to Harlow again. "This means you're staying, right? And you ain't selling the house?"

Harlow went still for a moment, her smile leveling out. "I... am. Staying, that is. And no, I'm not selling the house." She bit her lip. "The whole thing scares me witless, but the truth is, with my mother's estate paying the fine I feel like I owe it to her to finally do something she wants." And not just for legal reasons. It was time to make some changes in her life.

Relief lit Lally's face. "You got to want it, too, child."

"I do. A fresh start would do me good and with Branzino around, I feel safer here with you and Augustine than in Boston on my own."

"That man is no good."

"No, he's not." Harlow knew she'd be doing more digging on him now that Augustine had helped her connect Branzino as the client that had gotten her in trouble. "If it's okay with you, I thought maybe I'd have a look at the rest of the house. Maybe my mother's room."

Lally tsked. "You don't have to ask if that's okay with me. It's your house. You go on and explore all you want. Your mama's room is on the second floor, same as yours. She took the elevator these last few years. Easier on the old bones."

"Thanks." A hint of sadness crept over Harlow at the thought of her mother growing old in this house and Harlow not being a part of those years. That regret would be with her the rest of her life. "I'm sorry we didn't get off to a better start. I'm glad you were here for my mother. That she had such a good friend with her." *When I wasn't.* But those words seemed implied.

Lally flicked the cleaning cloth at her. "Go on, now, before I go all weepy." But she smiled and nodded like she understood.

Harlow climbed the stairs to the second floor and found her mother's room on the first try. The moment she entered, the fragrance of her mother's lemony perfume greeted her, making her feel like Olivia might walk in the room at any moment. The master suite was impressively furnished, although a bit over-done for Harlow's tastes. Olivia's had always run toward the dramatic, so the ivory, green, and purple that swathed the space was no surprise.

Mementos of the movies she'd worked on were scattered throughout; pictures from some of the sets or Olivia in costume, shadow boxes containing small props, the Oscar she'd won for supporting actress for the last role she'd taken before retiring.

Harlow's gloved fingers traced the gleaming statuette. There was so much she'd missed out on in her mother's life. Harlow opened a set of double doors and walked into the most amazing closet she'd ever seen.

The air was thick with the scent of her mother's perfume here, but there was comfort in that lemony tang. She walked past the racks of clothes, her fingers trailing over the gorgeous fabrics. The back of the closet held the fanciest dresses of all.

Harlow stood there for a moment, admiring the gowns covered in crystals and feathers and sequins. "Ooo...shiny."

A soft breeze slid past her bare ankles.

She glanced down. How was there a breeze in here? Lally's statement about the house being haunted echoed through her head, but she refused to believe what she'd felt had anything to do with a ghost. She crouched down to look. One of the gowns had feathers down the skirt. They fluttered just enough to make her even more curious. She dug her hands between the dresses and shoved them back.

A seam ran up the wall. She followed it with her fingers. It outlined the shape of a small door. There was no handle, so she pushed on it. Nothing. Not even a creak. She pushed the clothes farther apart and leaned her ear against the door. The breeze she'd felt made a whispering noise on the other side. One that almost sounded like words. She stood back and stared.

As much as the space intrigued her, she supposed it wasn't that unusual. Old houses all had secret rooms, right? And they were drafty. Didn't mean there was anything in there. Probably just led into the closet in the next room. Plus, she'd come up here for more than just looking at her mother's room. Harlow wanted to try a little experiment. She spread the dresses back over the space, covering the hidden door, then left the closet to look around for an item that would work—and found something perfect on her mother's dresser.

A handful of costume jewelry was strewn over the velvet-draped surface, but in the center sat a large fleur-de-lis marcasite pendant on a chain, just the sort of sparkly bit her mother would like. Harlow picked it up and sat in the ivory silk club chair in the suite's sitting area.

She laid it on her lap, then pulled her gloves off. Staying in New Orleans meant accepting who she was. No more running from being fae, something that was almost impossible in a place where everyone already knew that's what she was. If she could use her gifts to help, then they couldn't be bad, could they? The only way for her to get really comfortable with her heritage was to learn to control—and use—these gifts she'd been born with.

Starting with the one that had crippled her.

She eased her bare fingers under the pendant, the cool metal warming as it touched her skin. Like a switch had been flipped, images began rushing through her mind. The scent of her mother's perfume intensified and distant laughter filled her ears. She dropped the necklace and took a few deep breaths. She could do this. She *would* do this.

Slipping her fingers beneath the pendant, she closed her eyes and mentally clamped down the same way she did when entering a fragged database.

This time the images slowed and the overwhelming scent of lemon faded to a tolerable level. The laughter seemed to gain clarity, enough that Harlow knew it belonged to Olivia. The first image that came through clearly was of Augustine, his horns as large as they'd been the night of *Nokturnos*, handing over a box. A feeling of joy followed, then a sense of loss that Harlow understood because she was the one who'd caused it.

She dropped the pendant, opened her eyes and sat back. The pendant had been a gift from him to Olivia. Harlow knew it with an undeniable certainty. The gesture had given her mother great happiness but had also reminded Olivia of Harlow's absence in her life.

Harlow tipped her head back and took a deep breath in an effort to stem the tears threatening to spill. A few leaked anyway, trickling down into her hairline. Is this what it was going to take to master this gift? Feeling things so deeply that it was like experiencing them as the person they belonged to? Having her emotions shredded?

She lifted her head and wiped at her eyes before putting her gloves back on, then she picked up the pendant and stared at how it caught the light. No wonder her mother had loved it.

Olivia had always seen the good in people, the bright side of every situation, the silver lining in every storm. Harlow shook her head, the lump in her throat almost impossible to swallow around. She'd never be her mother, but maybe, if she really worked at it, she could become a fraction of the person her mother had wanted her to. The *fae* her mother had wanted her to be.

Harlow fastened the chain around her neck. The metal warmed to her skin. She sat, letting the emotions from the piece run through her until there was nothing left. At least this way, she could feel like a part of her mother was still with her.

It was the only way Harlow could think of to make peace with the past.

Chapter Thirty-one

D amn it." Augustine stared at the body dangling from the railing of the second story of the Garden District house and shook his head. Dreich, his lieutenant and Khell's cousin, had hung himself. "What happened?"

Fenton sighed. "Guilt, I guess."

"Over what?"

"He left a note confessing to letting the vampires in."

"Dreich?" Augustine shook his head. "I'm not buying it. He might have been involved, but I have good reason to believe Branzino is in on this. Where's the note?"

"On his tablet. It was left open and unlocked."

"That's convenient."

Fenton nodded. "Agreed. You really think Branzino is part of this?"

"Yes. I found out a hell of lot more about him from Livie. He's raptor fae, but basically lives as human mafia."

Fenton's brows shot up. "That's doubly bad. Why would he get involved in all this then?"

Augustine mapped out the conclusions he and Harlow had come up with.

Fenton sighed. "It's convoluted, but I've heard worse." He pushed his glasses up his nose. "We have a lot of work to do getting to the bottom of this. Do you think Branzino suspects you're aware of his involvement?"

"No. And we should keep it that way."

"Agreed. Why don't we spin this then, let Dreich shoulder the whole burden of guilt until we know otherwise."

Augustine nodded. "I don't like letting a potentially innocent man be the fall guy, but it's a solid plan."

"I wouldn't say potentially innocent. A cursory check of his bank account showed several large deposits recently." Fenton swiped at his mouth. "He looks good for at least being involved. Maybe he was jealous of his cousin's position, who knows. It'll come out as we investigate further."

"I never figured him for this." Augustine stepped aside to let a police officer pass. "What's the human take going to be?"

Fenton's gaze followed the officer until he was out the door. "Same as our story. Just as it looks, a suicide."

Augustine raised a brow. "Let's say he is involved. This suicide is awfully neat. So either Branzino is still in town or he's got people here."

Fenton blew out a sigh.

Augustine waited for a second cop to go by. "It's just too convenient we now have a confession that leads to an instant dead end—excuse the expression. Other than these deposits, we don't have any other evidence that points to Dreich. All I know is that Giselle is the witch behind the spell on the cross and she claims to have done it for a fae named Dell, so am I supposed to think that Dell is Dreich and consider this case closed? Because I don't. Not until I do more digging."

Fenton shook his head. "It stinks."

"Damn straight it does. Can we trust the police to work with us on this?"

"Yes. They don't want vampires in this city any more than we do." Fenton held up a finger. "But for now, we move forward like we believe this is exactly what it appears to be. That we have our vampire connection sewn up."

Augustine nodded. "Hopefully whoever he was working with

will think they're off the hook. All they need to do is feel comfortable enough to slip up." He glanced around the police officers. "Who's in charge of the human side of this investigation?"

"Come with me." Fenton led him into the office. Dreich's tablet was on the desk, black dust covering all the surfaces. If the cops were looking for prints, they didn't think this was a suicide, either. Or they were at least going through the motions. A familiar-looking man stood in one corner, his rumpled sport coat making him look like he'd yet to get to bed, as did the cup of takeout coffee he was nursing. The officer he was talking with left as they approached. "This is Detective Grantham. Detective, this is Augustine Robelais. He's our newly appointed Guardian."

Grantham stuck his hand out. His skin was a shade or two darker than Lally's, and his knuckles showed a matrix of scars. "Good to meet you."

Augustine shook the man's hand. "Are you...J.J. 'One Punch' Grantham?"

The detective laughed. "I haven't heard that name since I forgot to take out the trash and my wife yelled at me. Yeah, that was me. Lotta years ago."

"Your last fight was at Harrah's, right? You were a legend."

"Around here, maybe, but..." He shrugged. "Time came to move on and do something that wouldn't turn me into a crippled mess in my old age." He sipped his coffee. "You knew the deceased?"

"I did. Not well, though. His cousin was the last Guardian, the one killed by vampires a week ago."

Grantham nodded. "That is one problem I'd like to eradicate. Immediately. I'm tired of seeing tourists in my morgue."

"It's not good for any of us, fae or human."

Fenton interrupted. "If you'll excuse me, I have work to do. Augustine, call me if you need me." He nodded at the detective. "Grantham."

Grantham nodded back. "Fenton." Then he returned his attention to Augustine. "You buy the confession Dreich left?"

Augustine shook his head. "Yes and no."

"Meaning?"

"Meaning maybe he was involved, but I questioned him a day ago before we raided the Hotel St. Helene on a lead that the vampires were holed up there. They were, but someone must have tipped them off..." Augustine glanced back toward the foyer, where the coroner was in the process of cutting the body down. "Damn it. I really don't want him to have been behind this."

"Then who?"

"I don't know." He wasn't ready to share his theory on Branzino with the cops. Anything they did could tip him off. "It feels bigger than one person, though."

Grantham nodded. "I'd buy that."

"The witches are involved. I don't know how deeply, but I know Giselle Vincent had her hands in this." Augustine explained how the vampire they'd taken into custody had gotten killed, about the cross he'd found and how he'd had it read, but left Harlow's name out of it. "If you and your guys find anything that links back to any of the witches, I want to know immediately."

"I'll make sure of it, but you really think Giselle Vincent is involved in this? Her father's a pretty big deal. Why would she do anything to muck that up?"

"Because she hates the rule the fae have imposed on the witches."

One of the forensic agents came in. "Detective, we found some kind of powder on the kitchen counter." She held up what looked like an empty glassine bag.

"Any idea what it is?" Grantham asked as he took the bag.

She shook her head. "No, and there was barely enough on the

counter to get a sample but we'll rush it to lab as soon as we get back."

He opened it and sniffed. "Hmm." Then he held it out to Augustine.

Augustine took a whiff, but shook his head. "Nothing I recognize, but it smells... earthy. And old. Like dirt, but not dirt."

"Good assessment." Grantham sealed the bag and handed it back to the forensic officer. "Smells like *bokura* to me."

"What's that?"

Grantham's face took on the kind of serious air Augustine recognized as that of a man about to go to war. "In layman's terms, zombie powder."

Augustine almost snorted. "Are you serious?"

"The practice of voodoo is just as prevalent in the dark corners of this city as the witches' magic is. Used in the right doses, *bokura* could make a man very pliable. A person could drug someone with *bokura* and get them to do all sorts of things they'd never consider sober."

Augustine swore under his breath. "Vampires, witches and voodoo. I picked a great time to become Guardian." He shook his head. "Voodoo is one thing I've always steered clear of. All the fae do, it's considered as off-limits as witchcraft to us, but not because we have any dark history with it. Because of that, I have no real sources to go to on this."

"I do," Grantham answered. "My grandmother is a mambo, a voodoo priestess."

Augustine nodded, happy he hadn't said anything about voodoo being crazy.

"I'll talk to her," Grantham said. "See what she can tell me about who might have made this powder, but more than that, who might have sold some recently. Fenton gave me your contact info before you got here, so I'll fill you in once I know something."

"I'd appreciate that." Although he had a feeling if the circles in the voodoo world were as closed as the witches', he wouldn't be getting much information. "Now, if you'll excuse me, I've got some vampires to kill."

Harlow knew something was up by the slam of the door. She dropped her laptop and raced downstairs, running into Augustine half a flight down. "What's going on?"

A hardness she hadn't seen before had taken over his face. "I've had enough. Too many deaths, too many damn vampires." He dug into his pocket and pulled out a small black amulet. "You said you'd read this for me. Are you okay with doing that now? If so I'll get Dulcinea over here as soon as—"

"No." The word came out before Harlow could stop herself. "I don't need her help. I can read it on my own."

The hardness softened a little into surprise. "You sure?"

"Yes. I've been practicing a little." Very little. Could once even be considering practice?

More surprise. "I'm game if you are. Library?"

"Sure."

She followed him down, nervousness making her jittery. Reading her mother's pendant once wasn't practicing.

Instead of settling into their usual places, Augustine sat next to her. With no Dulcinea to act as buffer, there was no reason for him not to sit that close. She peeled her gloves off and held her palms up.

"Ready?" he asked.

She nodded, knowing he must be able to hear her heart knocking against her rib cage. "Just be close to grab it out of my hands if...you need to."

He laid his hand over her forearm, his warmth easily

penetrating the sleeve of her shirt. "Hey, if you think you can do this, then I fully believe you can, too. And I'm not going anywhere."

"Thanks." She gave him a little half smile that revealed nothing about how calming his presence actually was. Even the subtle, smoky traces of him that lingered in the house when he was gone had become small pockets of comfort to her. She'd lived alone so long, she'd come to think that's what she preferred. The way she felt being in this house made her question that. And a lot more. She wiggled her fingers. "Let me have it."

He lowered the amulet into her bare palms.

The second it connected, she closed her eyes and tightened down on her control, but not before a sharp metallic zing snapped along her bones. She gasped in pain.

"Are you okay?"

She nodded. Sweat beaded along her spine. "There's...there's metal in this."

"We think silver."

"I don't know enough to tell yet." She opened herself a fraction and let the images hit her. A shudder ripped through her. "Vampires," she whispered, an angry sob following close behind. More anger built as the visuals came through, snippets of the creatures who'd killed her mother, of them laughing and drinking and hunting down humans like prey. The rage edged her senses in a red-hot haze but also served to clarify the information as she received it.

The scents and sounds that came through reminded her of Bourbon Street. She forced herself to concentrate harder, to find something that would give Augustine what he needed.

His hand was on her arm again. "Harlow, maybe that's enough—"

"No." She loosened her control even more, opening a floodgate of new sensations and sights. Teeth sinking into flesh so real pain shot through her neck. She opened her mouth so she could get enough air.

"Harlow, enough."

His fingers brushed hers but she clamped her hands over the amulet to shut him out. "Not yet," she insisted. Then she got what she'd been searching for. A building. She grabbed hold of the image, letting it burn into her mind. The stream of information fought her, pushing at her to let go, to let the rest through, but she clung to it.

"*Enough.*" Augustine tore the amulet from her grasp. "Harlow, your nose is bleeding. What the hell did you just do?"

"I found them." She slumped back against the couch, gulping air and doing her best to ignore the throbbing ache in her head. She wiped at her nose, her hand coming away streaked red.

Augustine ripped tissues from a nearby holder and gave them to her. Concern masked his face. "At the moment, I don't care. Are you okay?"

She dabbed at the blood. "I'm fine." Actually, she had no idea. "I saw a building—"

"I don't care if you saw a pink giraffe." He turned toward the door and yelled for Lally. "Just sit still for a minute."

Lally came rushing in. "What's the matter?"

"Harlow needs an ice pack."

"I'm fine." She took the tissues off her nose.

Lally slapped a hand over her heart. "Oh my. Be right back."

"You." Augustine pointed at her. "Pinch the bridge of your nose and sit still or I will never ask you for help again."

She tried not to smile and failed.

He frowned. "I'm not being funny."

No, but he was being protective and sweet and although it wasn't something she was used to, she kind of liked it. "You're being bossy."

When Lally returned with the ice, he made her sit for a few more minutes with it over the bridge of her nose. At last, when he was satisfied the bleeding had stopped, he let her talk. Stress still creased his forehead. "Tell me what else you saw."

"I don't know it, but I can describe it. I feel like it's in the Quarter. I got images of Bourbon, but I don't think that's where this place is. It's tall. Three and...a half stories. Yellow with white trim and simple black railings on two floors." She closed her eyes, the image reappearing with little effort. "It's on a corner. The bottom floor has a shop. A café maybe. There's an oval sign hanging above the door. I can see the silhouette of a black cat. A small alley courtyard with some tables and chairs." She opened her eyes again, her gaze flicking from him to the amulet he now held. "Do you know the place I saw?"

He nodded. "Sounds like a place near Conti. The Chat Noir Café is on that street, that's black cat in French. That's got to be it." He sat back. "Those damn vampires are holed up right beside the Supreme Court building. They must have a good laugh over that one." His gaze wandered over her. "Are you sure you're okay? That looked pretty intense."

"I promise, I'm fine. Dulcinea said it would get easier with practice." Easier, maybe, but right now she felt like she'd been run over. "They're in there. I can feel it." She sat up a little. "I'm going with you."

He blanked for a moment, then snorted. "Like hell you are. This is real life, not a video game."

If it was an RPG, she would have decimated them ages ago. "They *killed* my mother. I have the right to be there."

"I'm aware of what they did. Which is why *I'm* going to kill them. Every last bloody one of them." He stood. "Rest, Harlow. What you did for me by reading that amulet was invaluable. It already makes you part of this hunt, but you don't have the

skills to defend yourself and I can't spare the manpower to protect you while you're out there."

"Then teach me."

He paused. "Teach you to fight?"

"Yes." She started to nod but her head hurt too much. "To
defend myself. To be an asset and not a liability."

"You really want to learn, huh?" He smiled. "We could turn
the ballroom into a gym of sorts...okay, you're on. But you're
still not coming on this mission." He stood. "And if you follow
me again, I won't train you."

She rolled her eyes.

"I'm serious. I can't have something happening to you. It
would...put me in a bad place." He started for the door.

His confession soothed a tiny bit of the ever-present ache in
her heart. "What about you?"

He stopped, his gaze straight ahead. "What about me?"

"What if..." She looked away for a moment. She should
shut her mouth, but the reading had left her emotions raw and
open. "What if something happens to you?" The idea of losing
Augustine—of being alone again—suddenly hurt worse than
the hammering in her skull. "Aren't you afraid of those vampires? They could hurt you."

He turned to face her, his eyes holding a light she'd not seen
before, his voice softer and filled with the kind of naked honesty
she'd last heard when he'd confessed to leading the vampires
back to the house. *To liking her.* He came back and kneeled
beside the couch so they were eye to eye. "I have to get rid
of these murderers before they hurt anyone else. It's the job I
agreed to when I accepted the Guardianship, but it's a job I've
been training for my whole life. They should be afraid of me. I
am by far and away the most frightening creature that lives in
this city."

He linked his pinkie with hers and the sincerity of his words radiated through her bare skin, soothing the pain left behind from the reading. There was no fear in him that she could sense, just the overwhelming desire for vengeance and the crystalline strength of his readiness. He looked into her eyes and smiled. "I *will* come home."

Chapter Thirty-two

In less than thirty minutes, Augustine had his lieutenants assembled in the war room at the Pelcrum. Fenton stood near the door while the lieutenants sat at the massive circular table. He planted his fingers on the tabletop and began. "Thank you for coming on such short notice."

"Whenever you need us, boss. That's what we signed up for." Sydra tipped her head solemnly and he got the sense they were all eager to show how loyal they were after Dreich's scheming had been outed. For the sake of further investigation, he was going to have to let them feel that way until he knew more.

"In light of recent events, I appreciate that." Beatrice was pale with stress, but her eyes held an unearthly fire. A few killings would do her good. "As to why I called you here. The vampires have been located."

Cy's deep baritone boomed over the others. "Let's go get 'em."

Augustine put his hands up. "Hold on. We have no intel this time, no way to know how many we're up against, so instead of storming the building, I want to set up surveillance and take them out one at a time. As one of them leaves the building, one of us follows, stakes them and returns to our post. This way we have none left behind, none that escape." He raised one finger as his lieutenants listened. "If I don't get the chance to go after him personally, the leader is to be spared until I can get there. I want the pleasure of killing him myself."

The lieutenants nodded. Sydra lifted a hand. He nodded at her. "Are we starting this mission immediately?"

"You mean in daylight? Yes. Since it doesn't restrict the leeches, there's no reason to wait until nightfall. Because of that, we need our takedowns to be discreet. Also, we're only carrying weapons that can be concealed. In other words, nothing happens in front of tourists who will only be too happy to whip out their LMDs and video such a thing. We don't want news of this mass slaying to travel because it could create the need for retaliation among other Young Blood members. I do not want vampires having another reason to seek out New Orleans." He sat back in his chair. "Any other questions?"

Shaking heads indicated there weren't. His gaze shifted to the fae by the door. "Fenton, the floor is yours."

Fenton approached the table, pushing his spectacles up on his nose. "I know you've all heard about Dreich."

Beatrice's nostrils flared and her bottom lip twitched once. Augustine swore he could see ripples of heat coming off her. It occurred to him she might need this more than he did, just so she didn't hurt someone else out of necessity.

Fenton strolled around the table until he came to a stop at the right of Augustine's chair. "The incident is under investigation and we have the full cooperation of the NOPD, as we always do with a crime that involves one of our own."

"He should be made *rek'vamus*." Beatrice's voice was soft but full of cruel intent, cutting through the quiet of the room like a snake slithering on sand.

Dulcinea sucked in a breath as Cy grunted and Sydra shifted uncomfortably at the declaration. *Rek'vamus* was akin to being unborn as fae. It was worse than being dead. Any fae so appointed would essentially disappear. They weren't spoken of, they weren't thought about, and every trace of their existence was purposefully erased.

Fenton swallowed. "I understand your pain, Beatri—"

"No, you don't." Strands of hair around her face lifted in the heat wafting off her. "My husband was killed because Dreich brought those monsters into our city so he could make some extra plastic. Because of his greed, I have no husband." Her hand cradled to her belly as her gaze dropped. "And my unborn child has no father."

There was a moment of utter silence as they took in her news. It didn't seem the right time to offer congratulations.

Sparks glittered in Beatrice's eyes. "I demand Dreich be made *rek'vamus*."

With a nod, Fenton acknowledged her. "I will bring this to the Elektos, but I must tell you nothing will be done until the investigation is complete." He glanced at Augustine. His apologetic look meant he must be about to go off book. "We cannot be certain that we are truly dealing with a suicide. Or that Dreich was not merely a scapegoat meant to end our search for the one responsible for bringing these vampires in."

Some of the fire left her face. "How soon before you know?"

Augustine jumped in. "Soon. There was some evidence discovered at the scene that needs analysis. We're hoping that gives us more to go on." He stretched a hand across the table toward her. "I miss Olivia every day. There is nothing I want more than her killers dealt with. For now, focus on that with me, because I need your head in this mission. If it's not, say so. I don't want you hurt out there. Especially since you're pregnant."

She dropped her gaze to the table. "I'm in. I'll be fine." Then quieter. "I need this."

"We all do."

"Thank you for not keeping me out of it because of my pregnancy."

"You're in until you tell me differently." He glanced at Fenton. "Anything else?"

Fenton looked them over with a sense of pride. "May fate fight with you." He lifted his chin a little, the stern set of his jaw giving him an even greater seriousness. "Now go ash every single one of those *bala'stro.*"

Setting up surveillance in broad daylight without being spotted by any of the vampire guards would be tricky. Augustine stopped the group when they were a few blocks from the townhouse. "Sydra and Beatrice, I want you to go up Conti and when you get to Royal, split off, come around the block and return here. I want the location of every guard you see called in as they're spotted." They all had their LMD set up as one big conference call, enabling them to hear each other and keep in touch with little effort. "As we kill off a guard, we take their place and use that as our lookout. Then any vampires that come looking for their gang members will come right to us. Those leaving the building will be trailed out of the area and dealt with away from tourist eyes. Remember, be discreet. We don't want to start a war of retaliation here."

"On it." Beatrice nodded and took off, Sydra jumping to catch up with her.

Augustine pointed at Cy. "Let's use your morphing ability to catch these buggers off guard. As soon as we get the first location, you're up."

Cy grinned, a frightening sight on his blocky frame. "I'm ready."

It didn't take long. Sydra's voice chimed through their com

cells. "Blue T-shirt, jeans, tan ball cap, lounging on the steps of the Law Library."

"Got it." Cy shimmered and a second later, a young girl stood before them. She gave them a little nod, then loped off in the direction Sydra had passed on.

"That is never not going to be weird," Dulcinea said.

"I can hear you," Cy called back.

Beatrice came in next. "There's one on Royal. Holding a takeout coffee with a *Times-Picayune* under one arm."

Dulcinea rubbed her hands together. "Here we go."

"Got another one," Sydra said. "I'll take him." Minutes later a soft *oof* filled their heads. "And done," she finished. She sneezed. "Sorry. Ash in my nose."

The sounds of two more kills followed on the heels of that one, leaving Augustine's hands itching for his turn, but there were no more guards, so everyone settled in for the haul, each in their predetermined spots to watch for incoming or outgoing vamps.

Hours passed, bringing the occasional vampire through their sights. "Boss," Dulcinea's voice filled his head. "I got a female headed right for you. Big straw hat and sundress."

Augustine grinned. "She must be all dressed up for our date." He stepped out of the alley he was in and spotted the vampiress coming toward him. He leaned nonchalantly against the wall, sunglasses hiding his eyes. He hoped he looked like a fae tourist out to get some.

As she approached, he made a show of ogling her with great appreciation, a big smile on his face. Let her think she was passing as human so well even a fae couldn't tell. That should stroke her ego.

It did. She slowed, a coy smile turning up the corners of her mouth. "Hello."

"Right back atcha." He peeled off the wall and took a step

toward her. "What's a woman as pretty as you doing all alone on a gorgeous day like today?"

She hesitated like she wasn't sure she wanted to play this game. Fae blood wasn't especially tasty to vampires, but many of them believed a fae's powers could be absorbed that way, making it worthwhile to some. "My lunch date stood me up." She wrapped a strand of blond hair around one finger, her indecision plain. "I don't know much about—what are you called? Fae, right?" She smiled.

He nodded, smiling right back because she was definitely trying to work him now. "That's right, fae." He decided to work her right back. "I can't say I know that much about you humans, either." He sidled in closer. "How about we do a little cultural exchange over lunch, since your date clearly wasn't man enough for you?"

She laughed and he could have sworn he saw the glint of bloodlust in her eyes. "Here's to lunch, then."

He took a step back toward the alley. "I know a great little place not far from here." He offered her his arm. "Shall we?"

She looped her arm over his, making his skin crawl. "Aren't you the southern gentleman? I've never had one of those before. I mean, known." She giggled. "You've got me all flustered."

"I have that effect on women." As they walked deeper into the alley his free hand went to the back of his waistband and got a grip on his dagger. The shadows of the buildings around them gave the narrow passage a soft gloom she didn't seem to mind.

"I bet you do." She continued the banter. "I get the feeling I'm being wooed by a real lady killer."

"You couldn't be more right." He bent her arm back behind her, threw her up against the wall and plunged the dagger into her heart. "That's for Olivia."

Her mouth dropped open a second before she went to ash.

Augustine wiped his blade clean on his jeans, then tucked

it into his waistband. He walked back to the mouth of
the alley as he spoke to his lieutenants. "Another one bites the
dust."

Nothing Harlow did seemed to make the day go by any faster.
She played Realm of Zauron for a few hours, but her head wasn't
in the game. After lunch with Lally, she swam some laps, but
the water was too cold to stay in long. Finally she flipped on the
holovision in the family room and scrolled through the channels looking for something mindless. Or better yet, a Star Alliance marathon. Captain Finn would make a great distraction.

She stopped scrolling as familiar opening credits filled the
screen. The movie was one she hadn't seen in years, but it seemed
like the perfect thing to watch. She sat up a little straighter.
"Lally! Lally, come here!" She hit pause.

Lally stuck her head in. "What's the matter, Harlow?"

"Look." Harlow pointed the remote panel at the holovision
where the image was frozen. "It's *The Vampire Queen*."

Lally's fingers went to the chain around her neck and her
gaze turned nostalgic. "That's the movie that really made your
Mama a household name."

"Will you watch it with me? It seems oddly appropriate to
watch this while we wait for Augustine to come home from killing the very creatures she made famous, don't you think?"

Lally nodded. "It does. And nothing I do today seems to
make the waiting any easier."

"Isn't that the truth." Harlow scooted over on the couch.
"Come sit with me."

Lally held up a finger. "I think we need some popcorn for
this."

"With butter?"

"Butter and hot sauce, 'cause that's how we do it in New Orleans." With a laugh, Lally headed to the kitchen.

Harlow left the holovision on pause and went to help, welcoming the distraction. Anything to help her ignore the fear that Augustine was in danger.

Or worse. That he might not come home at all.

Chapter Thirty-three

Afternoon stretched into evening and still no sign of the gang leader. Augustine hoped that Scarface, as they'd nicknamed the vamp leader, hadn't caught wind of their systematic wipeout of his gang.

"Got one leaving the building," Cy called out. "Not Scarface. You want me to question this one before I kill him? See what I can find out?"

"Couldn't hurt, boss," Beatrice answered. She'd mellowed considerably with a few kills under her belt.

"Sure," Augustine said. "See what you can get."

They all listened while Cy did his job. After a little physical motivation, Cy started with the questions. "Where's your leader?"

"Idiot. Vampires don't have a leader."

A thump, followed by a moan. "The one with the scar on his face. Where is he?"

The next sound was unmistakably that of spitting. Then a sharp cracking, which Augustine envisioned as Cy's fist breaking the vampire's nose. The howling that followed confirmed his theory. Cy's voice was as low and gravelly as distant thunder. "Answer me, leech."

The vampire's curse came out nasally, perhaps due to his collapsed sinus cavity.

Augustine couldn't place the wet, sucking sound that came

next. The yelp of pain meant Cy was still pursuing his line of questioning, but in what manner…

"My fang!"

Cy grunted. "Answer me and I'll let you live so you can grow another one."

The vampire whimpered, his missing canine giving him a lisp. "He'th in the townhouth getting ready to hunt."

"How many are in there altogether?"

"Him and three others. Now leth me go."

"You're going all right." The shooshing of flesh turning to ash was unmistakable. "You got all that, boss?"

"Yes. Too bad we don't know how many more are still out there."

"Sorry," Cy said. "I should have asked that."

"No worries." Augustine hesitated. "Did you really rip his fang out?"

A few seconds went by before Cy answered. "Should I not be taking souvenirs?"

"It's all good." Augustine laughed, relief coming with the knowledge that Scarface was close at hand. "When Scarface comes out, I'm on him. If he comes out in a group, I'll take Sydra and Beatrice with me."

He could hear the smile in Sydra's voice. "The drunk girl-friends routine?"

"That's the one. Cy, switch places with us so we can watch the entrance."

"You got it, boss."

Half an hour later, under the pale light of the crescent moon, Scarface emerged from the townhouse. "Here we go," Augustine whispered as he crossed himself. "And he's got two with him. That leaves one in the townhouse and who knows how many yet to return. Cy, get back here. You and Dulcinea are on point. Sydra, Beatrice and I are on the hunt."

With the women at his sides, they followed after Scarface and his bodyguards. Sydra and Beatrice played their roles perfectly, laughing, missing a step here and there and keeping up the perfect amount of low-key chatter. To any passerby, the three of them would appear like a tipsy trio out for a night of carefree fun.

"Damn it." Augustine kept his voice low. "They headed into Lucky Frog's."

"We've got this," Beatrice answered with soft reassurance. She trailed a hand down Augustine's chest as she went back into character. "I want to dance!"

Sydra let out a whoop. "Me, too!"

Augustine swiped his LMD across the credit strip to pay their cover and in they went. The noise level in Lucky Frog's made his sensitive fae ears ache. How could humans stand such racket? But there were humans everywhere, packing the place until walking from one end to the other was like wading through the bayou.

He gave Sydra's and Beatrice's hands a little squeeze to get their attention, then gestured for them to go after the bodyguards and draw them away from Scarface. The women nodded and headed into the crowd, Beatrice unbuttoning her top a little as she went while Sydra yanked the clip from her hair, letting her burnished red mane fall free around her shoulders. If either of Scarface's bodyguards had the slightest interest in redheads, they'd have a hard time ignoring the fiery duo coming their way.

While the women went toward their targets, Augustine pushed through the crowd and up the steps to the elevated bar and walkway that ran around the top half of the club. It was less crowded and gave him a better vantage point, but he still found himself brushing off the advances of interested females every few steps. He located Sydra and Beatrice. Even with their red hair, the strobing lights and pulsing colors made them hard to pick out in the crush. They were closing in on the bodyguards.

He worked his way toward that side of the bar and stayed close to the stairs. Somehow, the women convinced the bodyguards to dance with them. Augustine watched for a minute, making sure they had things handled. Each one was maneuvering her vampire into a separate corner of the club. Things were definitely handled.

Scarface had some female company of his own. Augustine hung back. Scarface was flirting hard and the human female was giving it right back. He bought her a shot, which led to another, which led to the woman's quick intoxication. Scarface acted drunk, but it took a lot more than that to get a vampire wasted.

Scarface took her hand and started leading her back toward the bathrooms. Augustine headed to the main level on full alert. He wasn't sure if Scarface would kill her or just drink a little, but Augustine wasn't waiting to find out. Scarface had already had his last meal, he just didn't know it.

Ahead of Augustine, they slipped into the unisex bathroom.

A shot girl stepped into his path. "Can I interest you in a Screaming Orgasm?"

He stopped. "What? No."

She smiled a little bigger and leaned forward to show off her cleavage. "How about a Louisiana Leg-Spreader?"

"Get. Out. Of. My. Way," he growled. "Now."

"Rude," she muttered as she lifted her tray and slid out of his path.

He rushed past, shoving through the crowd to get to the bathroom before it was too late for the female victim. He threw his shoulder into the door, cracking it open. The woman was up on the counter and Scarface had a fistful of her hair, pulling her head back. His other hand was traveling up her thigh, hiking her dress up. She moaned—fear or ecstasy, Augustine couldn't tell. Didn't matter.

He grabbed her arm and yanked her away. "Get out," he snarled, his eyes on Scarface.

"What the hell?" She swatted at him as she stumbled, trying to get her balance. "You get out, perv."

Scarface zipped his pants as he turned around. "Listen to her or I'll—" He ran a tongue over his fangs. "Get yourself a drink, honey. I'll find you when I finish with our *intruder*."

Muttering to herself, the woman took off.

Scarface raised a brow. "Well, well. Look who finally grew a pair. Took you long enough to track me down, but then I guess that's to be expected with your inferior senses."

Augustine almost laughed. "Nothing you say or do will change your fate tonight. But tell me the name of the fae who let you into the city and I'll *think* about letting you live." For like two seconds, right before putting a blade through his heart.

Scarface snorted. "You think you and your stubby little horns scare me? I'm a vampire, son. My gang and I will tear this city up if you so much as sneeze in my direction." He pushed away from the counter. "Get out of my way."

Augustine didn't budge. "The rest of your gang have either been staked or are about to be. Including the two bodyguards you came here with. Now it's your turn for killing Olivia Goodwin."

"Is that so?" Snickering, Scarface pulled an LMD out of his pocket and unlocked it, then tapped something and started calling out names into the receiver. No one answered him. His unnaturally pale skin took on a slightly green hue.

The swish of metal being unsheathed didn't help the vampire's complexion. Dagger in hand, Augustine stepped closer, grimacing as the vampire's sour tang overloaded his nostrils.

Scarface threw his hands up. "Okay, you've killed my crew, you've proven you're serious, how about we just call it even and I agree never to come back here?"

"I have a better idea. It ends with a pile of ash unless you give me the fae who brought you here."

"There he is!" The shout behind him was followed by a burst of movement. Two burly men rushed into the bathroom behind the female Augustine had saved from Scarface's clutches. "He assaulted me."

The bouncers grabbed Augustine's arms. "He's got a weapon," one shouted to the other. Augustine jerked away, but it was too late.

Scarface took the opportunity and jumped through the bathroom's single frosted-glass window, sending a spray of glass into the air and ripping the bars off the other side.

"Hell no." Dark, angry heat shot through Augustine. He lunged after him only to be jerked back by the bouncers. He shoved his elbow into one's face, breaking his nose. That got his right arm free to punch the other in the throat, taking him down. The drunk woman sobered up enough to make a run for the door.

Augustine leaped out the window after Scarface, but the street was empty. "Scarface is in the wind. Last seen in the alley behind Lucky Frog's."

From their posts around the city, his lieutenants checked in and the hunt got under way.

But an hour later there was still no sign of him.

Augustine growled, knowing the sound would carry through his com cell and not caring. "Damn it. Time to call it."

"You sure, boss?" Cy asked.

"Yes. Looks like he's long gone. At least we got the rest of his crew. I doubt we'll ever see his face again." The urge to punch something was strong. "And if I do, I'll kill him on sight."

"At least he won't remember he's been here after he gets outside parish limits," Sydra added.

"Yeah, I guess." The mission had been a success, but not killing Scarface sucked every bit of triumph out of it. Augustine hated losing and this was one job he'd definitely lost. He let fly a blue tangle of the worst faeish curses he knew. Someday, somewhere, he'd find Scarface and put an end to him once and for all.

As if sensing Augustine's darkening mood, Dulcinea spoke up. "Let's go to Stella's and celebrate with a round. We've earned it."

"I'm going home," Augustine answered. "I've had enough."

"Come on, boss," she cajoled. "Just one."

"*Belle's*," Augustine countered. If he had to be miserable, so did Dulce.

She sighed on the other end of her com. "*Fine.*"

The rest of them cheered and Augustine smiled a little. Scarface might have gotten away, but they'd cleaned the vamps out of the city. That was something.

Too bad it wasn't enough.

Harlow woke with a start to find the holovision still on, although the sound had been turned down, and the throw from the back of the couch pulled over her. Lally must have covered her up when she fell asleep. They'd watched *The Vampire Queen*, then *Return of the Vampire Queen* and lastly *The Vampire Queen's Revenge*. That must have been when she'd fallen asleep.

She tapped the screen of her LMD. After midnight. Augustine would have woken her up when he'd come home, wouldn't he? He had to know she'd want a full report on how things had gone. She sat up and rolled the stiffness out of her shoulders. Her neck ached, too. That's what she got for sleeping in such a weird position.

A noise made her go still. Was that a car door? Augustine must finally be home. She tossed the throw off and ran for the back door. She slid across the kitchen floor in her socks, grabbed the knob and yanked it open. The tiniest sliver of moon offered little light and the house was dark. Closing the door behind her, she stepped outside. No car lights, either. He must have parked in the garage. "Augustine?"

She moved closer to the steps, trying to see better. But as her eyes adjusted, she realized the garage door was down. Whatever she'd heard, it hadn't been him coming home. A sudden foul odor made her wrinkle her nose. There must be a dead thing in the garden.

Turning to go inside, she ran into something. *Someone.*

A hand clamped over her mouth, the skin as smooth and cold as a piece of meat. She tried to scream but the hand muffled most of it. She struck out. A hand caught hers, then an arm came around her, pinning her. *Vampire.* Somehow, she knew. He spun her so her back was to his chest.

"Hello there." His voice was low and breathy and filled with pleasure at her discomfort. "Is that horned freak home? I know he lives here."

She shook her head and thanked her twisted bloodlines that her gifts did not apparently extend to reading dead people. Instead of feeling emotion or getting images from him, all she got was a void. And the longer he touched her, the deeper that void became. The nothingness burrowed into her, found the hole in her heart and gnawed on the edges, widening the abyss inside her.

A new panic clutched at her. The feeling that the void might overtake her, that she might lose herself in the nothingness. His deadness was spreading through her like a cancer.

She struggled, loosening one arm just to have him pin her again.

He wrapped her tighter, making her fight for every inhale. "Keep it up and I'll squeeze until I break ribs."

She went still. What would Augustine do in a situation like this? Probably something she couldn't. His gifts were a lot more powerful than hers.

"That's a good girl," the vampire purred in her ear. His breath stank like decay. He settled into the corner of the porch. "We'll just wait here until that fae freak gets home. Then I'll let him watch while I kill you just like I did the old broad who lived here."

Rage surged up through Harlow hot and liquid. She strained against him as the desire to cause him pain for what he'd done to her mother made her vision go red. She became a creature of retribution in that moment. The living, breathing embodiment of vengeance. Her skin crackled with the need for revenge as her emotions bled out of her.

He shoved her away like he'd been shocked. "What the hell? What did you just do?"

She had no idea, but she was happy for the opening. Focusing on every fighting move she'd ever played out on Realm of Zauron, she spun around, her fist connecting with his cheek.

He cursed and backhanded her, knocking her to the porch floor. She pushed to her knees, then something hard connected with the back of her head and everything went black.

When she came to her head felt like it had been split open and the vampire had her in his arms again, this time with a blade pressed to her throat. She whimpered at the touch of steel. The knife had killed more than once and the emotions leaching into her skin made her nauseous.

"Oh good, you're awake," the vampire said. "I was just telling your boyfriend here how I'm going to kill you for what he did to my family."

"I don't have a boyfriend." Her world started to narrow in like she might pass out again, but she forced herself to look into the yard.

"I don't care who he is, he's going to watch you die," the vampire snarled.

Augustine stood in front of the Thrun, parked haphazardly, the driver's door still open.

"Harlow." He looked like he wanted to say more. His eyes burned with the kind of anger she'd felt right before the vampire had knocked her out, but more than that a brutal sort of darkness shadowed him. Like he was on the verge of losing control. Or giving himself over to everything raging inside him.

She held on to consciousness as best she could. "Augustine, he killed Olivia."

"I know." Even Augustine's voice held an edge. "And now I'm going to kill him. Just like I killed the rest of his gang. Unless he tells me who he was working with."

The vampire's laugh grated against her ears. "Why should I? I have the upper hand here."

"I'll ask you once more," Augustine said. "Tell me who helped you gain entrance to the city. Tell me, and I'll personally guarantee your safety to the parish line."

"Like I'd believe you." The vampire's arm came up, causing the blade against her neck to bite deeper. The metal's sick history coiled through her, filling the widening nothingness inside her with its dark poison.

"Last chance, vampire."

"Last chance, fae." Pain radiated from her neck and the metallic tang of blood filled her nose.

Augustine's face contorted, manifesting every bit of rage she'd imagined inside him. He flickered. His image changed and he became a phantom, so transparent that even the thin moonlight filtered through him.

He charged forward, moving at a speed only othernatural eyes could see. The smoky apparition he'd become lunged over the railing, passed through her and sank like a dagger into the vampire.

The force yanked the leech off her and threw him to the porch floor. Wood cracked and splintered beneath him. Lally's bedroom light came on.

The vampire clawed at himself, digging his nails into his own flesh and shrieking. Augustine had disappeared. The vampire's eyes bulged, his body convulsing, back arching like he was possessed. "Get out," he moaned.

"Who hired you?" The words came out of the vampire's mouth but the voice was Augustine's.

Was Augustine *in* the vampire? There was no other explanation.

"Fae," the vampire growled. Then he got up, grunting and gnashing his teeth, then jerked down the porch steps and into the yard. Unnatural bulges rippled beneath his skin. He scratched at himself, shredding strips of flesh that went to ash as he tore them away.

"Fae hired you?"

The vampire muttered something Harlow couldn't make out. Then, with the soft whoosh of a flame being extinguished, the vampire turned to ash. In his place stood Augustine, as solid as when she'd first seen him. Ash drifted down over him like a hellish snowfall. He brushed the sooty bits from his hair and clothes before walking back onto the porch.

Harlow bumped into the wall of the house. She wasn't

aware she'd backed up. "What…what just happened? Are you okay?"

"I'm fine." He wiped more ash off his face. "Are *you* okay?" He rubbed at her throat with his thumb. "You have a little blood on your neck, but the cut has already healed."

She lifted a hand to feel her throat.

"You're shaking." He came nearer but didn't touch her again. "I'm really sorry you had to go through that. If anything had happened to you…" He swallowed. "I never want any harm to come to you. Never."

She nodded, a little numb. "Thank you." The void created by the vampire still lingered, making her wonder if it was something she was stuck with. She wrapped her arms around her torso, trying to will it away and stop herself from shivering. "He said fae hired him. Do you think…"

Augustine took a step closer. "That it was Branzino? Yes." He looked toward the pile of ash. "He said something right before he died that could have been Branzino's name, but it wasn't clear. Still, it's enough for me to pursue that angle further."

"Did you really kill the rest of his gang?"

"With help, yes." He was half a foot away, maybe less.

"Good." She flicked her gaze sideways. Lally's light was still on. "We should probably go in and let Lally know everything's okay."

"She knows. She's watching from the kitchen window." He turned toward the house, the shimmer of power surrounding him like a visible aura. "Go to bed, Lally, it's all taken care of. We'll talk in the morning."

A few seconds later, the bedroom light went off.

Harlow tilted her head slightly. "Are you going to explain what you did to that vampire?"

"Yes, but not right now." His eyes took on the gleam of relief and something...else. "Remember when I said if you wanted me to kiss you again, you were going to have to ask?"

She nodded. Heat rolled off him in waves.

His hands broke the lock of her arms to slide around her waist. "I lied."

Chapter Thirty-four

Augustine met Fenton at the Pelcrum early, right after he'd made a trip to the bank to meet Cuthridge and access Livie's safety-deposit box. Before he'd left the house, though, he'd stuck his head into Harlow's room. He needed to know she really was okay. That she hadn't been so spooked by the vampire's attack that she'd run, but she was still there, deep in sleep and the kind of beautiful that made him understand how the world had become infatuated with Olivia. Like it or not, Harlow was her mother's child. She was, however, also very much her own woman. A woman he'd come to enjoy kissing too damn much for his own good.

He smiled, thinking of last night. The thunk of Fenton putting a mug of coffee in front of him pulled him from his memory.

Fenton sat next to him at the war room table. "I take it the mission was a success?"

"To the best of my knowledge, New Orleans is vampire-free. Unless our traitor lets another wave in." He sipped the coffee.

"Do you think that will happen?"

"I think it's a possibility until we know for sure who did it and deal with them." He planted his fingers on the table. "Both Harlow and I fully believe that Branzino is behind all this. Not maybe, but definitely. Which means Dreich was working for him. Whether Dreich knew exactly who he was working for, I have no idea but we need to move forward with Branzino as our main target."

Fenton nodded. "Do you have something new to share?"

"We know Branzino is using some kind of magic to pass as human. Can you research that, maybe come up with a list of the fae who'd be willing to do that kind of work?"

"Absolutely. Anything else?"

"Yes, but for right now, this stays strictly between us." He slid the data card across the table.

Fenton picked it up. "What's on here? Can you tell me that much?"

"Evidence that will put Branzino in the Claustrum once we have him in custody. That's not the only copy, but keep it safe."

"I will." He slipped the data card into his inside jacket pocket.

"Also, I need Olivia's house warded immediately."

Fenton frowned. "Did Branzino show there? Is that how you got this new info?"

"He's part of why I want it done, but he hasn't been back. Yet. However, the leader of the Young Bloods showed up there last night. He attacked Harlow and would have killed her, but I took care of things." He tapped a finger on the table. "I want a weaver there as soon as possible."

"Nekai is the best weaver for home protection, but he's on loan to another Haven city. As soon as he returns, I'll make it happen." Fenton used his stylus to scrawl a note in his tablet.

"Thanks. Speaking of Branzino, how's the investigation into Dreich's death going?"

Fenton shook his head. "Slowly. I spoke with Detective Grantham yesterday and while the lab confirmed the powder found in the kitchen was *bokura*, he hasn't been able to speak with his grandmother yet as she's been ill."

Augustine leaned forward. "I think it's time to label Dreich's death what it is. Murder. See if we can—"

"Hold on." Fenton raised his hand. "We don't have enough evidence to back that up. All we have is guesses. Even if Dreich was working for Branzino, he could have purchased that *bokura* to use on someone else."

"Then who did he use it on? Because there wasn't enough left to be useful. And who did he purchase it from? Bokura is a voodoo thing. That's not something our kind typically messes with. I think by revealing some of our suspicions, we might be able to get some new intel. Maybe someone saw him talking to a known voodoo priest or priestess."

"I think it's too soon. Let's give Grantham a chance to find out what he can before we upend this can of worms." Fenton tapped his tablet to turn it off. "As for you, take the day off. You've earned it. Your lieutenants, too. The city can go a few hours without you patrolling the streets."

"What if—"

"Augustine, everything is under control. And if something does happen, we still have the NOPD. Take some downtime. Do something to relax. Or do errands, or do nothing, but take the day off."

"There is something I should do." Augustine stood. He'd never thought the day would come when he'd feel this sense of responsibility to a job he'd never wanted. "Call me if you need me."

"I won't." Fenton made a shooing motion with his hand. "Go."

Fifteen minutes later, Augustine parked the Thrun outside the Ursuline Convent and walked through the front gardens to the visitors' desk. The austerity of the place never failed to make him feel like a schoolboy.

The sister on duty looked up at him. "Can I help you?"

"I'd like to see..." It took him a moment to remember what his mother had changed her name to when she'd come here. "Magdalena. She's a...I think it's called a postulate?"

"Just a moment." The sister picked up the handset on an old corded phone and dialed. "Magdalena, there's a visitor here to see you." She paused. "I'll ask." The sister put the handset to her shoulder. "Who are you and what is your business with Magdalena?"

"I'm her son and I'd just like to talk." The nun relayed that information. Some small part of him thought that if his mother understood the kind of work he was doing now, how he'd changed for the better and taken on some responsibility, she might soften toward him and they could have some kind of relationship. Olivia would approve. In fact, he hoped to be able to tell her about this next time he saw her, which would be soon. Olivia *had* to let Harlow know she wasn't really gone. He was going to insist.

"All right." The sister nodded into the phone, then looked up at him again. "I'm sorry, she doesn't wish to see you."

He stood there a moment, feeling like he'd been slapped. He'd been a fool to think this time would be any different. That she'd be any different. He closed his mouth and walked back to his car as it began to drizzle.

He pulled his collar up. Getting through to his mother was an impossible task. It might never happen. And yet, he couldn't bring himself to stop trying, no matter how many times he failed.

She was his mother. They were blood. Shouldn't that matter for something? Not to her, obviously. His LMD vibrated since he'd silenced it before entering the convent. "Answer."

"Augustine, where are you?" Harlow's voice was husky with sleep. She must have just woken up.

"I had an errand to run."

"Well, hurry up. Lally's making bacon pecan pancakes and says we can't eat until you get home. Also, pick up some orange juice." She snorted like something funny had just occurred to her. "Are bacon pecan pancakes a thing in New Orleans? You people eat some weird stuff."

"I guess we do. You're one of those people now, you know."

A few seconds of silence passed between them. "That's going to take some getting used to."

"I know the feeling." He opened the car door and slid into the driver's seat, staring at the rain streaking his windshield. Family wasn't about the blood that connected you to other people, it was about the people who chose to be connected to you. The people who stood at your side, who faced the demons, fought the battles and helped patch you up afterwards. The realization put a smile on his face. "I'll get the juice and be right home."

Without another look at the convent, he drove off. His family was waiting.

Acknowledgments

Writing is the hardest job I've ever had. Granted, I've never been a neurosurgeon or a tightrope walker, so I know it's all relative. Still, trying to get through the writing of a book without a support system is like trying to baptize a cat. Someone's going to end up in tears. So for all those who've helped me along the way—thanks! My apologies to those I've forgotten, please forgive me.

Here are a few of those people: My amazing, supportive agent, Elaine. My editor, Susan, and the entire publishing team at Orbit. The fabulous Writer's Camp chicks—Leigh, Laura, Rocki and by proxy, Louisa and Amanda. My House of Pain Street Team—namely Captain Melanie, Co-Captain Laura, super-member Amanda Masters and my betas, Dianna J. especially! And of course, my readers, who are the reason I do this.

Lastly, huge thanks to my family for their continuous support and to my husband, who is not only an amazing guy but one who can make me laugh like no one else. Y'all rock.

extras

orbit

meet the author

Kevin Roberts, Intimate Images

KRISTEN PAINTER likes to balance her obsessions with shoes and cats by making the lives of her characters miserable and surprising her readers with interesting twists. She currently writes award-winning urban fantasy for Orbit Books. The former college English teacher can often be found on Twitter @Kristen_Painter and on Facebook at www.facebook.com/KristenPainterAuthor, where she loves to interact with her readers.

interview

When did you first start writing?
When I was a kid! One of my first stories was about my cat. I'm still rather cat obsessed as some of you may already know.

Augustine is a side character in your original House of Comarré series—what drew you to him to write his story?
He's a really interesting character and not the sort I'd written before. He's laid-back, loves life, hates responsibility but harbors some really deep wounds that he's basically chosen not to deal with. There's so much there to work with I knew I had to explore him further!

What was your inspiration behind Harlow?
Harlow's a little like me in that she likes her books and her computer and is perfectly at ease with time alone. That part of her I really relate to. But I also wanted someone with some real challenges to overcome. Harlow was born out of that combination.

Why New Orleans?
New Orleans is a really magical place for me. I've visited more times than I can count, but never lived there (yet). I

feel so at home in that city and so inspired by it. Getting to set a series there was like a gift.

Who was your favorite character to write?

I'm enjoying all of them for different reasons! Lally's a lot of fun, though—she says what she thinks and doesn't take sass off anyone. I love that about her. Plus she's got layers yet to be discovered.

How did you come up with all the different types of fae? Did you have to do a lot of research for this book?

The different types of fae were all born in my head, so do what you will with that. I do a lot of research for everything I write—this book was no exception.

If you could pick one othernatural to be from your world, which would it be?

Augustine's got some pretty cool skills. I could see spending a day or two as him.

What's next for Augustine and Harlow?

Chaos! Mayhem! Banter! Kissing! You know, all the good stuff.

introducing

If you enjoyed
HOUSE OF THE RISING SUN,
look out for

CITY OF ETERNAL NIGHT

Crescent City: Book 2

by Kristen Painter

Chapter One

*Life is an unwinnable game. Only the playing
time may be prolonged.*
—Elektos Codex 13.4.1

New Orleans, Louisiana, 2068

Harlow woke gasping, her heart thumping. Sweat glued her
tank top to her body. She swallowed, trying to get air. A few
deep breaths eased the nightmare's grip on her, but its claws
still dug deep into her subconscious. Slowly, the sharp edges
wore away, leaving her with the kind of residual fear that clung
like secondhand smoke.

She forced herself to take a few more measured breaths. *It was just a dream.* Already the coolness of the dark room eased the heat of her skin. *This is reality, not that other horror.* She grabbed her Life Management Device off the nightstand and tapped the screen to show the time. A little after three in the morning.

Tossing the LMD onto the nightstand, she kicked the covers off and lay back beneath the whirling ceiling fan. The cool air wafted over her as she tried to concentrate on something besides the terrifying dream that had yanked her from sleep. She failed. The nightmare filled every synapse. She couldn't recall exactly what the dream had been, but the dread of it remained, impossible to shake. Something—or someone—had tried to drag her into an abyss. Or had chased her toward it.

Either way, she never wanted to feel that bone-deep sense of fear again.

Minutes slipped by, taking most of the panic with them. At last, she closed her eyes, praying the nightmare wouldn't return.

It didn't, but neither did sleep. She focused on the whirr of the ceiling fan. The subtle hum drowned out most other sounds. Except for one.

The unmistakable eddy and lap of water.

She got up and padded barefoot across the room, pushed back the sheers, opened the balcony door and stepped out into the cool night air.

Augustine was swimming laps in the pool below.

She sighed. Seeing him anchored her firmly in reality. His lean, muscled form cut the water cleanly, sending smooth ripples to kiss the pool's edge. In the submerged light, his skin seemed a darker gray, sleek and seal-like against the water's aqua blue.

She walked closer to the railing. There was something other-worldly in the way he slipped through the water, the effortless way he spun and pushed off the wall as he turned, the bone-less way his body undulated. Even if his horns hadn't grown back, with his gray skin and the six fingers on each hand—and now she could see six toes as well—no one would mistake him for human. He was utterly, completely, regrettably fae.

And she was utterly, completely, regrettably attracted to him. She exhaled the breath she'd unwittingly held. Sure, she was fae, too, but she'd spent her entire adult life trying to live like she wasn't. And her new life in New Orleans made those bloodlines impossible to ignore. She was the daughter of the city's most famous fae, movie star Olivia Goodwin. And she now shared a house with the city's fae Guardian.

Who was practically naked in the pool below her.

Steam rose from the water but the trails evaporated before reaching her second-story balcony. He must be using some of his fae skills to heat the water. That would be a wicked cool power to have. Unlike hers, which were mostly bothersome.

She leaned against the metal railing, causing it to creak.

He lifted his head, twisting seamlessly into a backstroke to smile up at her. "Hey, Harley. Come on in, the water's fine."

She pulled away from the railing. "I was just going back to bed." *And don't call me that.* But those words never left her tongue.

"Funny. Looks like you're standing there watching me." With a smug look, he ducked under, flipped around and pressed off the wall to glide underwater across the length of the pool in one long, easy movement. The water calmed, bringing into definition just how very small his black trunks were.

When he surfaced, he picked his head up and made eye contact again. "You can't sleep or you'd already be doing that. You might as well swim." He spread his arms out and floated lazily.

"I don't have a swimsuit."

His wicked grin returned. "I can ditch mine if it makes you feel better."

She bit her bottom lip and tried to keep her gaze from traveling below that smile. "Okay. Wait. No. Keep your suit on. I meant okay I would come swimming." Her tank top and boy shorts would work fine. It was dark. Sort of. And all that seemed to matter at the moment was that she get in the water.

She slipped back into the house, wrapped herself in a towel from her bathroom and then went down to the first floor as quietly as she could so she wouldn't wake Lally, the housekeeper. Outside, the grass muffled her steps. She shivered despite the towel. The unseasonably warm weather they'd been having was gone. At the pool's edge, she stopped, clutching her towel. She shouldn't be down here. She should be in bed. Asleep. *Alone.*

Augustine stood in waist-deep water. Vapor trails rose off his sleek gray skin to mingle with the steam from the surface, making him look like some kind of horned god of the underworld. He coasted his fingers over the surface, but his eyes stayed on her.

She shivered again. Standing beside a pool shouldn't feel this dangerous. This *wicked.*

He sank down to his neck and pushed back, sending out a small wake. "I can make the water as warm as you like."

If she didn't move forward, she was going to turn and run. She willed herself to drop the towel, then forced her feet down the steps. She could do this. She could be this bold. The pool was like a bath. She kept going, sinking down until her hair floated around her. "It's warm enough."

Warmer toward Augustine. Like the heat was radiating off him, which she guessed it was. She didn't know exactly how his power worked, but as skills went, this was a pretty good one.

He kept his distance, drifting about an arm's length from her. "Couldn't sleep, huh?"

"No." When he didn't say anything, she filled in the space with "I had a nightmare."

He nodded. "Those suck." Then he moved a little closer, his brow furrowed. "You okay?"

She stayed put. "I'm fine. I'm not eight. I can deal with it." She hoped.

He shrugged. "I had nightmares after your mom died that felt as real as anything."

She dropped her gaze to the water's surface. "It wasn't that. I don't even remember it now, really." Mostly true. Just the sense of that dark, threatening abyss remained.

"Cylo and Dulcinea should be back with your stuff today."

He was less than a foot from her, his voice soft. Lally's room was on the first floor, not that far way. She nodded, keeping her voice down, too. "I appreciate you sending them to Boston to clear out my apartment."

His face went serious. "Not something you needed to be doing with Branzino unaccounted for."

She backpedaled to lean against the pool wall and rest her head on the coping. "I don't want to talk about him." Her biological father was a monster, not someone she wanted in her brain after that nightmare.

"Me either." Augustine joined her on the wall, his shoulder barely kissing hers. The heat coming off him felt like a blast furnace. He pointed skyward. "See those five stars forming that wide W shape? That's Cassiopeia."

"Who was she? Some Greek goddess, right?"

"Close. A Greek queen."

"They're very pretty." She glanced over at him but his eyes were still on the sky. "How do you know about the stars?"

He turned toward her. "I like beautiful things."

A dark light flickered in his eyes. The look knotted her insides with rare, unused feelings. She faced him, gripping the coping with one hand while she pushed at him with the other. It was like trying to shove a stone wall out of the way. "Nice line, but I'm not falling for it." He'd have to try a lot harder than that.

He inched closer. The steam rising off him left little droplets in her bangs. "It wasn't a line. You're beautiful."

She swallowed, unsure how to respond. She didn't have to. His mouth closed on hers, the kiss unexpected, but not entirely unwelcome. His hands slid up her arms, stopping below her shoulders. She leaned into him, into his warmth. Into the press of a mouth both soft and firm. The surge of emotion she expected never came. Had he figured out how to squelch her gift? Or maybe he'd found a way to control what came through him.

She kissed him back, pleased that for once the only emotions skin-on-skin contact made her feel were her own.

His fingers tightened on her arms and his mouth bore down on hers. The pressure became painful. She pulled back to end the kiss and failed. He forced his mouth against hers harder. Panic jolted down her spine. She opened her eyes and struggled to break away. The water chilled.

A shadow passed in front of the pool light, causing it to sputter.

Except it wasn't a shadow. Like a crack opening in the earth, the blackness widened and spread toward her. She hit Augustine with her fists, but he didn't budge. They were locked together. She screamed into his mouth. The abyss came closer as a great emptiness opened inside her.

Augustine was sucking the soul out of her, draining the light and spirit from her body. She could feel it leaving as the blackness reached her. The water lapped over her, climbing up her arms, covering her body, choking the breath from her—

She bolted upright, gasping for air, clutching handfuls of the sheet like they were a lifeline. She was still in bed. It was just another dream. But the pounding of her heart was very real. She panted openmouthed to get enough oxygen into her lungs. Just a dream, she repeated. *Just a dream.*

She checked the time on her LMD. Quarter after four in the morning. Her pulse was easing, but the panic was slower to subside. The water, the kiss, the heat of his skin...it had seemed so real. She jumped out of bed, ran to the balcony doors and peered out. The pool was empty and dark, lit only by the moon.

She turned and crumpled against the door, her back flattening the sheers to the glass. She spread her hand over her heart. The darkness was still there. Darker than the room she was in. She could *feel* it. Feel the way the hole inside her widened with every nightmare. She'd lived with a sense of emptiness all her life, a longing she thought had been created by not knowing her father, but she'd met him and that introduction had done nothing to take away that ache. Maybe because Branzino had turned out to be a horrible, manipulative monster of a man, but maybe there was another reason. Maybe she was defective in some way. Like a part of her was missing.

Either way, touching the vampire who'd killed her mother had caused the hole to widen, creating a darkness in her she'd thought temporary. Obviously, she'd been wrong. Touching that undead creature had left permanent damage. Some kind of supernatural scar.

She slumped down and hugged her knees to her chest. Was this what it meant to be fae? To be this vulnerable? She wasn't tough and street-smart like Augustine; she was a computer geek who preferred the indoors to direct sunlight and email to actual conversation.

What would her mother do in a situation like this? Olivia had been strong and fearless. The kind of woman Harlow would love to be someday, but getting there was going to take courage. Something she wasn't sure she had. At least not in the kind of quantities she was going to need.

Maybe she should talk to Augustine. He'd promised to teach her to defend herself. Maybe that would help. And if it didn't... he'd know what to do. Or someone who would. He was the Guardian of the city. It was his job to protect the citizens of New Orleans and now that she lived here, that included her.

She got to her feet, shaking off the last bit of fear left by the nightmare and ignoring the darkness around her. "Just a dream," she whispered. She reached for her robe. It was somewhere on the bed's footboard, but her hand came in contact with something else.

A towel. Just like the one she'd wrapped around herself in her dream.

A tremor ran through her she was powerless to control. The towel wasn't hanging in the bathroom where she'd left it. And it was damp. "There's no way," she whispered. She lifted it to her nose and inhaled. She threw the towel down, but the scent stayed with her. The unmistakable tang of chlorine.

Augustine came down to breakfast to find Lally cooking eggs and Harlow already at the table. She was bundled in Olivia's old chenille robe, her cranberry-black hair knotted on top of her head. Even rumpled with sleep she intrigued him. He wanted to plant a kiss on the side of her neck. Instead, he grabbed a mug for coffee. "Morning. Cool out there, today, huh?"

Lally nodded. "Morning, Augie. I like that cool weather. Makes for good sleeping, don't you think?"

"It does, but Mardi Gras's going to be on the cold side this year if this spell doesn't pass."

Lally grinned. "Guess that means people just have to drink a little more to keep warm."

He glanced at Harlow. She'd yet to reply. "You okay?"

She nodded, but said nothing. Her gloved hands were wrapped around her coffee cup as if she were afraid it might try to get away. Purplish gray semicircles sat like bruises beneath her eyes.

He took the chair next to her. "Didn't sleep well, huh?"

She shrugged, her gaze never leaving her coffee. "I was...up late playing Realm of Zauron." She sipped her coffee. "My stuff should be here today, right?"

The sudden change of subject wasn't lost on him. He pulled out his LMD. "Yep. I got a text from Dulcinea around seven a.m. She figures they'll pull in sometime this afternoon." He'd sent two of his lieutenants, Cylo and Dulcinea, to Boston to pack up Harlow's apartment and truck her stuff back to New Orleans.

"Thanks for taking care of that." She raised her head a little, but still didn't make eye contact. She seemed shy around him this morning and he had no idea why. He hoped whatever she wasn't telling him wasn't serious.

"Of course. With Branzino who knows where, it was the smartest way to handle it."

Lally set a platter of eggs and bacon on the table, followed by a basket of biscuits and a bowl of grits sprinkled with cheese. "I'm glad that man has stayed away. I'm guessing he knows when he's been beat."

"Let's hope so." Augustine took a biscuit and slathered it with mayhaw jelly. Truth was, it was more likely Branzino was biding his time. "That reminds me, I can't hang out too long this morning. I've got to meet Fenton." Fenton Welch served as the Elektos liaison to the Guardian, a role the member of the fae's high council took very seriously.

Harlow sighed.

"I know, I owe you a lesson. I'm sorry."

She nodded. "It's okay. I know the Guardian stuff comes first."

Damn it. She seemed really disappointed. He had to figure out a better schedule.

Lally sat at the end of the table and helped herself to a spoonful of scrambled eggs. "Do you have a lot to do to get ready for Mardi Gras? As Guardian, I mean."

"Some." Mostly he was going to nudge Fenton about getting the house warded before they returned to the ongoing investigation into the death of Dreich. The fallen fae had been the late Guardian's cousin *and* one of his lieutenants. Hard to believe the man had been involved in letting vampires into the city. Vampires who'd not only killed some tourists and the last Guardian, but Harlow's mother, Olivia Goodwin.

But the man both Augustine and Harlow truly suspected to be behind the whole thing was Joseph Branzino, Harlow's biological father, raptor fae and known killer.

He shifted his attention to Harlow. She stared at the tabletop, taking a sip of coffee now and then and looking very much like a lost soul. Maybe he should tell Fenton he needed a day off. "Are you sure you're okay?"

Lally pushed the platter of eggs toward her. "Eat something, child. You need the strength to keep yourself warm."

"Thanks." She took a piece of bacon, then finally made eye

contact with Augustine. Briefly. "Yeah, I'm fine. Just tired. And thinking about how nice it will be to have all my stuff back. If it's okay with you two"—she turned her gaze to Lally—"I'd like to set up shop in one of the spare rooms."

"Shop?" Lally asked. "You're not going to get yourself into trouble again, are you?"

"No. Nothing like that." Harlow glanced at him. "But I still have clients and I need to work. I can't just live off my mother's estate. I need to do something. I realize New Orleans may not have the same kind of business going on that Boston did, but I don't just have to do penetration testing. I'm thinking I could do some Web work. There have to be people in this town who'd like a website designed. Most businesses here still have them, right?"

Lally shrugged. Augustine raised one shoulder. "I guess. Is that a thing most businesses do? My LMD is the closest I've been to a computer in a long time." The Great War had created a huge divide in who could afford things like electricity and technology. Once upon a time, connectivity had been an almost inherent right. Now it was a luxury for those who had the funds.

Harlow sighed. "I hope so. I'd like to do something with my time besides read my way through my mother's library. Not that that's such a bad way to pass the time..."

"You'll be plenty busy when we get this training schedule figured out." Augustine had promised to teach her to fight, but that didn't mean he wasn't having mixed feelings about it. On one hand, it would be good for her to be able to defend herself and would probably do wonders for her self-esteem; but on the other, he worried she'd get overconfident and do something with lasting results.

"I know." She chewed a piece of bacon. "But I still want to start this new business."

"I get it," Lally said. "No shame in wanting to feel productive."

"Take whatever space you want. It *is* half your house," Augustine added. "And I'll work on setting up the ballroom as a training space, too. I promise." If lack of activity was behind Harlow's unhappiness, then he was all for her starting up a new business. How busy she'd actually be, he had no idea, but it would give her something to do. With that and the training, she should be well occupied. He popped the last of the biscuit in his mouth and pushed his chair back. "I should be back before Cy and Dulcinea get here."

He pulled his coat on, covering the sword that hung at his hip, and headed out to the Thrun, the amazing piece of machinery he now drove thanks to his position as Guardian. He trailed his fingers over the car's sleek black hood as he approached the driver's side. He tapped the unlock icon on his LMD, then opened the door and slid in.

He smiled at the quiet-as-a-tomb interior when the door shut. Being Guardian came with a lot of headaches. This was not one of them.

His LMD vibrated with an incoming call. "Answer."

The com cell behind his ear allowed the conversation to take place in his head, something that was still taking some getting used to. "Augustine, it's Fenton."

"I'm on my way." He started the engine and pulled the car out of the garage. The Pelcrum, their headquarters, was only a few blocks away. "I'll be there in five."

"Meet me at Loudreux's." Fenton sounded tense.

"What's up?"

"I can't discuss it on an unsecure line."

"This is an unsecure line?"

"In this situation, yes."

Augustine rolled his eyes. Hugo Loudreux's position as Prime, head of the Elektos, had certainly filled him with a grand sense of importance. What the man wanted now Augustine could only imagine. "On my way."

But he kept the car going in the same direction. Being called to the Prime's house was a lot like having the police come to your door. Even if they weren't there to arrest you, they probably still weren't bringing you good news. And that could wait a little while longer.

With Dulcinea out of town, he felt duty bound to check in on Beatrice. The late Guardian's widow had agreed to become one of his lieutenants, only finding out afterward that she was pregnant. Now she and Dulce lived in the Guardian's house. He certainly didn't need it since he'd become half owner of Olivia's estate, and when Harlow had asked him to stay, he couldn't turn her down. *Wouldn't* turn her down. Especially not since the beginning of something had blossomed between them.

Besides, he'd promised Olivia he'd protect her daughter. Hell, as Guardian it was his job to protect every citizen of New Orleans. Getting to live with Harlow was just a bonus. A really good bonus. Now if he could just figure out what was bothering her.

He pulled into the driveway at the Guardian's residence and turned off the engine. Something was up with Harlow and he was determined to figure out what. Since the night the leader of the vampire gang had taken her hostage, she'd changed. Pulled away from him a little.

Was it because she'd seen him slip inside the vampire and destroy the leech the way only a shadeux fae could? Harlow had shied away from all things fae when she'd first arrived at the house, but he'd thought she was opening up to her heritage more and more with each passing day.

He tipped his head back against the seat. He'd vowed to protect her and yet he'd killed that creature right in front of her. That had to be it. No wonder she'd been acting so cold toward him these past few days. He'd scared her. Damn it. That had not been his intention. He smacked the steering wheel, his anger at his own stupidity blinding him.

If she needed some space, he'd let her have it, but there was no way he was walking away from her completely. There *was* something between them. Something he wasn't about to give up on unless she told him to.

And even then, not without a fight.

introducing

If you enjoyed
HOUSE OF THE RISING SUN,
look out for

THE SHAMBLING GUIDE
TO NEW YORK CITY

The Shambling Guides: Book 1

by Mur Lafferty

*A travel writer takes a job with a shady publishing company
in New York, only to find that she must write a guide to
the city—for the undead!*

*Because of the disaster that was her last job, Zoë is searching for a
fresh start as a travel book editor in the tourist-centric New York
City. After stumbling across a seemingly perfect position though,
Zoë is blocked at every turn because of the one thing she can't take
off her résumé—human.*

*Not to be put off by anything—especially not her blood-
drinking boss or death goddess coworker— Zoë delves deep into
the monster world. But her job turns deadly when the careful
balance between human and monsters starts to crumble—with
Zoë right in the middle.*

Chapter One

The bookstore was sandwiched between a dry cleaner's and a shifty-looking accounting office. Mannegishi's Tricks wasn't in the guidebook, but Zoë Norris knew enough about guidebooks to know they often missed the best places.

This clearly was not one of those places.

The store was, to put it bluntly, filthy. It reminded Zoë of an abandoned mechanic's garage, with grime and grease coating the walls and bookshelves. She pulled her arms in to avoid brushing against anything. Long strips of paint dotted with mold peeled away from the walls as if they could no longer stand to adhere to such filth. Zoë couldn't blame them. She felt a bizarre desire to wave to them as they bobbed lazily to herald her passing. Her shoes stuck slightly to the floor, making her trek through the store louder than she would have liked.

She always enjoyed looking at cities—even her hometown—through the eyes of a tourist. She owned guidebooks of every city she had visited and used them extensively. It made her usual urban exploration feel more thorough.

It also allowed her to look at the competition, or it had when she'd worked in travel book publishing.

The store didn't win her over with its stock, either. She'd never heard of most of the books; they had titles like *How to Make Love, Marry, Devour, and Inherit in Eight Weeks* in the Romance section and *When Your Hound from Hell Outgrows His House—and Yours* in the Pets section.

She picked the one about hounds and opened it to Chapter Four: "The Augean Stables: How to Pooper-Scoop Dung That Could Drown a Terrier." She frowned. *So, they're* really *assuming your dog gets bigger than a house? It's not tongue-in-cheek? If this is humor, it's failing.* Despite the humorous title, the front cover had a frightening drawing of a hulking white beast with red eyes. The cover was growing uncomfortably warm, and the leather had a sticky, alien feeling, not like cow or even snake leather. She switched the book to her left hand and wiped her right on her beige sweater. She immediately regretted it.

"One sweater ruined," she muttered, looking at the grainy black smear. "What *is* this stuff?"

The cashier's desk faced the door from the back of the store, and was staffed by an unsmiling teen girl in a dirty gray sundress. She had olive skin and big round eyes, and her head had the fuzz of the somewhat-recently shaved. Piercings dotted her face at her nose, eyebrow, lip, and cheek, and all the way up her ears. Despite her slouchy body language, she watched Zoë with a bright, sharp gaze that looked almost hungry.

Beside the desk was a bulletin board, blocked by a pudgy man hanging a flyer. He wore a T-shirt and jeans and looked to be in his mid-thirties. He looked completely out of place in this store; that is, he was clean.

"Can I help you?" the girl asked as Zoë approached the counter.

"Uh, you have a very interesting shop here," Zoë said, smiling. She put the hound book on the counter and tried not to grimace as it stuck to her hand briefly. "How much is this one?"

The clerk didn't return her smile. "We cater to a specific clientele."

"OK...but how much is the book?" Zoë asked again.

"It's not for sale. It's a collectible."

Zoë became aware of the man at the bulletin board turning and watching her. She began to sweat a little bit.

Jesus, calm down. Not everyone is out to get you.

"So it's not for sale, or it's a collectible. Which one?"

The girl reached over and took the book. "It's not for sale to you, only to collectors."

"How do you know I don't collect dog books?" Zoë asked, bristling. "And what does it matter? All I wanted to know was how much it costs. Do you care where it goes as long as it's paid for?"

"Are you a collector of rare books catering to the owners of... exotic pets?" the man interrupted, smiling. His voice was pleasant and mild, and she relaxed a little, despite his patronizing words. "Excuse me for butting in, but I know the owner of this shop and she considers these books her treasure. She is very particular about where they go when they leave her care."

"Why should she..." Zoë trailed off when she got a closer look at the bulletin board to the man's left. Several flyers stood out, many with phone numbers ripped from the bottom. One, advertising an exorcism service specializing in elemental demons, looked burned in a couple of places. The flyer that had caught her eye was pink, and the one the man had just secured with a thumbtack.

Underground Publishing
LOOKING FOR WRITERS

Underground Publishing is a new company writing travel guides for people like you. Since we're writing for people like you, we need people like you to write for us.

(continued)

Pluses: Experience in writing, publishing, or editing (in this life or any other), and knowledge of New York City.

Minuses: A life span shorter than an editorial cycle (in this case, nine months).

Call 212.555.1666 for more information or e-mail rand@undergroundpub.com for more information.

"Oh, hell yes," said Zoë, and with the weird, dirty hound book forgotten, she pulled a battered notebook from her satchel. She needed a job. She was refusing to adhere to the stereotype of running home to New York, admitting failure at her attempts to leave her hometown. Her goal was a simple office job. She wasn't waiting for her big break on Broadway and looking to wait tables or take on a leaflet-passing, taco-suit-wearing street-nuisance job in the meantime.

Office job. Simple. Uncomplicated.

As she scribbled down the information, the man looked her up and down and said, "Ah, I'm not sure if that's a good idea for you to pursue."

Zoë looked up sharply. "What are you talking about? First I can't buy the book, now I can't apply for a job? I know you guys have some sort of weird vibe going on, 'We're so goth and special, let's freak out the normals.' But for a business that caters to, you know, *customers*, you're certainly not welcoming."

"I just think that particular business may be looking for someone with experience you may not have," he said, his voice level and diplomatic. He held his hands out, placating her.

"But you don't even know me. You don't know my qualifications. I just left Misconceptions Publishing in Raleigh. You heard of them?" She hated name-dropping her old employer—she would have preferred to forget it entirely—but the second-biggest travel book publisher in the USA was her strongest credential in the job hunt.

The man shifted his weight and touched his chin. "Really. What did you do for them?"

Zoë stood a little taller. "Head researcher and writer. I wrote most of *Raleigh Misconceptions*, and was picked to head the project *Tallahassee Misconceptions*."

He smiled a bit. "Impressive. But you do know Tallahassee is south of North Carolina, right? You went in the wrong direction entirely."

Zoë clenched her jaw. "I was laid off. It wasn't due to job performance. I took my severance and came back home to the city."

The man rubbed his smooth, pudgy cheek. "What happened to cause the layoff? I thought Misconceptions was doing well."

Zoë felt her cheeks get hot. Her boss, Godfrey, had happened. Then Godfrey's wife—whom he had failed to mention until Zoë was well and truly in "other woman" territory—had happened. She swallowed. "Economy. You know how it goes."

He stepped back and leaned against the wall, clearly not minding the cracked and peeling paint that broke off and stuck to his shirt. "Those are good credentials. However, you're still probably not what they're looking for."

Zoë looked at her notebook and continued writing. "Luckily it's not your decision, is it?"

"Actually, it is."

She groaned and looked back up at him. "All right. Who are you?"

He extended his hand. "Phillip Rand. Owner, president, and CEO of Underground Publishing."

She looked at his hand for a moment and shook it, her small fingers briefly engulfed in his grip. It was a cool handshake, but strong.

"Zoë Norris. And why, Mr. Phillip Rand, will you not let me even apply?"

"Well, Miss Zoë Norris, I don't think you'd fit in with the staff. And fitting in with the staff is key to this company's success."

A vision of future months dressed as a dancing cell phone on the wintry streets pummeled Zoë's psyche. She leaned forward in desperation. She was short, and used to looking up at people, but he was over six feet, and she was forced to crane her neck to look up at him. "Mr. Rand. How many other people experienced in researching and writing travel guides do you have with you?"

He considered for a moment. "With that specific qualification? I actually have none."

"So if you have a full staff of people who fit into some kind of mystery mold, but don't actually have experience writing travel books, how good do you think your books are going to be? You sound like you're a kid trying to fill a club, not a working publishing company. You need a managing editor with experience to supervise your writers and researchers. I'm smart, hardworking, creative, and a hell of a lot of fun in the times I'm not blatantly begging for a job—obviously you'll have to just take my word on that. I haven't found a work environment I don't fit in with. I don't care if Underground Publishing is catering to eastern Europeans, or transsexuals, or Eskimos, or even Republicans. Just because I don't fit in doesn't mean I can't be accepting as long as they accept me. Just give me a chance."

Phillip Rand was unmoved. "Trust me. You would not fit in. You're not our type."

She finally deflated and sighed. "Isn't this illegal?"

He actually had the audacity to laugh at that. "I'm not discriminating based on your gender or race or religion."

"Then what are you basing it on?"

He licked his lips and looked at her again, studying her. "Call it a gut reaction."

She deflated. "Oh well. It was worth a try. Have a good day."

On her way out, she ran through her options: there were the few publishing companies she hadn't yet applied to, the jobs that she had recently thought beneath her that she'd gladly take at this point. She paused a moment in the Self-Help section to see if anything there could help her better herself. She glanced at the covers for *Reborn and Loving It, Second Life: Not Just on the Internet*, and *Get the Salary You Deserve! Negotiating Hell Notes in a Time of Economic Downturn*. Nothing she could relate to, so she trudged out the door, contemplating a long bath when she got back to her apartment. Better than unpacking more boxes.

After the grimy door shut behind her, Zoë decided she had earned a tall caloric caffeine bomb to soothe her ego. She wasn't sure what she'd done to deserve this, but it didn't take much to make her leap for the comfort treats these days—which reminded her, she needed to recycle some wine bottles.

EXCERPT FROM
The Shambling Guide to New York City

THEATER DISTRICT:
Shops

Mannegishi's Tricks is the oldest bookstore in the Theater District. Established 1834 by Akilina, nicknamed "The Drakon Lady," after she immigrated from Russia, the store has a stock that is lovingly picked from collections all over the world. Currently managed by Akilina's great-grandaughter, Anastasiya, the store continues to offer some of the best finds for any book collector. Anastasiya upholds the old dragon lady's practice of knowing just which book should go to which customer, and refuses to sell a book to the "wrong" person. Don't try to argue with her; the drakon's teeth remain sharp.

Mannegishi's Tricks is one of the few shops that deliberately maintains a squalid appearance—dingy, smelly, with a strong "leave now" aura—in order to repel unwanted customers. In nearly 180 years, Akilina and her descendants have sold only three books to humans. She refuses to say to whom. ∎